"I have no reason to believe you. I hardly know you," Kitty said.

"We were pretty close back there for a little while," he said with a roguish smile. "A little while longer, and we might have got to know each other real good."

"That . . . that has nothing to do with it. And if you won't agree to take me with you, we'll just forget the whole idea."

"Hell, woman," he exploded, "you're going to throw away a chance at a fortune because you won't trust me."

She looked at him then, a quick dart of fury. "No. You're throwing away a chance at a nice reward because you're like most men—you can't accept a woman being able to think for herself and make her own decisions."

"That's crazy. You're just afraid I'll find the gold and keep it all for myself."

"Well, if that weren't your intent, you'd have no objections to me going with you. I've damned well proved myself—but *you* haven't proved anything."

# Lords of Desire

# Arizona Gold

## Maggie James

A SIGNET BOOK

SIGNET
Published by New American Library, a division of
Penguin Putnam Inc., 375 Hudson Street,
New York, New York 10014, U.S.A.
Penguin Books Ltd, 27 Wrights Lane,
London W8 5TZ, England
Penguin Books Australia Ltd, Ringwood,
Victoria, Australia
Penguin Books Canada Ltd, 10 Alcorn Avenue,
Toronto, Ontario, Canada M4V 3B2
Penguin Books (N.Z.) Ltd, 182–190 Wairau Road,
Auckland 10, New Zealand

Penguin Books Ltd, Registered Offices:
Harmondsworth, Middlesex, England

First published by Signet, an imprint of New American Library,
a division of Penguin Putnam Inc.

First Printing, August 2000
10  9  8  7  6  5  4  3  2  1

# Chapter 1

The Parrish family cemetery, situated on a grassy knoll, was ringed by the cool, green mountains of Virginia's Shenandoah Valley. Dogwood trees were bursting into spring bloom, and delicate white flowers laced through the twisting blackberry bushes on the hillsides. The air all around was sweet with the fragrance of the first honeysuckle blossoms.

It was, Kitty Parrish supposed, a nice day for a funeral. But she was not about to say so. The few people there would not understand how struggling to find something, anything, good in a bad situation had always been her way of coping with life's miseries.

Even her mother, at eternal rest inside the pine coffin being lowered into the ground, had been baffled by Kitty's often bizarre method of rising above sadness or disappointments. She had accused her at times of being flippant and sarcastic, never knowing, of course, that, even though Kitty managed to smile in the face of adversity, she would be crying within.

Ezra Bynum, the preacher, bent and picked up a clod of dirt from the ground. Crushing it in his hand, he began to sprinkle it over the coffin as he said something about ashes to ashes and dust to dust. Then, a few murmured words of prayer, and it was over.

Kitty dusted her straw hat on her leg and put it back on her head against the hot sun. She supposed it would have been proper to have worn a dress, but the fact was she didn't have one. She had one other pair of overalls besides the ones she was wearing and a couple of threadbare shirts. That was the extent of her wardrobe. But what the heck, she told herself, it wouldn't matter to her mother if she could know, and there were only five others at the funeral. Preacher Ezra Bynum and his wife, Mildred, and the hired hands—Jabe and Loweezy and Roscoe—were as poor as she was and dressed no better.

Preacher Bynum walked to where Kitty was standing at the foot of the grave. He was a tall man, thin, with dark eyes that seemed forever condemning of the world around him. He wore a black suit, white shirt, and string tie. "If there's anything me or Mildred can do for you, Kitty, let us know."

They both knew it was merely lip service, just as they both knew the reason he had come was that Kitty had sent Jabe to fetch him with the promise of two dollars if he would give her mother a decent burying. Otherwise, Preacher Bynum would have stayed away like everyone else in the Shenandoah Valley that hated her mother like the plague.

"And you know you're welcome to stay with us." Mildred Bynum, standing next to her husband, stepped to put her arm around Kitty's shoulders and gave her a hug. She was the only person Kitty could remember ever being kind to her, and that was probably because she was an outsider—a Yankee. Ezra had met her during the war, when he was wounded and captured. She had been working in the hospital he was taken to. Afterward, when he was freed, he had married her and brought her home to Virginia to live, and folks had forgiven her for being a Yankee because she was married to a preacher.

But they had never forgiven Kitty's mother for what she had done in the war—not that Rosalie Parrish had ever asked them to. She had held up her head and gone about her business, not caring that she was ostracized for having sold horses to the Yankees instead of giving them to the desperate Rebs. It was a matter of survival, Rosalie had explained to Kitty when she was old enough to understand, not loyalty.

Sadly, Kitty had grown to realize what it meant to struggle to survive. The children at the one-room schoolhouse had taunted her and called her names. No one had wanted to play with her, and even though she'd begged to quit and stay home, her mother refused. Kitty was going to learn to read and write and cipher, she'd declared, and she might as well learn to stand up to those who would beat her down.

And Kitty had done so, but there were a few bloody noses along the way—hers as well as others'.

Mildred Bynum knew all that, because she was the schoolteacher. Many times when parents would demand punishment for Kitty's brawling ways Mildred had taken up for her by pointing out that she never started the fights.

"I'll be fine, Miss Mildred," Kitty said, shaking off the memories. "I don't plan on staying around here, anyway."

Ezra cleared his throat and held out his hand. "I reckon we'll be going now."

Kitty knew he wanted his money. Fishing in her pocket, she brought out two crumpled one-dollar bills. It was all she had until she could sell the two horses she had managed to save from the fire that had also killed her mother.

Ezra stuffed the bills in his pocket and, with a mumbled "Let's go" to his wife, started walking towards his buggy.

Mildred hung back, brow furrowed with concern. "I don't like you being here alone, especially after all the trouble. Those men might come back."

Kitty turned from the grave. She did not want to

watch Jabe and Roscoe shovel dirt on top of the coffin. "If they do, I'll be ready for them. I would've got a couple that night if Momma hadn't run out on the porch and stumbled into me and made me drop my rifle."

"Well, I'd just feel better if you'd come stay with us for a spell."

"Like I said, I'll be leaving as soon as I can make all the arrangements."

Mildred made a tsking sound. "You're still planning to go look for your uncle, aren't you? Oh, child, that's such a long trip for a young girl, all alone."

Kitty managed a laugh. "Now, Miss Mildred, you've always told me I don't even look like a girl."

"That's because you've never tried to. And you could be so pretty. I remember when you were in school I offered to buy you a dress and a pinafore and a ribbon for your hair. But you wouldn't hear of it. And neither would your mother."

"She wasn't one to take charity, and I felt like if I didn't look and act like a girl the boys would leave me alone. A pity it didn't work with Tormey Rankin," Kitty added, making a bitter face at the thought of that awful night.

Mildred patted her shoulder. "Now, now. It wasn't your fault, and you shouldn't blame yourself no matter what folks say. Those devils ought to be caught and punished for what they did, and—"

"Mildred, we have to go." Ezra was in the carriage, holding the horse's reins and glaring impatiently. "We need to stop by and see how Sadie Postner is doing. She's been down with her back, you know."

"You know I don't care what folks say about me," Kitty said to Mildred. "What happened wasn't my fault. I didn't mean to put out Tormey Rankin's eye with that pitchfork, but if I hadn't got my hands on it after he sneaked up on me in the barn, he would've had his way with me. As for the devils that set fire to the barn, they'll never be punished for it, and the sheriff knows who they are, too—Tormey's kin and the rest of the bastards who ride around at night wearing hoods over their faces, burning crosses and scaring the negroes to death."

Mildred shook her head and made more tsking sounds. "Maybe it's best you do leave these parts, child. You've got too many bad memories of your life here, and you're filled with rage."

"Perhaps I am. If it had been up to me, we'd have left here years ago, but Mother said she'd never run from the land that had been in her family for so long."

Ezra shouted, "Mildred, I mean for you to come now."

Both women glanced at him briefly, then Mildred fretted, "But can you be sure you can find your uncle?"

"My *stepfather*," Kitty corrected. Actually, she thought of Wade Parrish as her father, because he was the only one she had ever known. Her real father had been killed in the war, when she was only two years old, and she did not remember him. "And, yes, I'll find him. I have his address where he stays when he's not out prospecting for gold with his partner, a man by the name of Dan McCloud."

"And that's a place called Tombstone, isn't it? In the Arizona Territory?" She shuddered. "Such a horrible name for a town. I don't want to think about the reason for it. And he's still looking for gold, is he?" Her nose wrinkled ever so slightly in condemnation.

"Yes, and one day he'll make a big strike. I just know it. Last fall he wrote that they were digging near a river called the San Pedro, in the southern part of Arizona."

"But has he remarried? I recall your mother told me a few years ago that she had scraped up the money

and got a divorce so he'd have no further claim on
the family land."

"I don't know if he has or not." And in that particular moment, Kitty did not care. All that mattered was
that she leave Virginia before she got herself in a
whole peck of trouble, because she feared if she laid
eyes on any of those responsible for the barn burning
she would take the law in her own hands.

"Well, he might have a wife by now," Mildred reasoned. "I seem to recall all his letters have been in
the same handwriting for the last year or so. For a
while, he was getting different folks to write for him."

That much was true. Wade had never learned to
read or write. When three letters had come in the
same script, her mother had sneered and said he had
probably taken up with some trollop, because he never
mentioned taking a new wife.

It was only natural Miss Mildred would have noticed the sameness. Ezra's father ran the general store,
and after school she worked at the post office in the
back and saw everybody's mail.

Ezra yelled louder, and Mildred waved at him to
shush, then said to Kitty, "Well, I wish you'd recon-
sider, dear. You know you have a home with us."

Kitty managed to keep a straight face and not scowl
at such a thought. Miss Mildred would be all right to
live with, but Preacher Bynum would resent her terribly, even though he might try to hide it. The situation
would not be pleasant, and besides, Kitty had been
waiting for the chance to leave. She just wished it
had not come in the wake of such a tragedy as her
mother's death.

"So when do you plan to leave?" Mildred asked.

"I have to take care of things around here first. I'm
turning everything over to Jabe and his family."

At that, Mildred Bynum's brows crawled up into

her gray hair. "You're giving your land to your negroes?"

"They aren't *my* negroes," Kitty was quick to correct. "And they never have been. Or my mother's, either. That's another thing that rankled folks, even before the war. Her family never believed in owning slaves. They paid the negroes by giving them a roof over their heads and making sure they had enough to eat, but they were always free to go whenever they wanted to.

"As for giving the land away," she continued, head high and chin set, "as bad as I need money, I'd rather give it away than see it sold to people around here who treated me and Ma like dirt."

Mildred shook her head. "So much bitterness, child. Perhaps it's best you do go. You won't be happy here."

"I never have been, so I've got no reason to think it would ever change."

"Well, you be sure to come by for supper one night to say good-bye."

"Maybe." Kitty looked beyond her to Ezra's angry face and knew it was out of the question.

A week passed. Kitty found herself filled with excitement to be leaving in only two days to begin her new life. Jabe had taken the horses to a rancher in the next county. He hoped to receive a better price there. All Kitty needed was enough money to get her to Arizona. She was confident her stepfather—whom she had always called Daddy Wade—would look after her once she got there. But she did not intend to be a burden. She was certainly willing to work for her keep.

With a bouquet of crab apple blossoms, Kitty made her way up to the cemetery for one last visit to her mother's grave. She missed her terribly and wondered if the sorrow would ever go away.

"Oh, Momma," she said out loud, staring down at the raw mound of earth. "You had such a hard life. I wish I could have made it easier for you, and I'm so sorry you had to die like you did."

Her mother said they had lived good during the war, thanks to the Yankees' money. It was afterward that things got bad, because when word spread that Rosalie Parrish had done business with the Yankees, no one wanted her horses. She might as well have been raising dogs for all the interest anyone had.

The horses Jabe had taken to sell should have brought top dollar, but Kitty knew she would be lucky to get enough for her trip. She would take the train as far west as possible, switching to stagecoach the rest of the way.

She had been to Richmond to ask about the schedule, then written Daddy Wade to tell him when to expect her. She had said only that her mother was dead, leaving out the sordid details. All that could come later, when they were together. He would be saddened, of course, but would feel no loss. After all, he had only married her mother out of a sense of duty to his dead brother.

Kitty had adored him and grieved when he had left five years earlier, the year she turned fourteen. They had been so very close. He had taken her hunting and fishing and taught her how to ride and rope and shoot as good as any man—much to her mother's disapproval. And, yes, Kitty smiled to remember, he had taught her how to fight, too, so she could take up for herself when boys got scornful or frisky.

The years when Daddy Wade was there had been good ones, but only for her. Kitty knew he was miserable, because her mother nagged him constantly and treated him as no more than a hired hand. Then one day he drew Kitty aside and told her he couldn't take it anymore, and he was going away, heading west to look for gold, adventure, and, perhaps most important of all—peace.

But he had not completely abandoned them. First of all, he asked her mother to go with him, saying that maybe they could be happy in a place where people didn't hate them on sight. She had refused, and he had stayed in touch by sending a couple of letters a year, enclosing money when he could.

Kitty wrote to him and told him one day she would join him, and he had replied by saying she would always be welcome, but he was sure she would marry and settle down right where she was.

No chance of that, Kitty thought grimly as she placed the flowers next to the wooden cross she had made. Boys from decent families would never dare court a girl considered white trash, and the others, like Tormey, only wanted one thing. If she stayed in Virginia, she would be an old maid—if she didn't wind up hanging for shooting the varmints responsible for her mother's death.

Hearing the sound of a horse coming up the road, Kitty hurried down from the ridge to see it was Miss Mildred in her carriage.

"I'm glad you came by," Kitty said when she rolled to a stop. "I'm leaving day after tomorrow."

Mildred looked surprised. "So soon? Oh, dear, I am going to miss you, Kitty." She handed her a letter. "I was on my way to take Sadie Postner some stew and thought I'd drop this off to you. It's from your uncle."

Kitty took it eagerly. She hadn't heard from him in quite a while.

"Same handwriting as last time," Mildred remarked, "so maybe he is married. I truly hope so. I'd like to think you're going to be part of a family, though you're old enough to be thinking about having one of your own.

"Especially," she added, "when you start dressing like the lovely young woman you are." Her eyes twinkling, Mildred handed her a package.

"What's this?"

"A little going-away present. I want you to look nice for your trip, so I talked my father-in-law into selling me two nice dresses at a bargain. Shoes, too. And a bonnet. You'll be so pretty, Kitty. I wish I could see you when you're all dressed up. Maybe I'll see you at the depot."

"Well, that's real nice of you, Miss Mildred," Kitty said awkwardly. Nobody had ever given her a present in her whole life, except for the shotgun Wade gave her when she turned twelve. But a dress? Good heavens, the last time she'd worn a dress was when she got into a fight with Billy Ledbetter, probably ten years ago, and it had got ripped up so bad her mother had said she could just wear overalls if she was going to carry on like a boy, and that had suited Kitty just fine.

"And there's more," Mildred laughed happily, handing down yet another bundle. "Undergarments and stockings. I didn't let Mr. Bynum see me buy those, of course."

Kitty thanked her, feeling awkward. She had not thought about wearing dresses in Arizona, hadn't thought much about anything beyond getting there, in fact. The ticket agent had told her it would be a grueling journey. Not only would the weather be unbearably hot and the roads rough and bad, but there could be danger from Indians, especially the closer she got to Tombstone.

Then something happened that had given her an idea. Stepping away from the ticket window, she had watched as a young woman inquired about passage to

Texas to meet her fiancé. The agent had minced no words in warning of the perils to be faced by a woman, and it dawned on Kitty how he had mistaken *her* for a boy. So that was when she decided that if she could fool him, she should also be able to deceive the potential villains he had warned the other woman about— Indians and outlaws who delighted in taking females captive to perform unspeakable acts of savagery.

So Kitty thanked Miss Mildred for the clothes but knew she would not be taking them.

With a promise to try and see her at the depot to say farewell, Mildred waved and continued on.

Kitty eagerly tore the envelope open. Money fell out, along with a piece of paper. Grabbing the bills, she was amazed to see there was nearly three hundred dollars, but she was puzzled by the paper, which looked to be part of a crudely drawn map.

Quickly, she began to read, then recoiled in horror as the words seemed to leap from the page to slap her full in the face.

Dear Kitty Parrish,
I am sorry to tell you that your uncle is dead. He and his partner were murdered. He told me before he died to send you this money and piece of map if anything happened to him. There was a ring he wanted you to have, too, but it wasn't on him when his body was found.

Opal Grimes

Kitty stumbled across the yard and to the porch and sank down on the steps as the world spun dizzily around her.

Dear God, it could not be so—her beloved uncle dead, murdered. But how? And why? And had the murderer been caught? There were no details, only cold, blunt words that broke her heart in a thousand pieces and ripped her world apart.

She was still sitting there in a daze as darkness fell. Jabe, returning from his trip to sell the horses, saw her and knew at once something was wrong. "Miss Kitty, what's happened? You sick? You want me to fetch Loweezy?"

She swallowed hard and straightened her spine. There was no need to worry Jabe or the rest of his family. Life had dealt another harsh blow, and she would face it as she had all the others in her past. "No. I'm not sick."

He nodded to the crumpled letter she held in a tight fist beneath her chin. "You hear something to make you sad?"

"Yes, but I'll be all right." She stuffed the letter, along with the money and piece of map, in her pocket.

"I got paid for the horses. Here it is," Jabe said proudly. "I wish it was more, Miss Kitty. I truly do. And I wish I could pay you for this place, too. Lord knows, your givin' it to us is a miracle of God."

"I'm glad for you to have it."

As she watched him walk away, it dawned that she had not, after learning of Daddy Wade's death, considered changing her plans. She would go to Arizona, all right, and find out exactly what had happened.

Maybe she would even find that ring, she thought, lips set in a tight, angry line. Probably she would find it right on Opal Grimes's finger.

She shook away the suspicion and scolded herself for allowing it to creep in. If Opal was that sort, she would never have sent the money. In fact, if not for her having written the letter, Kitty would not have found out Daddy Wade was dead until she got there.

Kitty still grieved terribly for her mother. Yet she knew she would try and concentrate on finding the person responsible for killing Daddy Wade. She wanted, by God, to see that he paid for what he had done.

Although the Indian camp was well hidden among the rocks and boulders of the dense and perilous Dragoon Mountains, Ryder McCloud knew the way.

He was aware he was being watched, but the Indian scouts would allow him to pass unharmed, even though he wore the garb of the white man. They knew him well. After all, half of the blood flowing in his body was as theirs—Apache . . . *Chiricahua*.

Ordinarily, he would have been glad for the trip to visit his people. Proudly he would have donned the knee-high moccasins and breechclout. Also he would have preferred to tie his dark brown hair back from his tanned face with a bandanna or beaded scarf and truly look like one of his own.

He would also have liked to live with the Chiricahua all the time. He loved his people but felt, however, that he could do more for them by passing for white. By so doing, he could warn them of any potential problems with the army. After all, they were renegades. They had escaped from the reservation in the White Mountains where the Arizona Apache had been forcibly moved six years earlier.

He was almost through the pass when the warrior dropped from overhead to land on his feet directly in front of him.

Holding a rifle, his cinnamon-colored face crinkled in a big grin, Coyotay said in greeting, "I could have killed you for a white man, my brother. We are not used to seeing you dressed like our enemy."

Ryder had known Coyotay all his life, and they were, truly, like brothers. "Trousers and a denim shirt don't make a man your enemy."

"True. But it can bring quick death in the Dragoon Mountains. Now, why have you been away so long?

Three moons have passed, and your mother has
started to worry."

"She knows I went to Mexico."

Coyotay's black eyes took on an excited sheen.
"And you saw the land where we can live in peace
from the white man? The land the great chief, Victorio, told us about?"

Ryder felt sadness at the mention of the great
chief's name. He had fled the reservation a year earlier, taking three hundred warriors with him. He had
been killed a few months later.

Ryder reminded Coyotay, "The white man cannot
cross the border to hunt for us. It's the Mexicans we
have to worry about, and, yes, I saw the land. We will
be safe there. Chief Victorio would have been, too,
had he not been killed."

"And when can we go there?"

"When we have gold, so that we will never have to
raid again."

Coyotay grinned. "Yes, and your mother has told
us about the gold your father has promised."

Ryder glanced away, unable to look at his face,
shining with hope. The situation had changed drastically, but he did not want to divulge anything until he
spoke with his mother. She had to be told first. "Is
everyone in camp?"

"Only the women. The men are out hunting."

He held up his hand, which Coyotay pressed in a
gesture of camaraderie, then rode on through the final
pass to follow the narrow path upward.

Soon he could smell the roasting pits. Stems of the
green and tender yucca were being cooked before drying in the sun for storing. He also caught the aroma
of white rootstocks boiling with rabbit meat for soup.

As he rounded one last boulder, the camp came
into view. Since it was a sunny day, the women were
cooking outside their wickiups. Children, most of them

naked, were running about, squealing as they played. Skinny dogs lurked, anxious for any scraps tossed their way. Deer skins were stretched out in the sun to dry, and a few women were still beating dirty clothes with rocks beside the stream that flowed from higher up the mountain.

Word spread quickly as Ryder rode through the camp, and by the time he reached his mother's wickiup, she was pushing aside the bearskin covering at the door to hold her arms wide, her face ignited in a wide grin.

"Oh, I have missed you so," she cried, hugging him. "I always worry when you stay away so long."

Releasing him and stepping back, she held up a string of colored beads. "See what I made so I will know how long you were away? They are counting beads. The six white ones are for the days of the week, and the colored are for Sundays, and . . ." Her voice trailed off. Brow furrowing, she looked at him with concern. "Something is wrong, my son. Tell me."

The other women were watching, so Ryder took his mother's hand and drew her back inside the wickiup.

He indicated they should sit, then bluntly said, for there was no easy way, "Father is dead."

With a little gasp, her hands fluttered to her cheeks, and she began to sway to and fro. Then, with the stoicism of the Apache, she took a deep, shuddering breath, lowered her hands, and looked him straight in the eye. "Tell me what happened."

"He was murdered. Him and his partner both."

She was silent for a long while. Ryder held her hand. Finally, she said, "The last time you saw him, when he told you about the gold he had found, he said he wanted to share it with me and my people to help us make a new life in Mexico."

"I remember."

"And he said he might even join us."

"I believe he would have. He never stopped loving you."

"And I always loved him. I just could not live in the white man's world. But now he is dead, and we have to go on without him, and you must find his gold. That way, good will come from the grave. And he would want us to have it."

"It will be hard. He never told me where he made the strike. All he ever said was that it was well hidden. He and Parrish had drawn a map and torn it in two and each kept half."

"Do you think whoever killed them has it? If so, they may have already found the gold. How long ago did this happen?"

"Two months or so, according to the sheriff. I was in Mexico. But I don't think the killer got them to tell him anything. The sheriff said Father was still alive when he was found, and the last thing he said was that he was taking the secret to the grave with him."

"And the maps weren't found on the bodies?"

"No. The sheriff said their pockets were empty."

His mother, called Pale Sky, thought a moment, then hesitantly suggested, "Your father might have told someone else about the gold. Did he have a woman?"

"Not that I know of. But Parrish did. Father once told me her name and said she works in a saloon in Tombstone."

"Men tell women things sometimes in the night, when they are close. Find her," she said sharply. "Make her tell you what she knows. Our people need the gold to keep from starving in our new home."

"I will try," he promised.

Then, after a gentle embrace, he left her to mourn privately the only man she had ever loved.

# Chapter 2

It was late afternoon when Ryder reached the outskirts of Tombstone, Arizona. A dust-beaten collection of tents and wooden shanties, it was perched on a high, treeless plateau between the Dragoon and Whetstone mountains.

Already the noise from the saloons and gambling halls could be heard as the town began to come alive for the night.

It was a rowdy, rambunctious place. Big, too. Ryder had heard at last count there were around eighty houses, nearly four hundred tents, and the population was climbing above two thousand.

Making up the growing number were miners in from prospecting for silver in the mountains and cowboys off the range looking for an oasis of pleasure in women, liquor, and gambling. Added to the crowd were confidence men who loitered about waiting to tempt strangers with offers of land that had no title or shares in gold and silver mines that had no ore.

Too many who drifted in were hell-raisers, ready to take umbrage at any affront, and hardly a night went by when someone wasn't killed and hauled off to Boot Hill. A wind-swept, rocky cemetery, it was reserved for the common folk. Those considered respectable had their own burying ground. All in all, the town undertakers, Ritter and Ream, enjoyed a good business.

The town was young—born just two years earlier. There was talk, however, that things were already slowing down. Water flowing into mine shafts was making it unprofitable to dig below five hundred feet.

But, for the time being, Ryder had found it a good place to stay abreast of everything happening in the Arizona territory. Fort Huachuca was nearby, opened when the Apache began threatening settlers and travelers in the San Pedro Valley. Passing for white, of course, Ryder hired on as a scout whenever he needed money. He never led the pony soldiers to the Apaches, however, instead trailing their enemy, the Comanche.

His father had also used the town as a base for his prospecting in the mountains rimming the San Pedro River. But Ryder had never visited him there. When they had met, it had always been at the farm out in the Madera Canyon.

Dan McCloud had always been a private person. Ryder suspected that had to do with him secretly pining for Ryder's mother and the life he might have had with her—if he had been willing to live as an Apache.

Not that his father had ever told him much about those days. The two were not close, anyway, but Ryder had sensed a change in him the last time they met. He had been in the vicinity of the farm and stopped by to see if his father was there. He had been, and that was when he confided he had found a rich gold strike.

He had also explained about his partner and how the two got together. By coincidence, they had, unknowingly, been prospecting in the area, and, on the same day, made the find in the same location. Both being wise, sensible men, they decided that rather than argue about it, they would pool their resources and work the dig together.

His father knew about Ryder and his mother having

run away from the reservation with other Chiricahua. He also knew that one day they hoped to go to Mexico to live in peace. When he told Ryder he wanted to share his gold to enable them to do so, indicating he might even go with them, Ryder knew for certain he still loved Ryder's mother.

Their story was sad. When he was seventeen, his father had been captured and made a slave by the Chiricahua band of the Apache. But, iron-willed and full of spirit, he had won the respect and admiration of his captors, and, as a result, they eventually made him a blood brother.

He had, along the way, fallen in love with Pale Sky, and the two married with the blessings of the tribal leaders. Ryder was born, and, for a time, it seemed Dan McCloud had settled down to his life as an Apache. But that was only on the surface. Inside, he longed to return to his own world.

When Ryder was seven, his father had taken him, and his mother, and left the band. But his mother had not been happy and longed to return to her people. His father would not hear of it, but his mother was determined. Finally, after three years of being homesick and desperate, Pale Sky took Ryder and ran away, only to have Dan catch them before she could reach the protection of her people. Enraged, he had told her he no longer wanted her, that she could go but could not take Ryder with her.

Ryder, however, loved his mother deeply. He also loved the ways of her people—*his* people. Finally, when he was around twelve years old, he ran away from the farm in Madera Canyon and found his way to her.

It was a long time before he saw his father again. When Ryder reached sixteen, he declared that he wished to be a novice and go through the four stages of the demanding rites to become a Chiricahua warrior. A year later, he was forced to the reservation along with all the Apaches in the Arizona Territory.

The desolate area in the White Mountains made the Indians anxious, restless, and angry. Prospectors and cattlemen moved in and unlawfully took possession of large parcels of land. Authorities in Washington condoned it. Soon the original Chiricahua were squeezed onto the poorest property in the area. That was when groups led by strong and experienced leaders began to escape. Once they did, they brutally killed and plundered anyone they encountered.

Ryder also escaped, and it was during a raid that he did not, at first, recognize the farm that had once been his home, nestled in a canyon. Then he saw his father charge onto the porch firing a deadly Henry .44.

Another warrior had been about to fell him with an arrow, but Ryder screamed at him to stop, then pleaded with all his Apache brothers to cease fire and abandon the raid. They did as he asked, not understanding until he later told them they were about to kill his father.

That night, Ryder had returned to sneak inside the shack. There was a brief scuffle, as Dan McCloud did not at first recognize his son.

Gradually, as Ryder visited from time to time, they came to know each other again, overcoming any feelings of ill will or resentment. When Ryder told his mother, her eyes had sparkled like crystal waters in moonlight, and she had urged him to continue seeing his father whenever he could.

It was along about that time that Ryder searched the part of his heart that flowed with white man's blood and made up his mind he could no longer go out with the war parties. He promised the leaders, however, that he would remain loyal to his chosen people by working for the white soldiers. Then he could pass along important information.

Like the Chiricahua, Dan McCloud accepted Ryder's double life, and they shared some good times together through the years.

Eventually, Ryder arranged the first meeting between his parents since their separation. They spent several days together but parted with nothing resolved. His father was not about to go back to the Apaches—who would not have welcomed him after his abandonment, anyway. And his mother still wanted no part of being a white settler's wife.

It had been a gut-wrenching blow when Ryder heard of his father's death. He had stopped in Tombstone after returning from Mexico and was having a drink when he overheard two men talking nearby about how Opal Grimes was having a hard time getting over the death of her lover, even though it had been several months.

Stunned, Ryder's hand holding his glass had frozen in midair. His father had said *Opal Grimes* was the name of the woman Wade Parrish was involved with.

When the men went on talking about it, speculating that Parrish and his partner had been killed over their secret gold mine, Ryder bolted from the saloon and went straight to the sheriff's office. Without divulging that Dan McCloud was his father, he learned that he and Parrish had been found murdered, and there were no clues as to who was responsible. With at least one violent death occurring every day in Tombstone, the sheriff had to think hard to even remember the incident Ryder was asking about.

He did manage to recall, however, that Dan McCloud was still alive when another prospector happened by the next day. He had lived long enough to proudly say he had never told where the gold was, and that he was taking the secret to the grave with him.

Ryder had not been surprised to hear it. His father would have held on to life tenaciously, along with his secret, for he had been a strong man, both in spirit and body.

Other than adding that the two had been buried in Boot Hill, there was nothing else the sheriff could tell him.

Pulling himself from reverie, Ryder rode on through the loud, lusty town. It was cluttered with saloons, some of which were nothing but tents with the bar made of a plank laid across two beer kegs.

Then there were the numerous jerry-built structures and shacks where brothels operated inside.

Like all boomtowns, Tombstone had its reputable section, which was, literally, one side of Allen Street, the main thoroughfare. Decent shops and restaurants occupied the south, while the saloons and gambling and dance halls claimed the north—right where Ryder headed.

Soiled doves—prostitutes—stood in doorways and leaned out of windows as they boldly called out early invitations for pleasuring. One called Ryder by name, and his eyes raked over her as he tried to recall having met her. She had big breasts, a tiny waist, and long, shapely legs. Her cheeks were bright with orange rouge, her lips painted the color of blood. With her hair piled on her head in ringlets and caught with a feathered comb, she looked like all the other prostitutes that worked the streets from the flimsy shacks.

"You don't remember me," she said, hands on her hips as she swayed from side to side in a disappointed rhythm. "And we was so good together, too. The name's Bonnie. And I remember yours"—she gave a lusty wink—" 'cause I thought it fit you perfect the way you rode me hard, Ryder. I loved every minute of it, too."

"Now, come on in," she pressed close, looping her hand through his arm. "I'll give you two for one."

"Sorry." He extricated himself. "But I've got some business to see to."

Her lower lip dropped in a mock pout. "Well, try to come by when you're done. For you, the offer will still be good."

He said he might, knowing all the while he wouldn't. He had too many other things on his mind.

He passed a section where higher-class establishments were situated. Pausing at the window of the Cosmopolitan Hotel's Maison Doree restaurant, his mouth watered when he read the menu of beef brisket and ham cooked in a champagne sauce. Supper for him would be boiled beans and bacon for six bits at Dawson's Saloon.

At Dawson's, he asked the bartender if he knew of a faro dealer named Opal.

"Oh, yeah. Everybody in Tombstone knows Opal. She's the best dealer and caller in town. Works at the fanciest place, too—the Oriental Saloon. It's owned by Wyatt Earp. He's the brother of the city marshal— Virgil Earp."

The bartender went on to eagerly share the story, "She lost her man a few months back, and she ain't been holdin' forth as many hours as she used to." He snickered. "You aimin' to try and win at faro tonight?"

"I aim to try to win at something," Ryder responded quietly, smiling to himself to think how it would be nice to luck up and learn something about the location of his father's gold strike, or a clue to his murderer . . . *something*.

He finished his supper and went directly to the Oriental Saloon.

It was crowded and noisy, air thick with the smell of whiskey, sweat, and perfume. But it was also a truly fancy place; the decor, stunning. Crystal chandeliers hung overhead, and the shelves behind the great carved mahogany bar were lined with a variety of whiskey bottles and expensive glassware. Paintings of enticing, buxom, nude women adorned the walls along with huge gilt-edged mirrors.

Saloons got shot up plenty in Tombstone, but Ryder knew the Oriental was in less danger because of the Earps. He spotted Virgil, wearing the badge denoting his position as city marshal, making himself quite visible as he walked about keeping an eye on potentially rowdy customers.

The faro area was a busy place, with three people running it—a dealer, a lookout, and a casekeeper, who was sitting at the table with a device that looked like an abacus, which showed what cards had been played.

Opal Grimes, he learned by hearing her name called, was the woman working as dealer. She was older than he had expected and not particularly pretty. Her bright red hair, however, was striking, and her blue eyes might have softened her hardness had they not been dulled with what could only be grief.

Unlike the other girls around in bright, flashy, low-cut gowns, Opal was more sedate, in dark blue velvet with a high neck and long, tapering sleeves. And she was all business, her attention focused on conducting the game.

Ryder watched and listened as a man who had just won called out to Opal, "Hey, gal. If you'll take me home with you tonight, I'll split my winnings."

She did not respond. Nor did she look at him.

The man standing next to the amorous winner laughed and jabbed him with an elbow. "There ain't enough money in all of Tombstone to buy Opal. Don't you know that, Barney? She's a one-man woman, fer sure."

"Only her man just got hisself killed," Barney irritably snapped. "And she might be lookin' for another, so mind your own business."

At that, Opal raised angry, scathing eyes. "Both of you got big mouths. Now, are you gonna play or flap your jaws?"

"They better play," someone else yelled. "I didn't come here for no foolish chatter."

"Nobody tells me what to do!" Barney, who had been sitting down, leaped to his feet. His chair fell with a clatter, and all around more toppled over as men hurried to get out of the way of brewing trouble.

Another man suddenly stepped from the smoke and shadows of a corner just behind Opal. In a deep, ominous voice, he barked out, "You'd best shut your pie hole and get the hell out of here, boy, or you're gonna wake up in hell."

Barney whirled on him, hand inches from his holstered gun but making no sudden moves that might trigger a draw before he was ready. "Who the fuck are you, and what's it to you? He's runnin' his mouth at me, and—"

"And you'd best shut up," Barney's companion said uneasily. "That's Nate Grimes, Opal's brother. He's a gunfighter, and he'll kill you without battin' an eye if you mess with his sister."

Ryder tensed, ready to get out of the way should there be any shooting.

Barney's Adam's apple bobbled as he swallowed hard. Carefully, he shifted his hand from his side to hold it in front of him in a pleading gesture. "Hey, I didn't mean no disrespect. I've always thought Opal was a looker, and—"

Nate Grimes brusquely cut him off. "I think you'd best just leave, Big Mouth."

Nervously licking his lips, Barney gathered up his tobacco pouch and winnings and retreated with a conceding nod.

Opal, furious, turned on her brother. "You had no

business doing that. I don't need you hovering over
me like a vulture."

"Hell, somebody's got to look after you," he mumbled, drifting away.

The excitement over, the faro game resumed.

Ryder found a table where he could keep an eye
on Opal without being obvious about it, and the night
wore on.

A few fights erupted, but Virgil Earp was able to
keep the peace. Every so often shots would ring out
from somewhere else in town, and he would rush in
that direction to see if he was needed. Most of the
time it was a drunk cowpoke kicking up his heels, but
around midnight there was a gunfight in the street and
both men involved were killed.

Ryder sipped his beers slowly. Time passed. Finally,
around three o'clock in the morning, he saw Opal
begin to put her gaming tools away—the spinning device known as the *goose,* along with the numbered
balls. Only a few men were still playing, and they
grumbled, but she declared she was tired and quitting
for the night.

When she left the saloon a short while later, Ryder
was waiting in a dark alley across the street. She never
knew that he followed her to her shanty at the edge of
town, for he knew well the silent way of the Apache.

Once he saw where she lived, he melted into the
night to retrieve the Indian garb he kept hidden in
the not too distant hills.

A white man might not be able to persuade her to
tell all she knew . . . *but an Apache would.*

It was another night when Opal could not fall
asleep. Thinking about Wade kept her wide awake
and staring into the darkness for long, miserable
hours. She missed him terribly.

Bothering, also, was how Wade's niece was on her

way west. She had sent a telegram advising approximately when she would arrive by stagecoach. She was bringing her half of the map, she said, in hopes that between the two of them they could figure out the location of the gold mine.

A few weeks after the telegram, Opal received the letter Kitty had written earlier. In it, she told about her mother dying and how she had nowhere else to go except to join Wade and would be leaving soon.

Opal felt bad for the girl and knew in a way how she felt. After all, Opal had no family except Nate, and he was a big pain in the butt, always getting drunk and causing trouble. Oh, he made like he was so devoted to her, because she was his sister, but the truth was, he only came around wanting money. They were not close and never had been.

Wade hadn't liked him, either. He said he was too possessive of her and didn't like his mooching. They had not got along, and it had made Opal so happy when Wade promised that once he had enough ore dug he would marry her and take her to California to live. Nate wouldn't have dared follow after them, and Opal hoped it would make him settle down and get married himself, maybe.

But it was not going to happen, she cried to think. She would never get out of Tombstone, because where would she go and what did it matter, anyway, with Wade dead?

Tossing and turning, she finally got out of bed and poured herself a stiff drink from the bottle of whiskey she kept hidden from Nate. There was a hole in the wall behind the stove he did not know about. Concealed there also was the telegram from Kitty. Opal was keeping it to remind her of the date she was expected. She planned to meet the stagecoach when it got in; the girl would not know a soul. But Opal did not want Nate to know about the girl's coming, be-

cause she was uncertain as to what he might do. He
had never approved of her being with Wade and probably wouldn't like her having anything to do with
his family.

The whiskey took effect, and she curled beneath the
covers once more, eyelids heavy. And, as she drifted
away, she decided maybe it was not a bad thing that
Kitty Parrish was coming, after all. She would love
her because she was Wade's kin. Perhaps they would
be close, like mother and daughter, and having Kitty
around would be like having a part of Wade, and . . .

She slept.

*Then awakened with a start.*

Someone was in the room with her. She could make
out a figure looming over her.

Anger overrode fear as she surmised that it could
only be her brother. "Nate, how dare you come sneaking in like this and scare me to death—"

Terror was a ramrod up her spine as she felt something cold and sharp pressed against her neck and
heard the husky, whispered warning, "Scream and
you die."

The first light of dawn was creeping around the
edges of the shuttered window above her bed. With
eyes so wide she could feel the skin tearing at the
corners, she saw the Indian holding the flint knife at
her throat.

His face was painted in streaks. She could not dis-
tinguish all the colors but saw red mostly, with a long
black swath down his nose.

He leaped, effortlessly, up on the bed to squat and
straddle her. Leaning into her face and still pressing
the knife, his breath was hot, harsh. "Tell me what I
want to know, and I will let you live."

He relaxed the pressure of the blade to allow her
to whisper in capitulation, "Yes. Anything. Just don't
hurt me, please . . ."

The Indian sank back on his haunches. His hair was pulled back from his painted face by a rag across his forehead. He wore only knee-high moccasins and a breechclout. "You were Wade Parrish's woman. He told you about his gold—gold that belongs to the Apache. Where is it?"

"I . . . I don't know," she stammered. "I swear it. He never told me exactly . . . somewhere in the mountains around the San Pedros."

"There was a map."

She licked her lips nervously and tried not to swallow, because she could feel the sharp flint threatening to slice into her flesh. "I . . . I never saw it. I mean . . . I never saw all of it. Only part. Not enough to tell where they were digging."

She had to swallow, and winced as she felt her skin tear beneath the blade, ever so slightly. "Please . . . ," she begged between clenched teeth. "You're cutting me."

He pulled the knife back a bit. "Where is the part of the map that your man gave to you?"

Stunned that he knew it had been divided, she managed to say, "I don't have it, anymore. He had a niece . . . back east . . . and he told me if anything happened to him to send everything I had of his to her. And I did. There was a little money, too. I don't have that, either."

"I want only the map."

"But I told you—I sent it to his niece. And I can't draw it from memory, and it wouldn't mean anything without the rest of it, anyway. He and Dan—that was his partner—they drew it tricky, so nobody could look at half and guess where the ore was. So it wouldn't help you, even if you had it. Now, please"—tears spilled down her cheeks—"don't hurt me. I've told you all I know. I swear it."

He disappeared so quickly that, for one crystallized

moment, Opal actually wondered if he had been there at all or if it were a horrible, horrible nightmare.

And then the moment of paralyzed astonishment passed, and she began to scream, over and over again.

Ryder heard the sound echoing as he stealthily escaped into what was left of the night.

Back in his hideaway he changed into trousers, shirt, and boots. Holster and gun replaced knife and case. Then, Indian garments stowed away till the next time they were needed, he washed the war paint from his face in a nearby stream. That done, he bedded down to sleep for most of the day.

That night he returned to Tombstone and the Oriental Saloon. He bought a drink and helped himself to the free supper on the bar—boiled eggs, spiced pigs' feet, and pieces of spit-roasted chicken.

As he ate, he listened to excited talk about the wild savage that had sneaked into town the night before, intending to rob everyone's favorite faro dealer. He was after her man's gold, it was being said, only he didn't find any. Nate Grimes was up in arms and swore if the red-skinned son of a bitch dared come back, he'd be ready.

Ryder's sleeves were rolled up above his elbows. He was deeply tanned, but there was little about him that looked Apache. Neither did he sound like one, having learned how to speak without a native accent—except when he did so on purpose, like when he had spoken to Opal Grimes. His father had seen to it he was educated in white ways, just as his mother had wanted him to learn those of the Chiricahua Apache.

He kept an eye on Opal and could tell she was nervous. Her face was pale, drawn, and her hands had a slight tremor.

He knew, without a doubt, it would take her a long time to get over her fright.

*He also knew she had been hiding something from him.*

Nate Grimes hovered nearby, casting suspicious glances about. It was as though he expected the savage Apache to appear at any second.

Finally satisfied that everyone was busy for the night, Ryder returned, unobserved, to Opal's shanty.

During raids on white settlers in the old days he had learned to take a homestead apart and discover every imaginable hiding place. He had no trouble finding Opal's. It seemed many people favored stashing things behind a stove.

There was not much. A half-full bottle of whiskey and a gold nugget.

He picked up the nugget for closer scrutiny. He knew very little about gold ore but thought it was good quality. Large, too. Probably worth several hundred dollars. He put it back. He had not come to steal gold.

Disappointed, for he had searched the rest of the shanty and not found anything significant, he was about to turn away when a piece of paper caught his eye. He dared think it might be the map but saw it was only a telegram.

Curious as to why Opal would bother to hide it, he began to read, and, once more, hope surged within him like a mountain stream in a flash flood.

It was from Wade Parrish's niece. She was on her way to Arizona and would arrive in only a few weeks.

*And she was bringing her half of the map with her.*

# Chapter 3

Kitty ached from head to toe and had never felt so tired in her life. Sleeping on a stagecoach, she had quickly discovered, was next to impossible.

In the past three weeks, the only time she'd had any rest was stretched out on the floor of a home station. Normally, the stagecoach did not stop overnight, but there had been times when bad weather forced them to do so. Passengers, however, were not given the luxury of the bunk beds reserved for stage drivers, conductors, and express messengers changing runs.

Kitty kept to herself. When she did talk to anyone, she was careful to make her voice deep, lest she sound like a girl. The name she was using was *Kit,* a masculine abbreviation of her own.

As it turned out, everyone mostly ignored her, not only because of her surly manner but also her unkempt appearance. Her hair was long, deliberately unruly, and fell across her face. She wove frayed overalls and a tattered shirt, with a gun and holster strapped about her waist. Big, masculine boots were laced on her feet, and she kept her felt hat pulled down over her eyes.

Kitty did not really mind being somewhat ostracized. She was still grieving over her mother and did not want to be bothered. Other than that, she was concerned only with reaching Tombstone, Arizona, without incident. There she would find Opal Grimes, who would, hopefully, provide her with a place to stay till she could find work . . . or Daddy Wade's gold mine. Her intent was to offer Miss Grimes half if she would help her find it. As for any kin of Dan McCloud that might have a claim, Kitty would share with them, as well. After all, they needed her half of the map— as she needed theirs.

"Get off of me, damn it."

Kitty jumped as the passenger seated across from her in the coach, Seth Barlow, yelled at another passenger, Sarah Humphries. She had dozed off and slumped against his shoulder. In the past few days, Seth had become increasingly irritable, constantly griping and grumbling and getting angry at the slightest irritation.

Sarah, face red and embarrassed, straightened herself and squeezed as far away from him as she could. "I'm sorry. I didn't mean—"

Seth growled, "Just keep away from me. I know what you're after—a husband, and I wouldn't have a bony old bag like you. So leave me alone."

"But I wasn't . . ." She fell silent, blinking back humiliated tears.

The man sitting next to her, Lloyd Pendergrass, said, "Pay no attention to him. Mr. Barlow has a touch of *stage craziness,* I'm afraid."

Seth angrily demanded, "Who are you calling crazy, mister? I got a right to ride this stage without some husband-hunting old maid throwing herself at me."

Sarah gasped. "Oh, Mr. Barlow, I'm not doing that, believe me. And I'm not an old maid. I'm a widow. I told you that. I'm going to El Paso to teach on the reservation and make a new life for myself. I still grieve for my late husband, and—"

"And don't waste your breath," Violet Proby, the woman next to Kitty, said with a sneer. "He's just hoping you *are* after him. Hell, he's been trying to feel of me ever since we left Waco."

"I most certainly have not."

"Oh, yes, you have."

"Oh, no, I haven't. You're nothing but a painted-up hussy, and—"

Lloyd Pendergrass yelled, "Stop it. Both of you. God, but I'm sick of all this bickering. Will we ever get to El Paso?" He poked Sarah with his elbow and nodded to the space between Kitty and Violet. "Why don't you just move over there so you'll be sure not to touch the old grump?"

Sarah blinked and looked at Kitty uncertainly. "I . . . I don't think there's enough room."

Kitty was staring out the window, refusing to be a part of it all. She knew she was the reason Sarah did not want to switch seats—she did not want to be next to her.

Lloyd said, "Then change places with me. I certainly won't fall asleep and lean on him."

Sarah shook her head. "No. I'll stay awake. We should be stopping soon."

Seth gave a snort. "I sure as hell hope so, because I'll ride on top before I'll spend another day with you idiots."

Kitty had heard Mr. Barlow say he was going all the way to Tombstone, while the others were getting off in El Paso. If no one else boarded, it would mean she would be alone with him the rest of the way, and, Lord, how she dreaded that.

Not only had the passengers been friendlier in the beginning, but the trip had been pleasant. They would stop every twelve miles or so at what was called a swing station, to change horses. Those stations were little more than a stable and a granary run by a couple of stock tenders. Stops were longer at the home stations, which were forty to fifty miles apart. Besides bunks for the line's employees, there was a dining room and a stage and telegraph office.

Food had been good back then, too. They would be served things like fried ham and potatoes, stewed veal, canned tomatoes, peas, and rolls and butter. Moving on, however, they had to subsist on two pitiful meals a day—fried salt pork of dubious age, corn dodgers, dried fruit, and bitter coffee with no sugar or milk.

They'd had good stages at first, too—Concords, which were the finest, almost eight feet long and five feet wide, with seats upholstered in the finest leather, and wood paneling with polished metal fittings. Curtains were also made of leather, which could better absorb the wind and rain.

Horses were nicer then, too, but as they left behind settled farms and breeding ranches, half-wild stock was pressed into service. Squealing, biting mustangs, barely broken, were forced into harness.

So, as the journey wore on, passengers became increasingly uncomfortable. There was a critical lack of sleep and the misery of close quarters and tedium. Legs swelled, muscles cramped, joints throbbed, and tempers flared.

Kitty knew Lloyd Pendergrass had been quite serious when he said Seth Barlow had a touch of stage craziness. It was a recognized malady of the West, and sometimes passengers became violent and actually had to be thrown off the stage in the middle of nowhere to keep them from harming others.

She sneaked a glance at Mr. Barlow. He was plenty mad, she could tell. His eyes were stormy, his face was red and puffy, and with one hand he was noisily popping the knuckles of his other.

Violet suddenly cried, "I wish you'd stop that, you old goat."

"And I wish you'd kiss my ass, you strumpet." He raised his hand as though to hit her.

At that, Lloyd Pendergrass lunged for him.

Sarah Humphries screamed as she was mashed back in the seat, caught between them.

"Atta boy, Lloyd!" Violet was bouncing up and down and beating her knees with her fists. "Teach him not to talk that way to a lady. Beat his ass."

Seth landed a punch on Lloyd's chin, and Lloyd grabbed him by his throat as they fell on top of Violet and Kitty.

"Somebody make them stop," Sarah screamed, hands covering her face.

Then she screamed louder as the stage hit a bump, knocking the fighters back into her, and she was struck in the face by a swinging boot.

Finally, the driver realized what was going on and began to rein in the horses.

But before he could come to a complete stop, Kitty saw the sudden glint of steel as Seth pulled a knife from his boot. In a flash, she drew her pistol. Firing inside a stagecoach might be dangerous, but she knew what she was doing and had to take the chance. Swiftly aiming, she pulled the trigger and shot the knife out of Seth's hand just as it began a downward arc toward Lloyd's chest.

The explosion was like a cannon in such close quarters. Smoke filled the cabin, making everyone gasp and cough.

Violet yelled that she was deaf.

Sarah fainted.

Lloyd threw himself against the door at his back and toppled onto the ground.

Seth fell right behind him.

Rufus Ward, the driver, leaped from his box. "What in thunderation is goin' on back here?" His gun was drawn.

Lloyd scrambled to his feet, knocking dirt from his coat and trousers before pointing at Seth, who had made no move to get up. "Him. He's stage crazy. That boy"—he nodded toward Kitty, who was still in her seat—"if he hadn't shot that knife out of Barlow's hand, he might've killed me."

Rufus looked down at Seth. "Is that true, Barlow? You pull a knife on Pendergrass?"

Seth made a hissing sound. "I'll cut them all if they don't leave me alone. The women are throwing themselves at me, and Pendergrass is taking up for them, and him"—he pointed at Kitty—"he's the worst. He tried to kill me."

Pete Dorcas, the guard, looked down from where he stood in the box. Shotgun in hand, he laughed and said, "He's a damn good shot, too. Blew that knife outta your hand without a scratch." Leaning over, he directed his voice to the inside. "Where'd you learn to shoot like that, boy?"

Kitty did not respond.

Pete shrugged at Rufus. "I don't think I've heard him say a word since we took over."

"He never speaks," Lloyd said. "But he saved my life."

Rufus grunted. "Well, it's a good thing he had a clear shot, or he might've killed somebody."

At that Kitty could not resist snapping, "If I hadn't, I wouldn't have fired."

Everyone looked surprised that she had spoken, then Rufus allowed, "No, I don't reckon you would have."

Violet had got out of the stage and was standing with her hands pressed to her ears.

Rufus shouted at her, "You'll be fine in a while, miss. It just takes time to get the ringing out." He glanced inside and saw Sarah had collapsed. "She'll be fine, too."

After asking Lloyd to see if he could bring Sarah around, Rufus called to Pete to throw down the handcuffs. "I'm not taking no chances before we get to El Paso."

Seth fought against the cuffs, and Pete finally had to jump down from the box to help subdue him.

"A gag would help," Violet snapped as he was wrestled back into the coach.

Rufus assured her that if he heard one more foul word or threat out of Seth, he would personally ram his bandanna in his mouth . . . all the way to his lungs.

With a black look of resignation, Seth settled into grudging silence.

When they were under way again, Lloyd held out his hand to Kitty. "Thanks for saving my life."

Fearing he now felt a sense of kinship and would want to make conversation, she ignored his outstretched hand and returned to her vigil at the window.

With a sigh, he left her alone . . . as did everyone else.

The home station in El Paso was a welcome respite to Kitty for many reasons. She was able to find a private place to take a bath and had time to wash her overalls and shirt and allow them to dry in the Texas heat without anyone seeing her undressed. There was also good food and plenty of cold milk and even a cot in an obscure corner.

She did not realize she had slept for so long till Rufus shook her awake and said they would be rolling soon.

"You were tired, so I let you sleep," he said, sitting down on the side of her cot as he rolled himself a smoke.

She fought the impulse to shrink away from him. After all, it was supposed to be just two men talking and not mattering that one of them was in bed.

He struck a match, lit the cigarette, and took a deep draw before confiding, "I slept quite a spell, too.

Thought I had a couple of days to rest up before the northbound stage got here—that's the run I was scheduled for. But word's come they busted a wheel and they're running late. Then the driver that was supposed to take the run on into Willcox and Tombstone got himself killed in a gunfight in a Mexican cantina.

"So . . ." He shrugged and took another draw. "I'll be taking the stage on to Arizona. Drivers are supposed to change every station, but there ain't nobody else. I'm just hoping for relief along the way, but I'm afraid there won't be any."

She wondered why he was telling her his troubles and decided it had to do with the shooting incident. Still, she did not want to get close to anyone and remained silent.

After a moment, he looked down at her and laughed. "You're a strange one, Kit Parrish, but you oughta do all right out here. You keep your mouth shut, so it's likely you'll stay out of trouble. Knowing how to use that gun will help, too. Tombstone is a rough and dangerous place." He stood. "Best get up and moving, boy. We're leaving soon as we eat breakfast.

"Afraid we got some shitty horses, too," he said on the way out. "Crazy, half-broke mustangs. It's them or nothing, though. Shortage of horses. With a hundred miles to go, we'll probably wind up with mules before it's over."

Kitty dressed quickly and joined him in the dining room along with the new guard, Hank Wallace. Antelope steak, eggs, and hot biscuits were served, along with coffee and milk. She ate as much as she could hold, knowing that with the rest of the way so rugged and barren they would be lucky to get bologna and cheese and tins of herring or sardines at the few and far between stations.

She was having one last helping of biscuits and honey when a commotion erupted in the corral adjacent to the station house.

Rufus and Hank kept eating, but as the noise of horses whinnying and men shouting and cursing continued, Kitty raised from her chair.

"Nothing to worry about," Rufus said around a mouthful of fried egg. "Just the Mexican vaqueros trying to get harnesses on them half-broke mustangs. They'll whip 'em into settling down, though."

Kitty heard the sound of leather striking horseflesh and cried, "They shouldn't do that. You don't have to hit a horse to get him to do what you want."

Rufus and Hank exchanged startled glances as she strode angrily from the room, then hurried to the window to watch as she stormed into the corral.

Kitty marched right over to the vaquero wielding the whip and jerked it from his hand. "You don't have to beat a horse to break him. There are other ways to persuade him—like being gentle."

The vaqueros looked at each other, then at Kitty and broke into gales of laughter.

"Then do it," the one she had wrested the whip from challenged as he pointed to the stamping mustangs, their nostrils flared and eyes wild with rebellion. "We will see how the gringo would do it."

Kitty spent the next few minutes patting the horses and talking to them in soothing tones. Then, when they had stopped their agitated prancing about, she ran her hands along the straps to confirm her suspicion that they were too tight. True, a team had to be firmly harnessed in order to perform as a unit, but a good driver could handle pairs of loosely hitched animals separately. And Rufus, she had seen, was a good driver. He had just made the error of allowing someone else to take care of his horses.

After she had retied all the straps, the team settled

down even more. By that time Rufus and Hank had
finished eating and were at the corral.

Rufus, impressed, said, "I can tell you know about
horses, boy."

"I raised them back in Virginia," Kitty could not
resist proudly sharing. "I never broke horses for harness to something as big as a stagecoach, but I have
for wagons and carriages. It's just a matter of
patience."

"Which you sure have got."

His beefy hand slapping down on her shoulder was
staggering, and she stumbled a few steps before
righting herself.

There were only two other passengers, a married
couple, going only as far as the home station near
the Arizona border. As they waited to board, they
introduced themselves to Kitty and tried to make conversation, but she was unresponsive, and they soon
gave up and left her alone.

She regretted having to be so unfriendly. It had
been a tedious journey, and it would have been nice
to pass the time chatting.

Thinking back, she realized that her whole life had
been lonely and friendless, due to everyone hating her
mother as they had. Maybe, she dared hope, things
would be different in Arizona. No one would know,
or care, about her past, and she could feel like a part
of things . . . a part of life.

Kitty started to get up into the coach, but Rufus,
who had been staring down at her from the driver's
box with a thoughtful expression, suddenly said to
Hank, "How about you ridin' below for a while and
lettin' Kit come up here with me?"

"Sure thing," Hank said. "He proved he can use a
gun if he has to."

Drivers, Kitty had learned along the way, could
share the box with others if they chose to. They would

ask the guard to yield his place temporarily to a favored passenger. It was an honor seldom refused, despite the precarious perch.

She did not want to get up there but hated to say so. After all, Rufus was one of the nicest drivers she had encountered. Some of them had been genial and outgoing, warming to the passengers right away. Others had been aloof, regal-acting almost, and coldly silent.

But she knew it was an important job, and not just any sort of man could drive a stagecoach. After all, it was a big responsibility to get nervous passengers through wild, lonely, and dangerous country—all the while handling a team of horses on rough roads in sometimes terrible weather.

She settled in beside Rufus and noted how he held the reins wrapped in the fingers of his left hand. The right he kept free for the whip or handling the brake.

"Think you'd like to drive one of these rigs?" he asked around a mouthful of chewing tobacco.

Kitty mumbled that she didn't think so.

He then proceeded to tell her his life's story and how he had wound up as a driver. She listened with interest, enjoying his tales, relieved he was such a talker that he did not mind her contributing nothing to the conversation.

In a few hours they reached a swing station. As Rufus had predicted, they were given mules.

There was time for a quick meal of corn dodgers and boiled eggs, handed out by the old man tending the stables. Then they were on their way again. Hank took his place in the box, and Kitty settled in with the passengers, realizing how much she had enjoyed being up top.

When they reached the Arizona border and the home station there, Rufus cursed to hear that neither his replacement, nor Hank's, had arrived. "Damn a bear," he roared to the station master. "This was a double run for me. I'm plumb wore out, and you're tellin' me I've got to take this god-danged stage on to Willcox?"

Hank joined the protest. "I don't like it, neither. This was supposed to be my last run. I'm quittin' and headin' to California. Hell, I'm tired of all the time worrying about gettin' an arrow in my back or a bullet in my head."

The stationmaster gave a helpless shrug. "Can't help it, boys. When that stage was attacked by Injuns near Silver Creek last week, it messed up everybody's schedule."

"I don't see why," Rufus said. "That was nowhere near here."

"But the driver was killed. Guard, too. Then a few days later another driver died when the stage turned over. We got a shortage now, but if you boys can finish up the run to Tombstone, the big boss himself says you'll get double pay between here and there."

Rufus and Hank exchanged nods. Extra money was too good to pass up.

"You only got one passenger now, anyway." The stationmaster glanced at Kitty. "And you ain't carrying gold—just mail. So if the Injuns do attack, just hand the box over and don't put up a fight."

Kitty hoped against hope they would make it without trouble.

Indians, she had decided after hearing so many horror stories, were something she prayed never to encounter.

Ryder looked at his warriors. He had asked Coyotay to gather only a dozen, and he had done so. He did not want a large band. He wanted to make it appear that only a few renegades were in the area; otherwise,

the army would think even more soldiers were needed
and increase their number, which he did not want.

The sun was just rising, and the land was colored
in radiant pinks and lavenders, as though liquid flowers had spilled from the horizon. A soft breeze was
blowing. The sky was clear.

It was a good day for a war party to ride.

Coyotay kneed his mustang beside Ryder. "We
are ready."

Like the others, Ryder had streaked his face with
red and black and yellow war paint and carried bow
and arrow, as well as rifle and war club. He was
dressed in full Apache attire—skin vest and shirt and
trousers tucked into knee-high moccasins.

Today he was not Ryder McCloud. He was
Whitebear, a name given him by the tribal council
when he became a man. *White,* for that part of the
people whose blood flowed in half his body, and *bear,*
after a revered Apache leader who had long ago
joined the Great Spirit in the sky.

"We are ready," Coyotay said.

Ryder swept the warriors with a satisfied gaze and
raised his voice to remind them, "We do not kill unless it is to save our life or that of a brother. Our
only reason for attacking this stagecoach is to take the
woman I am seeking."

They raised their hands in salute.

Ryder lifted his as well, then kneed his horse about
and shouted, "Let's ride."

# Chapter 4

"**Y**ou sure don't talk much, do you?" Rufus said to Kitty with a sigh. He had allowed her to ride in the box again since Hank was keeping watch in the rear.

"I don't have anything to say," Kitty mumbled, careful, as always, to make her voice deep. They had just left Willcox, drawing ever closer to Tombstone, and she was anxious to complete the journey for many reasons, one of which was being able to stop pretending to be a boy. She supposed she could have confided in Rufus but saw no point. Besides, it might have made him mad to learn how she had fooled him.

Rufus shot her a glance. "Well, it'd help pass the time away if you'd make a little conversation."

"I just don't have anything to say," she repeated, then added, hoping he would take the bait, "I'm afraid I just haven't had an exciting life like you have. I don't have any tales to tell."

His chest swelled with pride as he settled down to brag about his exploits once more. "Well, I reckon there's not that many folks that do. I've been everywhere and done everything, boy. Fought Yankees. Killed a few, too. And I've left a few Injuns to feed the buzzards along the way."

Kitty cast a wary eye at the red and orange cliffs of ancient volcanic rocks above them. It was easy to imagine a savage Indian watching from behind the green groves of Ajo oaks, piñon pines, and junipers.

"Do the Indians ever attack towns?" she suddenly felt the need to ask, as she wondered how safe she would be in her new home.

Rufus guffawed. "Hell, boy, they've wiped out entire settlements. They burn everything to the ground, steal the livestock, rape and kill the women, torture the men to death, and take the young'uns for slaves. The army will wipe 'em all out sooner or later, though. Till then, folks just have to be on the lookout."

Pointing at a dark, scraggly bush by the side of the road, he said, "See that? The Mexicans call it *sangre de drago,* which means dragon's blood, because of the reddish colored sap. The Injuns use it to make dye for their war paint."

He showed her other things as they rode—signs of coyotes and javelinas, and they spotted jackrabbits and deer along the trail. Red-tailed hawks and prairie falcons wheeled in the sky, and there were flocks of piñon jays, juncoes, and chickadees flitting among the bushes at the base of the cliffs.

"So tell me about raising horses back in Virginia," Rufus prodded when he had grown tired of doing all the talking.

"My family had a farm."

"So how come you left it? Seems to me a body would be a fool to leave a nice farm to come out here and maybe wind up scalped."

"My mother died recently, and I didn't want to stay."

"What about the rest of your family?"

"There was just the two of us. The only family I have left is an uncle in Tombstone."

"Which explains why you're going there. What's his name? What's he doing there?"

The conversation was getting too personal, and

Kitty smoothly changed to another subject. "I notice your gloves are awfully thin. Seems to me you'd want thick ones to keep from getting blisters."

He flexed his fingers. "Yep, they are, but that's so's I can feel the ribbons . . . feel how the animals are responding. If I pull too tight, and it's not needed, they'll dance around. I've got to keep 'em moving smooth.

"Now, these gloves," he went on, "are made of the finest, softest buckskin, but they're cold in winter. I don't dare wear anything warmer, though, like fur, because then I couldn't feel the ribbons. I've known some drivers who got frostbit and lost a finger or two, but that's how it is. You got to be able to feel them ribbons."

Kitty marveled aloud that it took so much dedication to drive a stage, and Rufus beamed. "That's a fact, boy. We got to be able to face any situation—blinding snowstorm, stream too full to ford, or a horse going lame. And not only have we got to be able to decide right then and there what to do, but we've also got to know all about the country we're passing through—routes and landmarks.

"And don't forget the Injuns," he was quick to add. "The times I've run up on 'em, I've managed to get away without me or my passengers getting hurt, 'cause I'll give 'em the gold or anything else they want to keep from having big trouble. And the way I did it was by learning their language—Sioux, Pawnee, Comanche. That's what it takes. Why, I even know of a few drivers who actually went and lived among 'em to learn their ways so's they could get along with 'em should they ever get attacked."

"That's really something," Kitty murmured.

"Oh, that ain't nothin'. Drivers are just tougher than most men, that's all. But you know somethin' else?" He jabbed her with his elbow and snickered. "They ain't all men."

"You mean there are *women* drivers?"

"Well, you never know, especially since it came out about Charlie Parkhurst. He could handle the reins as good as anybody and fought off a goodly number of bandits and mishaps in his day. Even when he got old and suffered with rheumatism and lost an eye from a horse's kick, he kept on driving. He finally retired to a farm in California, and nobody knew he was actually a woman till he died of cancer in '79, and they started getting his—or I should say *her*—body ready for burying."

He paused to lean and spit tobacco over the side. "Now, I never met Charlie, but I can tell you if I had, he wouldn't have fooled me. Ain't no woman smart enough to pull the wool over ol' Rufus's eyes. I'd have spotted him right off for what he was."

Kitty turned her head as she felt her lips pull in a smile.

Reaching a stream, they stopped to water the mules and have a drink themselves.

Kitty made sure to hang back, pretending to empty her boots of sand as Rufus and Hank relieved themselves. That part of her ruse had been especially trying since the drivers and guards, as well as the men passengers, naturally saw no reason to be modest around *Kit*.

Taking care of her own needs had also presented problems from time to time, because she could not let anyone see her. It took some doing, and a lot of anxiety, but she had managed.

"Hey, boy," Hank called as she slipped behind a bush. "You ain't got to be ashamed around us. We don't care if you got a little pecker."

*Soon,* she told herself, *soon all the pretense will be over.*

"You think we'll make Tombstone by dark?" Hank asked Rufus.

Rufus grunted. "We could if we had horses instead of mules. Mules can't cover eight miles an hour like horses, especially stubborn old bags like these. Right now I just want to get through Dragoon Pass. I've heard a band of renegade Chiricahua are holed up in the mountains around there."

"But there hasn't been any trouble around here lately. It's them Mescalero Apache over in New Mexico."

Rufus allowed that was so but said he would not rest easy till they got through the Dragoons and reached the home station on the other side. From there, he anticipated an easy ride to Tombstone. "And if we're lucky, they'll have replacements waiting for us there. Lord knows, I'm worn out."

He called to Kitty as she came out of the bushes. "Boy, you get back on top with me. I know you're a paying passenger, and I ain't got no right to ask you to help out, but I'll feel better with three pairs of eyes watching for Injuns instead of just two."

Kitty did not mind. Actually she preferred being up top to know what was going on. She also had confidence in her ability to use a gun and, if the truth be known, figured she was probably a better shot than either of the men.

When they were rolling again, with Hank covering the rear, Rufus said, "I'm probably worryin' for nothin'. I've been through the pass a hundred times and never run up on an Injun. But I'm still not taking any chances."

He talked on, and Kitty listened. His tales, though sometimes horrifying and oft-repeated, helped pass the time. She was also learning things about her new world.

Still, her mind drifted to thoughts of Tombstone,

what kind of life she might make for herself there, and how she would try to find the gold. The piece of map was well hidden. She had put it in the bib pouch of her overalls, then sewn it shut. But, without the other part, it might be worthless, which, she cynically decided, was probably the only reason Opal Grimes had sent it to her.

Kitty wondered if her uncle and Opal had been in love with each other. She hoped they had, because then Opal would be more inclined to help her till she got on her feet. If the strike could not be found, then she was going to soon run out of what little money she had left.

She wondered if she could find work on a ranch without having to pretend to be a boy, but the stock tenders she had seen at the swing and home stations were all men. And so far she hadn't seen a woman who looked like she could tend a horse, anyway. They all dressed so feminine, in fancy gowns with lots of lace and ruffles and bonnets with silk ribbons.

As if he sensed she was pondering the future, Rufus asked, "So what are you going to do in Tombstone? Look for gold like everybody else? You ain't big enough to be a carpenter."

She gave a shrug. "Work on a ranch, I suppose."

"Then you're headed to the wrong place, boy. Ain't no ranches around Tombstone. It's a boomtown, full of prospectors and hell-raisers. You might find work at a livery stable shovelin' shit, though," he said with a snicker. "Or at a corral. Other'n workin' as a store clerk or carpenter, there ain't many jobs. Now if you was a woman, it'd be different."

She tried to appear only mildly interested. "How's that?"

"Oh, you could make money lots of ways. The gambling halls hire women to deal cards. And if a gal ain't more'n a little bit ugly, she can get a job at a dance hall. You know, dancin' and being nice to the men to get 'em to buy drinks."

"What if she didn't want to do any of those things?"

"She could always be a soiled dove. They make lots of money." He slapped his knee and gave a nasty laugh. "Hell, I've sure spent my share with 'em through the years."

"What's that?"

He looked at her in wonder. "Well, what do they call 'em back in Virginia, boy?"

"Call who?"

"Whores."

Once more she turned away, this time to hide a blush, though it was doubtful he could see her face the way her hair hung so straggly.

"They call 'em soiled doves out here. But while they might make a good living, it's rough. Some of the prettier ones usually find a husband." Suddenly he slammed a beefy hand on her shoulder, and she nearly fell out of the box. "I'll bet you ain't never had a woman, though, have you? How old are you, anyway? Seventeen?"

"Nineteen." That, at least, was not a lie, Kitty thought morosely.

"And you never had any?"

She stiffened. "I really don't like talking about it."

He began to slap his knee over and over as he cackled, "I knowed it. I knowed it. I knowed it. You ain't never had a woman. Well, I'm gonna make you a promise since you been so good about helpin' me out on this run. When we get to Tombstone, I'm gonna take you to see Jenny Lou, my favorite whore. She'll fix you up just fine. I'll even talk her into givin' you a special price, too, and—"

Suddenly, screams split the air like knives ripping canvas, as Indians dropped from the boulders above.

Taken by complete surprise, Rufus was felled by

one blow of a deftly swung war club and toppled over
the side.

Hank, also caught off guard, was struck and pitched
to earth without so much as a grunt.

Kitty, however, had caught a glimpse of movement
just as the shrieks erupted. She twisted in time to miss
being struck by her attacker, and he landed on his
back, then bounded up and toward her. She kicked
him in the groin, and he stumbled backward and fell
off.

The reins were flopping loose, the mules out of control as they began to gallop recklessly ahead in the
wake of all the screaming.

Kitty was reaching forward, trying to retrieve them,
when she heard a shriek and thud as another Indian
dropped behind her.

She drew her gun and fired just as the wagon
lurched wildly, nearly tossing her off. She struggled to
hang on, but the Indian, with a loud oath, grabbed
her as he fell.

Kitty felt a sharp pain as she hit the ground. Then,
from far, far away, beyond the gray, smothering fog
that seemed to wrap about her, she heard voices
speaking a language she did not understand.

"How bad is it?" Ryder asked Coyotay.

Coyotay was already back on his feet, blood streaming from his shoulder. "It is a clean wound. The bullet
went through me. I can still ride."

The other warriors had surrounded the stage. One
of them opened a door, then turned to look at Ryder
in wonder. "It is empty. There are no passengers."

Ryder swore. He had checked the stage schedule
himself—passing for white, of course—and it was the
same as he had read in the telegram. Kitty Parrish
was supposed to be on it, damn it.

He nudged Kitty with his foot. She did not move.

"Go see if you can wake the others and bring them to me," he yelled to his warriors.

Yanking off the scarf that held back his long hair, Ryder began binding Coyotay's wound. "We must get back to the camp and have this tended. You are losing too much blood."

"I will live," Coyotay said between tightly clenched teeth, "but not this one—"

Drawing his knife, he dropped to his knees to straddle Kitty as she lay in a dazed stupor. Fingers twisting in her hair, he brought her head up and was about to slash her throat when Ryder acted swiftly to squeeze his wrist in an ironlike vise and sternly declare, "No. We do not kill. We came to find the woman, not shed blood."

Coyotay spat and turned on him with blazing eyes. "Pah! He drew my blood. For that, he must die."

"No. There will be no killing."

"You cannot expect me to let him live."

"We agreed, Coyotay, not to kill needlessly."

The two locked fiery gazes, and the tension was broken only when one of the warriors reported that the big man, the one who had been holding the reins, could not be roused. "The blow of the war club was mighty. He will sleep for a long time."

"This one is awake," a warrior named Oconee said as he dragged Hank by his shirt collar and dropped him at Ryder's feet.

Ryder spoke to him in English. "Where are your passengers?"

"Only had one . . ." Hank, terrified, pointed at Kitty. "That boy there. He's been the only one since we crossed into Arizona. Now please, let me go . . ."

Ryder cursed the foul luck. Kitty Parrish would, no doubt, be on a later stage, and it would be impossible for him to know which one. He could not risk another attack, anyway, because when the army heard about this one, they would increase their patrols in the area. So all he could do was keep an eye on Opal Grimes, as Kitty Parrish would surely be in touch with her when she eventually arrived. And though it might be difficult to get his hands on her, he was not about to give up.

"Go in peace," Ryder mumbled and turned away, leaving Hank to gratefully retreat, on hands and knees, to take refuge beneath the stagecoach.

Ryder saw that Coyotay was yanking the boy, who had started coming around, to his feet. "What are you doing? I told you—no killing."

Coyotay's chin jutted in defiance. "I take him for my prisoner. He drew my blood. It is my right to do with him as I wish. You say I cannot kill him, but I can take him for a slave."

Ryder had always tried to keep the part of him that was white from conflicting with the tradition of his chosen people. He also had to remember that they were not educated in civilized ways, and it was necessary to tread lightly in order to keep them from becoming resentful of his mixed blood.

He stared at the boy, who was groggily trying to stand. He was a scruffy thing—hair hanging all over his face, baggy overalls, an empty holster strapped around him. He was on the small side and would not make a strong slave. Still, he could be taught to haul water, clean game, and tan hides.

"We have no slaves in our band," Coyotay reminded him. "Not since we escaped the reservation. We can use him."

Ryder caught a glimpse of the boy's eyes as he pushed his hair aside long enough to glare at Coyotay. There was no fear, only anger, for he was too young, too foolish, to know when it was wise to surrender. His spirit would not be easily broken, but Ryder knew Coyotay would try—even if he had to kill him.

And he could not allow it.

"All right," he said finally, "we will take him. But he will be my slave. Not yours."

"But it was *my* blood he drew. He should belong to *me*."

"I am leader, Coyotay. I say how it will be."

Coyotay could not argue with that. The tribal chiefs had named Ryder head of the young warriors group that had fled the reservation, and no one could challenge him and remain in favor with the council.

With an angry jerk of his head, Coyotay strode quickly to his waiting pony.

Ryder looked at the boy uncertainly. If not for the custom of making captives walk, he would have allowed him to ride with him.

"Do as I say, and you won't be harmed," he said quietly as he pulled Kitty's hands in front of her and began to bind her wrists.

She was jolted to hear him speak her language but did not respond as she fought to hang onto her sanity . . . her consciousness, for how easy it would be to faint and escape the madness.

They circled her—men with long hair streaming down their backs, garish stripes and symbols painted on their faces—all staring with black, piercing eyes, lips tightly set and grim.

Except for the one who bound her wrists. His hair was not quite as dark, or as long, and his eyes were the color of cinnamon and were not cruel or harsh as he looked at her. He was different, somehow, but she still loathed and feared him.

"You will walk behind my horse," he said.

Kitty prayed not to stumble . . . not to fall.

She had no idea what the future held at the hands of the savages, but for the moment she had to concentrate on one thing only.

*They could not find out she was a woman.*

# Chapter 5

Ryder could feel the boy's hot, hate-filled eyes glaring at his back. They had been riding for several hours, but the boy was keeping up. Not once had he stumbled. Neither had he made a sound.

They had wound their way higher and higher into the mountains. Ryder kept the rope slack, and his horse's pace slow. He did not want to be unnecessarily cruel, but he knew he could not show any concern for the boy's misery.

They had paused briefly at a stream to water the horses and eat handfuls of pemmican. It was late in the day, and they were all hungry. Ryder offered a portion of his to the boy, but he shook his head.

"You need to eat," he coaxed. "We still have a long way to go, and I cannot go any slower. You have to keep up with us or be dragged."

Kitty was speared by a hot jolt of rage as she hissed between clenched teeth, "You would like that, wouldn't you?"

Ryder shrugged. "No. But if you cannot stand up, then you give me no choice. Now I am offering you food—"

"I don't want that . . . that garbage." She looked at the bag and shuddered. It was made of some kind of skin, and the concoction the Indian was pulling out of it made her stomach roil.

"Dried buffalo meat and berries is not garbage."

Stubbornly, she continued to shake her head.

"As you wish. Now relieve yourself while you have a chance."

Feeling color creep to her cheeks, Kitty noticed how all around her the Indians were taking care of their personal needs. "Not here," she whispered.

Ryder threw back his head and laughed. "So. You are shy. Well, you will soon get over that, but go ahead." He had dropped the end of the rope when he dismounted. "But if you try to run away, you won't get very far.

"And if we don't catch you," he added with a crooked smile, "the wild animals will—mountain lions, grizzly bears, bulls and pigs, and snakes and lizards. They are all out there waiting for fresh meat like you—fresh *white* meat."

She was not about to do something so foolish as to let him think she was even considering escaping. If he, and the others, thought she was too frightened to go plunging into the wilderness by herself, then sooner or later they would turn their backs . . . and she would be ready.

When she returned from the bushes, the Indian who had taken charge of her was talking to the one she had shot. She could not understand what they were saying, but it was obvious they were arguing over her.

Ryder felt like yanking the boy up and throwing him on the back of his horse so they could make better time, but he knew that would make Coyotay even madder than he already was.

Damn it, why couldn't the woman have been on the stagecoach like she was supposed to be? Then he would not be stuck with trying to keep a scrawny boy from being mistreated by Coyotay and the others. In the triumph of doing what they had set out to do,

Coyotay would not have cared about making the boy suffer for having shot him.

And where was the woman, anyway? he thought, fuming as he gave the end of the rope a vicious jerk to bring the boy stumbling forward. There wouldn't be another stagecoach for over a week, and he would have to wait till then to ride into Tombstone to find out if she was on it.

Till then, he would watch over the boy. As long as he was his slave, Coyotay would not harm him. Maybe, in time, he could make Coyotay see it was best to let the boy go. After all, when they left for Mexico, they did not need to be bothered with taking slaves. They would be busy enough dodging army patrols.

Ryder saw how the bottom of the boy's overalls were in tatters from all the weeds and briars. His arms were also scratched and torn. Now and then he stumbled, but never did he cry out or complain.

With a disgruntled sigh, Ryder stared ahead, wishing the day had turned out differently.

The sun was a blazing ball of fire over them, beating down relentlessly, but gradually it began to sink into the west. The day was ending . . . but not soon enough for Kitty. The rope chafed her wrist, and her heels inside her boots were rubbed raw with blisters. The trail they were on was a steep incline, and she was painfully heaving for breath with every step. Her legs were shaking, and her mouth was as dry as the dirt beneath her feet. She wondered how much longer she could go on before falling to be brutally dragged over the sharp rocks.

Wearily raising her chin, Kitty looked at the Indian—Whitebear, she had heard someone call him—sitting astride his horse. He was tall and broad-shouldered. His back, bare now that he had taken off shirt and skin vest, was a deep bronze color.

Though a deadly and dangerous foe, he had seemed to take up for her, and she dared hope he might keep her from being tortured or killed.

But, she acknowledged with a deep, deep shiver, if they found out she was not a boy, Whitebear would not be able to save her from a woman's most dreaded fate.

Her toe struck a rock. Losing her balance, she pitched forward and fell.

Ryder stopped the horse and turned to look down at her. "Can you get up? We are almost there."

Kitty stared beyond him but saw only scrub pines and bushes and big boulders. Nothing resembled a camp of any sort.

"I asked you if you could get up," he repeated sharply. "We are almost there, but if you can't walk, then so help me, I will drag you, boy."

Kitty was close to tears and dangerously near the point of breaking. She was determined, however, not to let the savages wear her down. She had to appear strong and sure of herself, if for no other reason than her own self-esteem.

Amid the pain of her scrapes and bruises and how her wrists were bleeding and her feet were hurting so bad, the image of the last year of her mother's life came to mind. For so long her mother had walked with head held high, ignoring the slights and shuns of her neighbors. But then it was as though her spirit, her mind, just slipped away. She began to cry about her lot in life, how badly she had been mistreated. And she had begun to try and win her neighbor's grace and favors. Kitty pitied how her mother would grovel in her yearning to be accepted. She'd made up her mind that she would never do the same. Not for anyone. And not even now, when her very own life might be at stake.

Slowly, she struggled to stand.

"Good." Ryder nodded approval. "Keep on your feet. The others are hoping to see you dragged the rest of the way."

Suddenly, anger got the best of her. "Then go ahead and do it, you bastard. If you think it makes you more of a man to drag somebody behind your horse, do it."

For a long moment, he merely stared at her, and Kitty fought the instinct to cringe, to wither, but instead stared defiantly back at him—as best she could through the tangle of hair covering her face.

Finally, expressionless, he declared, "You will make a good slave once your spirit is broken, and I think to save you from yourself when I am not around to look after you, I had best see to it right away.

"Now come." He gave a hard tug, almost making her fall again. "And so help me, if you hit the ground again, you'll stay there."

He dug his heels into the sides of his horse and continued on up the grade.

Kitty staggered, stumbled, and nearly fell, but managed to keep on going. Perspiration ran into her eyes to sting and momentarily blind, and she wiped at them with the back of her tied hands.

She heard the sweeping of brush and had noticed how the Indians at the rear of the line used branches to remove any trace of their having passed by. They continued to do so even though they had traveled a long way since leaving the road where she had first been taken.

And then a path appeared, seemingly out of nowhere. The ground was smoother, and as she kept her gaze downward, she could see many tracks.

Without warning, Kitty's knees buckled. She went sprawling into the parched dirt and, with a cry of

panic, realized she was sliding straight toward the edge
of a boulder on her way to plunging into the canyon
below.

Ryder, having let the end of the rope go slack in
his hand as they topped the final hill into the Indian
camp, did not realize the boy was falling in time to
grab hold. The rope slipped from his hand, and he
whirled about to see the boy plummeting headfirst
down the incline and straight toward the edge.

Leaping from his horse, Ryder dropped to a squat
and let the bottom of his slick moccasins and the seat
of his pants take him in a rapid slide down the rocks
to catch the rope and grab it. Digging in his heels, he
held tight as the boy went toppling over.

Kitty was too terrified to scream and went sailing,
paralyzed, over the brim—only to be abruptly held
back by a sharp, painful jerk. Her arms were yanked
above her head and felt as though they were being
pulled from their sockets.

"Use your feet to climb the rocks," Ryder yelled.
"Push yourself upward."

But Kitty was too weak. Her legs felt like wet loaves
of bread—mush. She had no power over them, no will.

Coyotay came running to help Ryder, grumbling all
the while. "I should have slit his throat when you
stopped me. He is nothing but trouble."

As the boy was finally pulled up, his hair parted
from his face for a fraction of an instant, Ryder could
see defiance and anger despite the close brush with
death.

Coyotay, he feared, was right. The boy *was* trouble,
and the sooner he found a way to get him back to his
people, the better. But that would take time and careful planning, because he could not risk annoying Coyotay more than he already was.

The camp was directly ahead. Word had spread

from the posted guards that they had returned, and a curious crowd was gathering.

Coyotay and the others rode ahead, while Ryder hung back, pretending to get the boy to his feet and secure once more. What he wanted, however, was a chance to make him see that his best chance for survival was to surrender his spirit. "If you want to live, you are going to have to humble yourself. I won't always be in camp to look after you."

Kitty's eyes narrowed behind her unkempt hair. "If you are so concerned, why in the hell did you take me prisoner? And what are you, anyway?" Her eyes swept him from head to toe. "You aren't like the others."

Once more, Ryder was reminded how it was easier for him to pass for white, but he offered no explanation, instead saying, "I took you for my slave to save you from Coyotay. He would have tortured you for shooting him."

"I wish I had killed him," she said defiantly.

Ryder shook his head at the boy's audacity. "It is a good thing the others understand little of your language, because they would cut your tongue out. Maybe I should just turn you over to them, anyway. You don't appreciate my trying to help you."

"So what do you want from me?"

"You're going to be my slave and do my bidding, and when I am not here, you will work for my mother. Right now, though, you're going to answer my questions. And none of your insolence." He gave the rope a hard jerk for emphasis.

She could not hold back a grimace of pain, for her wrists were torn and bleeding.

He saw, and loosened his hold. "My mother will take care of your wounds in a little while. Now tell me about the women passengers that were on the stagecoach with you earlier. Did any of them become ill and leave before their destination? Do you remember anyone named Kitty Parrish?"

He might as well have hit her across the face with a war club, because Kitty was jolted so hard to hear him say her name that she actually took a few stumbling steps backward. Then, seeing how his eyes went wide at her reaction, she knew she had made a serious error and sought to cover by pretending she was about to collapse again.

His hand shot out to catch her. "What's wrong? Can't you stand?"

"I . . . I haven't had anything to eat. I'm weak." *Dear God*, she thought in surging panic, *they were looking for me.* That was why they had attacked the stage and it also explained why they had not bothered to take the strongbox or rob Rufus and Hank. But what did they want with her? And how did they know about her, anyway? Her mind began to spin, making her dizzier than she already was. Had Opal Grimes asked them to kidnap her—maybe even kill her—to keep her from getting to Tombstone? Maybe Opal had found the gold and didn't want to share, but if that were true, why would she have written in the first place and sent half of the map? None of it made any sense.

"It's your own fault," Ryder snapped. "You were offered food, and if you don't learn to eat what you're given from now on, you will starve." He began to untie her wrists. "I think you've got sense enough not to try and run away. Now walk behind my horse."

Mounting, he turned to ask, "What are you called?"

She thought of one of the stock tenders she had met along the way. "Billy Mingo."

"Very well, Billy Mingo. Keep your mouth shut when you meet my mother, because she understands and speaks English as well as I do. And if you dare sass her, I'll give you the beating you deserve to teach you obedience. Understand?"

"How . . . how long are you going to keep me here?" she stammered to ask.

"I haven't made up my mind yet."

He started the horse forward, keeping his gait slow. Kitty tried to follow without stumbling, aware that curious faces were beginning to line the path on either side. She did not want to appear any weaker than she already had, lest they think her too scrawny for a boy. And now it was more important than ever to keep her secret.

Kitty seethed as she plodded along behind Whitebear. Opal Grimes was responsible for her plight. Opal was the only person who had known she was on her way and when she would arrive. Well, heaven help her when she did escape, Kitty vowed, because she was going to find out exactly what was going on . . . and why Opal wanted her dead.

Her head jerked up as she heard a loud, angry voice and saw a woman rushing toward Whitebear. She was wearing a dress made out of some kind of animal skin, with beads on the front and fringe along the ankle-length hem. Kitty thought she might be pretty if her face were not twisted in an angry scowl. And, oh, how she wished she knew the Apache language so she could understand what was being said. It was about her, she could tell, because the woman was looking from her to Whitebear and speaking loudly, crossly.

"Why have you taken this boy captive?" Ryder's mother demanded. "You, who always preach that the Chiricahua must stop the savage ways of the old world, and now you dare bring a slave."

Ryder knew that his mother's reaction was motivated by the terrible memory of how his father had been captured and mistreated until he accepted his plight.

"If I hadn't taken him," he endeavored to explain, "Coyotay would have, to punish him for shooting him. As it was, I had to stop him from slitting the boy's throat."

"But he is too small to make a good slave. And what of the woman you were seeking? Where is she?"

"She wasn't on the stagecoach. I don't have any idea where she is." He dismounted and handed his horse over to one of the youngsters who were anxiously waiting to do the bidding of the returning warriors. "All I can do is wait awhile and then ride into Tombstone, find Opal Grimes, and see if she's arrived and living with her."

Kitty bit back a gasp to hear Opal's name. So, it was true, she raged to think. Opal had, for whatever reason, enticed the Apache to keep her from reaching Tombstone.

Ryder went on, "All I can do is keep trying, Mother." He put his arm around Pale Sky. "And I promise you when Kitty Parrish does reach Tombstone, I'll find her and make her tell me what I want to know."

Hearing her own name again, Kitty yearned all the more to know what they were saying.

"Meanwhile, you must do something with that pitiful boy," Pale Sky said.

Kitty could not help cringing as Whitebear and the woman turned to stare at her.

"He needs to eat," Ryder said. "He's being stubborn, though. He also needs those rope burns on his wrists tended to."

"Bring him to my wickiup. "He will eat," Pale Sky said with a determined nod. "And then I will see to his wounds."

Ryder walked over to Kitty. "You will go with my mother, and you will eat. Then she will tend your wounds. After that, come to me. I sleep in that tent over there." He pointed.

Kitty mustered the bravado to say, "I don't want to sleep in there. I'd rather sleep by myself."

"I don't give a damn what you want," he fired back. "But don't worry, I don't want you sleeping in there, either. I'll have enough company tonight as it is. Now go with my mother, and she'll show you how to boil water for my bath."

Kitty gulped, swallowed. "Your . . . your bath?"

"Yes," he said, turning away. "That's one of the things I learned to enjoy in my father's world—the pleasure of a hot bath, and *you* are going to give it to me."

# Chapter 6

Kitty had to stoop to get through the low doorway of the dome-shaped shelter. Bear grass, brush, yucca leaves, and rushes had been placed over the framework of poles and limbs tied together for support. Canvas stretched over that, but there was an opening at the top to allow smoke to escape from the fire pit near the center.

As she followed the Indian woman inside, a thick piece of bear fur slapped shut across the opening after them.

The woman gestured to Kitty to sit down on the floor. Glancing about uneasily, she noted that the furnishings were sparse—animal skin rugs, crockery of different sizes and shapes, baskets filled with herbs and vegetables.

The woman handed her a clay platter heaped with tortillas and curtly said, "Eat."

Kitty did so ravenously. At one of the home stations she had watched the cook as he made the stiff dough from flour, baking powder, water, and salt. He had pulled off a lump about the size of a biscuit, rolled it, then slapped it between his hands till it resembled a pancake. It had then been baked dry on the bottom of an inverted fry pan over the fire. Kitty found it a bit bland tasting but filling nonetheless.

"My name is Pale Sky. By what name are you called, boy?"

She repeated the lie. "Billy Mingo."

"And how old are you, Billy Mingo?"

"Fifteen," Kitty lied again. She reasoned if the Indians thought she was older they might expect her to work harder even if she was small.

A shadow crossed Pale Sky's face. "That is the same age as my husband when he was taken captive." Stiffly, she added, "I wish my son had not brought you here. You will only be in the way."

Kitty laughed uneasily. "Well, ma'am, I'll be glad to leave any time you say."

"You will stay until my son says you may go. For now, you are his slave, and you will do his bidding . . . and mine, as well. But if you do as you are told, I will not mistreat you. Do you understand?"

Kitty assured her that she did, grateful that the woman seemed borderline friendly. "I will do the best I can, but I don't know your ways. I don't know what you want me to do."

"I will teach you."

Kitty continued to eat, although her stomach was in knots as she wondered what the future held. She was in the hands of savages, who would kill without batting an eye. She would have to be very careful, toe the line, and try to do everything she was told. It was the only way she would survive—that and not let them discover she was a woman.

She wiped at her forehead with the back of her hand. It was very hot, and she was sweating.

Pale Sky noticed and said, "I know it is warm, but we cannot make the cooking fires outside. The smoke might lead the pony soldiers to our camp."

*Maybe that's the key to being rescued,* Kitty wryly thought—*setting the camp on fire.*

"You are fortunate my son took you."

Kitty shot her an incredulous look. "You think I should be grateful I was captured?"

"My son told me when he stopped Coyotay from killing you, Coyotay then wanted to make you his slave. My son saved you from a fate worse than death."

Kitty snorted. "Whitebear could have just left me where I was. Then I'd be *real* grateful."

Pale Sky frowned. "Eat. You have much work to do this night. My son learned from his father to like baths and you must bring water from the creek to heat over the fire to fill his tub in his tepee."

Whitebear had called it a tent. His mother called it a tepee. Kitty did not know what it was, nor did she care. All she was concerned with was having to lug big buckets of water and trying not to be around Whitebear when he was naked.

"Hold out your wrists."

Pale Sky towered over her with a small pot smelling of pine and clover. Smoothing its contents over the chafed skin, she said, "Your wounds are not bad. My son was gentle when he tied you."

Kitty felt like saying she would hate to see what he was like when he tied *rough*. Then she chided herself, because he could have made her suffer a lot more than she had. She would just have to keep reminding herself that things could be a lot worse. It was best not to antagonize anyone.

"Thank you," she murmured when Pale Sky finished smoothing on the ointment. "I appreciate your kindness."

Suddenly Pale Sky dropped to squat before her, gazing intensely upon her face. "Continue to be obedient, Billy Mingo. I do not want to see you mistreated. I saw what being taken from the white man's world did to my husband. I do not wish you to suffer the same way. Perhaps in time, I can persuade my son to set you free. Until then, I pray you do not make trouble for yourself."

Kitty was curious about a lot of things, like who was Whitebear's father and where was he? But she dared not ask about that just yet. Instead she decided to try and learn the real reason the stagecoach had been attacked. "Whitebear was looking for a white woman," she said. "Did he intend to make a slave of her, too?"

Pale Sky's expression turned to one of surprise. "He told you this—that he was searching for a woman?"

"Yes. Her name was"—Kitty pretended to flounder to remember—"'Kitty Parrish.'"

Pale Sky stood. "It is none of your concern."

*Not much it isn't,* Kitty thought, her anger smoldering over what Opal Grimes had done.

Pale Sky handed her two buckets carved from logs and threaded with rope for carrying. "I will take my son his food while you make ready his tub."

Kitty took the buckets. "He said he would have lots of visitors tonight."

Again, Pale Sky was astounded. "He told you about the girls? It seems my son tells you much, and you are a stranger as well as a slave."

"He only told me because I said I didn't want to sleep inside with him, and he said he didn't want me to, anyway, because he would have enough company."

Pale Sky nodded. "Adeeta will more than likely be the only one. She wishes to marry him, so she makes sure to visit him first, then sleeps the night so that Meena, the other maiden who also wants him, cannot go to him later."

It sounded terribly primitive to Kitty, and she figured her shock must have shown on her face, for Pale Sky said defensively, "It is the custom. Mating before marriage is not punished or considered wrong. And it is not the young boys who encourage it but the girls. It is common, you see, for the more mature unmarried girls to slip into a boy's tepee and teach him the art of lovemaking. It is supposed to be a secret, as the girls wish not to be called immoral, but Adeeta and Meena have been pursuing my son for so long that everyone knows it."

Kitty was exhausted. Her rope burns hurt despite the salve. The tortillas had not satisfied her, and she was still hungry . . . not to mention thirsty. She would like to have a bath herself and wanted nothing more than to fall down on one of the cozy-looking fur pieces on the floor and sleep for days. Yet she had grueling work ahead of her hauling water, not to mention having to bathe a man, and the last thing she wanted to hear about was his lovers. "I'll fetch the water," she said drily and turned toward the entrance and lifted the fur piece.

Behind her, Pale Sky snickered. "Do not worry, Billy Mingo. The maidens will not visit you. You are a slave. They know to have nothing to do with you."

*Thank God for that,* Kitty thought. Amorous Indian girls creeping into her bed were the very last thing she needed.

She counted a dozen trips to the stream to fill the pot on the stove inside Pale Sky's wickiup.

The Indians stared at her curiously, some with open hostility. A girl stepped from a wickiup and shook her fists and screamed words Kitty did not understand, but she sensed it was a threat. Then she saw Coyotay in the background and knew the reason.

Carrying the hot water to Whitebear's tent as steam rushed into her face was extremely difficult, and her weary legs staggered under the weight.

Whitebear, munching on what looked like a roasted rabbit leg, watched her come and go, urging her now and then to go faster.

She felt like telling him if he was in such an all-fired hurry to get started rutting two girls all night long, to just go ahead. Why bother with a bath first?

But she said nothing, doggedly continuing until the tub was amply filled.

"How did you get a tub out here, anyway?" she could not resist asking as she emptied another bucket.

He regarded her coldly. "It was at our last camp, before we were forced to the reservation. It belonged to my father. I found it and brought it here.

"Would you like to use it after me?" he surprised her by adding. "Or do you prefer to stay dirty?"

Kitty's gaze dropped to take in her overalls, filthy from the long walk as well as the tumble over the rocks. Her arms were streaked with grime. She had taken off her boots because her feet were so sore, and she could see they were nasty, as well. Her hair was probably the worst—greasy and smelling like a horse. The thought of warm water, even dirty, was enticing, but, of course, she could never indulge due to her secret. "I will bathe in the stream later."

"As you wish. And by the way, you can have the run of the camp, because you won't get far if you try to run. There are sentinels all over the place."

She would remember that—just as she would not forget to make sure it was pitch dark before stepping into the stream where she had just filled the buckets. It was narrow and not too deep, and she could manage a bath in the dark.

"If you could let me borrow some clothes till I wash my own, I would be appreciative," she dared request.

He threw back his head and laughed long and loud before sweeping her with mocking eyes. "If you wore my clothes then I would lose you, because they would swallow you—skinny bird that you are. But don't fret. I'll have my mother borrow things from one of the younger boys, though you'd come nearer fitting into a girl's dress."

Kitty scurried out, lest he think about what he had just said and wonder more about her diminutive size.

She returned with the last of the water. Bending and pushing the tent flap open with her hip, she turned and, with a soft cry, nearly dropped the bucket.

Whitebear was naked.

His back was to her, and she was thankful he could not see her face, which had to be the color of blood.

Transfixed, she stared, her gaze dropping to his muscled calves before slowly moving upward. She had never seen a naked man before, but she doubted many could be as glorious as the one standing before her. She even reached with trembling fingers to part her hair for a better view.

His thighs were also hard-muscled, corded and strong, stretching to his high, well-molded and cupped buttocks. Her eyes lingered there, and she nearly choked, biting back a gasp as he bent forward to scratch his ankle, giving her a brief glimpse of his manhood.

His back rippled as his moved, and his shoulders were incredibly broad and sinewy. His arms looked powerful, as though he could crush with one mighty embrace, and, for a dizzy instant, Kitty imagined how it might feel to be so deliciously imprisoned.

She shook her head to clear it, still mesmerized, and he turned and saw and bellowed, "What are you standing there for? Pour the water."

She did spill it then, all over her legs, because as he turned around, she retreated a few steps, making the water slosh over the rim.

"What is wrong with you?" he roared, yanking it from her. He poured the rest in the tub. "For a boy who knows how to shoot a gun like you do, you're acting like a sissy. It's a good thing I did take you captive, because you'd likely get yourself killed, foolish as you are."

"I . . . I'm sorry," she managed to stammer, keeping her eyes turned away as he stepped into the tub.

He settled into the water, leaned his head back, closed his eyes, and gave a satisfied sigh.

Kitty just stood there, not knowing what to do. She wanted to turn and run but knew if she did it would only make him angrier.

"Well?"

He was glaring at her.

"I don't know what you want me to do," she said in a thin, frightened voice.

He snapped, "What I want you to do is give me a bath, damn it. Now, listen to me, Billy"—he pointed his finger—"I am not an unnecessarily cruel man, but you try my patience. Annoy me one more time this night, and I don't care what my mother says, I will give you a sound thrashing to teach you your place."

Kitty swallowed nervously. He would do it, too, and then he would discover her secret, and there was no telling what would happen then. "I'm sorry," she whispered.

He pointed to a small bowl nearby. "My mother makes good soap from the aloe roots. She pounds them to a pulp. Work it into a lather with some water, then soap me all over."

"All . . . *over* . . . ," she echoed, heart pounding.

With an annoyed grunt, he settled back again.

Kitty picked up the bowl and mixed the aloe into a sudsy paste.

"Start with my hair so it can be drying," he ordered.

She worked the lather into his dark hair, using her fingertips to work out the tangles.

"Massage my scalp."

She did so, trying to focus on what she was doing and not look at the rest of him.

"Now shave me."

Timorously, she admitted, "I don't know how."

He looked at her—or tried to. Her face was obscured by the mat of hair hanging over it. "I don't suppose you do. And I shouldn't trust you with a sharp blade, anyway. Never mind. I'll do it myself when you're done. Work on getting done now."

She endeavored to work fast, moving her hands in circular motions, not rubbing too hard but enough to cleanse him.

As she touched his chest, his nipples, she prayed for her fingers not to shake, for something she did not understand was moving over her. Sensations. Feelings. Emotions. From head to toe and settling in her loins, a stirring . . . a hunger.

She moved over his shoulders, down his arms. He leaned forward so she could scrub his back.

And then it was time to go lower, and Kitty wondered if she could do it . . . if she could actually wash him *there*.

Stalling for the inevitable moment, she bathed his feet and legs, again experiencing bizarre, hot waves as she touched his thighs and hips.

"I'll do the rest," he said suddenly, taking the bowl away from her to pour the contents into the water. "Now get me a towel."

She glanced around but did not see anything that even remotely resembled a towel. Actually the tent was sparse. There were no cooking utensils or pottery as in Pale Sky's. A bow and some arrows were stacked to the side, along with a rifle. Other than a few animal skins piled about and a bearskin rug on the dirt floor, there was nothing.

"There," he said impatiently and pointed. "The small woven blanket. I dry with it."

She rushed to obey but, when she returned, he was standing, and her eyes locked on a scar she had not noticed before. It was shaped almost like a star, low on his abdomen.

He took the blanket from her and began to dry himself. Noticing how she was staring at the scar, he said, "I almost died when I got that. I suppose you wish I had."

"Yes," she said, matching his sarcasm, "along with all your people."

He quirked a brow. "Really? My mother, too? I passed by her wickiup when the two of you were talking, and it seemed she was being unnecessarily nice to you. Why would you want her dead?"

"I . . . I don't know." Kitty felt her temples begin to throb. She was so tired, and it was hard to think straight. She should not have made such a terrible remark, because despite the horror stories she had heard about Indians, they could not all be savages. Then there were the children. She had seen them clinging to their mothers as she made her trek to and from the stream, eyes wide with curiosity but shining with innocence, as well. "I'm sorry."

He continued drying himself, watching her thoughtfully as he did so.

Kitty folded her hands behind her back and stared at the ground. He was only a few feet away, still evoking emotions in her that she did not understand. What was wrong with her? She was his slave. He was her master. And here she was wondering what it would be like if he were to take her in his arms and—

"Go and fetch the *tulapai* from my mother."

She had no idea what he was talking about but hurried to get whatever it was.

Pale Sky was waiting to give her a clay jug filled with something that reminded her of the way Tormey Rankin smelled the night he had attacked her in the barn. "Whiskey," she said to herself out loud.

"It is called *tulapai*," Pale Sky said. "Tomorrow I will show you how it is made. My son is one of the few warriors who can enjoy it without going mad."

"That's nice to know," Kitty quipped. "He's sure been mad enough at me tonight."

Pale Sky smiled. "You will learn to please him, as all the slaves before you have done."

"There are other slaves?" She had not seen any other white people around, but it would be nice to have company in her misery.

"Not anymore. Not since we were taken to the reservation. You are the first in a long time. I pray you will be the last. Now, hurry so my son will not again be mad with you. He likes the *tulapai* to relax him before his visits from the young girls."

The *young girls* again, Kitty mused as she trudged back to Whitebear's tent. Only now when she thought of them it annoyed her to feel a twinge of jealousy, and she told herself she was the one going mad—and she'd not had one drop of the *tulapai*. She did not care how many girls or women he had. All she wanted was to escape.

When she reentered the tent, Whitebear was just finishing shaving himself. He had wrapped something around him and between his legs, and, as she stared at it, he said, "It's called a breechclout. It is what we men wear when we are not hunting or on a war party. Perhaps I can make one for you tomorrow."

"No, no, I—" Kitty scolded herself for appearing upset, but if he made her wear one of those diaper-looking things it was all over. She was as dead as that bear he was lying on. "Thank you, but I prefer my own clothes."

"For a time, I guess it's all right." He took a long sip from the jug, then gave a satisfied sigh. "Ah, my mother makes the very best." He held it out to her. "Would you like some? It will make you sleep better."

"I . . . I'll sleep just fine," she said, once more uneasy as she added, "wherever that might be."

"You'll sleep right outside. I might have need of you during the night. Take one of the skins and make your bed. And remember what I said about trying to run away."

She did not have to be reminded, because there was no way she was going to try to get down out of the mountains till she knew the way. If wild animals didn't kill her, a fall would—or leave her injured and unable to continue. No, she would just have to endure as best she could until the time was right. But at least Pale Sky was apparently not the cruel sort, and Whitebear would not mistreat her as long as she obeyed him.

The night was dark. There was no moon and not a star in the sky that she could see. The air was humid and smelled as if rain were coming, and she worried what she would do if it did. The only shelters were the tents and wickiups, and if Pale Sky did not invite her to hers, then she would just have to lie there and get soaked.

She found her way to the stream and took her bath quickly, then put her dirty clothes back on. With nothing to cover herself, there was no way she could wash them and leave them to dry. She walked back to the tent, made her bed as Whitebear had directed, and lay down in it.

From somewhere too close for comfort she heard a howl. That, and other strange and unfamiliar noises coming from the woods, reaffirmed her decision not to run away just yet. And she was going to need a weapon when she did. Perhaps Whitebear would eventually take her out hunting with the warriors, and she could watch them with their bows and arrows and learn enough to use one herself. They did not look too terribly hard to make. She could work on it when no one was watching her, and—

She froze to hear voices from inside Whitebear's tent.

Rising up on an elbow, she heard a girl talking but could not understand what she was saying because she was speaking Apache. Whatever it was, she sounded giggly and happy.

For a few moments, there seemed to be some kind of conversation going on, and the girl kept giggling, shrilly, sometimes. Then things got quiet, but only for a little while. Then the girl was making moaning sounds, and Kitty did not have to understand Apache to know what was going on then.

Yanking the deerskin from beneath her, Kitty wrapped it so she could burrow her ears into it and muffle the sounds.

And all the while she wondered why hearing them filled her with—what? Jealousy? Anger? She told herself she had no right or reason to feel either. Whitebear was nothing to her—except a savage holding her prisoner.

Still, she could not deny that she also thought of him as a man . . . a very desirable man.

But one she could never have.

# Chapter 7

In the days that followed, Kitty had little difficulty maintaining her ruse. The Indians, who at first had stared at her for the oddity she was in their midst, eventually paid her no mind. She was, after all, the slave of their leader, Whitebear, and he had made it clear that no one other than his mother was to have anything to do with Billy Mingo.

Fortunately for Kitty, Pale Sky seemed glad to take her under her wing. "To help you stay out of trouble," she said.

But she had no intention of getting into trouble if she could help it, because she did not want to call attention to herself. She reasoned that if she appeared to surrender to her fate, no one would suspect she was chomping at the bit to escape as soon as she could figure out how to go about it.

As for Whitebear, Kitty was thankful he had not asked her to bathe him since that first night. The experience of seeing him naked, touching him, had left her shaken.

She tried to avoid him as much as possible, which was not hard, for he kept to himself. He seemed to be brooding over something, and she knew it was probably over not having found Kitty Parrish. No doubt Opal Grimes had promised him a lot of money to get the job done, and since he had failed he could not collect.

Kitty did some brooding over Opal, as well, and it made her all the more determined to escape, so she could find out why the woman had wanted her abducted. But there was little time during the day to think about it, because, like all the Indian women, Pale Sky worked hard, and expected *Billy Mingo* to do the same.

"I know you probably hate woman's work," she said one day as Kitty watched the men ride out of camp to hunt. "But you cannot go with them. You are not a warrior."

Kitty was pounding dirty clothes on a rock in the stream but paused to look at Whitebear, who rode in front of his men. "Whitebear could take me if he wanted. He's the leader of the pack, isn't he?"

"Pack?"

"Like a wolf pack. He's the leader, true?"

Pale Sky chuckled at the comparison. "Yes, but I've never thought of the warriors as wolves, though I can see how a white man would. But why would you want to go? They won't let you use a gun . . . if that is what you are thinking," she added, eyes dark with suspicion.

"No, it's not that. It's like you said—I hate women's work." Kitty commended herself for quick thinking. She could not let Pale Sky guess her reason for wanting to join the men—to learn the countryside around her so that when she did escape she would know in which direction to go.

"You are not strong enough for men's work. And he would not want to be bothered with you, anyway. He has other concerns just now and is content to leave you to me."

Boldly, Kitty asked, "What kind of concerns?"

"None that are yours."

"Well, I wish he'd consider letting me go. You said yourself I'm not strong enough for men's work, and

I'm not very good at this." She pounded a warrior's
shirt against a rock, deliberately doing a sloppy job.
After all, as a boy, she should not know about things
like washing clothes.

"If he let you go, you would tell the soldier ponies
about our camp."

Kitty objected. "I don't know where I am. How
could I tell anyone else?"

"There are ways. You would make sightings on the
trip out, and the pony soldiers would learn from
them."

"Then he plans to keep me here forever."

"I do not know what he will do with you. As I said,
he has concerns . . . worries. For now, he is not thinking of you."

Kitty knew that for a fact. He ignored her, leaving
her completely to his mother.

"He will be leaving soon," Pale Sky said. "Then it
will be my turn to worry."

"But why? You are well hidden here. The soldiers
can't find you. And you have sentinels everywhere,
and—"

"It is not the soldiers that I worry about."

Kitty followed her gaze and saw that she was watching Coyotay as he rode by. He was staring back, but
at *her,* not Pale Sky, and she could almost feel the
heat of the anger shimmering in his black eyes.

"He hates me for shooting him," she said quietly.

"It is not only that. He is angry because my son
took you from him."

"And you're worried he will make trouble when
Whitebear leaves?" If Pale Sky was concerned, then
Kitty knew she should be, too.

"I cannot be sure. He and my son have always been
like brothers, but Coyotay was not pleased when the
council chose my son leader over him, because he is
only half-Apache.

"But that did not matter to the council," Pale Sky continued. "They chose my son because he has proved he is a great warrior. But when he is away, Coyotay is the leader."

Kitty felt a stab of apprehension. With Coyotay in charge, she could, indeed, be in danger.

"I will take care of you," Pale Sky said suddenly, sharply.

Kitty looked at her and thought she saw the glimmer of tears in her eyes.

"You remind me so of my husband, when he was taken captive. He, too, was hardly a man, but he was so full of spirit, despite being mistreated. They even tortured him, because in those days none of our people were civilized, and they hated all white men. But he endured and won their respect . . . and my heart."

Kitty dared ask, "What happened to him?"

"He is dead. Killed by one of his own. Come now." She trailed out of the creek, the hem of her buckskin dress wet and dripping. "We must see to the *tiswin*."

The tender moment had passed as quickly as it came, and Kitty said, as though disgusted, "You're teaching me to cook something else? I hate cooking." Always, she endeavored to maintain her pose of indignation over female tasks, and, so far, it was working.

"It is not food. It is drink. Like the *tulapai* you carry my son every night. But that is gone. And there is no more corn to make it. So I make *tiswin* from the cactus called mescal.

"My son does not mind that the *tulapai* is no more," Pale Sky continued. "Coyotay and the others drink too much, and it makes them crazy. Besides, we need what corn we have for eating and baking. Food is scarce for us when we have to stay here, in the mountains, and cannot make camp where the land is more fertile, the game more plentiful.

"How long will you have to hide?" Kitty could not

help being curious over the Indians' plight. Renegades, they fought to keep from being forced back
to the reservation. But beyond that, she knew, and
understood, nothing else about them.

"Soon we hope to make a new life elsewhere. Until
then, we do whatever we must to survive. As you must
do also," she added with a sharp glance.

Kitty nodded. *That,* she understood.

Entering the sweltering wickiup, Pale Sky went to
the big kettle that simmered constantly on the fire
when she was not making something else. "I have
been cooking the heart of the leaf clusters of the mescal," she explained as she stirred the strange-smelling
concoction. "Now it is only pulp, and we will pour it
into jugs where it will ripen in a few more days.

"I do not worry about it making my son crazy," she
added with pride. "He knows how much to drink.
Others are not as smart. They dance and fight and do
bad things with the women, who sometimes also drink
it and go just as mad. Sometimes, if it is winter and
cold, a few will fall unconscious and lie outside, away
from warmth. They get sick and die. But my son does
not allow that to happen with his people. He has
banned them from drinking it since Coyotay and some
of the younger warriors hurt each other fighting. One
was killed."

"So you keep this well hidden from Coyotay?"
Kitty wanted to assure herself.

"That is not necessary. Coyotay knows I make it
only for my son and that it is forbidden to him. He
will not disobey."

"Let's hope," Kitty said under her breath. If Coyotay got drunk without Whitebear around, it could
mean big trouble.

And *she* might be the one who wound up getting
killed.

"I'm curious about something," Kitty said. "Why

do you always call Whitebear your son and never by his name?"

Pale Sky's smile was tender. "It is the way of the Apache for a mother to do so."

Emptying the kettle, Pale Sky had to scurry about and find more jugs, for she had made more of the brew than she had realized.

"Far too much," she fretted. "I should have tended it better and poured some off, but I was busy with you and now I hate to waste it. Perhaps I should hide it, after all. If Coyotay were to see how much there is, he might be tempted to think he could take some, and it not be missed."

Kitty was glad Pale Sky had changed her mind, until she saw where she was hiding the jugs—under a bear-skin rug. Coyotay would have no trouble finding them, but, as Pale Sky pointed out, it was taboo to enter a woman's wickiup without being invited. Still that was little comfort to Kitty, for Coyotay seemed the sort who did what he wanted when he took a notion. The more she thought about Whitebear going away for a spell, the more worried she became and the more determined she became to stick close to Pale Sky as much as possible.

As always, Kitty was exhausted by mid-afternoon, but Pale Sky had much she wanted to teach her. "It is time you learned to tan the deerskin. My son will likely bring in another today, so we must work on the one I have had buried."

Kitty did not understand what she was talking about but quickly found out. Pale Sky had buried a deerskin in moist earth several days earlier. After digging it up, she had soaked it in warm water, then stretched it over a pole, fur side out.

Dried in the sun, it was ready to be worked into a supple material. Pale Sky gave Kitty a clay pot and told her to rub its contents into the skin with her hands.

Kitty sniffed the pot and immediately gagged. "What is this?"

"The brains of the deer. Now, busy yourself, Billy Mingo. I will be watching to see that you do it properly."

Kitty got down on her hands and knees, fighting nausea as she worked the bloody pulp into the deerskin. After a while, she became used to the odor and could not help but marvel at how the concoction actually did make the skin softer, pliable. She could understand and see why it was necessary, because it made the skin compliant for sewing into clothing.

"You learn quickly, boy."

Kitty, down on her hands and knees, working hard and fast to get the distasteful job done and over with, had not noticed that the warriors had returned. Nor was she aware that Whitebear was standing watching until he spoke.

She paused for only a second but did not look up, then continued working.

"My mother says you obey her and give her no trouble."

Still she did not speak.

"She says you want to go hunting with the men."

Kitty stopped then to peer up at him through the hair stringing down over her face. "Yes. I would. This is"—she made her tone mocking—"women's work."

"Which is all you are good for—puny as you are," he said with a sneer. "But perhaps it will be good for you to see what it is like with the warriors, and then you will be glad to serve my mother."

"I . . . I like your mother." She felt the need to make clear. "She has not been unkind to me."

"You're lucky that you remind her of when my father was a slave. You're also fortunate she is somewhat educated and more civilized than the others."

"Yes, I realize that." She went back to working the skin, uncomfortable because he was staring at her so intently.

"I was going to leave in the morning but saw some elk as we were returning just now. I'd like to get one so my mother can be curing the meat while I'm away. I'll take you with me and clean it where I kill it so I won't have to bring the whole carcass back."

She gulped and swallowed. She knew about such things. She had grown up watching pigs slaughtered, cows butchered, and chickens cleaned, but had never done it herself.

"Well, I don't know how," she said lamely, looking at her blood-slick hands and wanting to wrap them around Opal Grimes's throat for getting her into such a mess. "And I don't know if I can."

"You can, and you will," he said sharply. "I think maybe my mother is being too kind to you. She makes you soft. Well, tomorrow, you will get a taste of what it's like to be a man. And by the time you gut an elk, cut his head off, and haul his meat on your back for a few miles, you won't look so pale over the sight of blood as you do now."

Kitty felt anger rising and told herself to calm down. So far, she had managed to hold her temper and had to continue to do so or risk a beating—and she had to keep him from touching her, lest he find out the truth.

She was exhausted, aching from head to toe. It was nearly dark, but she had to keep working the skin until Pale Sky told her to stop. Then there would be supper, and she was starved. Afterward, when everything quieted down, and no one could see, she would go to the creek and wash. Only then could she fall into her miserable bed on the ground and sleep.

"When you finish that, you can prepare my bath. I have blood all over me, and I want hot water."

In that instant the red Kitty saw before her eyes was not entirely the blood from the brains she was rubbing into the deerskin. The thought of hauling heavy buckets of water from the creek to the stove to Whitebear's tub was overwhelming. She was not sure she could do it.

Hearing splashing sounds, she turned to see several of the warriors had stripped naked and were running through the creek to rid themselves of blood stains from the hunt. She knew it had nothing to do with cleanliness, for few Apache bathed. It was because of the biting gnats and flies that came after the blood that they wanted to rid themselves of it.

Suddenly, Kitty flashed with rebellion. She was tired, damn it. Her hands were blistered and raw from washing clothes and rubbing deer brains into the hide all afternoon, and just thinking about hauling all those buckets of water to the stove and then to the tub made her back hurt all the worse. Neither did she relish the idea of soap in the broken skin on her fingers.

"I am tired," she said, teeth clenched and jaw set. "Too tired to haul bucket after bucket of water when you can go splash off with your friends, and—"

In a flash, she was grabbed by the nape of her neck and yanked to her feet, and, besides sudden fear for her life, she worried he would somehow discover her secret as he held her close and shook her so hard her teeth rattled.

"You try my patience, boy. You are a slave. You do not question my orders. I think maybe my mother has been too easy on you, and you forget your place."

An icy dread swept through her as cold, dark eyes bore down on her.

He was holding her by one hand and she winced

and prepared herself for the blow as she saw him raise his other, but just then Pale Sky screamed out to him in their language.

He lowered his arm and dropped her to her feet, releasing her. "She saves you again," he said between clenched teeth, "but next time, nothing will save you, boy. You are long overdue for a sound thrashing."

Kitty wanted to kick herself for losing control. Now he was mad—furious—and there was no telling what he might do.

She scrambled to her feet and scurried to get the buckets.

It seemed to take forever to fill the tub, and each time she carried water to the stove for heating, Pale Sky lashed out at her for her insolence.

"Next time he will beat you, Billy Mingo. You must watch your tongue or risk having it cut out of your head. My son is the leader of his people. He cannot tolerate a slave talking to him so impudently. The only reason I was able to save you is because no one else heard. If they had, he would have had to beat you to save face. Now I warn you—tread lightly . . . or I will beat you myself."

Kitty had the idea she was not bluffing and cursed herself again.

Yet, despite the aches of her weariness making her feel as though she had already been whipped, apprehension crept in when she thought of seeing Whitebear naked once more. He was her captor, her master, and her life was in his hands, but still she felt helplessly drawn to him as a man.

When the tub was filled at last, she was relieved when he waved her away. "Go. I can bathe myself."

He had emerged from the shadows of the tent and stood in the glow of a small fire. Kitty could not tear her eyes from the glorious sight of him, bathed in gold like some kind of god, every muscle taut and shining.

"Did you hear me?" he snapped. "I don't enjoy being bathed by a man. I only made you do it that first night to humble you, but I see it didn't work. Now get out of here and get to sleep. We leave at dawn."

Cheeks flaming, Kitty fled from the tent and threw herself down on her bed.

She chided herself for her weakness, for her desire, but could no more dispel it than turn back the winds.

She was a woman.

And he was a man . . . a savage in some ways . . . but she wanted him as she had never wanted another.

Realizing that, accepting that, Kitty knew it was all the more important that she escape.

But, dear God, it seemed so hopeless.

"Get up."

Kitty awoke to the sharp nudge of Whitebear's foot in her side. It was still dark, but a pale hint of dawn began to appear on the horizon.

"Can you ride a horse?" he asked as she struggled to her feet.

Running her hands through her tangled hair, she jerked at her overalls to straighten them. Instinctively, she felt for the map and was startled not to feel it hidden in the pouch, then remembered she had removed it to slip beneath a marked rock. Often she got wet during the day and could not risk ruining it, so she had taken it out.

"I asked you a question, boy."

Kitty was still groggy, "Yes. Yes, I can ride."

"Then let's go. I want to get this over with so I can leave."

She followed him to the corral where the horses were kept. Selecting a mustang, he handed her a bridle. "We don't use saddles."

"I don't need one. I know how to ride bareback," she said, and he quirked a brow in surprise.

The sky was getting ever lighter, and she followed him down the trail. The way was precarious, but the mustang seemed to know it, so she gave him his head and let him set his own pace.

As they rode, she tried to get her bearings, as well as sight several places where she might hide once she did escape. She would not try to make it off the mountain all at once, as the Indians would expect her to do in her panic to reach safety. Instead, she planned to take it a bit at the time to throw them off. They would be looking all over, and she would be sequestered and nibbling the food she would hoard to take with her when she went.

"Do you know anything about hunting?" he asked.

"A little."

"Well, what you did back east was nothing like the Indian way. We hunt rabbit and turkey on horseback as well as on foot. Our horses are trained to follow rabbits running full speed, so we can swing down and hit them with a club. At a distance, we'll kill them with a throwing stick. Same as with turkeys. We don't waste arrows or bullets. Today I'll kill the elk with my lance."

Kitty hardly heard him, for the sun was up, and her gaze was helplessly drawn to the way his body seemed to undulate in a sensuous rhythm as it yielded to the softly jarring movements of the horse. His back was bare, as were his legs, for he wore only a breechclout in the summer warmth.

She watched the taut muscles of his thighs, the way his hips rocked gently from side to side.

She began to perspire but told herself it was from the heavy overalls and shirt she wore.

They waded through a mountain stream, and she longed to throw herself into the cool, crisp water in an effort to douse the rising heat she could not hold back.

Seeing a fish, she seized the opportunity for conversation in an effort to quell her rising longing. "We could catch fish," she suggested brightly. "I know how to cook them, and—"

"The Apache don't eat fish. They believe they're filled with bad spirits."

"You don't think that, do you?" she asked, astonished.

"No. But I'm different. I lived for a time with my father in his world and learned the white man's ways. He also saw to it I was educated, along with my mother."

"Then why don't you teach your people that it's all right to eat fish? With so many streams and rivers, they would never have to go hungry."

"I try not to argue with their taboos. I explain what I have learned, what I believe, but they have to make up their own minds. I am their leader, but I don't try to change their way of thinking. Not now, anyway. Maybe when we begin our new life elsewhere."

Kitty, yielding to sudden impulse, said, "Then will you let me go? You aren't going to keep me forever, are you?"

He was quiet, thoughtful for a moment, then said, "I have other things on my mind to worry about besides you, Billy Mingo. Besides, the only thing you need to worry about right now is doing as you're told."

She fell silent, sensing he was annoyed with her prattling.

They rode on in silence, and finally he spotted a small cluster of elk. "Stay here," he commanded, then charged right into them to fell one with his lance.

Afterward, he showed Kitty how to gut and clean it, and it was all she could do to keep from being sick to her stomach. She worked fast, wanting to get it over with.

Finally, the meat cut the way he wanted it, they returned to camp.

"You did well," he told her as he left her at his mother's wickiup.

And then he was gone, disappearing down the mountain once more without a backward glance.

Pale Sky called to her, "Come inside. I have food for you. Then we will work with the meat."

Kitty turned to go in but something made her turn around, and she was jolted to see that Coyotay stood nearby glaring at her.

He pointed to the scar on his shoulder, then at her, and raised his fist and shook it as he yelled something in Apache.

Pale Sky, coming out of the wickiup in time to hear, yelled back at him, and he turned and walked away.

"I'm scared of him," Kitty said as she followed Pale Sky back inside. "I worry he wants revenge so bad he won't obey Whitebear's order to leave me alone now that he's gone."

Pale Sky assured her, "He is not a fool. He will obey. He may be angry, but as long as he does not drink the *tiswin*—the white water as some call it—he will not have crazy thoughts."

*Then pray he doesn't get into it,* Kitty thought with a shudder of foreboding, *because he looks like he has enough crazy thoughts without it.*

# Chapter 8

"I think it is time you had new clothing."

Kitty stared at Pale Sky in horror. "I . . . I like my overalls," she stammered. "I don't want to change."

"They are torn and tattered." Pale Sky held up a pair of baggy white cotton trousers. "These will be better for you. I also have a breechclout and a calico shirt for you." She looked at Kitty in scrutiny. "I think it is time you tied your hair back from your face like the men."

Kitty's heart dropped all the way to her ankles. Without the thick bib of the overalls, the swell of her breasts might show. And if she had to tie her hair back with a headband like the Apache, her delicate facial features would be obvious. If anyone became suspicious and began to look closer, it would just be a matter of time before she was exposed.

After Whitebear had left the camp two days earlier, Pale Sky had directed Kitty to move her bed outside her wickiup. When it rained the previous night, she had her take it right inside. Kitty was grateful, for she had spent a few wet, miserable nights in the past. Finding Pale Sky standing over her with Indian clothing, however, had been a rude awakening. "I really prefer to wear my own clothes," Kitty continued to protest.

"You will do as I say," Pale Sky said in the no-

nonsense tone Kitty had learned to dread. "It is also too warm these days for such heavy clothing. Indeed, you might not even want to wear the shirt but go bare-chested."

*Now, that would cause some eyes to bug out,* Kitty thought with an inward groan.

"Go now." Pale Sky waved her toward the opening of the wickiup. "Take care of your morning needs and change. We will be leaving soon."

Kitty felt excitement surge at the thought of another opportunity to learn the trail down the mountain. "Where are we going?"

"To gather berries, grapes for drying—raspberries, hackberries, and mesquite beans. Chokeberries, also, though it may be too early."

"Is it a long way?" She hoped it was.

"Far enough that the men must go along to protect us. The scouts went yesterday to make sure there are no soldiers in the area. We will be going to the bottom, to a brushy pass where many berries were seen.

"Summer harvest is important to us." Pale Sky dropped the clothing and went to her cooking fire. She was making a stew of deer meat and white root stocks that would simmer through the day. "We have to prepare for the winter by drying and storing as much food as we can."

Kitty did not immediately get up. Instead she watched Pale Sky, thinking what a pretty woman she was. Always clean and tidy, she wore her long, shining black hair hanging loosely down her back, and rather than buckskin, she dressed as many of the other Apache women did, in a voluminous skirt that brushed the ground. The one she wore today was of a bright blue shiny fabric. Sateen, Kitty decided, with flounces and rows of ornamental braid for trim. Her over-blouse, which hung to her hips, had a high neck, full sleeves, and was also trimmed with braid.

Despite the stress of having to hide from soldiers that would force her and her people back to the reservation they hated, Pale Sky seemed content in her own way. She appeared to enjoy her life, and Kitty was well aware of her devotion to her son and how she worried when he was not around.

Kitty hated to admit it, but she worried about him, too—and not for his welfare. He was keenly intelligent and extremely strong and powerful and well able to take care of himself. What bothered her was how she could not deny being inexplicably drawn to him—and not just because seeing him naked had birthed strange, new feelings within her. It was more than that, and she wanted to attribute it to him having saved her life. No matter that he was her captor and a dreaded savage Indian. She was in his debt. Still, there was a part of her that would not accept that theory . . . the hungry woman part of her that he, as a man, had awakened and that now demanded be fed.

Rolling to her side, she was stricken by the futility of it all and the desperation of her plight. Her pretense of being a boy—a man—could not go on indefinitely, and she had to find a way to escape despite the risks involved.

Pale Sky chattered on about how they needed sycamore bark for making tea, and the leaves from the squawberry bush to make medicinal drinks as well as material for baskets. Wild potatoes, onions, bananas, and the fruit of the saguaro cactus were also in great demand.

"In the old days, when we roamed our land freely, we hid food in secret caves, usually near a water hole. We even left our clay cooking pots there, along with bolts of calico cloth. This was so that when we moved from one place to another to hunt game, or to flee our enemies, we would have important things that we needed."

Suddenly Kitty found herself asking, "Why doesn't Whitebear take a wife?"

Pale Sky, continuing to stir the stew, shrugged. "I suppose he has not fallen in love."

Kitty pointed out, "But what about Adeeta? He favors her over the other girls who try to sneak into his tent at night. I know, because when I was sleeping outside, I would hear them, and he turned them away, except for the one named Meena. He let her come in once."

"If he were to marry, he would choose Adeeta, I suppose, but he does not like her mother."

"What difference does that make? I mean, he could just stay away from her after they were married, couldn't he?"

"Oh, an Apache man does that, anyway. It is custom for him not to speak to his mother-in-law, because the Apache say that the mother of the wife is the cause of all trouble between a man and his wife and is to be shunned. He never enters her wickiup, and if she goes to his, he leaves and does not return while she is there."

"Then why—"

Pale Sky chuckled. "Adeeta's mother is so mean-spirited that my son fears one day Adeeta will be just like her. Now she is young, pretty, and kind, because she wants him for her husband. He fears that will not last."

"Then what about Meena?"

"Her father is old, and she has four sisters, and some of them are difficult to look at."

Kitty figured that was a kind way of saying they were ugly. "But what does that matter?"

"It is custom that if a man's wife has many unmarried sisters, he should marry them also. My son says he would have a hard enough time with one woman trying to tell him what to do. He would not want *five*."

Kitty doubted any woman would ever be able to boss Whitebear, but she kept her thoughts to herself.

"Now, go and put on your new clothes." Pale Sky waved her wooden spoon. "If you are not ready, they will leave without us."

Actually, Kitty was looking forward to going, and not merely because it was another opportunity to prepare for when she would attempt escape. The reality was, she enjoyed being with Pale Sky and learning the Indian ways. It was interesting to see the preparation of different foods, like dough bread baked in ashes, and a kind of coffee made from mashed walnut meats, shells, and hulls.

Still, it was necessary to keep up the facade of resentment, and irritably she said, "Let them. I don't like doing women's work."

Pale Sky's eyes snapped with sudden anger. "Pah. You are a stupid, ungrateful boy, Billy Mingo. How many times must you be reminded that if you were the slave of Coyotay you would be constantly beaten for your weakness? You should fall on your knees to my son for his kindness in giving you to me, for I have seen many slaves suffer through the years."

"As your husband did," Kitty interjected to stall for time as she tried to think of a way out of changing clothes.

"Ah, yes, as he did," Pale Sky murmured sadly.

"You loved him a lot, didn't you?"

"Yes. And I was glad that he was young when he was taken, otherwise he would have been killed as the older men were.

"For a time," she went on, "we were happy. But he longed for his world, and I longed for mine. We could not stay together. The worst part was when he kept my son from me, but he finally ran away and found me. Maybe that is why I am better to you than I should be, because I feel cheated not to have had my son with me all that time, and I am trying to make up for the lost years with you."

Kitty was moved. "Then I won't complain about working for you any longer, and I will do my best to please you."

Pale Sky smiled. "It will please me for you to wear the things I borrowed for you. They should fit. The son of my friend I got them from is about your size."

Kitty knew she could not put it off any longer. Gathering the garments, she raised the bearskin that covered the opening and was about to go outside but hesitated as she saw one of the warriors walk by. He was wearing a buckskin vest. Turning about, she asked Pale Sky, "What about a vest? I need one. Even if it is summer, I am not used to the early mountain chill."

"You wish to wear a vest?"

Kitty nodded.

"Very well. I will get one for you. Now go. Time grows short."

Hidden from view by a thick clump of brush near the stream running down from above, Kitty dressed in the Indian garb. Thankfully, the shirt was big and baggy and revealed no curves. Still, she did not breathe easy till she returned to the wickiup to find that Pale Sky had found a vest for her.

After pulling back her hair and securing it with the cloth headband, Kitty had streaked her face with dirt. Pale Sky, used to such uncleanliness among her people, said nothing, if she even noticed. Kitty breathed a bit easier. For the time being, her secret was still safe.

When they joined the women, Kitty was dismayed to see Coyotay barking orders.

"Do not worry about him," Pale Sky said, noticing how Kitty kept darting anxious glances in his direction as they began walking. "He will not harm you."

"It still bothers me how he looks at me—like he wants to kill me."

"He does want to kill you," Pale Sky agreed with candor. "You tried to kill him. Therefore, you are his enemy."

They walked on down and around high, jutting boulders. Kitty tagged obediently behind Pale Sky but kept pace. She did not want to call attention to herself by lagging back and was careful to keep her glances quick and furtive lest someone see and suspect she was memorizing the trail.

As they moved along, Kitty dared to think she might make it all the way to the bottom when she escaped, but only if she started early in the night. Still, there were the elements of the wild to be considered. Now and then they could hear the ominous sound of a rattlesnake somewhere in the brush at the side of the trail. There were also many wild animal tracks.

She thought of the bow Whitebear had left in his tent. Without being obvious, she had watched some of the young boys practicing with theirs. It did not look too difficult, and she had always been quick to learn. No one would notice if she took Whitebear's bow and a few arrows, and she hoped to be far away by the time he returned, anyway. It was taking a chance, but far less risky than continuing to stay with the Apache, especially with Coyotay chomping at the bit to take revenge against her. And once on the main trail, she planned to hide out, living off the land, and wait for a stagecoach to come by.

It took over two hours, she estimated, for them to get down off the mountain, then another to walk to the brushy pass where the berries had been located. The women began picking, while the men dismounted to lounge around and talk among themselves.

As the blazing sun rose higher in the sky, Kitty became increasingly uncomfortable in the heavy vest, but dared not take it off. The warriors, she noted, had stripped to their breechclouts.

She was soaking wet with perspiration and dying of thirst, but there was no stream nearby. She noticed that the men were drinking from bags of some sort and asked Pale Sky what it was.

Pale Sky was bent over a cluster of low-growing chokeberries she was delighted to have found. She straightened to whip her head about and look in their direction, then scowled. "It is not plain water they drink. Hear how loud they speak? See how they laugh and push at each other like silly fools and stumble when they do?"

"White water?" Kitty asked fearfully.

"Yes. Coyotay must have been hiding it until my son left. But there could not have been very much. All the corn has been used and there will be no more until autumn. So perhaps they will not become too crazy."

"A *little* crazy is too much for me," Kitty declared with brow furrowed. "Do you think we can start back earlier? Maybe the hard ride back up will sober them."

"No. We must harvest now that we are here. And I sense that you are thirsty or you would not have asked about the men drinking. Come, I will show you how to find water. Do not look at them any longer."

Leaving the others, Kitty followed Pale Sky out of the pass and to the flat area where barrel cactus grew.

Hoisting up her skirt, Pale Sky drew a long knife from where it was strapped to her thigh.

Kitty's eyes went wide. Pale Sky did not seem the sort to carry a hidden weapon, but she reminded herself that despite her kind and genteel ways, Pale Sky was still an Apache.

With one blow, Pale Sky knocked off the top of a cactus. From her pocket, she took a long, thin reed and stuck it into the pulpy innards. "Drink," she urged

Kitty as she stood back. "It is good when there is nothing else."

Kitty sucked out the liquid from the cactus. It was slightly bitter, but truly better than a parched throat.

Returning to the pass, the men had become louder. The other women seemed not to notice or, if they did, were unconcerned. They were used to the warriors drinking the white water whenever they could, especially when Whitebear was not around. In addition, none of them had anything to fear. The men would not mistreat them.

The day wore on, and when the women's sacks filled, and the sun began to drop to the west, Coyotay shrilly screamed and motioned that they were leaving.

"Not soon enough for me," Kitty muttered, dragging the bulky bag of chokeberries and seeds Pale Sky had shown her how to gather.

"I have told you—do not be afraid," Pale Sky said as they fell in with the others. "You are safe with me."

Kitty wondered whether her nervousness was getting the best of her or if Pale Sky sounded less sure of herself than before.

"And they have no more white water, anyway," Pale Sky went on to say. "By the time we make the high, hard climb back to camp, the wildness in them should pass."

Kitty hoped she was right, because Coyotay was openly glaring at her, eyes fiery with rage. The Indian whiskey had set his resentment to boiling, and she feared if he did not soon sober, he might lose all control and toss aside Whitebear's edict that she be left alone.

"I want you to stay beside me," Pale Sky said when they reached camp at last. "We will put the berries away, and you will not stray from my side."

Kitty knew then that she had been right in suspecting that Pale Sky was also starting to worry about Coyotay exploding.

Pale Sky showed her how the berries and other vegetation gathered were to be hidden in a small cave in the rocks to keep animals from eating them during the night. During the day, she explained, when the sun was shining, they would be spread outside to dry.

They did not immediately return to the wickiup. Pale Sky visited another woman to get scraps of deerskin. "I will show you how to make moccasins, Billy Mingo," she said cheerily, as though to get *his* mind off Coyotay. "They will be more comfortable than those heavy boots you wear."

Kitty did not want to make moccasins. She liked her boots fine but knew it was pointless to argue with the woman when her mind was set.

Pale Sky dawdled, chattering, and soon other women joined them. Kitty did not try to figure out what they were saying, for she was too busy wondering whether she should try to get away that very night. Having to sleep inside the wickiup presented a problem, however, because Pale Sky might hear her leave. Then, too, she would have to take time to find her way in the dark to Whitebear's tent to steal the bow and arrows. She could not just bolt out into the darkness with no weapon of any kind.

She also realized she would have but one chance, because if she were caught, the consequences would be great. Never again would she know any kind of freedom at all, and, worse, Pale Sky might be so angry with her for violating her trust that she would turn her over to Coyotay and no longer care what he did to her.

Pale Sky was enjoying socializing with the other women. One of them had fresh-baked tortillas, and they all nibbled. Kitty declined and drew away from them as she tried to make up her mind what to do.

At first, no one paid any attention to the sounds of the warriors' revelry. Amid the laughter, someone would yell out once in a while, but it was not unusual for them to carry on as twilight fell.

But then a fight broke out, and the women exchanged anxious looks as they moved in the direction of the noise.

Kitty was following Pale Sky, curious as to what was going on, but suddenly Pale Sky stopped short. Kitty almost ran into her as she held up her hand and spun about to warn, "Do not go any closer."

Kitty looked beyond her and saw that it was Coyotay and another warrior who were fighting. Coyotay was winning, having knocked his opponent to the ground, and was jumping up and down on his chest.

Another warrior rushed forth to push him away from his victim. Swaying drunkenly, Coyotay turned on him instead.

Pale Sky cried in horror, "Look at the opening to my wickiup. See how it is torn even wider . . . the bearskin ripped away? They have found the *tiswin* that I had hidden. Coyotay reasoned that I would be making more for my son, and he has taken it."

Kitty recognized the jugs the warriors were tipping to their lips as the ones she and Pale Sky had filled with whiskey. "Can't you put a stop to it?" she cried. "They stole from you."

"It is too late to attempt reason."

Kitty watched, her spine rigid with panic. Coyotay had stopped fighting and appeared to be leading his warriors in dance. Raising their knees up to their chest and bending forward, they whooped and hollered and stomped about in a frenzy.

"Wh-what are they doing now?" Kitty asked,

Sadly, sickly, Pale Sky explained, "It is a war dance. He wants to lead them on a raid. But by morning, they will be passed out and no danger. It is now I

worry about—when he remembers you and his thirst
for revenge."

"I can hide," Kitty said quickly. "Just show me
where—"

"No. He will find you. He would have the warriors
chop down trees and move boulders if that is what it
takes to find your hiding place. He will not stop until
he finds you, and then he will make you beg to die.

"No!" Pale Sky suddenly cried. "I will not let him.
You are but a boy. I cannot let him do this horrible
thing. Come with me."

Grabbing her hand, Pale Sky led the way around to
the rear of her wickiup. Stooping down, they crawled
inside as she said, "He might see us if we went in
the front." She gathered up rawhide bags filled with
pemmican and handed them to Kitty. "Now we must
go quickly, before he starts looking for you."

"Go where?" Kitty was terrified to think of trying
to hide after what Pale Sky had said. She had no
weapon, and—

"I am going to set you free."

Kitty, about to crawl under the canvas, froze to
stare at her in disbelief. The flames of the cooking
fire glowed softly in the gathering darkness within the
wickiup, and she could see Pale Sky's tightly set face.

Beside her, on her knees, Pale Sky repeated, "I will
set you free."

"But . . . but why?"

"Because I do not want to see you killed, and that
is what will happen if I do not take you away."

"But are you sure?" Kitty prayed she was, that she
would go through with it. "Coyotay will be angry with
you, and—"

"You think I fear his wrath? My son would kill him
if he dared raise a hand to me. Now we must go before he starts looking for you."

But Kitty hesitated long enough to say, "I will never forget you for this."

"And I will never forget you, Billy Mingo." Pale Sky smiled. "You are truly like the son that was lost to me for so long. So I will take you to safety, to where you can find your own people. I will give you my knife to protect yourself should need arise. Then I will return. You do not know the way back. You cannot tell them how to find our camp."

In a voice tremulous with her sincerity, Kitty whispered, "I would not do that even if I could."

"No," Pale Sky said softly. "I do not think you would. Now come. The way is long. It is dark. And we must move quickly."

"Wait for me." And before Pale Sky could protest, Kitty bolted into the shadows.

She could not leave without retrieving the piece of map she had hidden.

Ryder sat in the shadows of the Faro section of the Oriental Saloon. It was late, and Opal Grimes was wrapping things up.

One of the men yelled out, "Hey, Miss Opal, if you'll give me the numbers I need this time around, I'll not only share the winnin's but walk you home, too."

"I don't need nobody to walk me home, Barney," she said wearily.

He snickered. "Well, I'd say you do, what with the Injuns after you."

She threw him a frosty glare. "That only happened once."

"Yeah, but what about your friend from back east you was expectin'?" someone else called out. "Don't it make you nervous to think how Injuns are close to you and your'n these days?"

"She wasn't no kin of mine. She was kin to Wade

Parrish, and while I feel sorry for anybody that gets themselves captured by Apaches, it had nothing to do with me."

Ryder had been tossing down the last of his beer. It hit his stomach with a dull thud and felt like he had swallowed the glass.

White dots of rage began to dance before his eyes, and a great roaring began to sweep over him.

Slowly, stiffly, he managed to turn to the man sitting at the table next to him. "What is she talking about?" he asked woodenly.

The man looked at him, obviously surprised he did not know. "Didn't you hear about the stage that was attacked by Injuns between here and Willcox?"

"No, I've been away . . . in Mexico," Ryder managed to say past the roaring in his ears.

"They took a woman—a girl—that Opal was expectin' from back east. And you know the funny part? The guard said they never knowed she was a woman. Said she wore baggy overalls and kept her hair stringin' down over her face. Lord knows, I just hope she can keep on foolin' them redskins." He turned to call to Opal, "What was her name? The girl them savages took?"

Opal spoke with lips trembling. "Kitty Parrish. Her name was Kitty Parrish."

"A shame, ain't it . . ." The man turned back to Ryder.

But he was no longer there.

# Chapter 9

It had been nearly dawn when Kitty and Pale Sky came down out of the mountains. The trek had been slow due to their having to feel their way along in the darkness, and Kitty, not as surefooted as Pale Sky, had fallen several times.

Kitty had feared Coyotay would realize they were missing and come after them, but Pale Sky told her not to worry. He would think they were hiding somewhere around the camp.

"I will probably meet him on my way back," she said, adding with a smirk, "*if* he is able to walk after so much white water."

Kitty had tried to express her gratitude, but Pale Sky waved her away. "Be gone with you, Billy Mingo. Return to your world in peace."

"But I owe you my life." Kitty reminded her. "And you've been kind to me when you could have made me miserable as hell, and we both know it."

"It is not my way to be cruel."

"I am still grateful, and I only wish there was something I could do for you."

"There is," Pale Sky had said quietly. "You can tell your people you were treated well . . . that not all the stories they hear about the Apaches are true."

Kitty assured her she would do so, adding, "Maybe one day there will be peace between our people. I hope so, Pale Sky. I truly do. But I come from a different place, and I don't understand all the troubles out here."

"It is not difficult to do so," Pale Sky explained. "The white man came to force us from our land, and when we refused to leave, the pony soldiers came and herded us like cattle into terrible places called reservations where the land is poor for farming and there are few animals to hunt. That is why my son led us to escape. It is why we must hide, for they would kill us.

"We only want what is ours by right of our birth—our land," Pale Sky went on to say. "Nothing more. Tell them, Billy Mingo, even though it will do no good, for they will not listen. They never have. But by so doing . . . by standing up for the Apache, you will testify that we are not all evil, that we can be peaceful when not provoked."

Kitty had promised and impulsively hugged her.

When Kitty stepped back, Pale Sky drew her knife from its hiding place and gave it to her.

"Go," she commanded. "Get far away fast. Move at night as much as you can. If you walk in that direction"—she pointed to a distant butte—"you will reach the road where the stagecoach passes. I do not know when one will come, but that is where you should go."

She then turned and disappeared into the brush.

Kitty had begun walking but all too soon succumbed to exhaustion. Finding a spot among some boulders, she slept the day away, then set out again.

The night was clear with a full moon. She could see her way and kept on going, stopping only to eat from the pemmican sacks and take a sip of water from the canteen Pale Sky had also given her.

At dawn, she reached the road. There were many boulders, and she had no trouble finding a place where she would be out of sight.

The walk had been arduous, for the ground was covered with rocks that had to be stepped over carefully. With the sun beating down, she had not rationed her water. Neither had she portioned out the pemmican. Both were gone, and she was hungry and thirsty and prayed a stage would come by soon but knew it could be days. Wondering if she could last that long, she wearily drifted into a deep slumber on the hard ground.

At first, she thought she was only dreaming that she heard a noise, then she awoke with a start to hear horses . . . the sounds of wheels churning in the rocks and dirt . . . a man shouting . . . and the popping of leather.

Scrambling up on top of a boulder, Kitty thrilled to realize it was a stagecoach. She began waving her arms in a frenzy and yelling, forgetting in her excitement that she was dressed—and looked—like an Apache.

The guard saw her and, with a shouted oath, raised his shotgun and aimed.

Realizing her blunder, Kitty threw herself down on the boulder just in time for the blast to whiz right over her.

"I think I got him. Hot damn, stop them horses. I'm gonna take me a scalp home."

Kitty heard the driver reluctantly call "Whoa" to the horses before arguing, "There might be more of them devils around. It's risky to stop."

"If there was more, they'd be all over us by now. So stop your frettin'. I'm gettin' me a scalp."

Kitty lay very still. She was pressed against the rock, face turned to one side. Peering through lowered lashes, she watched as the guard approached. He carried his shotgun in one hand, a knife in his other.

She knew if she let him know she was not injured and tried to explain who she was, he might shoot again, which she could not risk.

Holding Pale Sky's knife beneath her, she waited until he was bending over her. Then, before he had time to realize she was not hit, she rolled onto her back in a flash to take him by surprise and press the tip of the knife to his throat. "Stop. I'm not Apache. I'm white—like you. They took me captive, but I escaped. Now, don't make me cut you, please."

"No . . . no . . . don't do that," he stammered, Adam's apple bobbing as he swallowed in terror against the flint blade pressing into his flesh.

"My name is Kitty Parrish," she said in a rush. "I was taken off the stage to Tombstone by Apaches— Chiricahua."

His fear-widened eyes blinked. "You . . . you're *her,* the one they took? They said you was passin' for a man . . ."

"Do you believe me? Can I let you go?"

"Yes . . . oh, yes. Don't hurt me, please . . ."

"What is your name?"

"Tom. Tom Culbreath."

"You don't have to be afraid of me, Tom."

She withdrew the knife, and he quickly straightened to yell back to the driver, "Hey, it's her—that woman them Injuns took a while back."

Kitty scrambled to her feet and tugged self-consciously at her vest and shirt. She knew she looked a sight—filthy, bedraggled, her hair stringier than ever.

The guard could only stare at her in astonishment, and then the driver scrambled up on the boulder. He took one look and cried, "That ain't no woman. That's an Injun."

He started to draw his pistol, but the guard held out an arm and said, "No, I believe her. She ain't got no reason to lie."

The driver squinted against the sun. "Everybody thought you was a boy," he said accusingly. "Nobody knew different till that woman in Tombstone said *Kit* Parrish had to be *Kitty* Parrish, 'cause she was expectin' you on that stage. So how come you lied all that time?"

Kitty thought of the irony and, with a soft laugh, explained, "Because I thought I would be safer traveling as a man."

"If you are able to fool the Injuns, then it was good that you did," he said. "Are you all right? I mean, did they hurt you? You sure look a sight. I'm Buck Hawley, by the way."

"I'm fine, Buck," she assured him. "Just tired and hungry and thirsty, and I'm real anxious to get to Tombstone."

They crawled down off the rocks, and Kitty groaned under her breath to see that the passengers—two women and three men—had got out. At the sight of her, one of the women collapsed into the arms of the man standing next to her, and the other turned and scrambled back inside to peer out the window in disgust.

Kitty made sure the passengers could not hear her as she warned Tom and Buck that they needed to be extra alert. "The Indians may be looking for me by now."

Tom was still in awe. "How did you get away from 'em?"

"It's a long story, and I don't want to talk about it."

Buck said, "Well, I don't blame you. And don't worry. We'll keep an eye out."

"I can ride on top to help out," she offered. "I'm a good shot."

"No. They'd pick you right off. It's best you get on inside." He handed her a canteen of water and a sack with soda biscuits and beef jerky. "Eat your fill, girl, and I'll get us to Tombstone lickety-split."

The passengers, quite vexed, had to make room for her, muttering among themselves all the while.

The stage began to roll. Kitty leaned her head back

and closed her eyes. The woman sitting next to her coughed and covered her nose with a lace handkerchief. Kitty did not care. Neither was she embarrassed. All she wanted was to get to Tombstone and have the confrontation with Opal Grimes that she had been yearning for.

Finally, one of the men, curiosity getting the best of him, asked, "Was it terrible . . . being with those savages?"

Kitty's eyes flashed open. She regarded him coldly. He did not care about her welfare. He just wanted to hear the gory details of her captivity. "No, it wasn't terrible at all. They treated me well."

The woman next to her made a face and said, "But everyone knows they're no better than animals—"

"All animals aren't dangerous," Kitty crisply informed her. "And the Chiricahua could hardly be called animals, anyway. Their ways are primitive to ours, true, but we have to remember they aren't civilized. They don't know about our way of life."

"They fled the reservation," another man said sharply. "They don't want to know. They'd rather live like the savages they are."

Fixing him with a condemning stare and remembering Pale Sky's words in parting, Kitty advised him, "They only want what is theirs—the land we drive them off of."

The woman beside her worked her lips silently, reproachfully, for a moment, then snapped, "Well, if you think so much of them, why didn't you stay with them? You sure look like you'd fit right in."

"Yes," the other female passenger said haughtily. "Why did you want to escape? If you must take up for them—dirty, ignorant barbarians that they are— then remain and be one of them."

She exchanged a smirk with the other woman.

With a sigh of disgust, Kitty leaned back and closed

her eyes again. Like Pale Sky had said—they would not listen. They never had.

She had slipped the flint knife inside her boot, glad Pale Sky had not made her wear moccasins, so she had a hiding place for it. She would keep it always as a memento of the kindhearted Indian woman who had set her free.

Whitebear would also be remembered. Though he had treated her, and regarded her, as no more than a pesky nuisance of a white boy, he had unknowingly awakened and stirred the woman part of her, and she feared he would haunt her dreams for a long time to come.

When the stagecoach reached the outskirts of Tombstone it was late evening. Tom stood up in the box and began shouting, "We found her. We found the girl the Injuns took. We got her . . ."

Kitty could see at once that Tombstone appeared to be unlike any other town she had passed through in the West. Busy, bustling, she sensed it was teeming with excitement.

She wondered what she would do after confronting Opal Grimes, which was first on her agenda. She supposed she would have to find some kind of a job fast. There had hardly been enough time to retrieve the map before fleeing the camp, and she'd had to abandon what little money she had left. But before she could look for work, she had to get herself cleaned up and find decent clothes. No one would hire her looking as she did.

By the time the stage rolled to a stop in front of the depot, a crowd was gathering.

Kitty stepped out to meet a sea of curious faces.

"Glory be, she looks like an Apache," someone cried.

"You sure it's her?" another man called to the

driver and guard as they got down out of the box. "Don't look nothin' like no white woman to me."

"It's her, all right," Buck assured him.

Kitty had got out and just stood there, unsure of what to do next. Then she saw a tall man pushing his way through the crowd. His expression was stony, and he wore a stiff-brimmed hat and a black frock coat. But, most importantly, a silver star was pinned on his chest.

She walked to meet him. "Are you the sheriff?"

He raked her with skeptical eyes. "I'm the city marshal. Virgil Earp's the name. Are you really Kitty Parrish?"

Kitty cringed at how everyone was murmuring among themselves as they stared at her like she was some kind of creepy, horrible thing. "Yes, I am," she said stiffly.

"Well, I think you'd best come along with me. The army will be wanting to talk to you."

He motioned her to follow, but she held back. "What for?"

"They'll be wanting to ask you questions to see if you can help them locate where the Apaches are hiding out."

"I'm afraid I have no idea," she said—although she did. She could probably lead the soldiers to the camp—or close proximity, anyway—but had no intention of doing so. "And I've no time to talk to them, anyway. I'm looking for a woman by the name of Opal Grimes. Do you know where I can find her?"

"She works in my brother's place just down the street—the Oriental Palace, but she won't be there for a while yet. However if I were you"—the play of a smile came on his lips—"I'd get out of those clothes you're wearing and into something else before I went walking around Tombstone. Folks don't cotton to Indians around here, ma'am, and you sure do look like one in that garb."

Kitty was undaunted. "I'd like nothing better, but, unfortunately, I don't have anything else to wear for the moment. Now, if you'll tell me where Miss Grimes lives, I'd be obliged."

He pointed. "You'll find some shanties down there. She lives in the second row on the end. She ought to be home at this hour, but if I were you, I wouldn't take her by surprise. After the scare she got a while back, she'd likely shoot on sight what she thought was an Indian."

"Seeing me will be a surprise no matter how I'm dressed," Kitty said, not bothering to explain that Opal probably thought she was long dead. Besides, she was not going to just walk up and knock on her door. If Opal saw it was her, she would likely barricade herself and never come out.

Kitty created a stir as she made her way through town, but by the time she got to the shanties there were few people out and about.

She stood back for a few moments to study the place on the end. Spotting an open window in the rear, she crept close and peered inside to see a woman sitting at a table. She was wearing a robe and sipping what looked like whiskey. She looked tired, old, and unhappy.

*Well, she's about to be* real *unhappy,* Kitty thought as she reached up to hook her fingers in the top of the window frame.

Taking a deep breath, she kicked off from the side of the shanty with her feet. Propelling her body backward and up, she then swung forward and through the window to land on her feet with a thud directly in front of the woman.

"Pleased to meet you, Miss Grimes. The name's Kitty Parrish."

Opal dropped the glass, whiskey spilling across the table and on her robe. Her face went white, and she tried to get up out of the chair but stumbled and fell, sprawling to the floor.

Kitty reached down and grabbed her arm and yanked her up, then roughly slung her into another chair.

"Now we're going to talk," she said, feeling angry blood rush to her face as she righted the fallen chair and sat down across from Opal.

"You . . . you're Kitty?" Opal clutched her throat with one hand, willing the words to squeak past the constriction of terror as she wilted before the blazing eyes. "But . . . but I thought . . ."

"You thought the Indians killed me like you paid them to do?" Kitty's laugh was harsh. "Well, you wasted your money, lady, because I'm free, and I'm here, and I want to know why in the hell you wanted to get rid of me."

"But . . . but I didn't . . ."

"It's my uncle's—my stepfather's gold mine, isn't it? With me out of the way, it's all yours. So when you heard I was coming, you got the Indians to attack the stagecoach."

Opal shook her head slowly from side to side. "No. No, I would never do that. And why would I have sent you his part of the map . . . his money . . . if I wanted it all for myself?"

"I wondered about that at first," Kitty said, "because it didn't make sense. But the Indians were definitely looking for Kitty Parrish, and the only way they could have known I was on that stage was for you to have told them. You were the only person who knew. Besides that, I heard them mention your name."

"My name?" Opal gasped, both hands slamming the table as she went rigid in the chair. "How could they know me?"

Kitty sneered. "They knew you, all right. Now enough of your lies. I want to know . . ." Her voice trailed off, seeing the expression on Opal's face. Opal looked deep in thought, forgetting Kitty was there.

And then she slapped her hands together and exclaimed, "Of course. That's it. That's why he was here—the Indian. He knew about the map to Wade's gold mine, and he wanted it. I told him I didn't have it, that I'd sent it to his niece—to you. He went away, but when I came home from work that night, I had a strange feeling he had come back.

"Your telegram and letter"—she pointed at the stove—"are hidden behind there. He must have found them, and evidently he could read, so he knew when you were expected. It all adds up."

"Not to me. How would he have known about the map in the first place?"

"I've no idea. But you have to believe me," Opal gestured helplessly, eyes imploring. "I would never do such a thing, Kitty. I wouldn't want you harmed for anything in the world. You . . . you're a part of Wade, and"—she swallowed and blinked back tears—"I loved him, you see. I could never hurt anything that was his."

Kitty was starting to believe her, because, after all was said and done, it just wasn't plausible that she would have gone to the trouble of even telling her about Daddy Wade's death if she wanted everything for herself. "But the Indian—Whitebear, he was called—I heard him say your name to his mother. And I know it was me he was looking for, because he asked me if I had met a passenger named Kitty Parrish."

Opal poured herself another drink with shaking hands. She offered one to Kitty, but she declined. "I don't know," she said. "Unless . . ." Her voice trailed off once more.

Kitty prodded, "Go on."

"Wade used to talk to me about his partner, Dan McCloud, and how he was a strange old codger. He had a little farm somewhere, and he'd disappear for days at a time, and that's where Wade figured he went. There was a woman somewhere, too, but he never talked about her except when he was drunk, and then Wade couldn't make out what he was saying. He had a son, and the reason Wade knew about that was on account of Dan saying if anything happened to him he wanted him to have his share of their strike.

"Wade figured the woman was Indian," Opal went on to say, "because he always wore an Indian amulet around his neck, and when he was drunk and mumbling about loving somebody, he would stroke it and cry. Wade suspected Dan had a son by her, and that he was a half-breed, and that's why he never came around."

Kitty paled.

"Kitty, what's wrong?" Opal got up and rushed to her side. She pressed a hand to her forehead. "You can't be well, not after being with those savages. Let me fetch the doc to give you a going over, and I'll fix you some soup and tea. We can talk about all this later. I just want you to believe me when I say I had nothing to do with you being abducted. I swear it, and you've got to believe me . . ."

"I do," Kitty cried. "And I think I know what's going on here."

"What . . ."

"Whitebear is a half-breed. His father was white, and I think"—she drew an excited breath—"I think Dan McCloud was his father. That would explain why he wanted the other half of the map . . . and why he wanted me."

Opal whispered raggedly, "Oh, dear Lord . . ." and collapsed to her knees.

\*      \*      \*

Ryder stared down at his mother, chest heaving with fury.

"I know you are angry," Pale Sky calmly said. "As I knew you would be. But I had no choice. Coyotay found the *tiswin* and became crazy. I knew if I did not take Billy Mingo from the camp and set him free, Coyotay would take the revenge he had been thirsting for. You were not here to stop it. I did what I thought was right.

"We have no business with slaves, anyway," she went on as she returned to her stove. "We have enough to worry about taking care of ourselves."

He had returned to the camp only moments before, moving his horse as fast as he dared up the last inclines after hearing from a sentry about the captive's escape. Everyone was sure Pale Sky was responsible, the sentry had confided.

He had burst into her wickiup and did not even have to ask, for she had faced him squarely from the onset to admit everything.

She began to stir the pot of chokeberries she was making into a kind of jam.

The only sound was Ryder's heavy, angry breathing.

"It is nothing to be upset about, my son. Now rest yourself, and I will make food for you. I know you are hungry after such a long ride.

"And tell me," she cast a smile in his direction and changed the subject in hopes he would calm down, "did you learn when the woman, Kitty Parrish, will arrive?"

"No. She's already arrived, Mother."

Pale Sky's head jerked up.

"She is probably in Tombstone by now."

"Are you sure? There must have been a stage you did not know about."

"No. I had the right stage. As a matter of fact, I had Kitty Parrish."

Pale Sky looked at him as though he were daft. "What nonsense is this?"

"Billy Mingo was not a boy. Billy Mingo was Kitty Parrish pretending to *be* a boy, and you," he said with cold finality, "let her go."

# Chapter 10

"I called him Daddy Wade and I couldn't have loved him more if he had been my real father."

Opal nodded with understanding. "And I know he loved you like the daughter he never had. That was why I wrote and did what he asked me to—sent you the map and the money. He talked about you a lot, Kitty. He was hoping one day you'd come out here. I'm just sorry things didn't work out."

She bit her lip, and Kitty patted her hand. Once she had been convinced Opal had nothing to do with Whitebear looking for her, Kitty had immediately taken a liking to her. True, she had a hardness about her, probably because her job required her to deal with men who sometimes drank heavily, but, also Opal had a gentle, caring side. Kitty thought she had probably once been very pretty, too, but now her face was lined, her eyes lackluster.

"I know you must have cared about him, too," Kitty said. "The two of you had been friends for quite a while, because I could tell you had been writing his letters for him the past few years."

"I loved him," Opal was quick to admit. "He was the finest man I ever knew. I would've married him any time he wanted me to, but he was hell-bent to get the money to get us out of here first."

Hesitantly, Kitty asked, "Do you feel like telling me how it happened . . . how he died?"

It was the morning after Kitty's arrival. The previous evening Opal had not had much time before having to go to work, and they had talked mostly about Whitebear. Now they were both sure he was Dan McCloud's son and the Indian who had terrorized Opal.

When Opal had returned in the wee hours, Kitty had been dead to the world, and Opal did not want to wake her. They were now having breakfast—eggs, salt pork, griddle cakes, and coffee. Opal had insisted on cooking a hearty meal over Kitty's protest that she should not go to the trouble.

"Yeah, I can talk about it," Opal said as she absently made circles on the table with her coffee mug. "But it still hurts. I think it always will." She glanced up suddenly. "Did you find everything you needed last night? I meant to tell you to take the bed. I would've been glad to make a pallet on the floor like you did."

Kitty could have told her there really wasn't much to find in the cramped little two-room shanty. The furniture was sparse, too—table, chairs, and stove in one room; a bed and chifforobe in the other. "I was fine, really. Actually, I'm used to sleeping lately with nothing between me and raw earth but a few animal skins. And, yes, I found everything. I had a nice bath, and your nightgown is a little large, but I'm grateful for the change." She gestured to herself.

"Well, we'll get you some decent clothes today. I thought after you eat we'd go shopping. There are a few nice stores in Tombstone where you can find fashions from back east, and—"

Kitty dismissed that suggestion with a quick wave of her hand. "Overalls are all I need. Maybe some new boots. I think I've worn mine out from all that walking, and . . ." She fell silent to see Opal's disapproving scowl. "What's wrong?"

"Kitty, you can't continue to dress like a man."

"Why not? I always have. It's comfortable."

"Folks will think you're odd."

"I've never cared what people think."

Opal looked her straight in the eye. "Maybe it's time you did . . . like it's also time you got that chip off your shoulder."

Kitty stiffened. "What do you mean?"

"Wade told me how it was for you growing up—the way folks shunned you and your ma for her siding with the Yankees during the war."

"She didn't exactly *side* with them. She did business with them in order to survive. She believed selling them horses was justified, but other folks didn't agree, and they wouldn't forget, and that's why we had trouble."

"Well, whatever the reason, Wade said it was tough on you, because you were all the time getting in fights. And lonely for you, too, on account of the kids not being allowed to have anything to do with you."

Kitty gave a bitter laugh. "It wasn't a matter of them being *allowed*. The fact is—they hated me, too. And, yes, it was tough, as well as lonely, but it's all behind me now. I'm going to make a new life for myself."

"Not as long as you got that chip." Opal pointed to Kitty's shoulder as though a block of wood was actually perched there.

"I don't know what you're talking about."

"I mean that you have to forget the past and start living like normal folk . . . like a *woman*. Besides, it's time you had a husband to take care of you."

Kitty was quick to object. "Getting married just to have a man look after me is the last thing I'll ever do. I can take care of myself, thank you, and probably better than most men. I can ride and shoot, and—" Again, the look on Opal's face threw her into silence.

"Maybe you can," Opal allowed. "But you have to

accept the fact that you are a woman, Kitty—and a very pretty one, at that. Look at you. With your hair all washed and shiny and hanging down your back, and your face scrubbed clean, you're very attractive. Why, the men are going to be beating my door down once we get you really fixed up."

Kitty sighed. "How many times must I tell you I'm not interested?"

"Well, then, what do you plan to do with yourself now that you're here? I've got a little money—not much on account of my brother managing to beg off of me what he doesn't steal behind my back—but you're welcome to it. And you've got a home as long as you need one. Heaven knows, the least I can do for Wade is look after you as best I can, but you've got to think about the future."

Kitty began to make circles with her coffee mug, as well, watching the wet swirls as she murmured, "Well, I'd like to look for the gold, but I guess I'd better think about finding a job."

"Doing what? You want to be a gambling dealer like me? That takes experience, honey. Years of it. And I'd hate to see you work the saloons, plying men to buy drinks, and you sure as hell aren't gonna be no soiled dove. Wade would turn over in his grave if I let you go bad."

"I would never do that. But there has to be something I can do. I'm good with horses. I thought maybe I could hire on at a livery stable, since I hear there aren't many ranches around here."

Opal sneered. "Who'd want to hire a woman for that? No, honey, we've got to find something else you can do. But tell me, what was your thinking in coming out here, anyway, once you knew Wade was dead?"

"I had no place else to go, and I guess I had it in the back of my mind that between the two of us we could find the gold."

"Believe me, I'd like nothing better, because from the way Wade talked, it was quite a strike. They weren't bringing any of it out, though, except for a few nuggets now and then when they needed supplies. They were hoarding it, because they didn't want to file a claim."

"How come? It seems to me they'd want to protect it by staking it."

"But if they did, other prospectors would hear and try to dig around it. They were also afraid of claim jumpers, robbers. They were"—she shuddered at the painful memory—"afraid of what eventually happened."

Kitty hated to have to remind her but wanted to know the whole story. "You said you'd tell me how it happened."

Opal closed her eyes momentarily, as though she had actually witnessed the horror, then looked at Kitty with sadness mirrored from her soul. "Marshall Earp came and told me another prospector had found Wade's body, along with his partner's, near the river a few miles outside of town. The prospector brought them both in on the back of his pack mule. Dan was alive when he found him but died after saying something about how he was taking his secret to the grave with him. So that means neither one of 'em told where their mine was—which is why they were tortured to death. The marshal said they'd have been killed, anyway, even if they did tell. It's just a damn shame they suffered like they did."

Kitty saw how Opal's hands shook as she lifted the mug to her lips to take a sip of coffee before continuing in a quivering voice. "I had to look at Wade . . . had to make sure it was him. He'd been burned, and one of his fingers was cut off."

Kitty covered her face with her hands to shut out

the image as she moaned, "Why didn't they tell? All the gold in the world isn't worth dying for."

"I agree with you, but obviously Wade and Dan McCloud were too stubborn. Wade wanted the gold for me and him to make a new life together out in California but said if anything happened to him that he wanted me and you to have his share. McCloud promised he'd see that we did, and, in exchange, Wade promised him he'd see that his son got his. That's why they made a map and tore it in two."

"But why did you send it to me? Didn't you want to try and find it yourself?"

"There's no way I could without the whole map. So I decided to just give it to you along with the money he left with me. I wish I could have given you the ring, too. He told me turquoise reminded him of your eyes, and now that I've seen you I know why. But it wasn't on him. The murderer took it."

Kitty raged, "There's got to be a special place in hell for somebody that would steal a ring off a dead man's finger."

Opal sneered. "Honey, the bastard not only took the ring—he took the finger. It was on the one he cut off."

Kitty gritted her teeth. "What did the ring look like?"

"The stone was flat and smooth and polished, and the band was wide, thick silver with a curving snake cut to twine all around it. He said he got an old Mexican to make it for him.

"But back to the map," Opal mused. "I think the only reason McCloud ever told Wade he had a son was because he wanted him to have his share of the gold. Otherwise, I don't think he would have said anything. According to Wade, he was a real loner . . . and unhappy, too. He was sure it had to do with the Indian woman."

"I think so, too. Pale Sky—that's Whitebear's mother—told me about the white man she loved and how he wanted his world, and she wanted hers. He took their son away from her, as I understand it, but he obviously found his way back to the Apaches—and her—when he was older."

"Well, I just wish I hadn't told him I sent the map to you, because when he came back trying to find it, he read your telegram I had hidden so my brother wouldn't see it. That's how he knew which stage to attack."

Kitty was puzzled. "But why did you hide it? Why would your brother care if I came out here?"

Opal was ashamed to have to admit, "Nate is a drunk, and I'm afraid I've always let him mooch off me. Sure, I get mad and run him off, but then I go soft and take him in when he's down and out.

"He didn't like me seeing Wade," she continued. "I guess he was afraid if we got married Wade would give him the boot for good. When I found out you were coming, I knew he wouldn't like it, because he'd figure I'd be giving you a hand instead of him. I didn't want to hear his mouth, so I didn't want him to know."

The last thing Kitty wanted was to cause family trouble. "He's probably heard by now. But don't worry, I'm going to get a job and get out of here quick as I can."

"He rode off a few weeks ago."

"Well, when he comes back, you won't have room for him if I'm around, which is another reason I need to get a place of my own."

"Don't worry about that. I been thinking it's best we both get out of here, anyway."

Kitty blinked. "You mean leave Tombstone?"

"No. I mean out of *here*"—she pounded the table for emphasis—"because I don't think it's safe. I been thinking while we been talking how you said that half-breed wasn't around when his mother let you go. Now he's bound to hear the real Kitty Parrish is in town after escaping from the Apaches, and when he realizes how you fooled him, and how his mother let you go, he's going to be mad as a wet hornet and come roaring back to find you."

"Then I need to get a gun," Kitty said, not about to be defenseless should Whitebear come after her. "I know how to shoot, so if you'll loan me the money to buy one, I'll pay you back as soon as I find work."

"We'll get you a gun, all right, but we're also getting out of here, like I said. I only took this place so's me and Wade could have privacy when he came to town. I also didn't like living around the soiled doves, but Mr. Wyatt Earp, who owns the Oriental, doesn't allow them there. He's got such a swanky place going he only lets important workers—like me—and special guests lodge up there. And right after Wade was killed, he offered me a room.

"So we'll do it today," she rushed on, enthused. "And then that damn Indian won't dare bother us, because there are always men with guns around. We'll be safe. And sooner or later he'll give up."

"But are we going to do the same thing—give up?" Kitty asked, disappointed. "I mean, just think. If Whitebear has his father's part of the map, and I could get him to agree to work with me, then we could find the gold and share it, and—"

Opal leaped to her feet, stunned she could suggest such a thing. "Are you out of your mind, child? Has living with those savages, if only for a little while, robbed you of your senses to make you think you could trust one of them, even if he is half-white? No. We forget about the gold and make sure he doesn't get anywhere near us, because once he got Wade's piece of the map, he'd slit your throat and mine, too.

Remember, honey. He's nothing but a savage. So get that notion out of your head right now. And I want us to keep this between us, too. We won't tell anybody what we figured out about why an Indian broke in on me. We don't want whoever murdered Wade and McCloud to think you've got any kind of a map at all.

"And where is it, anyway?" she asked suddenly, sharply. "What did you do with it?"

Kitty had stuck it in her boot when she left the camp. She went and got it and laid it on the table. It was crumpled, but none the worse for wear.

"Thank goodness, you didn't lose it," Opal said. "When we go into town, I'll put it in the bank."

"The bank? I thought that was just for money."

"Not anymore. One of the banks here has something new—little boxes that you can put important papers in, like wills and deeds. Things like that. Then they put it in the big safe for you. You might need it later on, and the dirty savage won't be able to get his hands on it there."

*Dirty savage.*

Kitty rolled the words around in her head. Whitebear did not exactly fit that description. She had no doubt he was a mighty warrior, but he was also well educated. He was also handsome in a rugged sort of way. As for him being dirty, that was not a fair description, either. She knew because she had bathed him . . . and now felt a rush of heat to think about it.

She could not help smiling to think how furious he would be when he found out that it had not only been a woman who bathed him, but the one he had been looking for, as well. She was glad she would not be around then.

Still, she wondered what it would have been like to have known him under different circumstances, for she could not deny feeling attraction . . . and *desire*.

"Kitty, are you sick?" Opal touched fingertips to her brow. "Your face is red, and you feel hot."

Kitty gave herself a vicious shake to dispel the image that filled her with heat. "No. I'm fine. Just anxious to get out of here before Whitebear realizes how I tricked him."

"Well, hurry and eat so we can do just that," Opal urged with a grin. "Your new life as a woman begins today."

Kitty did not share her enthusiasm about the woman part. Not that she wished she were a boy, but life would be simpler if she were. She knew nothing about styling her hair or dressing feminine, but she could shoe a horse and help a mare with a difficult foal. And while she was ignorant when it came to cooking and sewing, she could shoot the head off a nail from thirty feet away, break a wild pony to saddle and bridle and teach him gaits, to boot.

So here she was, in a strange town in a strange land. It was like being born all over again, and she was struck to realize she was suddenly more frightened of having to learn how to be female than she had been in the hands of the Apaches.

Opal disappeared into the other room and returned a few moments later with a gown draped across her arms. "I knew I'd find a use for this sooner or later," she said proudly as she held it up. "One of the dance hall girls left this behind when she ran off with some man. I found it before any of the other girls. It's too small for me, but I kept it because it's so pretty."

"Indeed it is." Kitty marveled at the creation of red and white gingham. It had short, pouffed sleeves and a high neck with a saucy lace trim meant to barely brush against the face. The bodice was form-fitting with a sash at the waistline. She liked best of all the skirt with its tiers of ruffles and more lace.

"Ruby Lee called it her *good-Christian-lady* outfit,"

Opal explained with an amused grin. "She'd wear it while she strolled down the street during the day when she wasn't working and ·stick her nose up at the ones who stuck their noses up at her because she was a saloon girl."

Kitty could picture that and laughed. "Well, I don't blame her. It's beautiful."

"And all yours if you can wear it. You're kind of scrawny, though," Opal remarked thoughtfully, then added, "But don't worry. We can take some nips and tucks. You're going to be one hell of a beautiful woman, honey. Just leave it to me. Why, you'll be married in no time at all. Men out here are foaming at the mouth like mad dogs to get themselves a wife."

Kitty bit back the impulse to remind her once again that she was not looking for a husband but decided not to waste her breath.

In good time, Opal, like any foaming-at-the-mouth men who dared come around, would find out for herself.

Pale Sky felt frustration and shame. "How could she have fooled me so? Why didn't I suspect something?"

Ryder sat on a bearskin rug, shoulders hunched, hands folded across his knees, which were drawn nearly to his chest. It had been three days since he had returned from Tombstone to find out his mother had unknowingly led Kitty Parrish to freedom. He had stayed in his tent, not wanting to face any of his people. Neither did he want the company of Adeeta or any other amorous girl. He wanted to be alone to think about his stupidity and try to figure out what to do next.

His mother, however, refused to give him the solitude he craved. She continued to berate herself for having been taken in by Kitty Parrish's deception.

Weary of listening to her, Ryder again tried to

soothe her in hopes she would calm down. "It's easy to see how she got away with it, Mother—her baggy clothes, the way she kept her hair hanging down over her face. I should have suspected something when she was so modest, always hiding in the bushes, making sure nobody could see her bathe. It all adds up now, but we didn't think anything about it at the time, because we had no reason."

"I'm just so sorry," Pale Sky wailed, crossing her arms over her bosom and swaying from side to side. She had brought him fresh tortillas and honey from a hive one of the young Indian boys had found somewhere. Pointing to the food, she said, "You must eat, my son. You cannot continue to starve yourself and brood. Let me get you some of the *tiswin* Coyotay missed when he robbed my wickiup."

Raising his head to glower at her, Whitebear could not resist the barb "*Tiswin* is what led to you letting her go, Mother. I don't think I can stomach the sight of it right now, though I'd drink myself into a stupor if I thought it would solve anything."

"So sorry. So sorry," Pale Sky moaned again. "I should not have let her go, but at the time I was afraid of what would happen if I did not."

Though Ryder loved and respected her and would never intentionally hurt her, he could not let her off too easy for her wrongdoing. "You could have taken her and hidden her somewhere. You know your way. By morning, Coyotay was probably too sick to do anybody any harm. You didn't have to let her go, and you know it."

"Yes, I admit that is so," she said with a nod. "I did not approve of you taking a captive in the first place, and that was wrong. I went against you, our leader, and for that, I ask forgiveness."

Ryder stood to give her a reassuring hug. "And you

have it. Like you said, you thought you were doing the right thing."

"As you did when you planned to take Kitty Parrish off the stagecoach and bring her here to try and scare her into handing over her piece of the map."

He raised a brow. "What else was I to do?"

Pale Sky spread her hands as though it were quite simple. "Wait until she reached Tombstone, then find her and introduce yourself. Tell her the truth and then offer to put your father's half of the map with hers and the two of you can work together to find the hidden gold mine."

For an instant, Ryder could only stare at her in wonder that she could suggest such a thing. But then he reminded himself that his mother had a pure, loving heart and wanted only peace. Yet he could not hold back a sardonic smile as he said, "You forget how important it is to our people that I am able to pass for white. We don't know that Father didn't get drunk and let it slip to Parrish that he had a half-Indian son. So had I approached Kitty Parrish as a white man, she would have been able to expose me if she chose to do so. I would not have been able to work as a scout again.

"And we both know she would never have agreed to an Apache for a partner," he concluded. "No. I did the only thing I could, and I failed, thanks to her disguise."

Pale Sky seemed to wilt in her despair. "So the gold is lost to us forever. We must go with empty hands to Mexico . . . where we will starve and die like so many of our people before us."

Ryder watched her go, then settled back on the bearskin rug once more.

He was not ready to give up, but neither had he come up with another plan to get his hands on Kitty Parrish's map. In all probability, she would have reached Tombstone safely. His mother had told him where she left her and the direction she told her to head. Based on his estimate of how fast she would have moved, she would have reached the stagecoach route and been picked up by the stage due to come along soon.

Once in Tombstone, she would find Opal Grimes, who would tell her right off about the savage Indian that had held a knife to her throat while asking questions about the map to Wade Parrish's gold mine. She and Kitty Parrish would add things up quickly and decide it could only have been Whitebear.

He tossed away the notion of going back to the shanty. They would expect him to do just that and have weapons ready and guards posted.

"Damn it," he cursed and slammed his fists together. A fool. That's what he was. Before his people and before the woman, because he had acted like she was a man, not caring whether she saw him naked, and, hell, he had even made her give him a bath. And now she was somewhere laughing at him for his stupidity while he was ashamed to look anyone in the eye. It would serve her right if he did the same thing to her.

He stiffened, jolted by a sudden thought.

There had been certain women in his past that needed persuasion to come to his bed, and he had coaxed them with warm caresses and a honeyed tongue. Perhaps he could do the same thing with Kitty Parrish. After all, she was young and might not have had much experience with men.

Then again, he might fail . . . might wind up looking like an even bigger fool.

But he had to try.

And, if he succeeded, he would enjoy a double triumph. He would have her half of the map.

And then *she* would be the fool.

# Chapter 11

"Say hello to *Miss* Parrish," Opal said proudly as she stepped back from the mirror to allow Kitty a full view of herself.

For a moment, Kitty could only stare in awe. She had not worn a dress since she was eight years old and certainly never one so fancy.

She turned slowly, loving the way the big red sash trailed down the back of the skirt. It matched the ribbon of the bonnet which was tied in a saucy bow beneath her chin.

"Well?" Opal prodded anxiously. "What do you think of yourself as a girl . . . a *woman*?"

Kitty found the curls Opal had fashioned with a hot rolling iron a bit strange. "Well, it's a different feeling. That's for sure."

Opal gave one of the sleeves another tug to fluff it. "You're beautiful, and you know it. Now, let's be on our way. Around noon is the only safe time to be on the streets, and then it's no guarantee bullets won't start flying."

As they walked along, Opal pretended to grumble, "I don't know why I'm even bothering to move you into the Oriental with me. You'll probably get a wedding proposal before we even reach Allen Street."

"Well, maybe you will, too," Kitty said, then added to tease, "After all, you're the one who said a woman needs a man to look after her."

"I didn't mean me. I do fine on my own. Always have. Always will. It's you I'm worried about."

"And I told you—I can take care of myself."

Opal snorted. "Don't look to me like you've done such a good job. If not for that squaw letting you go, you'd still be with the Apaches."

Kitty felt a prickle of resentment, then steeled against it. It was only natural Opal would be concerned about taking responsibility for her. After all, she had descended on her penniless and homeless. "Well, you don't have to worry. I'm going to do just fine on my own."

"Hmph. That remains to be seen," Opal grumbled, twirling her parasol as they walked along.

As they left the rows of shanties and entered the main part of town, Kitty forgot about Opal's nagging and sought to acquaint herself with her new home. When she had arrived the day before, she had been too exhausted—and, yes, angry and anxious about confronting Opal—to notice anything around her. Now, however, she drank in the sight of the bustling town.

The streets were crowded with cowboys and prospectors. Mule- and horse-pulled wagons lumbered in and out, wheels sometimes miring in the thick mud of the street.

Opal lifted her skirts to step over a puddle as she said, "This is when folks usually start waking up after a long night of gambling and drinking. It'll take 'em a while to get going again, but they will. And it's a rare day when there's not trouble of some kind. Tombstone is different from any place you've ever lived, honey, so don't be surprised at anything you see."

"I've only lived in one place my whole life, and that was a farm—not a town."

"Then you better get ready to go around with your

eyes bugging out of your head for a while, 'cause this place can get real wild. At last count, we've got two dance halls, twelve gambling houses, and twenty saloons." Opal pointed to some nearby construction under way. "I've heard that's going to be a real fancy place. They're going to call it the Bird Cage Theater, and it'll have a little bit of everything—dance hall, gambling, saloon, *and* brothel. The whores are even going to have little stalls like birdcages hanging from the ceiling."

"Good afternoon, Miss Opal."

Kitty and Opal stopped short as a cowboy suddenly straightened from where he had been leaning against a rain barrel enjoying a smoke. He tipped his felt hat to Kitty, eyes shiny with interest. "And who might you be, pretty little lady? I don't recall seeing you around town before, and to be sure I would, lovely as you are."

Opal promptly poked him in the chest with her parasol. "You get out of our way, Hardy Poe. We've no time for your foolishness." To Kitty, she said, "Hardy is a good-for-nothing. Lives for the price of a drink."

"Aw, don't talk like that, Miss Opal. You know I'm working a dig up in the mountains."

"And finding just enough ore to get drunk."

"Oh, that ain't so. Now, I'd appreciate your introducing me to this li'l lady proper, 'cause she's about as cute as a speckled pup."

Kitty bit back a giggle as Opal snapped, "If the truth be known, Hardy Pope, you'd *marry* a speckled pup if you could find one that would have you." To Kitty, she said, "Didn't I tell you men in these parts are desperate?"

Hardy held out his hand. "Now that you know my name, how about telling me yours since Miss Opal ain't gonna be polite."

Opal gave Kitty's arm a tug. "Come along. He's not worth your time."

Kitty thought Opal was being needlessly unkind. She felt the man, despite his unkempt appearance—scruffy beard and rumpled clothing that had seen better days—had behaved politely and deserved like response. She took his hand. "My name is Kitty Parrish, Mr. Pope. I'm pleased to meet you, but I'm afraid we are in a hurry."

She started around him, but he quickly stepped in front of her, eyes suddenly wide. "*You're* Kitty Parrish? The one the Apaches had hold of? I don't believe it. Some of the boys that saw you when you got into town yesterday were talking last night about what a sight you were. Didn't look nothing like a girl, they said. Looked just like an Injun boy. Now look at you. Why, they ain't gonna believe me when I tell 'em how you look now."

"And you're not going to believe it when I whack you over the head with this parasol." Opal held it up in threat. "Now, get along with you, Hardy. We've got business to tend to, and Miss Kitty just hasn't been here long enough to know it don't pay to be nice to you rowdies."

She poked him again with the parasol, and he stepped aside, still shaking his head in wonder as he stared at Kitty.

Opal was annoyed and walking so fast Kitty had trouble keeping up with her. The high button shoes Opal had insisted she wear were a bit too large and slipped up and down on her feet. They were also awkward, because she had never worn anything but boots in her life.

"I told you the men would flock around you like flies to sugar," Opal said, maintaining a firm grip on Kitty's arm. "and all they want is a wife to take to bed when they feel like it, wash their dirty clothes, cook their grub, and have a baby every year."

Kitty laughed. "And you dare wonder why I don't want to get married?"

"For you, it'd probably be better than starving. You just need to be particular, that's all. You ought not even be seen talking to white trash like that, much less shaking his hand. You've got a lot to learn, honey. You—"

Shots rang out.

Kitty froze in terror, but Opal reacted quickly, shoving her in the doorway of the store they were passing as she cried, "I hate it when they have these damn shoot-outs in the street. Some innocent soul is always getting killed. You got to learn to be ready to duck, honey, or you're gonna be one of them."

The firing stopped as abruptly as it had begun. Kitty dared to peer around the corner of the door frame to gasp, "Oh, no . . ."

An innocent soul *had* been shot—Hardy Pope.

He lay on his back in the mud. Sprawled nearby were the two gunmen, who had ultimately hit their targets—each other.

Kitty started toward Hardy, and Opal tried to hold her back. "Don't. There's liable to be more trouble. You could get shot yourself. It's best we keep going . . . not get involved."

Kitty struggled against her. "But look. He's alive. He's trying to raise his head." She could see blood on his chest. The other two were facedown and not moving.

"No. You got to learn to mind your own business."

After running for cover, people had started to return to the street, but no one made any move to help Hardy Pope. Neither did anyone yell for a doctor or move to find one.

With a mighty tug, Kitty yanked her arm free of

Opal and, pulling her skirt up above her ankles, took off running.

Opal wailed, "Kitty, come back here."

Reaching Hardy, Kitty dropped to her knees, unmindful of the mud.

With a great, rasping cough, he looked up at her with dazed eyes. A feeble smile touched his lips. "Why . . . glory be . . . ," he whispered. "It . . . it's an angel. I see an angel. I . . . I guess I didn't lead such a bad life, after all. I reckon I'm goin' to the promised land . . . praise the Lord . . ."

Kitty jerked his shirt open. He had been hit in the right side of his chest. Quickly untying the bandanna around his neck, she pressed it against the bullet hole. Over her shoulder she yelled, "Please . . . somebody get a doctor. Hurry."

"An . . . angel . . . ," he repeated. "I see an angel."

"Don't try to talk, Mr. Pope. A doctor will be here in a minute. Just be still and save your strength."

"It don't . . . don't matter. Angel . . . come to take me home."

She cradled his head to try and help him breathe better. Tears stung her eyes. It was not fair. He had just been standing there, watching her walk away and not bothering anybody.

"Why . . . why ain't you singin' to me, angel?" He looked at her with glazing eyes. "I . . . I thought there was music when somebody goes to heaven. I . . . I thought the angels would sing. Maybe"—he coughed and blood flowed from his mouth as his smile faded to a worried grimace—"maybe I ain't goin' to heaven, after all. Maybe . . . maybe I'm goin' the other way . . . to the bad place."

"No. You aren't going to the bad place," Kitty said, heart twisting with pity. If he knew he was dying, he did not need the anguish of thinking he was going to hell.

She began to sing a hymn her uncle had taught her—"Amazing Grace." He had always said she had a beautiful voice, that she should sing in church, but she never did because she never felt welcome there. So she had sung for her uncle, sung for herself, as well as the animals, whenever and wherever she felt like it.

Soon she was lost in the poignant words and spirited melody, unaware of the crowd gathered to watch and listen curiously. Neither did she notice when Marshal Earp appeared, along with his brother, to stand out from the others in their black frock coats and tall hats.

It was only when she finished the last verse that she saw that Hardy Pope's eyes were fixed, unseeing, upon her face.

He had died smiling contentedly, truly believing that an angel was singing to him on his way to heaven.

Opal, who had pushed her way through the throng to take up position directly behind Kitty, leaned to say, "That was beautiful, honey, but he's gone now. You can put his head down."

Kitty did so, then yielded to someone gently trying to help her stand.

Dusting her skirt, she saw the muddy stains and said, "I'm sorry, Opal. I'll take care of it, and if I can't get it clean, I'll try to replace it, I promise."

She turned to the man who had helped her up. He had dark, hooded eyes and a tightly set mouth beneath a pencil-thin mustache. She fought the impulse to cringe before his grim expression as she said, "Thank you, sir."

"Oh, this is Wyatt Earp." Opal was quick to introduce her. "I told you about him, remember? He owns the Oriental Saloon. And I'd like you to meet his brother, Virgil. He's the city marshal."

To the two men, she said, "And this is Miss Kitty

Parrish from Virginia. She's going to be staying with me for a spell."

Wyatt Earp's expression changed to one of incredulity. "*You're* the one who was abducted by the Indians? I heard you escaped and arrived in town yesterday, but I'm afraid my brother's description of you was quite different than what I'm seeing."

Virgil Earp laughed. "Well, I'd say looking like an Apache when she got here *was* different."

Kitty said, "Well, Marshal, I took your suggestion to change clothes."

"Oh, you've already met?" Opal asked, pleased.

Virgil confirmed, "Yes. I asked her to go with me to talk to the army, but she refused." His tone was condemning.

Kitty was firm. "It's over, and I don't want to talk about it. I'm here. I'm fine. That's all that matters."

"Isn't she something?" Opal was beaming, well aware of the admiring glances of the men standing about and also the jealous stares from some of the women. "I fixed her up good, didn't I? And that's Ruby Lee's gown," she said to Wyatt.

"Which I may have ruined," Kitty interjected with a sad gesture. Then she glanced down at Hardy Pope to add, "But I had to do it. That poor man . . ."

"I'm afraid it happens nearly every day in Tombstone," Wyatt said. He took her arm and began to lead her away, leaving the gruesome scene to his brother. "You're going to have to learn to be very careful when you're out on the street, Miss Parrish. You must observe everything going on around you and be ready to duck for cover without warning. Especially do not be out after dark." He shot a meaningful glance at Opal. "I keep telling her the same thing, but she won't listen—not even after one of those savages paid her a visit. She still walks herself home alone every night, no matter how late it is."

Opal said, "Well, I'm going to remedy that if your offer is still good to let me have a room over the saloon. I think me and Kitty would be safer staying there."

"Yes, you would, but the rooms aren't large," he pointed out. "The two of you would be crowded. I can rent one to Miss Parrish, however, at a special rate."

Kitty bit back a groan. If he wouldn't let them squeeze in together for a while so she could share Opal's free room, they would have to stay at the shanty and wait for Whitebear to come sneaking around. Opal would never move without her.

"We don't mind being crowded for a little while," Opal declared. "When Kitty gets a job, she'll get her own place."

He shook his head. "I don't know. I prefer one person a room. What kind of job is she looking for?"

Kitty responded before Opal had a chance. "I'm good with horses, Mr. Earp. I used to raise them back in Virginia. We had a farm—my mother and me. I can shoe and bust broncs, clean stables, anything. And once I start work, I can pay for my own room."

They had reached the boardwalk in front of the Oriental. Wyatt pulled a cheroot from inside his coat, ran it under his nose for a checking sniff, then lit it and took a draw before explaining, "I don't think I can do that, Miss Parrish. You see, I keep those rooms for special guests and employees, like Opal. Now, if you worked for me . . ." He trailed off, his meaning clear.

"Wait a minute." Opal leaped to object. "She's just a kid. She doesn't know anything about gambling, much less dealing. And it'd be like throwing a lamb to lions to put her to work serving drinks. She's still wet behind the ears. She wouldn't know how to handle them drunk rowdies. Now, I know it's going to be next to impossible for her to find a job working in a stable, but I thought I'd introduce her to some of the store owners. Maybe they can put her to work as a clerk."

Wyatt smiled. "I doubt that. I can't imagine a store owner's wife allowing somebody as pretty as she is to work around her husband. Besides"—he drew on the cheroot again—"I wasn't thinking about her dealing or working the bar."

Both Opal and Kitty stared at him expectantly.

"I was thinking of hiring her to sing."

Kitty was sure she'd not heard right. "Did you say—*sing*?"

"That I did. I heard you just now, singing to that dying man. You have a lovely voice, but, of course"— he paused to chuckle—"you wouldn't be singing *hymns* at the Oriental. But I'm sure that Jim—he's the piano player—could teach you some songs the patrons would like. So what do you say, Miss Parrish? I think you would be a great addition to my establishment. And you can have your room free, too, like Opal. I'll also pay you, but we can discuss that later."

"Oh, say yes," Opal urged, bouncing up and down on her toes in delight. "It's your lucky day, honey. The Oriental is the nicest place in town. Everybody will flock to see you. I just know it. We've never had anybody as pretty as you."

Kitty knew it was a wonderful opportunity, but thinking about actually standing up in front of people to sing made her shudder. "I . . . I don't know," she said uncertainly. "Maybe I'm not that good. They might not like me. And I've never done anything like that before."

"You just did," Wyatt said. "And you'll do fine." He looked at Opal. "You know your way around. Show her upstairs. Find two empty rooms, and they're yours. I don't know what's available. I leave that to someone else to take care of. Then take her to see Madelaine Dubosene, the dressmaker up the street.

She sews for my wife. Tell her to make Miss Parrish
a complete wardrobe and send me the bill."

He turned to go, then snapped his fingers and
turned about with an excited grin. "Tell Madame Dubosene that I plan to feature Miss Parrish as 'The
Singing Angel.' After all, that dead man back there
thought she sang him right into heaven."

With a tip of his hat, he left them.

They stared after him, and Opal exulted, "I don't
believe it. Free room, free wardrobe, and a job, to
boot. This is truly, truly, your lucky day."

Kitty felt the same, until some of the sparkle faded
upon visiting the second floor to try and find a room.
Most, they were told by a boy mopping floors, were
occupied by high-rolling gamblers from out of town
who showed no signs of moving out any time soon.
The only two empty were at opposite ends of the hall.
She and Opal would not be next to each other.

Opal said it wouldn't matter. "We'll be working
nights, and we can visit back and forth during the day.
Do you have any preference as to the front or the
rear?" She rushed on before Kitty could respond,
"Okay. I'll take the one in back."

That left Kitty with a room overlooking the noisy
street. She knew she would have a hard time sleeping
but thought maybe once she got to making money she
would find somewhere else to stay. Living upstairs
over a saloon, no matter how fine the establishment,
was not very appealing.

While Opal went to look around her room, Kitty
went to her own. There were two windows, and the
curtains were thick enough to keep anyone from
seeing in from below when they were drawn. The bed
was long and narrow with a carved cherry headboard.
Beside it was a table and lantern. A stack of fresh
linens were on top of the small dresser, and a chiffo-

robe on one wall would provide storage for the clothes she did not yet have.

The wallpaper had a beige background with roses and leaves. The pine floor was almost covered by the burgundy and gold rug.

It was a pleasant, bright room and, aside from its location, was quite nice.

"Ready?" Opal stuck her head in the door. "We need to go see Madame Dubosene and get you fitted, and then we can go back to the shanty and start packing. I'd like to be out of there by night, and if we hurry we can. And believe me," she said with a grimace, "now that we know who that Apache is and what he's after, I can't get out of there fast enough. He'll never try to bother us here. Not with so many people around. You're safe now, honey. We both are."

Kitty hoped . . . prayed . . . she was right.

Madelaine Dubosene was delighted to have the assignment to create a performing wardrobe for Kitty. "You have a nice figure, mademoiselle," she said in her thick French accent. "And I can make you shimmer on the stage with my imported satins and taffetas.

"Combs for your hair," she delighted to continue as she lifted a strand of Kitty's dark hair, "and feathers and pearl tiaras. You will be even lovelier than you are now. So tell me. When is your first performance?"

Opal answered for her. "Mr. Earp didn't say, but I figure right away, as soon as you can get her fixed up."

Kitty was quick to protest, "Oh, I hope not. I need time to practice with his piano player he talked about, to learn songs."

"I will have your first gown ready tomorrow," Madelaine said. "I have been experimenting with a new creation that I think will be perfect for you—white satin covered with seed pearls and soft pink net overlay." She kissed her fingertips. "You will look like an angel, for sure."

Kitty did not want to look like an angel. She did not even want to be a singer. But she had no choice. Not for the time being, anyway.

Leaving the dressmaker's, she asked Opal if they had time to go to the cemetery. "I want to visit Daddy Wade's grave."

Opal's mood turned somber. "Well, if you'd really like to, I guess we can. I usually try to go on Sundays, and we do need to get busy if we're going to get out of the shanty by dark."

"We won't stay long."

"Sure. I understand." Opal gave her a hug. "When I go there, it gives me comfort. Maybe it will do the same for you."

But Kitty felt no solace as she looked down at the mound of dirt and rocks Opal led her to. Only rage—cold, deep, and throbbing. Her uncle was the only person she felt had ever truly loved her, and she would have no peace until his murderer was punished.

Opal gestured to the crude wooden cross at the head of the grave, on which had been carved *WADE PARRISH, MARCH 10, 1881.* "I plan to get a nice monument later on. I just had that put down real quick so the spot where he's buried wouldn't be lost. As you can see, this place gets bigger and bigger."

Kitty saw that the graves in the section known as Boot Hill were dug one after the other in procession. Her uncle had been dead only a few months, but she quickly estimated there had been over a hundred new graves since he was buried.

"So sad," Opal said with a shake of her head as she brushed tears from her eyes with the back of her hands. "We were going to have a new life, away from all the hell-raising and killing. And I tried to tell him we should go on and get out of here and not worry about gold, but he said he'd be a fool to do that. He had a rich strike. We were going to have money to live like royalty the rest of our lives. Lord knows, I'd rather have lived in squalor if it meant keeping him alive."

Kitty's gaze locked on the grave next to her uncle's. There was no marker . . . no cross. "Is this where Dan McCloud is buried?"

"Yeah, it is," Opal said with a scornful sniff. "but I guess that half-breed son of his doesn't care enough to give him a marker. All he wants is his gold, but at least we can take comfort in knowing he won't get it."

"And neither will we," Kitty said quietly.

Ryder felt an inward cringe to see Coyotay blocking the trail. He had been hunting, wanting to ensure that his mother had meat during the time he would be away from camp. He had left before dawn and returned on a back trail, still avoiding the others in his chagrin.

Coyotay was astraddle his mustang, his expression stony.

Ryder braced himself. No doubt Coyotay was chomping at the bit to laugh in his face and deride him for his stupidity. Might as well get it over with, he thought, reining his horse to a stop alongside him.

Coyotay nodded to the ten-point buck strapped across the horse Ryder was leading behind him. "You have made a good kill, my brother."

*Brother?* Coyotay had hardly spoken since the stagecoach incident and then hadn't called him brother. "I plan to be away for a while. I wanted to make sure my mother has enough to eat so the braves won't have to look out for her."

"You know I will take care of her as I always have. You need not worry." He held out his hand. "And

I want to offer you my apology for what I caused to happen."

Ryder was stunned.

"Pale Sky would not have been frightened into setting the girl free had I not been crazy from the *tiswin*," Coyotay said sheepishly. "Then she would have been here when you returned. I am truly sorry, my brother. Sorry, too, that my anger poisoned my mind to all reason."

Ryder let out a long sigh of relief and smiled. "I always did consider you a man of strength and honor, Coyotay, and for you to admit you were wrong reinforces that belief."

"And you are no longer angry with Coyotay?"

"No. We are brothers once more."

"I am glad. So where do you go now? What do you do? The woman called Kitty Parrish is lost to us, along with her part of the map. Is this not so?"

"I'm not ready to give up, so I'm going into Tombstone, as a white man, to try and figure out what to do next. I'm taking this buck to my mother, and then I'm on my way."

Coyotay reined his horse beside Ryder's as they rode on toward the village.

From the corner of his eyes, Ryder saw how the corners of Coyotay's mouth twitched as though he were suppressing a smile. Finally, just before turning their separate ways, he could not resist saying with good humor, "All right. So I was a fool not to see Billy Mingo was really a woman. Go ahead and say it, because I can tell that's what you're thinking."

At that, Coyotay's lips spread in a wide grin. "No. That is not what I was thinking at all. You have no reason to be embarrassed because you did not see through her disguise. None of us did."

Irritated, Ryder countered, "Well, if that's the case, why are you snickering at me? You just said I had no reason to be embarrassed. All the warriors were fooled just like me."

"That is true." Coyotay's black eyes were twinkling with his mischief. "But they did not make her give them a bath, either."

Laughing with glee, Coyotay kneed his mustang and galloped away.

Ryder stared after him, fury worming through his body, but not at his friend. Oh, no. Coyotay was jesting and meant no harm. All their lives they had provoked and teased each other, but always in good nature. So Ryder had no animosity for Coyotay's glee. It was Kitty Parrish who stabbed at his masculine pride for having bested him—something few men had ever succeeded in doing . . . and something no woman ever had.

Till now.

# Chapter 12

Kitty flashed with annoyance as she tugged at the low neckline of her gown. "I told Madame Dubosene she should have made it higher. My bosoms are practically hanging out," she fretted.

Opal slapped lightly at her hands. "Stop it. You aren't singing in church, you know. You're performing in a saloon, and you're supposed to look, well, fetching," she said with a shrug.

"Fetching?" Kitty yelped. "Opal, if I walk out there on that stage in front of all those drunken rowdies, there's no telling what they're liable to do."

"But the gown is fashionable."

"Not for me. And what about you?" She gestured to Opal's gown. It had a high neck with little buttons down the front. "You look like a . . . a *schoolmarm,* and *you* work here. So how come you aren't"—she wrinkled her nose—"*fashionable?*"

"I'm sort of running a business," Opal replied defensively. "The men are supposed to pay attention to the game—not me."

They were in a small room behind the stage. Primarily it was for storage, but the girls working the dance hall and saloon used it to change costume when necessary or take a short rest.

Glancing at the clothes scattered about, Kitty snatched up a red feathered boa from the back of a chair and draped it around her shoulders and down her chest. She said, "Madame Dubosene said I'd look like an angel in this gown, remember? But I feel like a soiled dove."

"You don't know what you're talking about. Soiled doves don't wear white satin with pink net, much less pearl tiaras. And you can't wear that boa. You look like a red chicken."

Kitty twisted about in front of the mirror. "I don't care. I'm not going out there half-naked."

"But you don't understand, honey. The men expect it. They want to see a pretty girl with a nice shape. You just aren't used to dressing up, that's all."

Kitty had to admit that much was true but pointed out, "I'll be so self-conscious I won't be able to sing a note."

"Now you're being downright silly. The men will boo you off the stage if you go out there looking like that."

"She's right."

They both whipped their heads around to see Jim Haynie, the piano player, standing in the doorway.

"Forgive me for barging in. I knocked, but you couldn't hear me for your talking." Sweeping Kitty with an admiring gaze, he added, "You should be proud of your beauty, girl. Don't be shy about it. And what Opal says is true. You walk out there smothered in red feathers, and they'll laugh you right off the stage."

Kitty guessed Jim Haynie to be in his sixties. He had a grizzled, time-worn face, gray hair, and a thin mustache. He was tall, rangy, and stoop-shouldered, with eyes the color of a larkspur and crinkled at the corners when he smiled, which was often. His long, thin fingers made magic on the piano, and his personality was very likable.

He crossed to put a friendly hand on her arm as he offered encouragement. "You have nothing to worry about. You've got a beautiful voice and a face to match. Just sing your heart out and forget about everything else.

"And forget the feathers, too," he added with a laugh. "Opal hit the nail on the head—you do look like a red chicken."

Glumly, Kitty took off the boa and stared at the swell of her breasts above the white satin. She felt almost naked.

Opal said, "Need I remind you what an opportunity this is for you, Kitty? You know you're welcome to anything I have, but I can't support you. If you're going to stay out here, you're going to have to learn to take care of yourself. And if you lose this job, you aren't likely to find another one like it. You'll have to settle for anything you can get . . . which won't be much.

"And," Opal added with eyes narrowed, "you won't have a roof over your head, either. You'll get kicked out of your room. You can't share mine. And somebody has already moved into the shanty, so we can't go back there."

"You'll do fine." Jim again assured Kitty as he walked out. "We'll start in fifteen minutes or so. I'm gonna get me a beer and then I'll warm up the ivories. Listen for your cue and then go out on stage. Somebody will open the curtains when I give the signal. You be ready."

"And it's time for me to get my faro game going," Opal said, following after him. "But I should be able to hear you singing if the applause don't drown you out," she added to encourage.

"Or the shouts telling me to get off the stage," Kitty mumbled to herself as the door closed behind them.

She was pacing about nervously when one of the saloon girls came breezing in a few moments later.

"You're Angel, right? We haven't met. I'm Lulamae."

"Angel?" Kitty echoed. "But that's not my name."

"Sure it is. Mr. Earp said it was. *Angel, the Singing Angel,* that's the name of your show. He had it painted on a big board outside. Everybody's talking about it . . . about you, 'cause lots of folks heard you singing to that poor dying bastard out in the street the other day. That was really something. I wish I'd heard you."

She lit a thin cheroot and took a deep draw before exclaiming, "God, I love these things, but Mr. Earp don't allow us to smoke out there. Says it's not ladylike."

"He wasn't dead when I started singing to him," Kitty said, not wanting it to appear that she went around screnading lifeless bodies, for heaven's sake.

"Huh?" Lulamae had already passed the subject from her mind.

Kitty nudged her memory. "The man I was singing to. He didn't die till almost the end of the song."

"Oh, well. I heard it was nice, anyway."

Kitty stared at her purple-shadowed eyelids, bright orange cheeks, and ruby-colored lips. Dropping her gaze, she noted that Lulamae's bodice plunged even lower than hers. She could even see a hint of her nipples.

Lulamae was also scrutinizing Kitty. "You're frightened. How come?"

"I'm not used to singing in front of people. If you want to know the truth, I'm scared to death."

"No need to be. The customers here are always a happy bunch, and everybody gets along most of the time. Everybody knows that at the first hint of trouble, Mr. Earp nips it in the bud.

"What you need," Lulamae said as she went to a far corner and reached behind a stack of boxes, "is a drink. I keep a bottle stashed here, 'cause Mr. Earp don't allow us girls to drink when we're working. He says we forget what we're supposed to be doing, which is make the customers spend money like water."

"But don't the customers buy you drinks?"

"Yeah, that's part of it, but what the bartenders fix for us ain't all whiskey. It's mostly tea with a splash of liquor for the smell. The customers don't notice. Besides, we got to stay sober so's we can get them drunk enough they won't realize how much they're spending. We also urge 'em to gamble, because they'll get so jack-fried on the hooch they won't care how much they lose.

"It's what it's all about," she said airily, waving the bottle. "So relax and get used to it."

Lulamae found glasses, which other girls had stashed away with their hidden liquor stock. She poured Kitty a drink. "Here."

Kitty looked at the amber liquid as though it were a spider about to spring and bite. She had never had a drink in her life. "I . . . I don't know. Maybe I'd better not."

Lulamae pushed it at her. "Go on. It can't hurt."

"If whiskey makes the men forget what they're spending and losing, it might make me forget the words to the songs."

"What are you singing?"

"Only three songs tonight—'Aura Lee' to start, because it's slow and simple. The 'Battle Hymn of the Republic' for the Yankees and 'Dixie' for the Rebs. Jim says it will balance things out, and he doesn't want me to do too much the first night, anyway."

"You probably know the words backwards. Now here. Drink up. You'll feel better."

Kitty took a sip. It burned going down. The next swallow felt better. By the third she was warm all over and not quite as nervous. By the time she emptied the glass, she was glowing.

"Feel better?" Lulamae asked, grinning.

"Much. But I think I've had enough." She held her hand over her glass as Lulamae tried to refill it.

"Yeah, you're probably right. If you have much more when you ain't used to it, you might fall on your butt out there, and then I'd be in big trouble." Lulamae poured another for herself.

She and Kitty were sitting on stools opposite each other. Tucking her skirt between her legs, Lulamae propped her elbows on her knees and leaned toward Kitty till their faces were mere inches apart. With fascinated eyes she asked, "What was it like with them Indians? I've heard they do terrible things to women. Was it real awful? Do you have nightmares about it?"

"Not really." Kitty would hardly call nightmares the dreams she still had about Whitebear . . . dreams she wished would go away because they left her feeling so confused.

"You see," she went on to explain to Lulamae, "they thought I was a boy. I dressed like one on the trip out here because I felt I would be safer if I did. As it turned out, I was right. The Indians never knew I was a woman."

"But it must have been a horrible experience just the same."

"No. Actually it wasn't. I had to do chores, and I slept on the ground on animal skins, and I didn't enjoy a lot of their food, but, all in all, I was well treated."

Lulamae poured herself another drink. She stared at Kitty over the rim of the glass as she took a swallow, then said, "I've just heard so many dreadful stories that it's hard to believe what you're saying."

"Some of the tales are probably true, but the Indians feel they are only fighting to keep what is theirs by right of their birth—their land. They aren't all evil. They're capable of love, and . . ." She trailed to silence when she saw Lulamae's condemning expression, and

was reminded once again of Pale Sky's sad words—
*They will not listen. They never have.*

Lulamae drained her glass then tapped Kitty's knee
with her fist. "I'm going to give you some advice,
sweetie. Watch what you say about the Indians. Some
folks have had relatives slaughtered by those devils . . .
tortured, scalped. And if you go around trying to de-
fend them by talking about the white man stealing
their land . . . shit like that . . . you're going to make a
lot of enemies. Best if you just keep your mouth shut.

"Besides," she said, refilling her glass, "Mr. Earp
don't want nothing else said about you having been
with them, anyway. From now on, you're an angel."
She lifted her drink in salute, then lowered her voice
conspiratorially to ask, "But I'm still curious about
some things, 'cause if they thought you were a boy,
you probably saw them naked, didn't you?"

"Yes, but I tried not to look."

Lulamae leaned even closer to whisper, "Did you
wonder what it would be like with one of them? I bet
it'd be terrible, them being such savages and all. I'll
bet they're like animals, and—"

A loud rap on the door made them jump. It opened,
and Kitty recognized Morton, one of the bartenders.
His face was screwed with anger as he spotted Lulamae and he roared, "I figured you'd be back here snea-
kin' a drink. You better get yourself back out here
and get to work or I'm gonna see Mr. Earp finds out."

Lulamae bounded to her feet. "If you do, you old
goat, I'll see to it your wife finds out you're sleepin'
with Jessamine every chance you get."

"You'd do it, too, wouldn't you?" he snarled.

"You tell on me, I tell on you."

They glared at each other in tense silence. After a
moment, Lulamae, cursing under her breath, got up
and went with him.

Kitty sat where she was and did not move. Lulamae

had sparked memories and her thoughts began to drift.

Whitebear had been a fine figure of a man, and with the whiskey making her mellow, she could fantasize without guilt or shame over what it would be like to have him make love to her.

He would not be brutal. Of this she could be sure, for she had heard him with the Indian girls . . . had heard their tender sighs and satisfied moans as he took them to paradise. There was no coarseness. No savagery. No animal grunts or cries. From where she had lain outside his tent, every sound was audible. Remembering, she felt a flood of desire in her loins.

She thought of the morning when she had awakened in the silent graying dawn to find him standing over her. Her vision had slid up long, lean legs, the flesh smooth and golden. Taut thighs stretched to a breechclout which hung low on his flat belly. A narrow waist veed up to a wide, solid chest, and he had stood with knuckled hands at his narrow hips.

He had ordered her to get up and fetch water for his mother, but Kitty had been unable to move . . . unable to tear her gaze away from him in that crystallized moment of realizing for the first time in her life what it meant to be a woman . . . and want a man.

The revelation had abruptly ended when he yanked her up, so effortlessly that it was almost as though she were floating until he set her down on her feet.

*Stop it,* she chided herself as she pulled herself back to the present. *Stop thinking about him, and if you're lucky, you'll never see him again.*

She had to go forward, not dwell on the past, for it was truly behind her—the brief episode of captivity, the grueling journey west, and, yes, too, the misery of her life in Virginia. All faded and gone . . . along with the dream of being with Daddy Wade again. Reality was a smothering thing, reminding her she had no

family and was completely on her own. There was no
one to look out for her, to care for her, and certainly
no secret gold mine to be found with half of a tattered
map. But now she had a chance to make money as a
singer and support herself. Otherwise, there was nothing left except marriage for the sake of survival or a
job trying to get men so drunk they didn't know what
they were doing.

With a deep sigh of resolve and determination,
birthed all the way from her very soul, Kitty got up
and returned to the mirror. Opal had styled her hair
in swirls atop her head, then capped it with the pearl
tiara. She had also applied her makeup—pink cheeks,
pink lips, and eyelids dusted with a blend of blue and
green to highlight her turquoise eyes.

Kitty felt as though she were looking at a stranger.

She heard Jim start playing the piano but no longer
felt any apprehension. Opal was right. She had no
reason to feel bizarre in her costume—and that was
what it was—a costume. She was a performer . . . a
singer . . . and she would entertain the men and give
them a show, and then walk away with head held high.

Mr. Earp had called her into his private office earlier and told her he was going to pay her twenty-five
dollars a month. Opal had nearly fainted when Kitty
told her. She only made fifteen, she confided, so Mr.
Earp had to have great confidence that Kitty was
going to bring in lots of new customers to justify such
high wages.

Jim had gone over the introduction music with her,
and as soon as she heard her cue she hurried up the
stairs leading to the stage.

Thick drapes of blue and yellow velvet shielded her
from the audience. She could hear sounds above the
music—glasses clinking, loud voices intermingled with
laughter.

The curtains began to open.

Kitty folded her hands beneath her bosom, fixed a smile on her face, and drew a deep breath.

She could feel the glow of the sparkling chandeliers above as a hush fell over the crowd.

She began to sing, drawn to the beauty of the melody and the sensual rhythm of the words. Pleasurable vibrations rolled over her in caressing waves. Something was being unleashed inside her, driving out all fear and making her want to open her eyes and face her audience.

The men staring up at her were mesmerized, entranced by her incredibly melodious voice. Some watched with lips parted. Others swayed in time, lost in sweet memories thought long forgotten but brought back by the sensuous balm of the song.

Kitty found herself smiling as she sang, and soon she began to walk about on the half-moon stage. She made eye contact with her patrons, as though singing to them and them alone. She gestured with her hands as if to fold them into the melody along with her.

She did not see Wyatt Earp watching from the railing upstairs, a pleased expression on his usually stony face. Nor was she aware of Jim's moist, shining eyes, or how Opal, along with her faro players, had momentarily abandoned the game as they were drawn to the music like everyone else.

When the song ended, the applause was deafening. Jim did not allow her but a brief curtsy, however, for he went immediately into the federal army's anthem. It was also received in a rousing way, and by the time she swung into the peppery stanzas of "Dixie," everyone was up and stamping their feet and clapping their hands.

Kitty pranced and whirled and threw her arms to the sky, feeling the rhythm, the music, all the way to her bones. The crowd no longer existed for her. She was lost in a world of her own and enjoying every second. And it was only when the song ended and the curtains swished open and closed again and again that she remembered where she was . . . who she was.

*The Singing Angel.*

Afterward, she collapsed happily in a chair in the dressing area. Her heart was pounding and her spirits were soaring. Lulamae charged in to hug her and tell her she had never heard anything so lovely. Jim was promptly there to declare he'd never seen such a reaction from an audience.

Opal, came, too, for a quick hug and promise that they would meet later to celebrate.

Then others came—all men—to vie for Kitty's attention and favor.

One man, wearing a diamond stickpin in the lapel of his gray striped suit, introduced himself with a bow and a sweep of his top hat and then proceeded to bluntly ask her to marry him.

Another shoved him aside to do the same.

A drunk staggered in insisting that she dance with him.

And then Wyatt Earp was there to usher them out and declare that, henceforth, he would post a guard outside the door so Kitty would not be bothered with such foolishness.

Finally, she was alone with nothing to do. Jim would keep playing off and on, but she would not sing again, although before he had left her Mr. Earp had hinted they needed to think about doing two shows a night.

Not about to join the revelry in the saloon, Kitty waited until things settled down, then went back to the stage. The curtains were closed, and there was a side exit where she could slip out, unseen, and make her way to the back stairs.

Once in her room, she peeled out of the gown, scrubbed the makeup off her face, and vigorously brushed the curls from her hair.

Someone had left tea cakes, fruit, and a pitcher of milk on the table beside her bed, and she ate ravenously. With her stomach in knots earlier, she had not wanted any supper.

Afterward, she lay down and tried to sleep, but the noise from downstairs kept her from doing so. Finally she got up and padded to the window to look down on the busy street below. Despite the bustling crowds of the night and the goings-on in the saloon, Kitty was struck to realize how truly alone she was.

She absently chewed on a fingernail as she wondered why, despite the successful evening, she felt so empty. When she was with the Apaches, even as a captive, she now realized that she had felt a part of things . . . a part of life. The cooking and hunting and tanning had all made her feel vital, as though she belonged somewhere . . . to someone. Here, she was something to be stared at, ogled, and, yes, prized, if some man could rope her in for his wife.

She thought of Virginia and the farm and Jabe, Loweezy, and Roscoe—the only friends she'd ever had.

And she thought of the horses, how she had loved working with them.

It was the kind of life she yearned for, longed for— not singing in a saloon, even if she had been well received.

Suddenly it dawned on her that she was trapped. With no other way to support herself, she had to be grateful for the opportunity at hand.

*But if she could find the gold strike . . .*

"Impossible," she said out loud and turned from the window and went back to bed.

The only way she might ever find it would be if she had Whitebear's half of the map. But he was not going to give it to her any more than she would hand over hers to him.

"So be it," she muttered sleepily, covering her head with the pillow to shut out all the noise.

"I'll just have to content myself with being the Singing Angel," she whispered . . . knowing she never would.

# Chapter 13

It was late afternoon, and Ryder was about to make his first attempt to find Kitty Parrish in busy, crowded Tombstone.

He had arrived early that morning and taken a room at a boardinghouse. Weary, he had slept most of the day, knowing the town did not come alive till late afternoon anyway.

Bathed and dressed, he scratched irritably at his beard. The itching was why he had never liked having one and tried to shave every day. It was necessary, however, that he change his appearance drastically. He was also assuming a new identity, for there was no way he could introduce himself to Kitty Parrish by the same last name as her uncle's partner.

So he had taken the name Sam Bodine. With a double holster strapped around his waist, he would present himself as a drifter . . . a hired gun. That way, most folks would steer clear of him, which was what he wanted. He did not need, or want, friends or camaraderie. He had one reason for being in town—to seduce Kitty Parrish and get her to turn over her half of the map. Everything else was a waste of time.

He felt no guilt or shame over his purpose. His people came first, and they needed gold to survive across the border without having to steal. He wanted no trouble with the Mexicans.

He had spent the past three weeks working as an

army scout in Texas. He needed the money, as well as the time to grow his beard.

He hoped his quest would not take long. Already it was mid-summer, and he wanted to get his people out of the mountains before autumn. They needed time to settle in before winter. In the spring, they could start their gardens and, hopefully, start herds of cattle, but food had to be found and stored for the harsh months ahead.

So it was important he move fast, for too much time had already been wasted.

He supposed it was arrogant to assume he could maneuver Kitty Parrish into his bed and charm her into handing over the map, but the fact was, he knew how to pleasure a woman.

*Katrina Stevens had taught him well.*

She was the daughter of one of the high-ranking officers at Fort Bowie. It had been built to fend off Indian attacks at a place called Apache Pass, through which the Butterfield Stagecoach line carried mail and passengers from Missouri to California. Ryder had gone there, passing as white and working as stable help to spy for the Apache leader, Geronimo, who was leading raids on both sides of the border.

At first, Ryder naively thought Katrina hung around the stables because she liked horses and was always coaxing one of the soldiers to take her for a ride. Because of all the Indian trouble, she was not, of course, allowed to go outside the fort without an escort and then could not go far.

When Katrina began to pay attention to him, he was too taken by her to notice the smirks from the soldiers. And, since they dared not speak disrespectfully of an officer's daughter, Ryder had no way of knowing that she was a spicy little vixen who enjoyed a good tumble in bed as well as any man, and he was merely a new conquest.

She asked him to take her riding, and he eagerly agreed. There was a creek within the boundaries she was allowed to go, and she directed him to a private hideaway among some boulders. To his surprise—and delight—she promptly stripped and proceeded to show him an ecstasy unlike anything he had ever known before.

Katrina's desire was insatiable, and she showed him a hundred ways to try and satisfy it.

Inexperienced and naive when it came to women— back then, anyway—Ryder stupidly thought what he felt for Katrina could only be love.

Little did he realize such thoughts were birthed in his loins—not his heart.

He could look back now and see where he went a bit crazy that summer. He forgot all about spying. In fact, he shirked his chores to be with Katrina any time she wanted him.

And all the while the soldiers were laughing behind his back.

Ryder was completely bewitched, and when Katrina began talking about how she was going back east in the fall, he felt his heart begin to crack. She hated the West, and so did her mother. Her father had put in for a transfer, and it was hoped by the end of summer he would have it.

The thought of her leaving drove him crazy, and one day, after a torrid session of lovemaking, he asked her to marry him.

At first, she had seemed stunned, then she began chattering about how he must be crazy to think she would live in the West. And hadn't he been listening all the times she had expressed her desire to go back east?

He had quickly assured her he understood how she felt and was willing to move there to make their home.

So many times Ryder had thought back on that day

and given thanks he had kept his mouth shut and not told her of his mixed blood and how difficult it had been for him to make the decision to leave his mother and his people and live forever in the white man's world. Had they married, he would have told her in time, but he figured his proposal was a big enough surprise for the time being.

As it turned out, he was the one surprised, for when he kept pressing her to say yes, arguing down all her reasons against marriage, she had finally, bluntly, told him that when she did wed, it would be to someone wealthy. He was nothing but a poor stable hand and would never be able to support her in the way she wanted.

He had dared hope that in time he could break down her resolve, still foolishly thinking she loved him, but, as it turned out, he was not to be with her again. She refused to have anything else to do with him and, the very next day, shunned him to ride with another soldier.

Fool that he was, he had continued to pine, until a sergeant drew him aside and said it was time he wised up. Katrina Stevens was a hot-blooded little whore, the sergeant confided, and had bedded half the cavalry. Her father was as blind to her immorality as Ryder had been.

It took a while, but he got over it, ultimately deciding the experience was not totally wasted. After all, he had learned how to give a woman the greatest sensual pleasures possible, and the knowledge had served him well, for the rewards had been great.

Now he hoped the erudition of it all would work for him in a different way.

He heard the sound of the dinner bell and went downstairs. By the time he got to the dining room, the other six boarders were ahead of him. Already they had heaped their plates with food, and elbows were flying as they eagerly forked it into their mouths.

He squeezed in at the end of the bench. Reaching for the last piece of chicken on the platter, he wondered if Cora Lucas, the owner, would bring more.

Breezing in with a plate of biscuits, Cora, a pudgy, no-nonsense widow, saw the disappointed look on his face and knew what he was thinking. "You'd better learn to be on time, mister," she snapped. "I feed, but I don't fatten, and what food is on the table when I ring that bell is all there is. If you're late, you're out of luck."

Ryder shot a glance at the plates around him, which were filled to overflowing. Probably the others had waited in the hall for the bell, then stampeded like cattle spooked by thunder. Now he had another reason for wanting to finish his business in Tombstone and be on his way, because he would sooner starve than fight for his food.

The men ate noisily, not talking or slowing until they had wiped their plates clean with a last bite of biscuit. Only then did they seem to relax and talk among themselves as they waited for Cora to serve dessert.

"What's your business in town?" the potbellied man next to Ryder asked. "The name's Wister Nichols, by the way."

The others turned to stare with interest.

Ryder took them all to be prospectors, in from their digs to buy supplies, maybe get a bath and a shave, and then wallow in whiskey and women before heading back to the mountains.

He was finishing up the peas he had managed to rake from the bottom of the bowl and did not look up as he said quietly, coldly, "I don't have any yet. But my guns are available for the right price."

Suddenly he had a few more inches of space on the

bench, as the man, along with those seated beyond him, shrank back.

His meaning was clear. He was a hired gun and would kill for a price.

Ryder thought for a second they were all going to bolt for the door, but just then Cora came in with a big apple pie and set it on the table. They could not resist and once more dove right in, only this time there was an ample portion left for Ryder.

The men began to talk among themselves once more. Ryder was only half-listening. Then Wister said something that caught his attention. He was in a hurry, he said, to get to the Oriental Saloon so he could get a good seat for the first performance. The Oriental was where Opal worked, which meant Kitty Parrish might be close by.

"Is that li'l gal as good as they say?" someone asked Wister. "I didn't get by there last night. I got tied up in a poker game, 'cause I was winnin' for a change."

"Yeah, what's she like?" another wanted to know. "I ain't much on sittin' around listenin' to singin'. I'd rather get a gal and dance."

"Oh, she dances," Wister told them, "but up on the stage. She don't mingle with the customers, and Mr. Earp has a guard posted so nobody can get to her."

"What is it they call her?"

"The Singin' Angel, and she dresses up like one, too. The other night she was even wearin' paper wings, painted gold, and the crowd loved that."

Cora came with a bowl of cream for the pie. Hearing the topic of conversation, she sneered. "Oh, she ain't all that good. My man-friend, Boozer, heard her the other night, and all he could talk about was how pretty she is. Didn't say nothin' about her voice. And I tell you one thing—Wyatt Earp better look out, or what he brought in to draw customers is gonna blow up in his face, 'cause everybody's goin' to be in front of the stage instead of gathering around the bar or gambling tables.''

''Well, she don't perform *all* the time,'' Wister said huffily. ''Just twice a night. There's plenty of time for gamblin' in-between.''

Ryder did not care about a stage show and asked, ''Does the Oriental still have the best faro in town?''

Wister said, ''I wouldn't know, mister. Faro ain't my game.''

Ryder glanced up and down the table. ''Anybody know anything about the faro game over there? I heard they had a woman dealer who's the best around. Can't recall the name,'' he added, not wanting to appear too knowledgeable.

''You're talking about Opal Grimes,'' a man at the far end volunteered. ''And she's pretty good, I reckon.''

That was all Ryder wanted to hear. He had ridden by her shanty on his way into town. Children had been playing outside, and when he saw a strange woman call them in, he knew for sure that Opal had moved elsewhere. It was a bad sign, and he had worried ever since that she might have left town and taken Kitty with her. After all, Kitty would probably have had no one else to turn to. But now he could relax. Opal was around, so maybe Kitty would not be far away.

He wished he could just come right out and ask about her, but there was always the chance she had not made it to Tombstone. She might have been so unnerved by her experience that she turned tail and headed back east. However, if she were in town, he did not want to draw attention to himself by making inquiries. So he had decided to locate Opal and go from there.

After supper, he headed straight to the Oriental. The faro game had not started up, so he had a drink at the bar.

A half hour passed, and he noticed how the place was starting to get crowded. Men were pushing into the rows of chairs lined up in front of the stage, and Ryder asked the bartender what was going on.

The bartender displayed a gold front tooth as he grinned to say, "You must be real new in town, mister, if you ain't heard of the Singing Angel. She really packs in the customers. I'll bet if you walk up and down the street, the other saloons will look closed down, 'cause everybody piles in here when it's time for her to perform."

"What makes her so special?"

"Well, for one thing, she's a damn pretty little gal, but she's got a way of making you think she's singing right to you and nobody else. She got the name Singing Angel, by the way, on account of how she sings to men in the street when they're dyin', and they think she's an angel come down from heaven to serenade 'em home."

"Oh, Morton, you got shit for brains," the man standing next to Ryder sneered. "She only done that once. You make it sound like every time she hears gunfire she runs out to see if anybody's shot and dyin' so she can sing to 'em. Hell, if that was so, she wouldn't have no voice left.

"Undertaker buried two this morning," he said to Ryder with a polite tip of his hat. "May they rest in peace."

Ryder downed the rest of his drink. He did not care about singing angels, or gunfights, or any other damn thing that went on in Tombstone. All he wanted was to find Kitty Parrish as fast as possible.

The bartender refilled his glass and went on down the bar to other customers.

Ryder took his drink and went back to the gaming room, which was still empty. It had become obvious that until the so-called Singing Angel performed, not much else would be going on.

Glancing about, he did a quick double take as Opal came down the backstairs. She looked stern, as usual, in a conservative gown of deep blue taffeta, the lace collar nearly brushing her chin.

"Evenin', Miss Opal," a man walking by called to her as she descended. "You're early. Guess you can't sleep as late now that you're livin' up there."

"Yeah," Opal confirmed, "but it's a hell of a lot better than staying awake worrying an Apache is gonna sneak in and slit my throat."

Ryder knew then that his visit as Whitebear was the reason she had moved out of the shanty.

Opal started by him, then paused to rake him with curious eyes. "I haven't seen you around before. You waiting to play, cowboy?"

"Maybe." He took a lazy sip of his drink. She started on by, and he casually asked, "Did I hear you say something about Apaches?"

"You sure as hell did. One slipped in on me where I used to live and held a knife to my throat. Scared the grits out of me, it did. But it won't happen again. Not with old Ben up there keeping an eye on things. Mr. Earp don't let nobody upstairs that don't have business up there."

Ryder had already spotted the man with a shotgun posted on the upstairs landing. "Do you have many Indian attacks on folks around here?"

"Well, no," she said hesitantly. "This was the first I knew of."

"So why would one threaten you?"

"I don't want to talk about it. What's your name, anyhow?"

"Sam Bodine."

"Where you from?"

He shrugged. "Anywhere. Nowhere. Wherever I can find work."

"And what might that be?" Her gaze fell on his guns. "Oh, I see. Gunman, 'eh? Well, you'll wind up like the rest of 'em—in Boot Hill."

"I doubt it. I'm good. Otherwise, I'd already be there. Besides, I don't go looking for trouble." He had tipped back in his chair to prop against the wall. With thighs spread and head cocked to one side, he looked anything but worried about getting killed in a shootout.

"Well, it'd be a shame to see a fine-looking man like you laid to rest"—she grinned and winked—"just like it's a shame I'm probably old enough to be your mama. Otherwise, I'd give you some trouble—but it'd be the kind you'd enjoy."

With hips swaying, Opal continued on her way.

He heard piano music, and the crowd started yelling and stamping feet.

Curious as to what had them so enthused, Ryder went and stood where he could see the stage.

He saw the Earp brothers leaning against the bar, keeping an eye on things. Then gunfire exploded outside in the street, and they took off.

He heard a man nearby say, "Wish they hadn't run off like that. There's always some rowdy who needs his head busted to keep the peace."

A roar went up as the curtains finally opened.

Ryder drew a sharp breath. The woman standing in the middle of the stage was pretty, all right. And she did kind of look like an angel in gold satin and lace, her chestnut hair curled in ringlets about her sweetly smiling face.

Her hands were folded beneath her chin as she began to sing. And, like the bartender had said, she did have a way of locking eyes to offer a personal serenade.

After her opening number, slow and soft, she went into a rousing song and began to prance about the stage. She did a jaunty little dance, lifting her skirt ankle-high to show her tapping feet.

The men sang along with her, clapping their hands over their heads.

"Sing to me, angel," a voice louder than any of the others cried out. "Sing me to heaven or hell. I don't give a damn."

Laughter erupted, and others began calling out to her, each trying to outdo with wit and praise.

Then someone shoved someone else, and things began to get out of hand. Chairs fell, and the Singing Angel quit singing and melted back to the far wall of the stage in fright.

The piano player banged all the harder, trying to get people back into the mood of music, but a fight broke out.

Suddenly a man began pushing his way through as he yelled, "I aim to hear my angel. C'mere, angel. We're goin' where I can hear you good . . ."

He bolted up on the stage. Ryder saw he had drawn his gun in warning to anyone trying to stop him.

"You get away from her," Opal screamed, then whipped around to yell at the guard upstairs, "Ben, get your ass down here now."

Ben was on his way, but the man on stage saw him . . . saw he was carrying a shotgun, and fired. Ben dropped his gun, grabbed his wounded shoulder, and tumbled down the steps.

Quickly, before anyone else got hurt, Ryder stepped up on one of the chairs. Drawing his right gun, he took careful aim. The man on stage had hooked his arm around the woman's neck and was trying to drag her off, and Ryder had to be careful lest he hit her.

He squeezed the trigger, hitting the gunman in his

wrist. With a shriek, he dropped his weapon and fell to his knees. Instantly, men rushed on the stage.

Ryder surged forward with the crowd, wanting to make sure the woman wasn't hurt.

Suddenly Opal screamed, "Damn you, Roscoe Pate, you old drunk. You're gonna get yourself killed one day pulling your crazy stunts."

The wounded man sat on the stage floor, his left hand gripping his bloody right. "Aw, hell, Opal, I didn't mean no harm, and you know it."

"You scared her half to death, you ninny. And it's a good thing the Earps weren't here, or they'd have shot you dead."

"Who did do it?" someone asked. "Damn fine shot, whoever it was."

Ryder saw that the Singing Angel, who was being comforted by the piano player, was staring right at him.

"He did," she said with a nod in his direction. Then she was ushered away, but she turned to look at him over her shoulder till she faded from sight.

Opal turned also and blinked in recognition. "Sam Bodine. Well, I thank you for what you did.

"And thanks, too," she added, "for not killing this worthless bastard. He really don't mean no harm. He just does stupid things when he's drunk." She turned back to Roscoe with a scowl. "I guess you being here means my no-good brother is back in town. How come he's not here raising hell, too?"

"He's took up with a *puta* south of the border."

"Well, it would suit me fine if he stayed there."

A deputy came to whisk him away to jail with the promise he would be there awhile. Ben was helped up and taken to a doctor to treat his wound.

Things began to settle down, and Opal walked over to the bar, where Ryder was having a drink on the house.

"Thanks again, mister," she said, slapping him on the back. "I really appreciate your coming to the rescue. Roscoe wouldn't have hurt her for the world, but he was scaring her to death."

"Glad to do it," he said. He was also glad to be in her favor, because he intended to figure out a way to ask about Kitty Parrish, and maybe she would cooperate.

"Yeah, Kitty has been through a lot."

Ryder's stomach slammed against his spine.

Opal slapped the bar with her palm. "Morton, give me a whiskey. After all that, I need a drink powerful bad.

"Kitty wasn't too sure she could do it," Opal continued, "but she needed a job. Now she's used to it, and I think she likes it, but many more upsets like that, and she'll quit."

Ryder took a sip of whiskey and rolled it around in his mouth a few seconds in hopes of slowing his throbbing pulse. Then he said, "That's her real name? Kitty?"

"Yeah, but Mr. Earp gave her the name Singing Angel, because a man shot down in the street thought that's what she was when she tried to help him. I'll have to introduce you later. She'll want to thank you proper. Right now I've got to get that faro game going, or I'll be out of a job."

She took her drink and walked away.

Ryder stared after her.

A coincidence, he repeated to himself. There was no way that woman on the stage could be the same bedraggled *boy* he had held captive.

"Lucky you," the bartender said. "Our little angel has been real standoffish with men since she hit town, but you'll be on her good side, for sure."

"How long has she been here?"

The bartender scratched his chin as he thought

about it, then said, "Oh, a month or more, I reckon. Real interesting story about her, too. She got captured by Injuns—Apaches—but managed to escape." He held up the bottle. "Want a refill? After what you did, Mr. Earp ain't gonna care how much you have."

Hand slightly trembling, Ryder covered his glass.

He did not need more whiskey.

The world was already spinning.

# Chapter 14

Damn the money, the fancy wardrobe, and all the attention and flattery that went with being a well-liked performer, Kitty was no longer enamored. In fact, she was fed up.

Stomping around in her room the next morning, she was churning with anger. Feeling life slowly ebbing away as Roscoe Pate's hold on her neck threatened to crush her windpipe, Kitty had known more terror than she ever had with the Apaches.

And what if the bearded stranger had missed and hit her instead? She would have been next in line at Boot Hill. Still, she could not chide him too harshly for taking the chance. After all, she had done the same on the stagecoach when she had shot the knife out of Seth Barlow's hand to keep him from stabbing Lloyd Pendergrass. So thank goodness the stranger was as good a marksman as she was.

She wished she'd had time to thank him proper. But maybe it was just as well. There had been something about the way he looked at her when their eyes met and held for the briefest of seconds that was strangely unnerving, for he made her feel that she was being looked *into* . . . not *at*.

Silly. She was being silly, that's all. He had come to her rescue, and she was grateful but would probably never see him again. Drifters came and went like the wind. She had to stop thinking about him, Roscoe

Pate . . . all of it. Because it was time, she decided, to think about leaving Tombstone.

Opal's call brought her from her musings, and she hurried to unbolt the door and let her in. Opal was still wearing her robe, soft blue satin edged in delicate pink lace. Setting down a tray of sandwiches and tea, she said, "I figured you didn't go down for breakfast this morning."

"I wasn't hungry."

"Still upset over last night, huh? Well, don't be. Ben's going to be fine, by the way. It was just a flesh wound.

"Stupid, stupid Roscoe," she snorted, disgusted. "He gets drunk and don't know what he's doing. He wouldn't have hurt you, though."

Kitty had been standing at the window, holding back the drapes to peer down at the street below. Whirling about, she cried, "How can you say that? He was choking me to death."

"But he didn't mean to."

"You just said he didn't know what he was doing—and he obviously didn't know he was killing me. If that man, whoever he was, hadn't acted when he did, there's no telling what might have happened. I just thank God he was a good shot. What if somebody else had tried to shoot the gun out of Roscoe's hand and hit me? No"—she shook her head so hard her hair flew about her face—"I can't dismiss it as easily as you, Opal. There's too much violence here. Somebody is always getting killed. And when I think of what happened to Daddy Wade, it makes my blood boil. I just don't like it here."

"Honey, it's dangerous all over the West. Outlaws, Indians. You're as safe here as you would be anywhere else, except maybe Virginia, and I don't think you want to go back there."

"No, I don't."

"Then forget about last night. You're making damn good money for a woman. More than me, that's for sure. And you've got a nice, clean place to stay. Everybody looks out for you. There's a lot you ought to be thankful for."

"But I'm not happy here, don't you see? And I've tried. I really have. I do my best to entertain, and I have to say the majority of the men in the audience treat me with respect. But I still don't enjoy it. I grew up outdoors, and I want to ride, raise horses, break them to saddle. I'd even like to learn ranching . . . maybe have one of my own one day. I don't want to spend the rest of my life standing on a stage hoping some rowdy doesn't decide to drag me off of it."

Opal spoke around a bite of sandwich, "Which is why I keep telling you to find a good husband while you've still got your looks and can pick and choose. Why, there isn't an unmarried man in that audience who wouldn't leap at the chance to marry you."

"I have told you over and over—I do not want to get married."

Opal threw up her hands. "Then all that's left for you, honey, is what you're doing or a job like I got. You aren't going to get hired on at a ranch to do man's work even if you're able. What rancher in his right mind would hire a pretty young thing like you? His hands would never get any work done and probably wind up killing each other over you, to boot. And forget pretending to be a boy. You might have got away with that on the ride out here and fooled the Indians, but you couldn't do it forever, and you know it.

"Settle down," she urged, pouring a cup of tea and holding it out to her. "You'll get over last night."

Kitty took the tea and sipped, hoping it would quell her rolling stomach. She was a bundle of nerves, thinking of her plight. "I feel like a prisoner here. There's nothing to do but hide out in this room when I'm not on stage, and it's hot and stuffy. I'm miserable here.''

"Go for a walk. It's safe during the day. Do some shopping.''

"I have been to every store in Tombstone. I know all the shopkeepers by their first names. There is nothing I need to buy, anyway. And I have walked this town till I could find every house, tent, and shanty blindfolded. What I want to do is go riding.'' She drained the tea and set the cup down with a clatter. "But I'm denied the privilege of even doing that. All the stable owners refuse to rent me a horse, because they say a woman has no business riding out by herself.''

Opal shrugged. "So ask a man to go with you.''

"I can't do that. If I ask someone unmarried, he'll think I'm inviting him to court me. And it would be improper to ask someone who is.''

"You're probably right,'' Opal allowed. "And I'm glad they won't let you go off by yourself. That Apache—Whitebear, or whatever you said his name was—might be out there.''

"He wouldn't know me if he saw me,'' Kitty pointed out. "Besides, we don't know for a fact that he ever found out who I really was, anyway.''

"True, but it's not worth chancing. That's why we moved up here, remember? Now relax. Things aren't as bad as you think.''

Kitty went to her chifforobe and yanked the door open. Rummaging through her clothes, she took out a citron cotton dress. "I am going to relax,'' she said. "I'm going for a ride. If I don't get out in the wide open spaces for a breath of fresh air and change of scenery, I'm going to go crazy. I've never felt so cooped up in my life.''

"But you just said they won't let you have a horse.''

"I'm going to rent a buggy.''

"They won't agree to that, either."

Kitty smiled. "They hinted they would if I'd hire one of the stable boys to go with me. They all look to be about thirteen or fourteen, so they're hardly married or looking to be any time soon."

"Well, I'm not going to argue. Your mind is set." Opal gathered cups and saucers, stacked the tray, and stood. "I just hope if you do run into trouble there's another gunslinger around to take care of you."

"That one last night," Kitty said, mind again hooked to the stranger, "who was he? Do you know? I didn't have a chance to thank him."

"Never saw him before. I talked to him a spell before you went on. Said his name was Sam Bodine."

"Well, if he's around tonight, I'd like to thank him for what he did."

Opal moved to the door. "He probably won't be. His kind never hang around for long. Good-looking fellow, though, wasn't he? Even with that beard covering most of his face."

Kitty allowed that, yes, the stranger had been good-looking, in a feral, rugged way. But Opal was right. She would never see him again. Perhaps it was just as well, for the way he had looked at her still needled.

Ryder had been standing across the street from the Oriental Saloon since noon.

Discovering that the popular so-called Singing Angel was actually Kitty Parrish had struck as hard as a mule kick to the belly. It had all but knocked the wind out of him, because it was too incredible to be true.

But it was.

And his self-confidence was shaken.

After all, he had not pictured Kitty as being pretty. She had been a scrawny, scruffy, dirty boy with long, greasy hair stringing all down her face. As a woman, he had imagined her to be shapeless and plain, easily falling prey to a man's attentions.

Hell, he never dreamed she would be the sweetheart of Tombstone, turning the head of every man in town. It was going to make his quest extremely difficult, if not impossible, but at least he had an edge, because she would be appreciative of what he had done.

All he had to do now was find a way to get to her without being obvious about it. So he had stationed himself across from the saloon to wait for her to come out, only he was beginning to think she wasn't going to. Most of the women who worked the gambling and dance halls stayed in during the heat of the day. And he didn't dare hang around all afternoon. It might arouse suspicion, and he did not want that . . . did not want it to appear he was stalking anybody.

And then he saw her. She came out the front door, pretty in a yellow dress and matching bonnet. With head held high, she walked purposefully down the boardwalk, and Ryder smiled as she cursed to stumble in her high-button shoes. A far cry from the boots she'd been wearing the whole time she was with him. Evidently she was not used to dressing up, but she did a fine job of it. She was a beauty, all right. No denying that.

He waited a moment, then began to amble lazily down his side of the street, keeping her in sight as she marched by the stores. Every so often she nodded to someone she knew, but she ignored the hoots and whistles from men who ogled as she passed.

When she reached the livery stable, she turned in. Ryder went down the alley next to it and entered from the rear door to stand in the shadows and listen.

He caught the tail end of her offer. ". . . pay you two dollars. All I want you to do is take me for a buggy ride."

While Ryder could not see Kitty, the stable boy was

visible. With head down, shoulders hunched, he dug into the straw-littered floor with the toe of his boot as he regretted to say, "Aw, I'd like to, ma'am, 'cause that's a lot of money, but there ain't nobody here but me, and the boss would kill me if I upped and took off."

Ryder heard an exasperated sigh, then, "All right. Let me take the buggy by myself, and I'll pay you anyway. And I assure you I can handle a horse. I used to raise them back home in Virginia, so you needn't worry. And I won't be gone long. I just want to go for a little ride. Maybe an hour or two."

The boy lifted his head to stare at her in horror. "I can't do that, ma'am. We don't let our buggies to women."

"I thought it was only horses."

"Buggies, too. If you was to get hurt, everybody would blame us. I'm sorry. Maybe I can go another time."

"But I need to get out of town today."

Ryder could not believe his ears. Throughout the time Kitty Parrish—or Billy Mingo, as she had called herself—had been held captive, not once had he heard her sound as though she were about to cry. Now it appeared she was close to breaking, and it made no sense, not over something as trivial as renting a buggy. Whatever her reason for desperation, he quickly decided to use it to his advantage.

He stepped from the shadows. "I'd be glad to take you, Miss Parrish."

Kitty took a step backward, then, in recognition, her hand fluttering to her throat. "You're the man from last night . . . the one who shot the gun out of Roscoe's Pate's hand."

Frightened by the sight of an ominous-looking stranger stepping out of darkness wearing the low-slung double holster of a gunslinger, the stable boy disappeared as though he had never even been there.

Ryder sucked in his breath as he looked her up and down. How stupid he had been not to see through her disguise. Delicate hands, neck pale and slender, the soft line of her jaw, and rosebud lips begging to be kissed. But he had not seen all that, because he had not looked for it. His view had bounced back from the dirt and grime and sheer messiness of Billy Mingo.

And her voice had been another deterrent to discovery. Always she had spoken low, husky, not soft and lilting as she did now.

"Sir?" Kitty prodded, tilting her head at how he was not saying anything . . . how he was looking at her once more in that strange, thoughtful way. "That *was* you, wasn't it? Last night? In the Oriental Saloon?"

He wiped his hand across his brow, which had become beaded with sweat. "Yes. It was."

"And how is it that you know my real name?"

"Your friend, the faro dealer, told me." He tipped his hat. "I'm Sam Bodine.

"I hope I didn't scare you too bad, having to shoot as close as I did," he added with a smile to lighten the mood.

She seemed to relax a little. "Oh, it gave me a start, for sure, but I'm glad you're as good a shot as me or I wouldn't be here to thank you." She laughed, soft and silvery.

The corners of his mouth pulled in a smile. "Are you saying you're good with a gun?"

"I am." Mischief twinkled in her sea-green eyes. "Want me to prove it?"

"Why not? It could be fun."

"Then I'll take you up on your kind offer to give me a ride out of this rough and tumble town, and we can find a place where we can shoot."

Ryder knew her real motive was to get him to take her for an outing she would not have otherwise. He called to the stable boy, figuring he was hovering nearby and listening in. "Get us a horse and buggy."

Kitty offered to pay since it was her idea, but Ryder declined and gave the boy the money himself, figuring the more indebted she felt toward him, the better.

"You picked a bad time to go for a ride," he said after they had rolled along for nearly ten minutes without conversation. "It's boiling hot."

She waved a hand to fan herself. "I know, but I thought if I didn't get away for a little while, I'd lose my mind."

He noted she was keeping her distance, squeezing as far from him as possible on the leather seat. "Do you want me to stop and pull the cover up for shade?"

"No. I want to feel space around me. Staying in my room all the time is positively smothering."

"Why don't you get out a spell?"

"Where would I go? And what is there to do? It's terribly boring, but as soon as I've saved up enough money, I'm going to buy a horse, and then I can come and go as I please."

He stole a glance out of the corner of his eye and wondered again how she could have fooled him so. Then the question struck—what if she hadn't? What if he had known who she was? Would he have been able to frighten her into handing over her part of the map? He doubted it, recalling how feisty she had been even though she was a captive. She was just not the sort to be easily frightened or intimidated. So maybe it was just as well he was going at her from another angle. After all, she was a strong woman . . . and also smart.

"Aren't you worried about Indians?" It was time to cut to the chase and steer the conversation in the way he wanted it to go. "The bartender told me last night you were captured a while back by Apaches. Seems to me you wouldn't go anywhere you might run into them."

For a heart-stopping second, he feared he had gone too far and crossed a forbidden line. Her face went tight. Her hand stopped fluttering and returned to clasp the other in her lap. With back rigid, head jerking up, she coolly said, "I don't let myself think about that. It's in the past."

He dared press on. "Was it so awful?"

She looked at him then, deeply, thoughtfully, as though deciding whether he was worthy of sharing her feelings.

He waited, again wondering whether he had gone too far.

Then, with a resigned sigh, she said, "Actually, it wasn't. I was disguised as a boy, you see, and since I made a very *scrawny* boy, the work they made me do wasn't all that hard. Besides, the Apaches have their reasons for being like they are."

He was struggling to keep his voice even, for it was a jolt that she was not condemning them . . . *him*.

Kitty repeated the parting words of Pale Sky.

Ryder was even more stunned.

She saw his expression and explained, "One of the women helped me escape, and when we said goodbye, she asked me to spread that message."

He listened as Kitty talked on and knew, somehow, that it was the first time she had so completely verbalized her feelings and reactions to her captivity. He sensed she had pushed it back in her mind but now welcomed the chance to let it out, and it flew eagerly, like a bird released from a tangled thicket.

Suddenly she pointed to an expanse on one side with a backdrop of boulders reaching to the sky. "We can shoot there. I'm going to prove I'm as good a shot as you, Mr. Bodine. Maybe even better."

He reined in the horse, then turned and held out his hand to her. "Call me Sam, please. I'd like to be your friend, Miss Parrish. And you don't have to worry about me doing anything to dishonor you. I may make my living with my guns, but I know how to treat a lady." Quite a speech, but he had no time to waste in trying to win her confidence.

She gave him a long, searching look.

Ryder bit the inside of his jaw to steady himself. He was remembering how she had bathed him . . . touched him. Lord, if he had known the truth . . .

"I'd like that," she said finally. "I could use a friend."

Then, scrambling from the buggy before he had a chance to assist her, she flashed an impish grin and said, "But right now I'm anxious to see if you can outshoot me, Sam Bodine."

He thought, in that moment, that she was, without a doubt, the most winsome and comely woman he had ever seen in his whole life. He liked the freshness of her, the wholesomeness. She was happy and perky and cute, and as long as he had been in her company she had made him feel good.

He also noted the swell of her bosom and marveled, again, over how she had managed to keep her secret. To think such a delicacy had slept on the ground outside his tent all those nights, listening as he—

"Well?"

She was frowning at his hesitation.

He forced buoyancy. "All right. Let's see how good you think you are."

"How good I *am*," she corrected, frown gone.

Ryder glanced around for a target. Even if there was a bottle to be had, he was not about to shoot toward the boulders for fear of ricochet. Then he saw the saguaro cactus with its human shape—round flat head, jutting arms to the sides. "There," he pointed.

"I'm going to set a rock on the top, and we'll see if you can hit from twenty paces."

"I can hit from forty."

"Think so?" He was amused by her arrogance . . . and also still very much smitten. "If you've got that much self-confidence, maybe you'd be willing to make a little wager."

The frown threatened to return. "What do you mean?"

He shrugged. "An innocent bet, that's all."

"I only have a few dollars with me."

"Fine."

He set the rock, marked off forty paces, then handed her his six-gun. "I guess I have the advantage, being as you aren't used to my pistols."

"A gun is a gun," she said confidently, then, without further ado, she aimed, fired, and hit the rock.

Ryder was impressed. The little gal could shoot, all right. But Coyotay could have attested to that. He did not have to see her hit a rock on top of a cactus to confirm his own belief. What he did have to do, however, was make her happy and at ease with him.

He set another rock, fired himself, and hit the target, then said, "Well, I guess it's a draw. Pardon the pun," he added with a chuckle.

"I still want to best you, Sam Bodine. How good are you with a knife?"

"Pretty fair." *He was damn good.*

"I'm better."

He sucked in his breath to see her whip a knife from where it was strapped to her ankle and send it whizzing through the air to hit the cactus dead center.

He gave a low whistle. "I think we'll declare you the winner." He did not want to show off too much and went to retrieve the knife—then froze.

"What's wrong?" she called when he continued to stand there, staring.

It was his mother's flint knife. He knew because he had made it for her.

He yanked it from the cactus. "Nothing. Just amazed at your skills. Not many women have them."

"Not many women were raised like I was."

"And how was that?"

He watched as a shadow passed over her face, erasing the happy glow. Something remembered was causing her pain.

Her shrug was forced, her tone flippant. "Oh, it doesn't matter anymore."

Then, to change the subject from herself, she pointed up and said, "Those beautiful yellow flowers, what are they?"

He followed her gaze. "Mexican poppies. The coral-colored ones are called *mallow*. And see that?" It was his turn to point.

Kitty took a staggering step backward as a zigzagging bee nearly flew into her face. "What in the world . . ."

"A drunk bee," Ryder explained. "They love the nectar from both the poppy and the mallow and switch back and forth, but the combination, for some strange reason, gets them drunk."

Kitty murmured, "Like an Apache drinking too much *tiswin*."

"Did you have a bad experience with it?"

"It's what led Pale Sky to set me free. Her son—Whitebear, he was called—was away somewhere. Otherwise, it wouldn't have happened, but the other Indians got to drinking, and one of them—Coyotay was his name—hated me because I shot him when I was captured. Pale Sky was afraid he might hurt me, so she led me out of the camp and told me which direction to go to reach the road where the stagecoaches traveled." She spread her hands and smiled. "So here I am, thanks to her."

They had begun to walk aimlessly, not noticing how far they had wandered from the buggy.

Ryder urged her to talk on and managed to keep a straight face as she described some of the more primitive sides of Indian life that she had not fondly embraced. But it was all interesting, and he listened keenly, hoping she would say something about her uncle, the gold mine, and, of course, the map.

But she mentioned none of that, and when the desert began to turn pink and purple in the shades of dusk, she gave a little cry and said, "Oh, my goodness. Look how late it's got. Opal will be in hysterics thinking something's happened to me."

Ryder also pretended concern to have let time slip away and wasted no time getting her back to town.

He pulled to a stop in front of the Oriental, saying he would return the horse and buggy.

Again, Kitty did not wait for him to help her down.

Her feet hit the boardwalk as Opal came charging out the front door to scream, "Where in the hell have you been? I just sent word to the marshal to get a posse out after you, and . . ." She trailed as she looked up at Ryder, then said, "Oh, Sam Bodine. She was with you?"

He tipped his hat. "Yes, ma'am. She was hell-bent on going for a ride, so I obliged."

Opal smiled, relieved. "Well, if I'd have known that, I wouldn't have worried. Thanks for looking after her."

He tipped his hat. "My pleasure, ma'am."

Kitty, he noted, seemed suddenly shy as she murmured, cheeks pinkening, "I really enjoyed the afternoon."

"We'll do it again."

"You come back for her show," Opal called after him as he snapped the reins and the buggy began to roll. "This time she won't be interrupted, and you'll see why all the menfolk are crazy for her."

Ryder smiled.

He already knew.

# Chapter 15

In the following days, Ryder became a permanent fixture around the Oriental Saloon. Attending every performance of the Singing Angel, he was right there to keep Kitty company when she was not on stage.

During the day they were inseparable, going for long rides on horseback, picnicking on the riverbank, and wading in the cool waters.

Others noticed and began whispering how they were sweet on each other and maybe wedding bells would ring soon.

Opal, keeping an eye on the situation, tried to hurry things along. "He's a good man, I can tell," she declared to Kitty one morning as she was dressing to go out on another ride. "Sure, he's a gunslinger, but you can change all that. Marriage will get him in a settling notion. You can get yourself a little spread somewhere, raise a family, and he'll curl up like an old hound dog. Wait and see."

"I'm not even thinking about that," Kitty lied. She was buckling her holster around her waist.

"Well, you're a fool not to. And how come you've got to strap on that gun? It's not very ladylike."

"We enjoy practicing now and then. Besides, I feel safer with a gun, even with Sam. You never know what might happen out there. If we were to run up on Indians, two guns would sure be better than one."

She was wearing one of the simple cotton skirts she

had bought for riding, and an off-the-shoulder blouse that was purposely fetching. She had new boots, too, of fine leather, and a suede, flat-brimmed hat.

"I'm ready," she said finally, pulse racing to think of Sam waiting at the livery stable. Never in all her born days had she imagined a man could affect her so. All he had to do was touch her or flash a smile, and her insides felt like she had swallowed Mexican jumping beans.

"So how long are you going to wait before you rope him in?"

There was tension in Opal's voice, and Kitty turned to see that her expression matched. "You've always wanted to get me married, but you're starting to sound almost desperate. Why?"

Opal did not say anything as she twisted the sash of her robe between nervous fingers. She still lounged most of the day, seldom dressing before time for supper and the evening's work to begin.

"Opal, something is wrong. What is it?"

"Well, I hate to say anything, but I've heard some gossip that's got me worried."

"What kind of gossip?"

"About you and Sam."

Kitty sighed and began pulling on her suede gloves with fringed cuffs. "I figured as much, and it makes me angry. Soiled doves can hang out the windows half-naked trying to entice customers, and nobody says a word. I go for a ride unchaperoned with a man, and everyone talks about it."

"No, it's not that."

"Then what?"

"Haven't you noticed anything about your audience lately?"

"No," she said with a shrug. The only person she had eyes for was Sam, and she sang for him. Oh, she tried to move around and look at others, but always her gaze flashed back to him. He had become so special, so dear. Yet, he had not even kissed her. Not even touched her, except to help her up and down off her horse, which always sent little rivulets of pleasure up her spine. He was being a perfect gentleman, but she was starting to feel like anything but a lady. And she wished he would shave his beard, so she could see what he really looked like. She had said as much to Opal once, but Opal pointed out that maybe he was using it as a disguise, because his clean-shaven face was on a Wanted poster somewhere. That would not be out of the ordinary for a gunslinger. Sometimes they killed people with important relatives who posted rewards. So Kitty did not say anything to him about the beard, allowing that it was his business.

"You haven't noticed anything?" Opal persisted, the sharpness of her tone puncturing Kitty's reverie.

"No, why?" Kitty was impatient, anxious to be on her way.

"It's getting smaller. Four nights ago, there was standing room for the first time since you started singing. Three nights ago, there were empty chairs. And there's more every night. Morton says Mr. Earp blames it on Sam hanging around."

"That's ridiculous."

"Not when you think about it," Opal said delicately. "You don't realize it, but you don't sing for the customers, anymore. Only for Sam. So you're no longer their sweetheart. You're his."

Kitty was aghast. "But my voice is the same, and that's why they come—to hear me sing."

Opal chuckled. "You silly goose. They never gave a damn about your singing. They just wanted to look at you, because you're pretty, especially in those fancy gowns. It was a lark, too, your being called the Singing Angel. But now I'm afraid the Singing Angel's days are numbered, because Mr. Earp is not going to keep you on if you don't bring in the customers. And when he lets you go, what are you going to do then? It'll be hard to get another singing job when word gets out you got fired on account of the audience dwindling."

"I . . . I don't know." Kitty floundered.

Opal rose. "Well, I'd say it's time you made Sam Bodine start hearing them wedding bells. Otherwise, you're going to be out on the street. I've got a little money put back, but I can't help you, because I'm saving to get out of here, too. I still got dreams of California. I'm afraid you'll be on your own if Mr. Wyatt gives you the boot."

Though Kitty had never really liked her job, she had never thought of it ending before she was ready. But the idea of marriage was terrifying. Besides, she pointed out to Opal, Sam had never given any inclination he wanted to marry her. "For all I know he's already got a wife and a family somewhere. We're just friends. We ride and shoot and laugh and play and have a good time. That's all. I've no reason to think he's in love with me. And besides," she added, "I don't know that I love him."

"Oh, you'd learn to. A good-looking man like him wouldn't be hard to love at all."

"If only it had worked out for us to find the gold," Kitty said, more to herself than Opal. "Then neither of us would have had to worry about the future."

"The only gold you'll ever see is a wedding band," Opal said with finality. "And that's what you better set your sights on if you know what's good for you."

Feeling as she did about Sam, Kitty was not opposed to the idea, but the reality remained that he had never given any hint he might be interested in her beyond friendship.

And the truth she dared not admit to Opal was that she was beginning to wish he would.

\*    \*    \*

Ryder could tell something was on Kitty's mind. Usually she was perky, talkative, interested in everything around them, asking the names of flowers, plants, birds, animals, anything he could tell her. Today, however, she was strangely quiet, brooding, as though waging some kind of inner war with herself.

Well, he could understand if she was, because he was having one of his own. Nights he lay awake telling himself he had to hurry and cozy her up and do what he had set out to do, but one day blended into the next and he had not made a move. And, bad as he hated to admit it, he knew it was because deep down he did not want their time together to end. He enjoyed being with her, delighted in every moment they spent together.

Slowly, it began to dawn on him that maybe he should not be so sure of himself, because maybe he did not appeal to her. She could be trying to think of an easy way to end their friendship. Or she might even have a fiancé back east who was on his way west.

They were riding alongside the river, and when they reached a bend, shaded by an overhang of mesquite growing in the rocks above, he signaled for them to rein in their horses.

He dismounted without asking if she wanted to, but she followed, then drifted over to the river to kneel and scoop water up in her hands and drink alongside the horses.

He waited a moment, then followed to gently grasp her shoulders and pull her to her feet to ask, "Is there something on your mind we need to talk about?"

"Well, I . . ." She stammered, caught off guard. "No, there's nothing."

He kept his hold on her, afraid if he let her go she would leap back on her horse, ending the quiet moment between them. "I believe there is, and that it has something to do with another man, and you just don't want to tell me."

She gave a nervous little laugh. "What makes you think that?"

"A girl as pretty as you is bound to have a beau somewhere, Kitty." His smile, meant to be warm and assuring, was thin, strained. The arrival of a fiancé would destroy his plan—unless he acted fast.

Kitty swayed ever so slightly, tremors rocking through her like a buggy on a bumpy road to have him stand so close and to feel his hands, so warm and possessive, on her bare shoulders. "No," she managed to push the word from her constricting throat. "No, I don't have a beau. I . . . I never have had," she suddenly admitted, then, in an embarrassed rush, confided, "Oh, Sam, you don't know how it was for me back in Virginia. I talk about it like I loved it, and certain parts of my life I did love and always will, like the horses, and the cool, green grasses and mountains, but the rest of it was miserable. People hated me and my family, and—" She faltered as the humiliating memories washed over her.

"Tell me about it," he urged. "Sometimes it helps to talk it out."

It seemed so natural for her to rest her head against his chest as he held her, and soon the entire story of her wretched past spilled forth.

"So I came here even though my uncle had been killed," she finished, "because I had no place else to go . . . nobody to turn to."

Though shaken by her nearness, Ryder reminded himself she had not yet confided about the map, and he could not let on he knew too much. Gently, hesitantly, he said, "It must have been the last straw to be taken by Apaches. I'm so sorry, Kitty."

"It was terrifying at first, but not as bad as it

would've been if they'd found out I was not only a woman but the one they were looking for."

Ryder pretended to be dumbfounded. "I don't understand."

"They were looking for me—Kitty Parrish—when they attacked the stagecoach. I was going by the name Kit, to go along with pretending to be a boy. But they didn't ask my name. Not then, anyway. They were just looking for a woman. And they would have left me behind except that I had shot one of them, and to keep him from killing me, their leader said he was going to make me his slave."

Ryder stepped away from her, fearing she would feel how his heart was racing. "Why would they be looking for you?"

"At first I thought it was Opal's doing, that she had arranged for me to be taken so she could have all my uncle's gold for herself."

"What gold?"

"I didn't tell you that part, how Opal sent me half a map to my uncle's gold strike."

"Why only half?"

"That's where the Indian attack comes in," she explained. "After I finally reached Tombstone and met Opal and realized she hadn't had anything to do with the Apaches looking for me, we were able to get to the bottom of things.

"You see," she rushed on to confide, "my uncle had a partner who had a son by an Apache woman. We figured out that's the one who took me for his slave, that Whitebear is actually Dan McCloud's son. He had sneaked into Opal's shanty on the edge of town a few weeks earlier to try and get my uncle's half of the map from her. That's when she told him she had sent it to me. We figure he went back later and found where she had hidden my telegram saying when I would arrive, and that's how he knew what stage I'd be on."

"But she lives over the saloon now."

"Yes. We were afraid once Whitebear discovered I had escaped that he might also hear Kitty Parrish had arrived in Tombstone and figure out what happened and come looking for me. We're safe at the saloon."

Ryder gave a low whistle. "That's an incredible story, Kitty. So what do you plan to do about finding the gold?"

"There's nothing I can do. Without Whitebear's half of the map, I could never find it."

"That's a shame. You both lose. But what if he had approached you in a different way, say to ask that you work together to locate the strike and then share it? Would you have agreed?"

"Probably," she said without hesitation.

Ryder cursed himself. But how was he to have known she would go along with such a proposal? She claimed to have had a miserable life, but he was used to getting kicked in the teeth himself.

"Maybe," he dared to say, "it's not too late. What if this Apache—Whitebear, you called him—came around again, this time in a civilized way, and asked if you'd work with him to find the gold? What then?"

She thought a few seconds, lips pursed, then said, "I don't think I could trust him. I'd have to say no. Besides"—she gave a little shiver—"I don't want to think of him getting close enough to me to ask."

"I suppose not," he murmured, mind spinning as he tried to analyze the situation.

She gave a little sigh and leaned to take up the reins of her horse. "It's a shame. Just think—somewhere, maybe even right around here—there's a rich gold strike that might never be found. Someone might find it sooner or later, true, but it's comforting to think it probably won't be the monsters who murdered my uncle and his partner. Opal said my uncle told her it was a tricky map, and without both parts put together, no one would be able to figure it out.''

Ryder's father had told him the same thing. And since he'd not seen his half, he could only take his father's word for it, even though he knew the area well.

"Kitty," he said suddenly, grabbing her arm and pulling her close once more. "I'd like to see your part of it. I know this country. Maybe I could figure it out."

"But it'd be a waste of time, I'm sure."

"I'd still like to try it." She would not know he had the whole map until it was all over. Then he would offer her half, which was fair.

Thinking like that eased his conscience. He had never felt really good about seducing her to get all the map and then keeping all the gold for himself. She was entitled to her uncle's part. He hadn't felt that way when he was angry and humiliated over her having fooled him, but a change of heart was inevitable, he supposed, being drawn to her as he was.

Kitty was staring up at him, her teeth biting into her lower lip as though she were trying to decide if she could trust him.

"You can," he answered, reading her mind. "You can trust me, Kitty. I swear it. And I really do want to help you."

But Kitty had learned, among other things, since coming west, to be leery of everything and everyone. "But why do you want to? I would pay you, of course, but to go to so much trouble, maybe even risk your life, for a nominal reward doesn't seem right."

His hand reached for hers. "Maybe I just want to help you, Kitty. You've been through so much in your life."

"But—"

He silenced her with his lips, arms going tight about

her, and he instantly felt himself grow hard as her breasts crushed into his chest. His tongue touched the corner of her mouth, coaxing her to open for him, then fiercely claimed possession.

Kitty moaned and swayed, would have stumbled had his arm not been tight about her waist. Heat unfurled in her belly, and she closed her eyes to let the delicious waves ripple up and down her body.

His tongue still exploring the sweetness of her mouth, he began to gently knead her breasts.

Suddenly frightened by the wild churning within, Kitty came out of the heated trance to tear her mouth from his and raggedly whisper, "We . . . we mustn't. Please —" She pushed at his chest, trying to free herself of his embrace.

"I'm sorry," Ryder said in a rush, releasing her and stepping back.

"There . . . there's no need to be," Kitty murmured thinly. "It . . . it was my fault. I shouldn't have let it go so far . . ."

Snatching up the horse's reins once more, she mounted and, still teeming with the desire he had ignited, said, "We have to be getting back. We've been away longer than usual, and I have to get ready for the first performance."

He also swung up in the saddle. "Don't you think we ought to finish the conversation I so rudely interrupted?" he asked with a reckless smile.

Kitty also smiled, pleased to have him so deftly take them from the tension. "Do you really want to help me look for the gold?"

"Not *help* you," he said carefully. "I wouldn't want you involved. It's too dangerous. Whoever killed those two men might still be looking."

Kitty's face went tight. "I'm afraid I'd have to insist on coming along."

"I couldn't allow that," he said, eyes growing darker

to think of having her exposed to potential danger. It was, truly, a distinct possibility that the murderer—or murderers, as the case might be—would be lurking around waiting for her to appear. Him, too. They could be followed, and he could not chance it.

"Then I'm afraid it's out of the question."

"And I'm afraid I feel insulted, because it's obvious you don't trust me."

"And it's obvious you don't trust my ability to look out for myself. I wouldn't be in the way, and you know it, just like you know if we run into trouble I can handle a gun. So I have to wonder what your real reason is for not wanting me along.

"Well?" she persisted when he offered no explanation. "What am I to think when you won't say anything?"

What could he say—that he would welcome the intimacy during the search . . . welcome the glory of emptying his passion into her sweetness every chance he got until she found out who he really was? Because once the gold was located, he would have to identify himself in order to demand his rightful share, and she would surely hate him forevermore.

*But why not enjoy her in the meantime?* a little voice within nagged. *What is the harm?*

The harm, he was pained to admit, would come because he feared he was falling in love. And even if she should love him in return, it could never work out between them. They came from two different worlds, and he would not risk things turning out like they had between his parents. It was best to end it now before they got more deeply involved. Once he located the gold, he would deposit her share in a bank and send her a note telling her where it was. Then Sam Bodine would drop out of sight never to be seen again, and they could both get on with their lives.

Finally, he said, "You can't go. It's too dangerous."

"Then forget it," she snapped, digging her heels into the horse's flanks to send him into a gallop.

Ryder pulled his horse alongside, keeping pace. "You're being stubborn, Kitty, I told you—I know the country around here. I'm certain I can find it."

Over the sound of hooves clicking on the rocks, she cried, "If I don't go, you don't get the map."

"What you're saying is that you think I'm going to swindle you. I'm not an outlaw, Kitty. And when I give my word, I keep it."

"I have no reason to believe you. I hardly know you."

"We were pretty close back there for a little while," he said with a roguish smile. "A little while longer, and we might have got to know each other real good."

"That . . . that has nothing to do with it. And if you won't agree to take me with you, we'll just forget the whole idea."

"Hell, woman," he exploded, "you're going to throw away a chance at a fortune because you won't trust me."

She looked at him then, a quick dart of fury. "No. You're throwing away a chance at a nice reward because you're like most men—you can't accept a woman being able to think for herself and make her own decisions."

"That's crazy. You're just afraid I'll find the gold and keep it all for myself."

"Well, if that weren't your intent, you'd have no objections to me going with you. I've damn well proved myself, Sam Bodine.

"But *you* haven't proved anything," she concluded angrily, popping reins across the horse's neck to make him go even faster.

They rode the rest of the way in frosty silence, and when they reached the livery stable, Ryder was so mad he turned away from her without a word.

Tossing a coin at the boy to wipe down his horse
and put him away, he headed for the nearest saloon.

Leaning against the bar, he ordered a shot of whiskey and quickly gulped it down.

He saw Kitty pass by the window. Her chin was up,
and her eyes were flashing.

*Stubborn filly,* he grumbled to himself. So sure of
herself with a gun. Hell, she didn't have sense enough
to realize shooting at a cactus was different than drawing against a man. True, she had hit Coyotay, but that
was in the midst of an attack. She did not know one
damn thing about tracking or sneaking up on anybody
or outwitting the enemy.

And who was to say when it came right down to it
she wouldn't do something stupid—like cry or faint?
No matter how good she was with a gun, she was still
a woman, and therefore, he felt, not competent to face
the dangers that might be waiting. After all, somewhere out there was the man—or *men*—who had
killed her uncle and his father, and they were probably
still trying to find the hidden gold strike.

But, despite everything, the fact remained that Kitty
Parrish was not some empty-headed female easily
swayed by a man's charms. Now he suspected that if
he had made love to her, it would have made no difference in her decision not to hand over the map unless she was part of the deal.

He ordered another drink and thought maybe he
should just give in and let her go along with him and
enjoy the hell out of her before going back to his
people. And so what if she did find out he was actually
Whitebear? What could she do about it except hate
him forevermore? He could take her, use her, and—

He gave his head a brisk shake and slammed his
glass down in signal for refill.

He couldn't do it, damn it, because he cared about

her. Like it or not, he cared. And the sooner he was rid of her and on his way, the better off he would be.

But not before he got hold of the map, because he had come too far to give up.

She had let it slip that it was hidden in her room. All he had to do was sneak upstairs while she was performing and find it. She might not even discover it missing till she got his note about the deposit in her name.

But he would have to wait a few days and let her think that Sam Bodine had ridden out of town and out of her life.

It was how it had to be . . . no matter how much he wished it could be otherwise.

# Chapter 16

"You should have given him the map and been done with it," Opal grumbled.

Kitty wondered how many times she had heard her say that in the four days since Sam was seen riding out of town. She wished she had never told her about his proposition.

"Hell, what did you have to lose?"

"The map," Kitty coolly pointed out—and wondered how many times she had said *that,* too.

"Well, it's sure as hell of no use to you."

"True. But at least now he can't try to find the gold and keep it all for himself."

"You don't know he would've done that."

"Well, if that wasn't his intention, why did he object to me going along with him to look for it?"

Opal was sitting on the side of the bed buffing her nails while Kitty dressed for the evening. "It would've been a gamble, but if you don't bet, you don't win. So now what have you got? Half of a worthless map and no money."

"Well, I've still got my job," Kitty said, but without enthusiasm. She liked her work less and less, and with Sam gone, she was lonely and back to having nothing to do all day.

"You won't have it for long if some of those chairs don't start filling up. Besides, I hear the Lucky Nugget down the street has got a dancer wearing nothing but feathers."

Kitty was quick to say, "Well, Mr. Earp better not get any ideas about changing my act to the Singing Chicken."

"Maybe you better start learning to deal or call faro."

Kitty hated the thought. She wanted, needed, to be outdoors, working with horses and enjoying the world, not stuck in a smoky gambling hall. "I guess I'd better get downstairs," she said, tired of conversation.

"Yeah. Me, too." Opal gathered her things, then paused to say in an accusing tone, "You know he was the pick of the litter, don't you? A fine-looking man like that, and you let him slip right through your fingers by insulting him and making him feel like an outlaw."

Kitty's shoulders sagged. Like it or not, Opal made sense. She *had* insulted him. She *had* been stubborn. And if she had it to do over again would react differently. Besides, the map was no good to her, anyway. She could not strike out on her own and make heads or tails of any of the clues and landmarks. It would have been better to trust Sam Bodine. And, beyond that, she was pained to think, there was always the chance that their feelings for each other would have grown. Now, sadly, it was over, and she was left to wonder how it all might have ended had she not been so obstinate and suspicious.

She was wearing a new gown Mr. Earp had insisted she have made. Fashioned of bright red satin, it was covered in thousands of sparkling sequins. And it was different from any of her other costumes, which were in soft pastel colors and lacy and fluffy in style. Obviously Mr. Earp was concerned about the dwindling audience and trying to spice things up.

"Lord have mercy," Morton said, wide-eyed, when

Kitty went to the bar for the glass of wine that always fortified her for the show. "I can't say as I've ever thought of an angel wearing red, but you're sure beautiful, Kitty."

"I think red goes with the other place." She pointed down and smiled.

She took the glass of wine he had waiting and walked toward the little table in an alcove to the side where she could observe without being seen or bothered. It was early. The saloon was nearly empty. Not a soul was waiting for her performance to begin and only a few weeks ago not a seat would have been left.

Morton called after her, "Oh, I almost forgot. Mr. Earp said to tell you he wants to see you in his office before you go on. He's waiting for you."

Kitty felt a shudder of foreboding. Mr. Earp never asked her to go to his office when he wanted to speak to her about anything. He would just walk up to her before or between performances.

She went to the very back of the saloon, where there was a long, narrow hallway. The office was at the end.

She knocked on the door and softly called, "Mr. Earp, it's Kitty Parrish."

"Come in," came the booming response.

He was seated behind his desk, elegant in satin-striped vest, white shirt with ruffled collar, and gray trousers. Smoking a thin cheroot, he waved her to take a seat as he leaned back in his oxblood leather chair.

Kitty sat down. "Morton said you wanted to see me."

He was a man of few words and got right to the point. "I think people have gotten tired of your act, Kitty. After tonight, that's it."

She pressed her hands together in her lap as she quickly calculated her savings. She would be all right for a little while if he did not make her give up her room.

He quickly destroyed that hope.

"I'll have to ask you to move. Like I said before—the upstairs is for special guests and hired help only. I'm not in the business of running a rooming house, but I have no objections if you want to move in with Opal till you find something else."

Kitty was not about to do that. She adored Opal and was grateful for her friendship, but it would not do to be around her all the time. Opinionated and prone to speak her mind, Opal also drank heavily and could be hard to get along with.

"I have a little money," Kitty said. "And I would appreciate it if you'd let me stay on a little while, at least."

"A *very* little while," he said, tapping ashes into a silver bowl.

Kitty hurried back outside, fighting tears of frustration and feeling sick to her stomach.

Opal had warned her it was coming, that Mr. Earp would let her go, but she hadn't believed her. Now she was swept with feelings of despair and desperation unlike any she had ever known. It was almost like starting out from Virginia all over again, except that back then she had not known the pleasure of a man's kisses or the delicious dream of loving and being loved, which made it all worse.

By the time she returned to the main room, Jim had started playing the piano. He did not miss a note as she whispered to him that she would be giving her last performance.

"I know, and I'm sorry," he said. "Mr. Earp told me. But don't worry. Maybe that beau of yours will propose."

"I don't know that I'd accept if he did. Besides, he's left town."

He continued to run his fingers over the ivory keys. "Ah, that's a shame. I could tell he was real sweet on you. Never took his eyes off you for a second when you were on that stage. Maybe he'll come back."

"I don't think so." She gave his shoulder a pat and made her way backstage.

She could have told him that, no, Sam Bodine would not be back, because she had not given him what he wanted, only he might have taken it the wrong way, and she was not about to explain.

Perhaps she had been hasty in rejecting his offer, because Opal had a point in saying she had nothing to lose. After all, if he had been able to find the gold and had kept it for himself, she would have had no less than what she had now—except for her pride.

So she would never know if she had made the right decision. But one thing she could be sure of—if he *had* cared anything about her, he would not have been so fast to leave. He would have stayed even if she had not been willing to hand over the map.

After a while, Jim began to play the opening number.

Kitty went up the steps and took her place behind the curtain for the last time. She was only going to do one show. If Mr. Earp did not like it, so be it. Her head was aching along with her heart, and all she wanted was to hide in her room and lock the door and cry her eyes out as she wondered what in the hell she was going to do with the rest of her life.

Most of the chairs, she was gratified to notice as the curtain opened, were filled. At least her last performance would not be for an empty room.

She began to sing, wanting to get it over with. She held up three fingers to Jim, signaling that was how many songs she would do. He nodded that he understood.

She was halfway through the second, which was

"The Battle Hymn of the Republic," when a man's loud, angry voice suddenly drowned her out.

"Hey, I ain't listenin' to that shit. Sing 'Dixie' or don't sing nothin'."

Jim, trying to head off trouble because he had seen both the Earps head out the door at the sound of gunfire in the street a few moments earlier, immediately changed to the melody the man had demanded to hear.

Kitty, however, did not switch to the other song and instead stopped singing. Glaring at the man, she said, "You are rude, sir. Now, sit down and allow me to finish."

He guffawed and waved his arms for her to come down into the audience. "I'll allow you to come here and sit in my lap and give me some sugar . . . *sugar.*"

The audience burst into laughter.

Kitty motioned to Jim to go back to the interrupted song, but he stubbornly swung his head in refusal.

"Now, sing, damn you," the man roared, stamping his feet and clapping his hands.

Suddenly, Kitty could stand no more. There was just no way she was going to yield to the drunken buffoon's demands. She had already lost her job, so why should she subject herself to such humiliation?

Lifting her skirt so as not to stumble, she walked across the stage and down the steps.

The man let out a loud, angry bellow and started toward her, bumping into people and knocking over empty chairs. "Hey, you ain't goin' nowhere till you sing 'Dixie' for me, you little strumpet."

Jim stopped playing and leaped to his feet.

Morton saw what was happening and reached for the gun he kept hidden under the bar, but the man was quicker. He drew his own weapon and warned, "Leave it be, Morton, or I'll blow you to hell."

Morton obeyed, eyes wide as he raised his hands

skyward in surrender. "Now, don't do nothin' foolish. Just take it easy. Kitty'll be glad to sing for you. We don't want trouble."

"I will not sing for that insufferable clod," Kitty said, bristling with fury as she stomped right past Morton and into the line of fire should the man pull the trigger. "I am through with all of this—"

"No, you ain't."

The man lunged over the last few chairs and caught her by her wrists, holding them pinned behind her. Pistol in hand, he bent her backward as he covered her face with wet, hungry kisses. "You be nice to me, sugar, and I'll be nice to you. We can have us a good time. You can sing just for me."

A loud clang resounded through the room as he was bashed over the head by a metal tray wielded by Opal. With eyes flashing fire, she screamed, "You let her go right now, Nate, or so help me I'll bash your skull."

With a cry of pain, he released Kitty, and she fell to the floor, stupefied.

Opal had called him *Nate.*

He was her *brother.*

"Now you get out of here," Opal warned, hitting him across his chest for good measure, "before the marshal gets back here and hauls your ass off to jail. That's what oughta be done with you, anyway, drunk as you are.

"And you oughta be ashamed of yourself," she railed on, holding the tray up as though to smack him again as he backed away, hands over his face. "Scaring Wade's niece that way."

"Wade's . . . niece . . ." He looked down at Kitty, who was still sprawled on the floor. "Well, I'll be cat scratched. What's she doin' here? And ain't she a pretty thing?"

Opal gave him a shove. "Yes, she's pretty, and you leave her alone and get on out of here."

Nate Grimes whined, "But, Opal, sugar, I ain't got no money. I need a stake. I got robbed in Mexico, and—"

"You got robbed by whichever *puta* you were laid up with all these many weeks, and I'm not giving you a cent."

"Hell, you won't even give me nothing to eat," he bellowed, "and how come you moved? I went to the shanty and some man run me off with a shotgun. I started to blow his head off."

"I live upstairs now. But that's none of your business. Now git."

Nate sneered at Kitty. "You ain't nothin' but trouble. I heard how you caused Roscoe to get a little crazy with your prancin' and flirtin', givin' him all kinds of notions."

He took a step toward her, stumbled, and fell.

Kitty scrambled to her feet and backed away from him, but then saw he was no longer a threat.

He was out cold.

"Help me get him upstairs," Opal said to Morton. "He's just had too much to drink. He'll sleep it off and be fine in the morning."

Kitty watched as Morton and another man pulled Nate to his feet, then slung his arms about their shoulders and proceeded to take him up to Opal's room.

"Now I've got to get to work," Opal said to no one in particular.

Kitty sat at the bar and had another glass of wine, feeling miserable to the tips of her toes. She had lost her job, had no place to go, missed Sam Bodine terribly and wished they had never quarreled. He had called her stubborn, and he was right. She was. And if she knew how to get in touch with him, she would tell him so.

Memories of how he had held and kissed her made her feel all the worse, and she sank so deep in her despair that she did not protest when Morton kept refilling her glass.

Finally, with heavy head and heavy heart, she went up to her room.

She did not notice that the door to Opal's room at the other end of the hall was standing open and that Nate could see her as she went to her own.

Neither did she think, light-headed from drink, to lock her door.

Promising herself she would make a new start in the morning, she undressed and got in bed, the wine making her fall asleep almost as soon as her head hit the pillow.

Ryder stood in the alley behind the Oriental Saloon. He knew Kitty's room was in the front. He had kept a vigil across the street with hat pulled down over his eyes until he managed to see her pacing in front of the open windows. Getting down the hall without being seen at such a late hour was no problem. The trick would be to scale the wall and enter through the window opening into it.

It was time for Kitty to go on stage for her second performance . . . and also time for him to get in her room, find the map, and get the hell out of Tombstone before anybody saw him.

Quickly, deftly, he took the tomahawk he had brought from his hiding place outside of town and tied it to a rope. Then, after several mighty swings over his head, he sent it sailing upward to land with a thud in the wall just below the window.

Giving it a tug, he decided it would hold, and proceeded to pull himself up as he walked the side of the building.

Crawling through the window, he dropped noiselessly to the floor.

A lantern on a nearby table cast a dim light up and down the T-shaped hall.

He crouched and waited for any sound, but heard nothing except the noise filtering from below.

He began to creep along slowly, lest someone in one of the rooms on either side hear him and investigate.

Her door would be locked, but he could pick it open. He knew he had to work fast once he got inside, but he figured there were not many places in the room where she could have hidden the map.

Suddenly a door began to open slowly just a few feet away.

Ryder pressed back against the wall and waited. The last thing he needed was to have to shoot somebody, but he drew his gun just in case.

A man stepped into the hall but did not look around. He began to shuffle along, lurching from side to side.

Ryder decided he was drunk and on his way to find more liquor. He was no threat. He would keep on going, turn at the end of the hall, toward the steps, disappear, and—

Ryder sucked in his breath.

The man went to Kitty's door, opened it, and walked right in.

Ryder could only stand there, staring in disbelief as the door closed after him.

Who the hell was he?

And why had Kitty obviously left the door unlocked for him?

His first impulse was to just get the hell out of there, but he reminded himself why he was there. If Kitty had a lover, it made no difference. He had come to get the map and be done with it, and that was exactly what he was going to do, by damn, as soon as the man left. Kitty was supposed to be downstairs singing. Surely he wouldn't hang around with her not there, and—

A scream ripped the stillness.

It came from Kitty's room, and Ryder forgot everything else as he charged down the hall.

Shoving the door open, he plunged into the room
to see Kitty struggling with her intruder.

Ryder clamped his hands on her attacker's shoulders, taking him by surprise. Spinning him around, he
clipped his jaw with a hard blow that knocked him to
the floor, unconscious.

In the scant light shining through the window, Kitty
looked from the crumpled body on the floor to Ryder
and gasped in recognition, "You . . . Sam . . . it's you.
Oh, dear Lord . . ."

Scrambling from the bed, she snatched up a robe
as the room suddenly began to fill with people who
had heard her screams and come running.

Someone turned up the lamp.

Opal was among the first to arrive. She took one
look at the man on the floor and screamed, "What
the hell is my brother doing in here?" Then she saw
Ryder. "And what the hell are you doing here?"

*Think fast,* Ryder commanded himself as all eyes
suddenly turned on him.

When he did not speak right away, Kitty managed
to say, "I guess I forgot to lock my door, and Nate
stumbled in. Sam was nearby"— she glanced at him
as though wondering why he would be—"and came
to my rescue."

Morton rushed in. Looking from Nate on the floor
to Ryder standing over him, his eyes clouded with
suspicion. "How'd you get up here? I didn't see you
run up in front of me."

Ryder shrugged. "It's like she said. I heard the
ruckus and ran up the steps. You just didn't see me."

"I told Mr. Earp he needed to get somebody to
take Ben's place on the landing. Anybody can get up
here looks like." Morton pointed to Nate and asked
Opal, "What do you want to do with him?"

Opal, hands on her hips, sighed and shook her head. "Just take him back to my room and lock him in this time." Giving Kitty a pat on her shoulder, she offered, "I'm sorry, honey. Nate gets crazy when he drinks. Otherwise, he wouldn't harm a fly."

Kitty did not look so sure about that.

Morton and another man lifted Nate by his feet and shoulders and carried him from the room, with Opal leading the way.

Everyone else had drifted out. Ryder suddenly felt very awkward to find himself alone with Kitty, but at least he had not been caught in the hall and did not have to come up with an explanation for that.

They looked at each other in challenge, each waiting for the other to speak. Finally, Ryder said, "Well, I'd best be going. It isn't proper to be in a lady's room," he added with the hint of a smile.

"It doesn't matter to the lady," Kitty said boldly.

His smile grew wider. "That's surprising, since the lady made it clear a few days ago she didn't trust me."

"You misunderstood. Trust has nothing to do with it," she lied. "I just wanted to go along. I still do. And now I have even more of a reason, because I no longer have a job, and I've been asked to move out of here."

He fought the impulse to put a comforting arm around her. "I'm sorry. So what are you going to do?"

She hesitated but a second, and then, with a twinkle in her eye, she said, "Search for a lost gold mine. Care to join me?"

The way she was looking at him made him feel like butter melting on hot pancakes. "Let's talk about it in the morning," he said, knowing that if he did not get out he was going to wind up taking her in his arms, and he was not sure how she would react if he did.

"We can meet at the livery stable and go for another ride. Around eleven?"

She did not hesitate. "I'll be there."

# Chapter 17

Sitting astride her horse, Kitty watched as Sam studied the trail that ran alongside the river. They had never ridden as far before, but they had been so absorbed in conversation that neither had paid attention to time or distance.

She felt warm inside, like after a cup of warm milk laced with brandy. They'd had a good talk and agreed to look for the gold together. As soon as they gathered all the supplies they would need, they would start out.

"It's that way," he said, pointing.

At first, she did not take in his words, for she was admiring the sight of his broad shoulders and narrow hips, the casual grace with which he sat on his horse. Finally she came out of her velvet trance to ask, "What are you talking about?"

"The spot where they found your uncle and his partner. It's maybe two miles up that trail."

A shudder went through her. "I thought it was near the river . . . on the riverbank."

"It is. There's a fork a little ways farther up that winds back through some sharp boulders. It's a real secluded spot. Prospectors use it for a short cut to the mountains, but others stick to the main trail because they worry about Apaches."

"Why don't the prospectors worry?"

"The Apaches tend to leave them alone. The prospectors give them things—beads, whiskey, trinkets, and whatever food they can spare. They're allowed to pass, because the Indians figure they're harmless."

"But maybe with my uncle and Dan McCloud they didn't."

Ryder stiffened. "What are you talking about?"

"Have you ever thought about the possibility that it might have been the Apaches who were responsible? After all, Dan McCloud had a half-breed son, remember? And maybe he told some of the warriors in his tribe, and they decided to hunt McCloud down on their own and make him tell where his strike was."

"No. That's not possible."

She wondered why he suddenly sounded so angry, but she maintained her theory. "Well, I think it could have happened that way."

"White men did it."

"How do you know?"

"I heard how their bodies looked. It could not have been the work of Apaches."

She did not want to hear details. "Since we're so close, I'd like to see the spot."

"Are you sure? We might ought to be heading back to town. We don't want to get caught out here after dark."

"Scared of Indians, are you?" she teased. She gave her holstered gun a pat. "Don't worry. I'll protect you."

"Like you protected the stagecoach?" he teased right back, for she had told him her version of the attack. It had been all he could do to keep from busting out laughing to listen to her describe him as a painted-up savage with wild eyes and how Coyotay, when he had wanted to kill her, had reminded her of a rabid dog she had seen once. He would have to remember to goad him about that.

Her head came up in a flash of indignation. "I put up a good fight. I was outnumbered, you know."

"And might be again, but if you insist, let's ride. Besides, this is the way we'll head when we start looking for the strike."

He turned his horse and rode up the trail.

Soon it began to narrow. They could no longer ride side by side. Kitty fell back to allow him to take the lead . . . and also to enjoy the view of his hips undulating in the saddle in rhythm with the horse's plodding gait.

She had thanked him for once more coming to her rescue, and he'd said he just happened to be where he could hear her. She had asked him what he was doing back in town, and his explanation was that he planned to try and gain her trust. Satisfied she would be joining him, Kitty had resolved to attempt to ease tension between them and felt she had succeeded. The relaxed camaraderie was back. They were friends once more.

An hour or so passed. They made small talk when the trail permitted them to ride closer, but mostly they ambled along in silence. She noted how he was ever alert, eyes forever darting about.

Intent on watching him, she was caught off guard when the branch of a low-hanging mesquite slapped her full in the face. She gave a little cry. He twisted about in the saddle, saw what had happened, and chided her to be more alert.

"That's something you're going to have to learn out here, Kitty. It will be no leisurely ride as we've had in the past when we stuck to the main trails. Not only do you need to keep an eye out for Apaches but you've also got to watch for outlaws. Then there are snakes, lizards, holes you need to steer your horse around so he won't stumble, and—"

There was no warning. Kitty's horse stumbled but

once and went down. Relaxed in the saddle and un-
prepared, she went sailing right over his head to land
flat on her stomach. She felt a sharp pain, and the
wind was knocked out of her.

Ryder quickly swung down to kneel beside her.
"Are you hurt?"

She tried to speak but could only wheeze, face
screwed in the anguish of struggling for breath.

He ran his hands up and down her arms and legs
and side. "I don't feel anything broken and don't see
any blood. You've just had your wind knocked out.
You should be okay in a minute or two. Just lie still.
I've got to see to your horse—make sure he didn't
break a leg."

Quick scrutiny revealed only a badly sprained leg
that would slow the horse down a day or two.

Ryder returned to Kitty. She had pulled herself up
to a sitting position but was still gasping. "He's going
to be lame for a day or two," he said. "Nothing serious, but you can't ride him."

He cast a wary look skyward. Dark thunderclouds
were gathering, and the wind had picked up. "I should
have been paying more attention to the weather. We
need to get out of here before that storm breaks. If
the rain gets heavy, this part of the river will rise
quickly."

Kitty glanced about helplessly but saw only boulders
and rocks with nothing hanging overhead to protect
them. "We can ride double and try to make it back
to town."

For a long, tense moment he said nothing, then,
"Too risky. Too many rocks on the trail. Having to
carry both of us, my horse wouldn't be as surefooted.
He could stumble like yours."

Kitty was breathing better but fear was threatening
to choke her. "Do we have any other choice?"

There was something in his face she could not quite

read as he stared off into the distance. "Maybe. I used to know of a cave not too far from here."

Kitty felt a surge of excitement. "Maybe it's an Indian cave, and we'll find food stored there. Pale Sky told me how in the old days, when the Indians could ride wherever they wanted, they would hide food and things in secret caves, usually near water, so they'd be there if needed."

She did not see how he frowned as he turned away, thinking how sometimes his mother talked too much. "I don't know about that," he lied, "but if I can remember where the cave is, we'll at least have shelter." He knew the exact location but was not about to let her know that.

"Are you all right now? Can you ride?" He held out his hand.

She took it and allowed him to help her stand. "I think so. I'm a bit sore, though." She rubbed her bottom.

"Some help you're going to be," he pretended to grumble. "You can't even stay on your horse."

Not entirely in jest, she crisply informed him, "I'll bet I could outride you with both legs broken."

"Well, let's hope we never find out." Her cockiness bothered him sometimes. He was afraid it might get her in a peck of trouble one day. After all, he had been confronted by many a young gunfighter with the same kind of attitude. He had, however, wounded them instead of killing them as he could easily have done.

He swung up in the saddle, then pulled her up to sit in front of him. "Your horse will follow after us."

He liked the feel of his thighs against her as she was squeezed up against him. Reaching around her to take the reins, he felt a rush of pleasure as his arms brushed her breasts.

The wind, which was steadily rising, caused her hair

to whip against his face as they rode, and he thought how good she smelled . . . how good she *felt*.

Kitty was silent, afraid if she talked her voice would give away the storm raging inside her. His nearness was overwhelming, and she drank in the masculine aroma of him, delighting in his firm chest as she leaned back against him.

There was a hardness against her buttocks, and she wondered, cheeks flaming, if it was caused by his desire. She did not know much about such things, could only guess . . . fantasize . . . and she fought to keep from shuddering, lest he sense what she was feeling.

Ryder attempted to force his mind to other things— like finding the hidden trail through Peralta Canyon. Spotting the creek bed, dry and brittle as old bone, he knew he was going the right way. Trees and brush were pale and dust-colored in the hot, hazy light, desperately in need of the rain that threatened. Soon they were wrapped in a world of stillness—canyon pools, birds, buzzards, and barrel cactus.

As they headed into a pile of boulders, Kitty turned to make sure her horse was following. "He doesn't look like he's limping very bad now," she remarked.

Ryder twisted about to see also. "I told you it wasn't bad. He just needs a bit of rest. Your riding him would aggravate it, and he could stumble again and do some serious damage then."

"Are we almost there?" The trail narrowed considerably, and she winced as her knees brushed against the rocks on either side.

"Just about."

"How on earth did you ever find this place?"

"If a man wants to live long in this territory, he has to learn his way. So I've done a bit of exploring."

The closeness, the intimacy, was overwhelming, and Kitty found herself wondering how they were ever going to be able to travel together, camp together, without him seeing how it unnerved her. But maybe he wasn't experiencing the same feelings, so it would not be on his mind. She told herself she only imagined the hardness pressed against her.

Daring to hope conversation would get her mind on other things, she pointed to a shrubby sort of cactus that appeared to be covered in gold and silver fur. "Oh, it's beautiful," she cried. "It looks so soft."

He chuckled. "That softness you think you see is actually thousands of tiny little spines—needles—and once they get on your clothes or in your flesh they're very painful and real hard to get out. You have to pluck them one by one."

Suddenly she yielded to impulse and said, "You're always eager to tell me about the land but never anything about yourself, like where you come from, or if you have a family."

"It's not important," he said uneasily.

"All I know is that you're a gunfighter."

"My past doesn't matter."

She continued as though he had not spoken. "Sometimes I wonder why you want to help me find my uncle's gold. After all, we might not be able to, and then it will be a waste of your time."

"I'm hoping it won't be. And don't forget," he interjected to allay any suspicions she might be having, "I'm expecting a reward."

"Don't worry. I'll be generous, I promise, but it all depends on how much we find."

Ryder was not worried in the least. Neither was he concerned over the amount of his so-called *reward*. He would take what was rightfully his—half. And it would not matter if, by then, she figured out who he really was, because he would be leading his people to escape across the border as quick as he could.

He would let nothing stand in his way.

And it made no difference that Kitty Parrish made

his blood boil with desire. She came from another world and could not be a part of his any more than he could ever content himself in hers. So he would take one day at a time, damn it, find the gold, and get the hell out of her life.

"You certainly can be mysterious," she said when he lapsed into a cold silence. "I answered all your questions about me, and—"

He cut her off. "The cave should be around the next bend."

"But how did you find it? What were you doing way back in here?"

"I told you—I explore a lot. I know my way around. Otherwise, I wouldn't have offered to help you find the gold."

Kitty was startled to hear what sounded like anger in his voice, and lapsed into an uncomfortable silence. Obviously, he did not like probing questions about himself, but perhaps his resentment was a good thing. It quelled some of what she was feeling, so maybe the answer to tension . . . desire . . . would be to provoke the cold side of his nature that seemed to close any doors of intimacy between them.

She pretended to be indignant. "Well, you don't have to snap my head off. After all, if we're to work together, we should try to get along."

"Then stop asking so many questions that have nothing to do with our work."

She noted he had pulled back from her, as though he did not like her pressed against him. Fine. She leaned forward, turning once more to make sure her horse was still plodding along behind them. He seemed to be much better, hardly favoring his injured leg at all. If they had to stay the night in the cave—*if* Sam actually knew where he was going—by morning she would be able to ride. Meanwhile, she would do as much sparring as necessary to keep that door closed

between them. It was her only defense—against
*herself.*

"Here it is."

They rounded one last, huge boulder, and Kitty saw
they were riding right into a gaping hole in the side
of a mountain.

He helped her down and then dismounted himself.
Kitty hurried to investigate the cave.

The opening was wide, and light poured in despite
the storm clouds that continued to race ominously
across the sky.

"It *is* an Indian cave," she cried, delighted to find
clay jugs with dried vegetables and fruits stored inside.
There was also water, blankets, and cooking utensils.
"We could stay here for weeks if we had to."

"Well, we don't have to," Ryder said curtly. "I
think we can rest a spell and be on our way. I noticed
your horse isn't as bad as I first thought, so as soon
as it looks like the storm danger is past we'll get out
of here."

But Kitty was paying no attention, too engrossed in
her surroundings. "Isn't this wonderful? Why, I'll bet
Indians come here all the time. It's like the way stations for the stagecoaches. They have their own place
to rest and eat."

Ryder ignored her excitement and set about to
make them a meal out of dried rabbit meat and
tortillas.

He also retrieved a jug of *tulapai* he had personally
hidden where no other of his band would find it. Filling a chipped crockery mug, he held it out to Kitty,
who had just declared she was dying of thirst.

She took a sip and made a face. "It's white water—
what the Chiricahua I lived with call *tulapai*. I should
have known by the smell."

"It's good," he said between swallows, trying not to
smile. "Whatever it is."

Kitty liked the way it felt so warm in her stomach, calm and soothing. She took another sip, and the taste was not as bad.

The sound of rain turned their gazes to the cave entrance. It was slow and cooling.

Kitty walked out to stand right in it, reveling in the feel upon her face.

"You're going to get soaked," Ryder said irritably.

"I don't care." Her lips parted and she licked eagerly at the refreshing drops. "It's been so hot, and this feels wonderful."

Ryder looked at her grudgingly. Her head was thrown back, hair wet and stringing down her back. He felt a tremor to see how her blouse stuck to her, nipples prominent beneath the damp clinging cotton. And it was maddening to watch as she licked at the raindrops with her tongue and made husky sounds of pleasure deep in her throat.

"I don't care how wet I get," she declared. "And if the river isn't too high when we start back, I think I'll jump right in for a swim."

She looked at him and grinned, face glowing. "I'd forgotten how it feels to stand in the rain. And I used to swim all the time back home. There was a pond right near my house, and I'd ride my horse into it and then dive right in, and—"

With a groan, Ryder crossed to her in swift strides, grabbed her, and crushed her against him.

One hand on the back of her head, he held her in a viselike grip as his mouth claimed hers.

She tried to wrench away. "No . . . don't . . ."

But then he felt her resistance wither as her lips yielded to his assault, parting to allow his tongue entry.

As he began to unbutton her blouse with deft, eager fingers, his hand at the back of her head moved to cup her chin, then trailed downward to make tiny circling patterns in the sweet hollows of her throat.

Hot tingles ignited throughout her body, and Kitty unconsciously pressed closer, surrendering herself to his sweet torture. She felt consumed by the ravishing hunger of his tongue and responded with a thirst of her own.

Ryder began to trail his lips downward, wanting to lick and taste all of her, inch by inch. Her hands moved to clutch his hair, twining her fingers in it, as she moaned and quaked beneath his touch. It was her own primal need, awakening and demanding to be fed.

Slowly, for he wanted to savor and enjoy, he pulled her yet deeper into the raging current of passion, the heated throbbing of her body urging him on.

With her blouse open, parted, their gazes locked as he cupped her breasts ever so gently, then harshly, almost painfully, in his possession of her as she sighed, smiling to urge him to continue.

"I want you." He rolled her nipples between thumb and forefinger, liking how they turned hard beneath his touch while she pushed herself against him, wanting more. "I want you, but I'll stop if you tell me to. I didn't bring you here to seduce you, Kitty, but I'd be lying if I said I didn't want you."

Her fingers moved from his hair to dance down his neck, across his shoulders, and finally down his back to clutch his buttocks tightly.

"And I want you," she whispered. "I may regret it later, but right now I want you more than I've ever wanted anything in my whole life."

Ryder felt as though his loins were on fire as he lowered his face to her breasts. He assaulted one taut nipple between his teeth to nibble deliciously, and Kitty twisted and writhed in joyful anguish, mesmerized by the fervid moment.

He released her long enough to unbuckle his holster

and lay it aside, and she did the same with hers. Then, embracing her once more, he lowered her slowly to the ground.

Kitty felt his hardness and knew she was not imagining anything this time. Long and hard, bulging in his trousers, it pressed against her belly.

She was stretched across him, and he pulled her upward, lifting her so that her breasts were above his face.

Sweetly, savagely, he assaulted each in turn, taking the nipple in his teeth, then rolling it with his tongue before taking as much as he could into his mouth.

She was on fire, trembling from head to toe, and he felt it . . . knew she wanted him . . . but had to be sure. "Tell me," he commanded, releasing her breast and rolling her to her side. "Tell me you want me, Kitty."

He was shoving up her skirt to yank down her undergarments. Her legs seemed to have a will of their own as they eagerly spread for him. He touched between, caressing the center of her desire.

"I . . . I do want you . . . ," she said in a voice she did not recognize as her own. "So much, Sam . . . so much."

*Sam.*

The alien name spoken, reminding him of his deception, was like a dash of cold water. For an instant, he hesitated, but then quickly thrust his fingers inside her. She closed about him, and he throbbed with a powerful urgency.

"I'll be gentle," he promised in a ragged, fevered whisper as he positioned her on her back. "If you've never been with a man, it hurts, and—"

"Never," she all but shouted. "I've never been with a man, Sam . . . never wanted to be . . . till now . . . till you . . ."

Quickly he peeled off his clothing, then straddled

her, and she opened herself to him, hips arching to maneuver herself closer. He mounted, eagerness hot and tense, charging from head to toe as he guided himself inside her.

He endeavored to be gentle, but she was clutching his back, nails cutting into his flesh as she urged him on.

Knowing that she matched his ardor, he pushed deeper, cradling her buttocks in his hands as he worked to put all of himself inside her.

She gasped, and he saw how her face winced with the pain of violation, but never did she pull back, even a little. Instead, she clutched harder, hips undulating and finally slamming against him to meet his every thrust. Her expression of rapture, the sight of her kiss-swollen nipples and heaving breasts incited him all the more, and it was all he could do to keep from ripping into her with hard, jabbing thrusts to take himself to glory. But he maintained control, working rhythmically, not wanting her to hurt any more than she had to and determined that she would know the ultimate joy.

He felt the shuddering deep within her and knew her release was coming. Pumping his hips harder, he felt his own crescendo building.

She made soft, whimpering sounds that grew louder with each propelling thrust he made into her.

Her legs went wider, then closed to lock about him as her heels dug into him. She was attached, clinging, and they became one, rocking in rhythm, each lost in the magic of their passion . . . their lust . . . their ultimate climb to the pinnacle of fulfillment.

They clung to each other . . . quietly, reverently.

Ryder was the first to speak, tone worried. "Did I hurt you very much?"

She managed a choky little laugh. "Your beard did." She rubbed at her cheeks.

Ryder saw the redness on her face, as well as her
breasts. His whiskers had not been kind to the delicate flesh.

"I'm sorry," he mumbled, feeling bad because there
was nothing he could do about it. If he were to shave,
she might recognize him, and he could take no
chances, not when they had come so far.

It had stopped raining.

Ryder rolled to lie beside her, his arm about her as
he cradled her head against his shoulder.

Turning to gaze toward the strange light that fell
across the cave entrance, he said, almost wistfully,
"I've always loved twilight in this part of the country.
It doesn't last long, just a few magic minutes when
the world seems to turn purple and lavender, as the
light bleeds over everything before melting to
darkness.

"Beautiful," he said, turning to brush his lips across
her forehead. "Like you."

Kitty snuggled yet closer to him, weariness creeping
over her. "At least there was no storm. Just rain. And
now it's gone. We can start back early in the morning.
I'd like to get the map, buy our supplies, and get
started.

"Do you think my horse will be all right to ride by
then?" She raised to look at him, wanting to see his
dear and handsome face so near.

His eyes were closed.

His breathing was even.

She knew he slept, and she smiled.

A cool breeze blew over them. Kitty shivered and
sat up to button her blouse and pull her skirt down
over her bare legs.

She looked at Sam. He was completely naked and
would be cold, but she did not want to awaken him.

She had spotted some woven Indian blankets
stacked to one side and scrambled up to get one. The

warmth would be welcome for both of them against the night chill.

She began to spread it over him, desire washing over her to gaze upon his broad chest, strong shoulders and arms, and . . .

With a warm flush, her gaze moved downwards—

A gasp ripped through her.

Surely her eyes deceived her.

Quickly she moved closer for better scrutiny, pulse racing and heart thundering.

It had to be a play of light, she told herself, or a blemish. It could not be . . .

But it was.

On his lower abdomen was a scar, like a puncture wound . . . in the shape of a star and identical to the one she remembered seeing on Whitebear when she had bathed him.

Kitty began to shake from head to toe, and she moved back from him lest she wake him, and, dear Lord, she did not want him awake now.

She leaned into his face. It was hard to tell what he really looked like with a beard covering it, but now that she was looking for resemblance, she found it easily.

The dark hair. Dark eyes. The lines, muscles, of his body. The very shape of him.

Sam Bodine, she realized with fury roiling like water boiling in a kettle, was actually *Whitebear*.

# Chapter 18

Ryder awoke to find Kitty straddling him and holding a gun in his face.

"What the—"

He lifted his head but lowered it quickly as she pushed the gun barrel right under his nose.

"Make a move, and so help me, I will blow you away," she said with jaw set, teeth clenched.

He knew at once she was not playing some kind of game. Her eyes were so hot with anger he could feel the heat.

He swallowed hard. "Kitty, what the hell is going on?"

"You tell me—*Whitebear.*"

He sucked in his breath and let it out in a whoosh. "How did you find out?"

"Did you really think I wouldn't? Oh, you were good, all right. The beard had me fooled."

He kept his eye on her trigger finger and hoped she wasn't cold-blooded enough to actually shoot. "Kitty, I was going to tell you eventually."

She sneered. "Sure you were—after you had all the gold for yourself."

"I wasn't going to take more than half, which is my share."

"Oh, of course. That's why you were trying to find me in the first place, right? When you and the rest of those savages attacked the stagecoach looking for me, you only wanted to ask if you could help me look for the gold so we could share it.

"Do you take me for a complete fool?" Her voice rose as she waved the gun, then stuck it under his nose again.

"Kitty, be careful. It could go off."

"Which is what I want it to do, you arrogant bastard. You seduced me thinking that once we made love I'd give you anything you wanted. Of all the conceit—"

He dared to remind her, "I didn't seduce you, and you know it. You wanted it as much as I did. Besides, we had already made a deal before it happened."

"But all along it's what you were leading up to." Humiliation made her hand tremble. "I ought to blow your lying head off here and now."

His arms were to his sides, and he started to raise one in a pleading gesture, but she warned, "Don't try anything. I swear I'll shoot you. Damn it, when I think how you deceived me . . ."

"Put the gun down," he coaxed. "And let's talk. I can explain everything."

"I know all I need to know, *Whitebear*." She spat the name. "Or should I call you *Sam*? And by the way, which name would you prefer on your tombstone?"

"Sam Bodine is not my name. And I grew the beard not only to keep you from seeing some resemblance but also because I've worked as an army scout using my real name—Ryder McCloud. I was afraid I might run into soldiers that know me. So it was necessary to create a whole new identity to keep you from finding out who I was—changing my voice, the way I walk . . . everything.

"You should be able to understand that," he added, venturing a crooked smile to remind her of her own deception. "You did the same thing."

"And thank God I did," she fired back. "Otherwise I'd have been raped . . . tortured . . . scalped."

"That's not true. I would not have let that happen."

Her laugh was bitter. "And I was your slave, remember? I had to do your bidding, wait on you hand and foot like you were some kind of god, and sleep on the ground outside your tepee while you made love to all those girls, and . . ."

He quirked a brow, pretending shock. "You mean that's what this is all about? You were jealous of those girls? But if you'd let me know the truth about yourself, I'd much have preferred you, and— "

Her face turned even redder. "Why . . . why of all the nerve . . ."

It was all he needed—a split second of diversion as she sputtered with indignation.

Moving with lightning speed, before she knew what was happening, his hand struck like a rattlesnake to wrap around her wrist and jerk it to one side.

The gun went off in a deafening explosion.

"You could have killed me, you little vixen," he roared, wresting it from her to toss into the far shadows.

Swiftly he rolled her over to pin her arms over her head. "Now it's my turn to talk, goddamn it, and you are going to listen even if I have to gag and hogtie you."

"I hate you," she hissed, eyes glittering like a wolf at prey. "I never knew I could hate anybody so much. You were using me. All you ever wanted was the map. You were never my friend."

"I was your friend. I still am. Now more than ever, because of what we just shared." His gaze went to her heaving bosom, and he fought the impulse to attempt to silence her with his lips.

"You never cared about anything but the damn map," she repeated.

"That's not true."

"And now I feel so foolish."

"*You* feel foolish?" He laughed incredulously. "How do you think I look to my people? Whitebear, their leader, could not tell his slave was actually a woman."

"I was trying to survive, damn you, not trick you so I could steal your share of the gold. And besides, if you had found out who I was you'd have taken my piece of map and then killed me."

"No, I would not have," he said quietly, soberly. "My intention when I attacked the stage was to find you and keep you till I could scare you into handing it over, then let you go."

"Oh, I'm sure it was, but when I was clever enough to escape, and you discovered later how I'd tricked you, you set out to seduce me and persuade me to take you in as my partner so you could swindle me."

"Not necessarily in that order." He smiled, a slow, lazy, taunting smile that infuriated her all the more. "As I said, we already had a deal before you wound up in my arms. And as for your claiming to be *clever* enough to escape"—he paused to sneer— "my mother was responsible for your getting away, and you know it. Otherwise you'd still be there giving me a bath whenever I told you to.

"And, oh, what a shame I didn't know the truth then," he goaded. "Think what fun we'd have had in the bathtub together."

"Damn you," she repeated as she struggled against him.

"But your secret would have been discovered sooner or later. You know that. You were lucky my mother took pity on you before it was."

Suddenly curious, she asked, "When did you find out the truth?"

"I went into Tombstone as Ryder McCloud and

overheard a conversation between Opal Grimes and someone else about how the young woman she had been expecting from back east had been taken by Indians and how no one on the stage knew she was a woman, because she dressed and acted like a man.

"You even changed your voice," he said, grudgingly impressed at how cunning she had been.

"When I realized what you'd done," he continued, "when I realized Billy Mingo was actually you, I rode back to camp like the devil was on my heels, but by then my mother had already let you go."

"And how did you find me after that?"

"It wasn't hard, and it didn't take long. I knew you'd head to Tombstone and straight to Opal Grimes, because you didn't know anybody else or have anywhere else to go. I went to her shanty. She had moved, but I knew where she worked."

"And you had earlier paid her a visit as Whitebear and held a knife to her throat, hadn't you?"

"I didn't hurt her. I just wanted to scare her into telling me what she knew. That's how I found out she'd sent Parrish's half of the map to you. It was later I discovered where she'd hidden the telegram saying when you'd arrive, and then I made my plans to attack the stagecoach."

"So the night you shot the gun out of Roscoe's hand you were actually at the saloon to spy on me and leaped at the chance to rescue me so I'd be grateful and let you get close to me."

He gave her a gentle shake. "If I let you up, will you be still and listen?"

"To what? You've told your lies. I don't believe you. So go ahead and kill me, because I don't have the map with me, and I'm not going to give it to you.

"In fact," she cried with a fresh roll of anger, "If I have a chance, I'm going to burn it. I'd rather not find one nugget than have you get your dirty hands on it."

His own rage ebbing, Ryder stood, easily lifting her with him. Standing her on her feet, he gave her a shove away from him along with a disgusted glare. "How dare you think I have no right to my share, you haughty little brat? I'm as much entitled to that strike as you are. Maybe more so, because it was my *father,* not an *uncle,* who was partner with yours. That's thicker blood."

Tears sprang to her eyes as she said defensively, "Uncle Wade was like my father. I called him Daddy Wade . . ." Her voice faded as she thought how childish the term sounded now, in the wake of so much bitter frustration.

"But it doesn't matter," she said finally. "We're never going to find it. We couldn't have with just my half of the map, anyway."

"Probably not," he said soberly. Retrieving his clothes, he began to dress, keeping a wary eye on her to make sure she did not go for her other gun. "But I never intended to look with just your half."

She exploded once more. "That proves it. You *were* going to take it and then desert me. Oh, damn you to hell, Sam . . . Ryder . . . Whitebear"—she stamped her foot—"whatever you call yourself. You are a liar and a crook."

He stepped into his trousers and calmly buttoned the fly. "I am going to try to explain it all to you one more time. First of all, I don't have my father's half, but I've got a good idea where it is. Second, I am still willing to split whatever we find, but if the deal is off now that you know the truth, I'll take you back to Tombstone and forget the whole thing. It's all I can do, because I'm running out of time. I have to get my people across the Mexican border before winter, with or without any money to make a new start. Otherwise, they will either starve to death where they are or be caught by the soldiers and taken back to the reservation. And believe me," he grimly added, "they'd rather die than go back there."

"My plan at first," he admitted, "was to take your map, but I changed my mind after I got to know you."

She snorted, "Likely story."

"It's true. You'll just have to trust me."

"I do not trust you," she said solemnly. "And I never will. Not now."

He strapped on his holster and, without looking at her, said, "Then let's get you back to Tombstone. It's over."

She made ready to leave, but when she went to retrieve her own holster and weapons, Ryder was quick to snatch them away.

"I'll just hang onto these till we get back to town," he said drily. "I don't want to get a bullet in my back."

"It wouldn't be in the back. I still think I can out-draw you." She strode out of the cave to where the horses were tethered.

Ryder swung up into the saddle and held out his hand to her almost grudgingly. "You still can't ride that horse."

Petulantly, childishly, she said, "Well, I won't ride with you."

"Have it your way. You can walk." He kneed his horse to start him forward, pulling hers behind.

Kitty stumbled along as they moved through the high, pressing walls of the path. Again and again, she relived the time when she had been his captive and felt so foolish to think how, afterward, she had been so drawn to him.

She mused, also, over the past weeks and how her feelings for him as Sam Bodine had grown so deeply. There had been moments when she actually wondered whether she were falling in love with him. Then, too, she had to admit she had likewise been drawn to him as Whitebear. But now she was rocked to her toes with humiliation, which made it all the easier to despise him.

It was getting dark. She imagined all sorts of monsters hiding in the brush, ready to pounce on her.

Soon she could barely see him in front of her, could only hear the steady clicking of hoof beats against the rocks as they became more distant.

Finally, she could stand it no more. "I've changed my mind. I want to ride," she called into the dimness.

Reining to a stop, he waited for her, then swung her up to settle her in front of him in the saddle. He cursed himself for the tremor that rocked through him as his arms went about her. With thighs pressed against hers, he willed himself not to grow hard . . . not to let desire rise once more at her nearness.

Her hair brushed his cheek, and he sucked in his breath and fought for willpower to withstand the emotions she so easily evoked. *Dear God,* he prayed, *make the ride go fast so I can get her out of my sight, out of my life, because having her close, touching her, feeling her, is torture too great to bear.*

He wished she had not found out the truth so soon, but he had not thought about the scar, damn it . . . had not thought it made such an impression on her that she would have noticed it so easily. But it was too late to worry about it now. All he could do was get her as close to Tombstone as he dared, then ride away before she sounded an alarm and got a posse after her.

He also hated that he could never again cross the line from Indian to white as Ryder McCloud. She would tell about that, of course, but he had felt it necessary to confide everything in hopes she would somehow sense he was baring his soul and come nearer trusting him. He had gambled and lost, but wondered if it really made any difference. His days of pretending to be a white man were behind him, anyway, for his people would need him in their new home.

Kitty was also lost in needling thoughts and waging her own inner battle, for, despite her choler at his treachery, there was no denying that she had found splendor in his arms. He had shown her what it meant to be a woman, and she would always remember him for it, despite her anger.

As they rode slowly into the night, Kitty wondered how things would have been for them had they met under different circumstances. There was no denying that they had got on well when he had taken her on daily outings.

But it had only been an act, she bristled to remind herself, all a part of his scheme.

"Were you really tempted to shoot me?" he asked, sounding amused.

"I sure as hell was," she lied. "You caught me off guard before I had the chance."

He laughed softly. "I don't think so. I think you just wanted to vent your rage and then leave me stranded."

She was not about to admit that that had been her exact plan.

He continued with a snicker. "You'll get your revenge when you scream to high heaven the minute we hit town that Sam Bodine is actually Whitebear, the Apache. I'll be hung as fast as they can get a rope around my neck. No trial needed. They'll take the word of a lady any day.

"Especially," he added to goad, "when she's considered an *angel*."

"The billing as an angel was never my idea," she curtly informed him. "It was Wyatt Earp's, only it got old after a while. That's why I now have no job and no place to go . . . that, plus the fact I lost my audience because they all thought I only had eyes for you. And as for telling everyone who you really are, don't worry. That's the last thing I'd do, because I don't want anyone knowing I was stupid enough to be taken in by you for so long."

Ryder sensed that some of her animosity had subsided, and it was now her wounded pride that was fueling her hostility. Daring to think there might be a chance he could still sway her to cooperate, he tried a different ploy. "My mother couldn't believe she was stupid enough to be taken in by you, either. She feels real bad about it."

Kitty stiffened. "Your mother isn't stupid. And it has nothing to do with being stupid, anyway. Everyone thought of me as a boy. They had no reason to suspect otherwise.

"Tell her that," she added. "I don't want her to feel bad. She was good to me, and I'll never forget her."

"So you liked my mother."

"I certainly did."

"Then why won't you help me find the means to give her a new life in Mexico? You know she only wants to live in peace."

Kitty tried to twist in the saddle so she could look at him in order to convey her sincerity, but when her breast brushed his arm, igniting a delicious tremor, she drew back. "I would like to help her, but not if it means letting you make a fool of me—again—which you would do. I'd never see any of the gold, and you know it."

"I told you—you have my word. And Apaches don't give their word lightly. Besides, you're cutting off your nose to spite your face, because you've nothing to lose. You can't find the gold without me. You're just being stubborn, and you know it. You also have nowhere to go and nothing to do. You've lost your job, and you've got to give up your room and probably don't have much money put back."

Everything he said was true, but Kitty was still leery. "I don't think I can take the chance."

"So what else is there for you?"

She forced a shrug, wanting to seem unconcerned, when all the while desperation was churning inside like cream into butter. "Don't worry. I can take care of myself."

"Then to hell with you," he said, losing patience as they rounded a knoll and the lights of Tombstone came into view. "It's obvious you don't give a damn about anybody but yourself. Hell, you'd rather see my mother and all my people perish than take a chance that I just might be telling the truth, all because of your silly pride."

Kitty winced beneath his angry outburst. She did care about his mother. She was in her debt.

He yanked the reins so hard Kitty lurched forward, but he made no move to steady her. "You can walk the rest of the way. I'm not going to be around when you start screaming."

Before she realized what was happening, he had grabbed her and lowered her roughly to the ground.

"I told you I'm not going to tell anyone," she said, staring up at him even though she could barely make out his face in the scant moonlight.

"Well, maybe I don't trust you any more than you trust me." He tossed her the reins to her horse. "Take him to the livery stable. Tell them how he injured his leg. They'll know what to do for it."

"When I first got to Tombstone, I didn't tell where your camp is, and I could have, you know."

He tensed. "What are you talking about?"

"I had almost memorized the trail, anyway, before your mother took me down it, because you had taken me out with you when you went hunting, and then Coyotay and the other warriors took the women to harvest food. I could have described the way to the soldiers, and any scout worth his salt could have found it."

He snickered. "You couldn't have learned how to mark a trail that quick."

"I already knew how. Back home, I didn't have any friends, so I spent all my time when I wasn't doing chores exploring the mountains. I learned real young and real fast how to keep from getting lost. So I most certainly could have led the soldiers to your camp had I wanted to."

"But you didn't," he said in sudden wonder. "How come?"

"Because of your mother. She was good to me. She made me see that the Indians have their good side, too, so I certainly wasn't going to sic the cavalry on her or your people.

"Not even Coyotay," she added with a disgusted wrinkle of her nose.

Ryder had to laugh. "He's not so bad when you know him. He was just mad because you wounded his pride as well as him—especially when it was found out you were actually a woman. That made it all the worse—that he had let a woman best him.

"But thank you for not telling," he said, lifting the reins and making ready to ride. "However, I can't take any more chances with you. So I'd best be on my way. I'll drop your guns and holster not too far away so you can find them."

He paused to smile and add, "But it was good while it lasted. I'll never forget you."

Digging his heels into the horse's flanks, he set him into a fast gallop and rode away.

Kitty stared after him in the deepening night.

It was hard to grasp, this all-consuming knowledge that the strong and mighty warrior she had lusted for was the same man she had given her body to so willingly, so freely.

Blended, also, into the maelstrom that consumed like a deadwood fire, was the concession that he was right in saying she was only spiting herself to refuse his offer. After all, she had no other hope at the moment, and should he prove treacherous she would be on guard and ready to leap to her own defense.

And, perhaps most of all, she really had nothing to lose.

Except her heart.

She took a few running steps and called out to him, but the sound bounced back at her in the night wind.

He was gone.

And never had she felt more alone.

# Chapter 19

After quickly looking the horse over, the stable boy confirmed what Kitty, having experience with such injuries, already knew. "He'll be fine after he rests a spell." Then, because she looked so dreary, he added, "Things ain't as bad as they seem, Miss Parrish."

*No,* she thought dismally, *they're worse.*

Leaving the stable, Kitty pushed her way through the crowds gathered on the boardwalk running in front of the busy saloons and gambling halls. It was late on a Saturday night, and the streets were teeming with cowboys and prospectors out for a wild time.

With head held high, she ignored the leers and crude invitations from the rowdier bunch and quickened her pace. An unescorted lady on the street at such an hour was asking for trouble.

The sounds of gunfire sent her scrambling for cover inside a doorway along with half a dozen other people. She waited a few moments till it got quiet, then peered out to see a man sprawled in the mud and another standing over him with a smoking pistol.

People went their way, and so did Kitty.

It was just another rip-roaring night in Tombstone, Arizona, and suddenly Kitty felt hollow and empty inside. She longed for the peace and tranquility of the country. Living in a bustling town or city would never be her cup of tea.

But where, the emptiness inside her cried, did she belong? Where could she go and what could she do?

For the moment, however, she worried that turning down Ryder McCloud's offer was probably the biggest mistake she had ever made in her life. She could have put her foot down and said it would be strictly business. No intimacy. No lovemaking. Just put the map together, find the gold, divide it up, and go their separate ways. It might have worked. She might have been rich.

But maybe it was just as well. She could not trust him, or herself, either. Not after the glory she had found in his arms.

There was a larger than usual crowd at the Oriental, and as soon as Kitty pushed through the swinging doors she saw why.

A new singer was on stage. Dressed all in red and black, she had enormous breasts that were pouring out of the drastically low bodice of her gown. She had bright ruby-painted lips. Her cheeks flamed orange with rouge, and her eyelids shimmered with purple shadow.

Kitty paused inside the door to stare in astonishment as the woman flounced around the stage, hiking her ruffled skirt up to her waist to display long, black-stockinged legs and unbelievably high, thin heels on her red shoes.

She was singing a bawdy song, the lyrics suggestive to the point of being vulgar.

Kitty walked over to the bar for a quick glass of wine just as the woman spun around, bent forward, and flipped up her skirt to show her nearly bare bottom.

The men went wild, stamping their feet, clapping their hands, and cheering at the top of their lungs.

"The Singing Angel never provoked that kind of carrying on," she said grudgingly as Morton poured her wine. "They'll be shooting out the chandeliers before it's over."

"Naw, they won't," Morton said easily. "Mr. Earp makes everybody check their guns at the door now. I'm surprised you got in with yours." He nodded to her holster.

Kitty turned to see, and, sure enough, a man she had not noticed before was methodically taking weapons when armed men entered. "I suppose he didn't bother to look, figuring a woman wouldn't be wearing one."

"As for all the hollering and carrying on," Morton said, "Mr. Earp's decided maybe he's been running too quiet a place, so he hired Ramona, there, to pep things up."

"Well, she's doing a good job."

"Hate to see you go, Kitty, and also hate to be the one to pass along bad news."

She tensed. "Let's hear it."

"Mr. Earp said if I saw you before he did to tell you he wants you to clear out of your room by morning. Ramona needs it. She's new in town and don't have nowhere to go."

"I know the feeling," Kitty said under her breath, then, with a sigh, "I suppose I'll have to ask Opal if I can crowd in with her till I find something."

He was making wide circles on the bar with his polishing cloth and punctured her bubble of hope with a brisk shake of his head. "Nope, you can't. She's got to get out, too, on account of her brother. Mr. Earp heard about her letting Nate sleep off his drunk in her room last night and blew his stack. Says he's not having men bunk in with women even if they are kin. Of course, he's never had any use for Nate anyhow, and I think that's the main reason he told her to move."

"I'm sorry to hear that." Kitty took her wine and

turned toward the faro table to tell Opal how bad she felt for her.

"She ain't back there," Morton said.

"But she's usually working at this hour."

"Not anymore. She got mad and quit."

Kitty stared at him, aghast. "You don't mean it. She loved her job here, and she's the best caller in the house, and you know it."

He shrugged. "You'll get no argument from me there. From nobody else, either. But when it comes to her brother, Opal can get real huffy. Nate might be a rowdy son of a bitch sometimes, and Opal might get real mad and bust him over the head once in a while, but she won't put up with anybody else bad-mouthing him. So when Mr. Earp told her that he didn't want Nate coming around here, she told him where he could stick his faro game."

Kitty groaned.

Morton laughed. "Oh, don't worry. As good a caller as she is, she won't have no trouble finding another job."

"I still want to talk to her. The Oriental is probably the nicest place in town to work. Is she upstairs?"

"Nope. She and Nate have been gone most of the day trying to find someplace for her to stay. She said if they found anything she was getting the hell out of here tonight."

"I wish I could do the same." Kitty finished her wine and went upstairs, feeling as though the whole world was tumbling down around her. She could not even turn to Opal, because she had problems of her own . . . as well as a brother Kitty did not care to be around.

Again, she was plagued with remorse to think how foolish she had been to let her pride and anger turn Ryder away. They should have just used each other and then gone their separate ways. No one would have been hurt, and—

She had reached her room, opened the door, and her hand flew to her mouth to stifle a scream.

It was a shambles.

The mattress had been slashed to ribbons and the stirring of the air from the door opening sent a thick cloud of feathers flying.

She batted them away from her face to see that the chifforobe doors hung open. Her clothes were strewn everywhere and some of the gowns appeared to have been ripped apart.

Behind her, footsteps clattered on the stairs, and then Opal was calling, "Oh, you're back. I'm glad. I wanted to see you before I left to tell you where you could find me, and—" She saw Kitty's expression as she stared into her room. "What are you looking at? What's wrong?" Opal hurried to join her.

"A robber . . ."

It was all Kitty had time to say before Opal let out a scream that lifted all the way to the rafters, followed by her shrieking, "Oh, God, he's been here again. That savage has been here again, and he's going to kill you and me both over that goddamn map."

She grabbed Kitty by the front of her blouse and began to shake her as she pleaded wildly, "Give it to him. Give it to him before he kills us, please . . ."

Opal had turned hysterical in the blink of an eye. Kitty slapped her to get her to hush, then immediately wrapped her arms around her to comfort and apologize.

At the sound of people rushing upstairs to see what all the ruckus was about, Kitty quickly told Opal, "It wasn't him. I know it wasn't him."

Opal, sobbing wildly, slung her head from side to side as she tried to pull from Kitty's tight embrace. "It had to be him. Give it to him, Kitty. It's not worth dying for. Give it to him and be done with it, child. You've got to."

Kitty was tempted to tell her that it could not have been Whitebear, because she had been with him all day long. She held back, however, for two reasons— one, because Opal was too panicked to listen, and, two, because Kitty did not, despite everything, wish to betray him. Revealing he was actually a renegade Apache would be a death sentence.

"It wasn't him," she repeated.

The room was filling fast, just as it had the previous night after Nate had stumbled in, and she did not want anyone to overhear Opal's raving.

"It was the Apache," Opal insisted.

Morton shoved into the room, a big scowl on his face. "I swear, I'm starting to agree with Mr. Earp that you women are nothing but trouble. What's all the yelling about this time?"

"Somebody was just looking for something to steal," Kitty said lamely, staring at Opal with eyes pleading for her to keep her suspicions to herself.

Morton glanced about and gave a low whistle before saying, "Well, Mr. Earp should have hired somebody to take Ben's place on the landing. I can't keep an eye on the bar and up here, too, especially on a Saturday night."

Opal began to calm down a bit but urged Kitty, "Come with me. Pack your things and come with me tonight. I found a place. It's not much, just another shanty, but there's room for you."

"What about Nate?" Kitty asked.

"Oh, he's not going to be around for long. He never is. He's just waiting now for Roscoe to get out of jail. Since he didn't kill Ben when he shot him, he's only doing thirty days. They'll ride out when he's free. So I'll help you clean up this mess, and then we'll both get the hell out of here.

"Nate's real sorry, by the way," Opal rushed to add. "He's just had too much to drink. He didn't mean no harm. Just like I didn't mean any when I bashed him over the head. He gets drunk and doesn't know what he's doing, and I've had to hit him before to stop him from going too far and probably will, again, but he's the only kin I got, and I have to look out for him."

*Your kin,* Kitty sullenly thought. *Not mine. And I can't be as understanding or tolerant.*

"We'll talk about it tomorrow." Kitty gently ushered her toward the door. "I need some time alone to think."

Morton started herding everyone out and advised Kitty, "Lock your door. I'll send word to the marshal to have someone come up and look around and see if anything is missing from the other rooms."

"I still think it was that Apache," Opal said as she left.

Kitty moaned to hear Morton say, as he walked Opal on down the hall to her room, "Now, why would that Apache come back, Opal? That's nonsense."

She prayed he would continue to think so . . . and that Opal would remember how they had agreed to keep it all between them.

After a near sleepless night, Kitty awoke feeling as though she had not even been to bed. A quick bath and change of clothes and she was ready to set out to find both job and place to stay.

A few hours later, however, she felt defeated and frustrated.

No store would hire her. There were either no openings, or it was as Wyatt Earp had predicted—owners' wives did not like the idea of a young, unmarried woman working for their husbands.

Neither could she find a decent place to stay. Not even a shanty. There were tents available for three dollars a night, but at that rate Kitty would soon be broke. And she did not want to stay in a tent, anyway, knowing she would be taken for a whore. So many operated out of the flimsy canvas structures.

When she arrived back at the Oriental late in the day, Morton again regretted having a message for her from owner Wyatt Earp.

"He says he'll give you today, and that's it. If you aren't out by morning, I'm to take your things and set them on the street. And you, too, if you refuse to leave. He got real mad when he heard about your room getting torn up last night, says you're some kind of a jinx and there's been nothing but trouble around here since you came."

"There's always trouble in Tombstone."

"Well, not *Injun* trouble."

Kitty forced a laugh. "Is Opal still carrying on about that? I swear, I don't think she will ever get over being scared out of her wits by an Indian who just happened to pick her shanty to break into. She's going to see Indians in every shadow the rest of her life, I'm afraid."

"She says it was him, all right, that he's looking for a piece of a map to Wade Parrish's gold strike that she gave to you."

Kitty had to speak around the sudden choking knot in her throat. "That . . . that's ridiculous."

"Well, she should know. She says he's the half-breed son of Wade's partner, Dan McCloud, and he wants your piece of map to go with his daddy's so he can find the gold."

Kitty ground her teeth together. Everyone in town would soon know, including whoever had killed her uncle and Dan McCloud. They might not stop to think her piece of map by itself would not lead them to the strike. After all, anyone who would torture and mur-

der could not be thinking rationally, anyway, which
meant she could be targeted for death, too.

"So you can see why Mr. Earp wants you out of
here," Morton went on to say. "He don't want Injuns
sneaking around. Somebody could wind up getting
killed.

"And you want to hear something interesting?" he
went on to ask with brows raised. "Some of the soldiers that Opal talked to—"

"Soldiers?" Kitty cried in horror. "What was she
doing talking to soldiers about all this?"

"Oh, they just happened to be having a drink at the
bar when she stopped by to tell me she had got everything out of her room. One of them had heard something about a robbery here last night and said he
reckoned she was glad to be moving, and she told him
she sure as hell was but only hoped the damned Injun
didn't follow her to her next place. That started questions, and you know Opal. She answered them.

"Anyway," he went on, "when she told them the
Injun was McCloud's half-breed, they said they knew
of a scout by that name and wondered if it was him.
You can bet they'll find out, too, 'cause they sure as
hell didn't like the idea of a half-breed pretending to
be white and working as a scout, and—"

Kitty had heard all she could stand.

Abruptly turning about, she walked back out of the
saloon and straight to the bank where she had depos-
ited her meager savings. Withdrawing it all, she proceeded to the nearest dry goods store. She was
wearing a nice blue gingham dress with lots of ruffles
and lace. She even had on a ribboned bonnet, which
she hated, much preferring the kind of felt hat cowboys wore. And her feet hurt terribly, because the
high-buttoned ladies' heels were so uncomfortable.
But she had wanted to look nice—*ladylike*—while

seeking a job and a room. That was, however, now behind her.

She selected a cotton shirt, denim trousers, suede vest, felt hat, and leather boots, and changed right in the store, abandoning the clothing she took off.

She also bought a rifle, ammunition for it as well as for her pistols, and a blanket, saddle, and bridle.

A canteen and a sack containing dried bacon, beans, and hardtack completed her purchases.

Proceeding to the livery stable, she was able to buy a fairly good horse with the rest of her money.

And then she was ready to go . . . ready to prove her boast to Ryder that she could track and find the Apache camp. Then she would tell him she had decided to accept his offer only because she was desperate.

In addition, she wanted to warn him that, thanks to Opal, he could no longer pose as a white scout. For reasons she did not like thinking about, Kitty could not allow Ryder to believe she had betrayed him.

"I'll need to stay the night here," she told the stable boy.

His eyes went wide. "I don't know about that, lady."

She glanced up at the hayloft. "I'll be fine up there and gone before first light. I've a long ride ahead of me."

"The boss might not like it," he argued, "you bein' a woman and all. We get old drunk bums sleeping around here sometimes, but never no woman . . . no *lady.*"

"I won't be any trouble," she said over his protests. "You won't even know I've been here."

He walked on out, shaking his head, and Kitty was almost up the ladder when she froze at the sound of an unfamiliar voice calling her name. Turning, she nearly fell to see Nate Grimes looking up at her, a big grin on his face.

"What . . . what do you want?" she asked nervously, wondering how she could go for her guns when she was clinging to the ladder.

"I need to talk to you."

He sounded pleasant, certainly not threatening.

"Don't mean you no harm, Kitty, and I want to apologize for scarin' you the other night."

"I . . . It's all right," she said uneasily. "You don't need to apologize." She began to back down the ladder. "How did you know where to find me?"

"I followed you," he said simply. "Saw you walking down the street carryin' all your stuff and figured you was gettin' ready to leave town, and I didn't want you to go before I had a chance to say I'm sorry about what I did and to tell you about my proposition."

"What kind of proposition?"

"I can find your uncle's gold. I know the land around here pretty good, and I might just be able to find it even with just half the map."

She dropped the last few feet to the ground, dusted her hands, then lowered them to her side, near her guns, just in case. Nate Grimes was a fierce-looking man, with cold, beady eyes like a lizard and a mouth that could probably bite the head off one. He was big, too, with brawny shoulders and a wide chest and a huge belly hanging over his gun belt.

"How did you know about the map?" She knew but wanted to hear what he would say.

"Opal told me this morning. She told me about last night, too, and how she's scared if you don't hand the map she sent you over to that Injun he's going to wind up killing both of you. Made me mad she didn't tell me before," he said with a shake of his beefy fist. "I would've made sure he never got near either one of you again."

"Well, it wasn't him," Kitty said uneasily. Even though she wasn't about to vouch for Ryder's whereabouts all of yesterday and how he couldn't have done it, she wanted to dispel the belief that he had as much as possible.

Nate argued, "It couldn't have been anybody else. None of the other rooms was touched. Just yours."

"And how would he have known which was mine?"

"He's probably been watching every move you make. Maybe he dresses like a white man. Opal says he's the half-breed son of Dan McCloud."

Opal, Kitty angrily decided, had a very big mouth. "I still say it wasn't him."

"Well, whether it was or wasn't ain't got nothing to do with my offer to try and find that gold for you. Everybody swore the two of 'em—McCloud and your uncle—made a big strike. It's just a shame they were so stubborn they gave their lives for it. So you just hand that map over to me, and I'll do my dangdest to find it for you."

The last thing Kitty wanted was to be involved with Nate. "I really don't need your help, but thank you for offering."

His lips twisted, as though he were fighting anger. "You ain't gonna give up, are you?"

She was not about to tell him her plans. "I haven't decided."

"There's no need to just throw the map away, you know."

"I wasn't going to."

"Then why not let me look? What have you got to lose?"

"I'll let you know if I change my mind."

"Well, don't say I didn't offer."

"Thanks again," she said in finality.

Kitty waited till he was gone before going back up the ladder. She was glad to be leaving Tombstone, glad not to have to be around the likes of Nate Grimes, but the next time she saw Opal, by God, she was going to tell her what she thought of her for failing to keep her promise.

Settling down in the hay, she willed herself to sleep quickly so the morning would hurry and come and she could be on her way to try and find Ryder.

She would not let herself think of the possibility she might not be able to . . . or that she might encounter danger along the way.

Clean-shaven, bare-chested, and wearing only a breechclout, Ryder was once again Whitebear as he settled on the bearskin on the floor of his tent.

His mother had been glad to see him—until he told her all hope of finding the gold strike was lost. Without the whole map, it would be a waste of time to look for it.

She had looked at him with a face as forlorn as a lost calf's and asked, "Did you try everything, my son?"

He said he had.

"Did you try to frighten her as you did Wade Parrish's woman?"

He explained how that tactic would not work with Kitty. She was too strong and too stubborn.

Next, his mother asked, "Then did you appeal to her as a man to a woman—gently . . . lovingly?"

Without revealing intimate details, he had assured he had done everything humanly possible, short of beating it out of her.

His mother had hung her head and sadly murmured, "I would not want you to do that. So it is truly over. We must go on without the gold."

Ryder had had a long talk with Coyotay and given orders that he was to have everyone ready to move out in a few days. They would make their way to

Mexico, destitute except for the provisions they already had, and hope for the best.

Word had spread through the camp, and everyone was heavy-hearted.

He lay on his back, arms folded behind his head, staring up into the darkness. Sleep would be a long time coming, if at all, as he pondered what the future held. It would be a bleak, hard time in Mexico, especially through the winter. His people would have to change their ways to survive. It would be a new life, new things to be learned, and he would do his best to teach them and encourage them to endure.

A surge of fury rolled over him, and he found himself clenching his teeth and his fists simultaneously.

Damn Kitty Parrish for being so obstinate and unforgiving.

And damn himself for being so stupid as to forget about the scar near his groin and not thinking how she would have seen it when she bathed him. Yet, despite his anger, he was able to smile at how embarrassing it had to have been for her. It was a wonder she had not given herself away and gone running out of the tent.

Suddenly he was struck to think how she had not run out of the cave, either. When he had been unable to conceal his desire for her any longer, she had yielded.

And it had been wonderful.

So wonderful, in fact, that he had allowed himself to ponder whether feelings other than merely lust could be growing between them.

*Ryder, you are a fool.* He grimaced, jaw going tight and aching with the force.

He meant nothing to her and never would, and he was best rid of her, because he could not allow her ever to mean anything to him, either.

Rolling over on his stomach, he pounded the rabbit

fur pillow his mother had made for his head. His father had liked a pillow, she'd said, so Ryder had
learned to enjoy one also.

He was almost asleep when the sound of someone
crawling under the back wall of the tent jolted him
to alertness.

A few seconds later he felt Adeeta curling against
his back, her hands dancing around to trail down his
chest, dropping lower.

He caught her wrist and held it. "Not tonight," he
said, trying to make his voice kind when inside he felt
grumpy as a bear bothered in his den.

"But—"

"I am tired," he said, turning over to give her a
quick hug before pushing her away. He did not want
to hurt her feelings, but the truth was he had no desire
for her, no desire for any woman except Kitty. He
knew he would have to get over that . . . knew that
eventually he would, but for the time being that was
how it was, and he could only, without explanation,
offer apology. "I'm sorry."

She left him, and he knew despite his best effort
she was hurt.

He could not help it, but damn it, how he wished
he could.

# Chapter 20

Kitty pulled her hat a little lower on her forehead against the relentless sun. Since leaving Tombstone the previous morning, she had finally reached the place where she had met the stage after Pale Sky set her free. She had moved slowly, not wanting to wear out her horse in the smothering heat.

Pausing, she shaded her weary eyes to look around at the rocky ground and sparse vegetation. She was exhausted, because she had been unable to sleep when she bedded down the night before not too far from the San Pedro River. The scream of bobcats and the howling of coyotes amid the inky blackness had set her nerves on edge, and she had stayed awake with gun ready.

Now she was nettled to be having second thoughts about her decision to find Ryder. She now wondered if it were such a good idea, born of desperation, after all, and whether she should have accepted Nate Grimes's offer instead. True, he was a drunk and a rowdy, but Opal would have kept him in line. Now Kitty wished she had at least talked to Opal about his proposition, but she figured Opal was still so terrified, believing Whitebear had returned, that she would have said to surrender the map to anybody to be rid of it, regardless of the consequences.

So perhaps she was doing the right thing after all, she decided, *if* she could find the camp.

She felt a ripple of fear, wondering whether she might have been overly confident. Tracking back in Virginia was not the same as here, in such near-barren country where the scenery could become monotonous in its similarity. Like cactus. For the most part, she had decided, all cactus looked alike, unless she took the time to differentiate in height and width. She had, however, set in her mind the saguaro cactus at the exact point where she and Pale Sky had come down off the mountain. It had two arms jutting to the left, toward the eastern horizon, and one to the west. Taller than Kitty by three heads, it was distinctive and she was sure she would know it when she saw it.

She gave the horse a pat on his neck. "Well, boy, this is it. We turn from the road to Willcox and head into real Indian territory."

She reached into her saddlebag and took out the piece of white cloth she had purchased at the dry goods store. Wrapping it around the end of her rifle, she held it up as she headed straight into the wilderness. She had overheard a prospector in the saloon one night telling how that was what he did when he passed through Indian territory. The Indians took it as a sign of truce . . . peace . . . and those that knew him would allow him to pass. Others would stop him, but had always let him go after understanding what he was doing there and how he meant them no harm.

Kitty would not allow herself to think of the consequences if the flag did not work.

She was hungry and reached into the saddlebag once more and took out a piece of beef jerky. She ate it, then washed it down with water from her near-empty canteen.

She patted the horse again and spoke out loud. She had got in the habit of doing that during the long, lonely hours of plodding along slowly with no one to talk to. "Don't worry. I remember there was a watering hole not too far from here. I was on foot then, and so thirsty I thought I'd die, and when I saw the water, I threw myself down and drank till I nearly popped. I won't let you do that, though. Drinking too much in this heat could kill you, fellow.

"I miss taking care of horses," she went on, slumping a bit in the saddle from weariness. Still she tried to be alert to holes the horse might stumble into, rattlesnakes that might make him shy and rear up to dump her to the ground, and, yes, for Indians, as well.

"One of these days I'm going to live on a ranch again. Surely there's somebody, somewhere, who will give me a chance to prove that even if I am a woman, I can handle a horse as good as a man, and—"

The arrow whizzed so close to her face she felt the heat and wind of it.

At the same time, a scream split the air, and Kitty whipped her head about to see the Indians on horseback, bearing down on her from behind a clump of boulders to her rear.

"Go!" She dug her heels into the horse's flanks to set him in a fast gallop for yet another cluster of rocks directly ahead.

Another arrow sailed by her, and she held the reins in one hand while holding the rifle aloft with her other to wave the white flag she could only hope they had not seen before.

Reaching the rocks, Kitty leaped from the saddle and threw herself, belly down, against a rock and pointed the rifle over it.

The Indians were still shrieking, and the arrows were still flying.

She waved the flag frantically.

The sounds died down.

And the arrows stopped coming.

With pounding heart, Kitty dared raise up and peer over the rock as she continued to hold the flag. There

were perhaps twenty of them, strung out on horseback, some holding war clubs, the others with bows
and arrows ready as they glared at her.

Kitty knew the same heart-stopping terror as when
the stage had been attacked. "I want to speak to
Whitebear," she yelled, hoping his name would make
an impression.

Her voice rang loudly, clearly, in the stillness of the
hot, desert day.

She saw how the Indians exchanged curious, incredulous glances. Probably they spoke little English, if
any at all, and suddenly she wondered in a rush of
panic whether they were even Apache . . . Chiricahua.
There were other tribes in the region, she had been
told, and if she had encountered any of them, she was
in serious trouble.

"Whitebear," she called again, voice wavering this
time as fear rocked her from head to toe. "Your
leader. Your chief—Whitebear. I must speak to him."

"Whitebear is not chief."

With a gut-wrenching gasp, Kitty rolled to the side,
back pressed against the wall. An Indian was standing
on top of the rock directly behind her holding a feathered tomahawk over his head in menace.

Kitty blinked against a flash of terror to finally focus
her eyes and, with yet another twisting wrench, saw
that it was Coyotay towering above her.

She tried to speak his name but no sound would
squeak from her tightly constricting throat.

He leaped from the rock to land flat-footed right in
front of her.

"Whitebear is not chief," he repeated.

Reason began to surface amid the terror boiling
within Kitty as she grasped that he spoke some English, then remembered from her days of captivity that
there had been times when he had muttered phrases
at her that she comprehended—phrases that had

chilled the marrow of her bones as he called her names and made threats of torture and maiming.

Coyotay did not, of course, recognize her, and it was with trepidation making her skin crawl that Kitty finally forced his name from trembling lips. "Coyotay."

Stunned, he took a step backward.

"You are Coyotay," she said softly. "I am a friend of Whitebear. You must take me to him."

She saw how his jaw tightened with confusion and indecision.

"Coyotay," she repeated, arms splayed over her head as she pressed back against the wall. She wished she dared attempt to draw her guns. Then she could keep him at bay while she tried to make him understand. But he continued to hold the ominous weapon above his head, and she knew that if she made any attempt at all to go for her pistol, he would bring the sharp club down to split her skull.

He worked his lips soundlessly for a moment, then said, "Name. You know Coyotay's name. How is this?"

Good, she thought feverishly. He knew enough English to communicate . . . if she was careful. "It does not matter how I know Coyotay. Coyotay must take me to Whitebear."

The other Indians began to appear, and Kitty looked at each vicious, threatening face and knew she had to make herself understood fast. "I am Kitty Parrish," she said in a rush. "The woman you thought a boy—Billy Mingo. You took me captive, and— "

"Aieeee . . ." Coyotay, his face suddenly twisted in rage, lunged for her, grabbing her about her throat with one hand while holding the tomahawk with his other as he held it above her in threat.

Kitty also screamed, sure he was going to kill her. She tried to draw, but one of the other Indians lunged to rip her holster from her, babbling all the while in his Apache tongue.

All of them began to talk at once, it seemed, loudly, angrily, and all the while Coyotay held her pinned down, as he seemed to wage an inner war over whether to slice her head open with the tomahawk and be done with it.

Finally, an older Apache appeared and seemed to have a calming effect on Coyotay as he caught his arm to lower it, speaking to him in firm tones.

Coyotay made growling noises of protest but finally let her go. He continued, however, to glower at her so intensely that she imagined she could actually feel his hatred for her.

The other warrior continued to talk to him—arguing, it seemed to Kitty.

She held her breath, sensing that her fate depended on the outcome of the debate.

At last, they seemed to come to some kind of agreement, nodding to each other, and she dared hope it was in her favor.

But hope became a fleeting thing as Coyotay, with another bloodcurdling shriek, lunged for her, hands going about her throat to squeeze tightly.

Kitty, legs kicking as she struggled to breathe, was lifted up off the rock as easily as though she were nothing more than the pitiful little white rag still fluttering from her rifle in the late-day breeze.

And the last thing she saw before losing consciousness was Coyotay's lips curled back from his teeth as he shook the last breath from her lungs.


Ryder was going over the map he had made on his last trip to Mexico when he heard the commotion outside and frowned to have his thoughts intruded upon. It was important that he plan exactly how he would lead his people to try and keep them out of sight, and he had much planning to do. That was why he had not gone with Coyotay and the others to hunt.

He tried to ignore the shouts and cries, assuming they had found plenty of game to clean and dry for food on the journey. Good. They would need it. But for the moment, he needed peace and quiet to look at all his notes and markings.

The covering to his tent swished open, and Adeeta poked her head inside. "Whitebear, you must come and see what Coyotay has—"

"Not now," he said irritably without glancing up. "I've told everyone I do not want to be bothered."

"But Coyotay has—"

"Not now," he repeated, loud and forceful.

The flap slapped shut.

He shook his head and wondered if any of them realized how serious the situation truly was. There was so much to do in preparation for the journey, most of which involved having enough food, not only as they traveled but also to do them until they could find more at their destination.

Which, he sighed to think, meant he had to hurry up and plan the way and wished everyone would leave him alone.

He also wished he had a clear head to think . . . wished, by damn, that thoughts of Kitty Parrish would go away.

Settling back and lighting one of the few white man's cheroots he had left, he admonished himself for allowing her to creep into his mind again.

Maybe he should have tried harder to convince her to keep their bargain. After all, she was just angry for having been deceived. It made no difference that she had made him feel foolish with her own deception. To Kitty, her situation had been a matter of life or death while his had been solely to trick her into giving up her uncle's map.

But to hell with her, he swore under his breath, and to hell with the gold. He and his people would survive somehow, although it would have been a damn sight easier had they had money to do so. And besides, it really rankled him to think that somewhere his father's gold lay hidden and maybe always would be . . . unless the murderer figured out where it was.

Reminding himself he had no time to dwell on the past, Ryder gripped the cheroot between his teeth and forced his attention back to his drawings.

The noise outside was louder, and he wondered about so much laughter, but figured everyone was in a jovial mood, which was good. The trek south would be hard, because he intended to penetrate deep into Mexico, so let them enjoy themselves while they could.

"My son."

He looked up sharply at the sound of his mother's voice, at the same instant she tore back the opening to rush into the tent.

"You must come at once."

He cursed inwardly and tossed the papers aside with an exasperated sigh. "What is it?"

"It is Coyotay—"

"I know, I know. He's back from hunting, but I don't care. I have work to do, and—"

"But—"

"But no one understands that I don't want to be disturbed."

Pale Sky lost patience and began to wave her arms frantically. "You must listen, my son, and you must come at once. Coyotay has brought a white captive."

Ryder bolted up, tossing the cheroot to the ground and stomping on it. "The last thing we need is a captive. The soldiers will be swarming all over these mountains again. Has he lost his mind?"

"Worse," she said coldly. "He has brought a woman."

Ryder stared at her in disbelief.

Pale Sky hesitated as though gathering her wits to concede that it could really be true, then solemnly informed him, "Coyotay's captive is the woman we knew as the boy slave, Billy Mingo."

Ryder was out of the tent in a flash, his mother right behind him.

He could not see Kitty for the crowd gathered around her. A few of the warriors were still on horseback, watching in amusement.

Ryder wasted no time pushing his way through, and everyone got out of his way as soon as they saw him and heard his angry curses.

Kitty lay on her back where Coyotay had dropped her, and she was staring about in terror.

He reached to take her hand and pull her to her feet. "What the hell are you doing here?"

"Oh, thank God, it's you," she cried, recognizing him.

The Indians had become silent and stood watching, listening, though most could not understand what was being said.

Despite her predicament and the fact that her throat still ached from how Coyotay had almost crushed it with his bare hands before someone had mercifully torn him away from her, Kitty managed a nervous smile. "I told you I could find the camp."

Ryder fought to keep from laughing. "Looks like you've found yourself a captive again instead."

She began to run her hands up and down her arms as she glanced about at the hostile eyes surrounding her. "Actually, I ran into some of your pals before I got to the camp."

"It was inevitable that you would. Did you really think you could just ride right in?"

"I was waving a white flag," she said, annoyed that it had been ignored.

"That doesn't always work. But you still haven't told me why you're here."

"I came—"

Coyotay suddenly interrupted. "She came because she remembered the way to us, which means she cannot be allowed to leave. This time she must die."

He had spoken her language, so his threat was quite clear to Kitty, who instantly beseeched Ryder, "Tell him he and the others have nothing to fear from me."

"I will later. Right now you and I need to talk in private."

He took her arm and began to steer her away from the crowd, but just then Kitty recognized Pale Sky and cried, "Pale Sky, I'm happy to see you. I've thought of you so often, and . . ." She fell silent as Pale Sky turned her back and walked away.

Ryder began pulling her along again.

Kitty turned her head to stare after Pale Sky. "Why is she angry with me?"

"She knows everyone blames her for letting you go in the first place, and now they'll be upset all over again because you were able to find your way back."

"But I never meant—"

"Well, what do you mean?" They had reached his tent, and he pushed her inside. Grasping her shoulders, he spun her around. "I'm asking you again—what the hell are you doing here? Don't you know you could have been killed?"

"I had to see you . . . had to tell you that you can't go into Tombstone as Ryder McCloud anymore."

Fury was a spider, creeping over his face. "So you did run to the law and tell them how I'd been passing for white."

"No. You have to let me explain. It was Opal. Someone broke into my room that last day you and I

were out riding, and she thought it was you—
Whitebear. She was terrified and started talking, telling everyone how you and I had figured out it was
Dan McCloud's half-breed son who broke in on her
in the first place. She even talked to some soldiers
who remembered a scout by the name of McCloud,
and—"

"Damn it to hell." He released her to curl his hands
into fists and slam them together. "You told me the
two of you had agreed not to talk about your
suspicions."

"We did. But like I said, she thought you were the
one who tore up my room, because you still want the
map, and she says if I don't give it to you, you'll kill
both of us. She just got so upset she started talking
to anyone who would listen."

"So who did search your room?"

"I don't know. A random robber, I suppose."

Ryder steepled his fingers as he stood with legs wide
apart, considering everything.

Kitty chided herself for feeling a rush as her eyes
flicked over his bare chest and well-formed buttocks
in the tight breechclout. Memories assaulted her, of
how he had held her and kissed her, and she shook
them away, forcing herself back to the issue at hand.
"I wanted to find you to let you know it isn't safe for
you back there, and, also"—she sucked in her breath
and held it as she offered a quick prayer that she was
not making a mistake—"to tell you I've changed my
mind. I want us to work together, and I'll share fifty-
fifty whatever we find."

A slow grin spread across his face. "That's real generous of you."

She did not like the insolence in his voice. "But we
need to get a few things settled first. I have a few
conditions I want you to agree to."

"Before you have your say, I want to know what made you change your mind."

"Finding out I really have no choice," she said with candor. "I figure I have nothing to lose."

"All right. Let's hear your conditions."

"I have two. First, you have to let me copy your father's half of the map so you can't run off with it and mine, too."

"Fair enough. What's your second condition?"

Kitty glanced away, unable to look at him as she said, "It has to be business. *All* business," she emphasized.

He bit back a smile, knowing what she meant but not about to let her off so easily. "I don't know what you're talking about."

She looked at him then, forcing herself to meet his mocking gaze. "I'm talking about what happened in the cave. It was a mistake. It cannot happen again."

He spread his hands in a helpless gesture. "I didn't force you then, so I doubt I'd try to force you next time, either."

Kitty stiffened, furious with herself over how, despite his arrogance, she was moved by the nearness of him.

"There will not," she said tightly, harshly, "be a next time."

"As you wish . . . ," he whispered, still smiling. "As you wish."

# Chapter 21

"I'm so sorry I couldn't let you know the truth," Kitty said to Pale Sky with all sincerity.

They were seated in Pale Sky's wickiup. It had taken much persuasion on Ryder's part to arrange the meeting, but he had finally succeeded.

"Please believe me," Kitty went on, fighting the impulse to reach out and take Pale Sky's hands in hers but knowing she would not allow it. "I felt I'd be safer pretending to be a boy on the way out here, and after I was taken captive I knew it was more important than ever that I keep up the ruse."

Pale Sky continued to sit in rigid silence.

"I know you probably wouldn't have let me go if I had told you my secret, and you've been embarrassed over having helped me, but you probably saved my life."

Pale Sky coldly said, "No. I would not have let you go. And, yes, I know I saved your life. Had Coyotay known it was a woman who had wounded him nothing could have stopped him from killing you. Not even my son."

"I know that, and I'm truly grateful and couldn't leave here without telling you so."

Pale Sky continued to regard her with cool suspicion. "My son tells me the two of you have made an agreement to look for my husband's gold."

"Your husband's and my uncle's," Kitty gently amended.

Pale Sky softened. "Then I am grateful to you, for if he finds it, my people will not go hungry in our new home. But I think it is wise for the two of you to leave right away. Do not stay here. It is not safe."

Kitty was baffled. "But Ryder—I mean *Whitebear,* as you call him—said he would tell the others of our agreement so they would understand and not hurt me. He wanted us to wait till morning to leave, so I could eat and rest.

"He said I could sleep outside your wickiup again," she added with a little smile.

"You would still be in danger. It is best you go. I will make food for you to eat on the way." She got up and began moving about her stove.

"But Whitebear said—"

Pale Sky looked at her with mischief in her eyes. "My son cannot control some things . . . like the jealousy of one who loves him."

"I don't understand."

"Do you not remember the nights you spent outside his tent? Do you not remember how the girl, Adeeta, slipped inside to lie with him?"

"Yes, but—"

"She is jealous of you."

Kitty argued, "But she has no reason to be."

"Perhaps she does not think so."

"Well, she is wrong." Kitty knew she had been nothing more than a passing moment of pleasure to Ryder. And she was trying hard to convince herself that all she felt for him was sentimentality, because he was the first man she had ever been with.

"Perhaps."

Kitty stared at Pale Sky. Was it her imagination or was she being flippant? Surely she did not think there was anything between her and Ryder, but Kitty was

not about to ask. "I suppose it's best we do go ahead
and leave then. I don't need more trouble."

"And you might have it if you stay the night. I saw
the look on Adeeta's face when you were walking with
my son a short while ago, and her eyes had the look
of a snake about to strike. She would do you harm if
given the chance. So go. And hurry with your quest,
for we must be leaving this camp before many
moons pass."

Kitty stood and started to leave, then hesitated before saying, "I want you to know that I've done what
you asked me to. Whenever I have a chance, I spread
your message."

Pale Sky nodded, but sadly. "And it does no good,
does it, my child? It never does. They do not listen."

"But I'll keep on trying. You have to know that."
Kitty yielded to impulse and rushed to throw her arms
around her. "I'll never forget you or your people,
Pale Sky."

"Go, my child." She pulled away, embarrassed by
the display of affection. "And help my son find that
which belongs to both of you."

Ryder placed his saddle on the ground and unrolled
a blanket. After leaving the camp late in the day, they
had ridden till well into dark, for he knew the way.
Then he had said they should bed down for the night
and get an early morning start in order to arrive in
Tombstone by mid-afternoon.

Kitty had spoken only when necessary as they rode.
He had made little attempt at conversation himself.
She was right. It was best that everything be strictly
business between them. They had enjoyed each other
once. That was enough. Anything else could compli-
cate their work . . . as well as the future. And she
played no part in his future, despite the memory of
how good it had felt to make love to her.

She was just a woman, he told himself over and
over. One of many he'd had, and one of many he
would enjoy in the years ahead, for he had no plans
to marry any time soon.

Adeeta had come to him as he was saddling his
horse and making ready to leave. She was angry that
he was leaving with a woman. He had told her she
had no reason to be, nor was it her right, that he had
never promised her anything. She had stalked away
mad. He did not care. When the time came for him
to marry, it would be to one of his own kind, but he
would do the choosing, regardless of custom.

"There's no need for a fire," he said as he settled
down with the tortillas and dried deer meat his mother
had packed for them. "It's a warm night, and we have
food. I don't think the coyotes will bother us, either."

He held the bag out to her and was surprised when
she helped herself. "I didn't think you liked Indian
food."

"I like your mother's tortillas."

"She is a good cook," he acknowledged, pleased,
then said, "I want you to know I'm glad you had that
talk with her. She feels better knowing you didn't just
use her to escape. Your changing your mind and
agreeing to work with me won her over."

Kitty made her own bed as far away from Ryder as
she could get without leaving the surrounding shelter
of rocks.

Ryder could barely make her out in the darkness.
She was determined to be as impersonal as possible,
but there was something he had to settle and then she
could ignore him all she wanted.

"Where is your half of the map, Kitty?"

He sensed her immediate tension as she responded,
"In a safe place."

"I'll need it as soon as we get to Tombstone."

She was bending over and scooping small stones out

of the way so she would not roll on them in the night, but at once straightened and turned to crisply remind him, "That was one of my conditions, remember? I get to copy your half before you see mine."

"Sorry, but it can't be that way."

"What are you talking about?" She walked over to him to stand with hands on her hips. "You agreed."

"I've decided otherwise."

"That isn't fair."

"Maybe not, but that's how it is, Kitty. I have to be sure you've got what I need before I go to the trouble of trying to locate my father's part."

She gasped. "You said you have it."

"I told you—I have a good idea."

"An *idea*? That's all? I went to all the trouble to find you, even risking my life, for God's sake, because I could have been killed by Coyotay and his bunch, and all you have is a *good idea* where it is? Thanks a lot, Ryder." She nodded her head vigorously and threw up her hands. "Thanks a whole hell of a lot. I've just wasted my time, that's all."

"Maybe not. Give me your half, and we'll see."

"I will not."

"Then I might as well go back to camp in the morning. You can head on back to Tombstone . . . or wherever you decide to go."

He rolled over on his side.

Kitty squinted to see the clear outline of his buttocks and thought about giving him a good, swift kick.

"You lied to me," she said, walking back to throw herself on her blanket in a despondent heap. "You lied all along. You don't know where your father's map is, and you want mine because you think you can find the strike with just it, because you know this country."

He said nothing and let her rage on, and, in a while, he fell asleep despite her continued mumbling.

He awoke the next morning to find her standing over him again, red-eyed and looking like she'd not slept a wink.

"I'll do it," she said, tight-lipped and angry. "I'll just copy it before I show it to you and hope I can use it to find you if you run out on me."

"Oh, I'm not going to do that." He yawned and thought how nice it would be if she were to take off every stitch of clothes she was wearing and stretch out beside him. They would make warm, sweet love, then splash around in the little watering hole beyond the rocks and then do it all over again. He wanted to wear himself out with her . . . take her to climax so many times she lost count, and—

"Ryder McCloud, I've reached the point where I don't believe a damn thing you say, and I wouldn't trust you any further than I could throw you, you arrogant—"

He caught her ankle and tripped her to the ground, then fell on top of her to taunt, grinning, "This is where I want to throw you, little one—right beneath me."

With a furious cry, she slapped her palms against his chest and gave him a mighty push that he could have resisted but did not, as he allowed her to shove him to the side.

"You don't intend to keep any of our bargain, do you?" she cried, leaping to her feet and dusting her bottom. "Maybe you're right. Maybe you'd better head on back to your camp, and we'll call the whole thing off."

"Relax. I was teasing." He got up and reached for his blanket and began to roll it.

"About all of it?" she prodded hopefully. "About wanting my map, too, before looking for your father's part?"

"No," he said solemnly. "I have to see it, Kitty, to

make sure it's what I need before I do something I really don't want to do."

Her curiosity was piqued. "Why all the mystery? Why can't you tell me what you mean?"

"If you knew, you'd understand. You'll have to trust me."

"That," she said sharply, tartly, "I will never do."

Instead of riding straight into town, Ryder led the way to the hideaway he had used when switching between identities. "I'll wait here," he said. "It might not be safe for me to ride in after Opal has spread the word about Dan McCloud's having a half-breed son. That's what I get, I suppose, for using his name. I should have taken another, but I never thought it would be necessary."

Kitty could not help voicing her compassion. "It must have been terrible for you having torn loyalties between two races."

"Not really," he said matter-of-factly. "I feel kinship with both, but I always knew my whole heart belonged to the Apache.

"But enough of that," he said to cut off the subject. "Go get your map and copy it or whatever you want to do with it and then meet me here. If you can make it before dark, fine, otherwise do it first thing in the morning. But don't let anyone see you head this way. If you think you're being followed, don't come. I'll find you somehow."

Kitty was suddenly apprehensive. "Why should I be followed?" She had not told him about Nate having done so before. Neither had she told him of Nate's offer, seeing no need.

"Because," he patiently explained, "I don't believe your theory that whoever ransacked your room was just an ordinary robber. I think it might have been someone looking for the map.

"Maybe even the murderer," he added.

The thought was disconcerting, but Kitty refused to allow herself to dwell on it.

She got to the bank just before it closed. A clerk took the little metal box she had rented from out of the big safe and gave it to her. Then, in a cubicle where no one could see, Kitty made a sketch of the map, which she put back in the box and returned to the clerk.

Hurrying, she reached Ryder's hideaway at dusk.

"Good," he exclaimed happily as she handed the map over. "Now let's see what we've got here."

There was scant light, but enough that Ryder could see the map. He studied it a few moments, then said, "I was right. I need my father's part. Otherwise, it will take a long time to figure out where they were digging.

"And there's something else, too"—he held the paper toward the sunset for better light—"some kind of writing that is also divided."

Kitty said, "I saw that, too, but I couldn't figure out what it says."

"It looks like numbers from a Bible verse. The chapter must be on the part my father kept. It must be a clue, but we'd need to know exactly what it is, then look it up in the Bible."

"I thought the same thing when I saw it, but it didn't mean anything to me, because my uncle wasn't a religious man, I'm afraid."

Ryder said he thought his father might have become one in recent years. "He was lonely. I'd stop by to see him and find him reading a Bible a missionary had given him. I wouldn't be at all surprised that this was his doing—using a verse in the Bible to give the most important clue of all as to where to find the gold."

"Which means," Kitty said worriedly, "that without his part, we'll never find it."

"Not necessarily. I think we can pinpoint the vicinity from just your uncle's half, but I've got a feeling it will take figuring out the Bible verse to find the actual site of the dig."

"So"—she threw up her hands—"go get your father's part. You said you had an idea where it is," she tartly reminded.

"In good time," he said quietly. "I'll set out first thing in the morning."

"And I'll go with you."

His expression told her he'd not changed his mind about that, and Kitty did not argue. She had made up her mind to follow him, anyway.

She had bought food   steaks, eggs, and fresh-baked bread. Afterward, they sat around the small campfire and made small talk. Kitty used the opportunity to ask him about his people, for she had realized she was fascinated by their ways and eager to learn more about them.

Ryder was only too willing to tell her, and time slipped by. The moon was high in the sky, and, despite herself, Kitty began to yawn.

Ryder said they should call it a night as he wanted an early start in the morning. "As soon as I get back, and we know we've got all the map, I'll give you a list of supplies we'll need, and you can go into town and get them. Then we'll head out."

Kitty snuggled down, but the awareness that he was nearby made her restless. Finally, she slept, but fitfully. Then something startled her, and she sat up to realize it was a coyote howling somewhere in the mountains.

She got up to tiptoe behind a rock to relieve herself, wishing she had not drunk so much water earlier.

And that was when she saw, in the radiant light of the full moon, that Ryder's bedroll was empty.

She told her racing heart to slow down, that there

had to be a reason. He had drunk a lot of water, too,
and perhaps he had needs, as well. But as long moments passed, anxiety began to creep up on her.

She groped her way to where they had left the
horses and could make out only her own in the
shadows.

He was gone, and she knew then that he'd had no
intention of waiting till morning. He had planned to
abandon her as soon as he got his hands on her map.

*Damn you to hell, Ryder McCloud,* she fumed to
herself as she hurried to gather her things and saddle
her horse. *Damn you for the traitor and liar you are,
and damn me for being so stupid as to think I could
believe a word you said.*

The only thing she knew to do was return to Tombstone and find Opal and see if she could stay the rest
of the night with her. It was not terribly late. Maybe
midnight. She would still be working. Kitty had heard
at the store where she had bought the food that Opal
had gone to work at the Oriental's biggest competitor,
the Lucky Nugget.

After that, she would just have to put Ryder out
of her mind, as well as the gold, and find a way to
support herself.

"But if I ever see him again," she swore into the
night, "so help me, I'll shoot him for the lying bastard
he is."

Everyone stared as Kitty entered the Lucky Nugget.
A woman dressed like a man and wearing a double
holster was not exactly a common sight.

When Opal saw her, she immediately yelled for
someone to take over the faro game, then grabbed her
arm and led the way to an empty table in a far corner.

Pushing her into a chair, she sat down opposite, and,
after signaling to the bartender to bring them each a
drink, she furiously demanded, "Just where the hell

have you been? I've been out of my mind worrying that savage got hold of you. I tried to get Marshal Earp to send out a posse to look for you, but once the boy at the livery stable told him you had a horse and took off on your own, he said it was none of his concern."

Kitty knew she was genuinely upset and hastened to explain, "I'm sorry, and I wish I could have told you, but the fact is, you were upset and doing a lot of talking, and I was afraid you couldn't keep it to yourself, and I didn't want anybody to know."

Opal's eyes slitted with indignation. "What do you mean—I was doing a lot of talking?"

"You told everyone about Dan McCloud having a half-breed son and how you think he's the one who came to your shanty and was also responsible for ransacking my room."

"So?"

"So we agreed not to talk about it."

"What difference does it make?"

"Not any now, I guess." Kitty took a sip of the whiskey that had been set before her. It felt like a fireball hitting her stomach but also went to work to quell the angry churning.

"Well, I would appreciate it if you'd tell me why you rode off by yourself and scared me out of my wits. Whether you believe it or not, I still care what happens to you."

"I know you do," Kitty said gratefully, "and maybe it's time I explained a lot of things, except that I'm embarrassed to admit I've been such a fool."

Opal looked troubled. "Why do I get the feeling this has something to do with Sam Bodine?"

"Because it does. You see"—she swallowed hard—"Sam is really Dan McCloud's half-breed son. His real name is Ryder McCloud. He's been passing for white and working as an Indian scout."

Opal banged her fist on the table, making their glasses rattle. "The lying son of a bitch," she shrieked. "I'd like to get my hands on him—"

"Opal, please . . ." Kitty held a finger to her lips. "There's no need for the whole town to know."

"I think you'd better tell me everything."

"I will. But later. Right now you've got to get back to work." A man in a black suit, white shirt, and string tie was watching them and looked annoyed. Kitty suspected he was Opal's boss.

Opal turned to see who she was looking at, then agreed, "You're right. I'm getting the evil eye." She downed the rest of her whiskey. "I quit at three in the morning. Meet me at my shanty. It's two rows up from the one I used to have, second on the left. The key is under a rock beside the door."

"What about Nate?" Kitty did not want to be around him and would spend another night in the hayloft before being under the same roof with him alone.

Opal airily waved her hand, "Oh, Roscoe got out of jail yesterday, and him and Nate are off somewhere raising hell."

"Well, I'd just as soon stay here and wait for you, if that's all right." She did not want to take any chances on Nate stumbling in.

"Suit yourself." Opal got up and went back to calling faro numbers.

And Kitty settled back to wait, dreading having to admit her mistake in having trusted Ryder.

The rest of her misery—how she had given herself to him so recklessly—she would keep to herself.

Ryder stood at the edge of the cemetery known as Boot Hill, the crosses and markers appearing to glow eerily in the streaming moonlight.

He had tied his horse behind a nearby barn, where it would not be seen.

He had also borrowed a shovel from the barn, which he held against his shoulder.

The grisly task ahead was one he had postponed until the very last, making sure that Kitty did, indeed, possess Wade Parrish's part of the map before he looked for his father's.

And now the time had come.

With a great, heaving sigh, wrenched from the very core of his soul, Ryder entered the cemetery . . . and began walking toward his father's grave.

# Chapter 22

"I'm not going to be here long," Opal explained as Kitty looked about the shanty uncertainly. "Just till I save a little money, and then I'm heading to California. There are fancier saloons out there, nicer places to live. Weather's better, too, I hear.

"But at least I've got room for Nate when he's around." She gestured to a curtain hanging in a doorway at the rear of the kitchen. "I keep thinking one of these days he'll settle down before he winds up in Boot Hill, but he keeps on drinking and raising hell."

Opal went to a crude plank shelf that ran along one wall and took down two glasses. She set them on the table along with a bottle of whiskey, poured them each a drink, then urged, "Tell me everything."

She sat down and motioned for Kitty to do the same.

Kitty took a sip of the whiskey. She never liked the taste but figured she needed it right then to give her the courage to admit, "You were right. Ryder is Dan's son. He's also Whitebear. I found that out the day my room was ransacked. That's how I knew he wasn't the one who did it—because he was with me."

Opal downed her drink in one gulp and slammed the empty glass on the table. "I knew it. I knew it. That's why he was honeying you up—to get your map. Well, thank goodness you were smart enough not to—" She had started to pour herself another drink, but her hand holding the bottle froze in midair as she saw the look on Kitty's face. "Oh, no," she whispered. "Tell me you didn't give it to him."

"I did," Kitty said miserably. "But not then, because I was furious. It was later, when I decided I really had no choice, that I set out to look for him at the Indian camp."

"And you found him?"

"Sort of," she sheepishly admitted. "I thought I knew the way, and maybe sooner or later I would've found it, but an Apache hunting party found me first and took me there."

"Then what happened?"

"We talked and made an agreement to look for the gold together and share it."

Opal finished filling her glass. "I don't see how you figured you could trust him."

"It's kind of hard to explain, but I did—then. He ran out on me last night, though."

"And, no doubt, took your map with him."

"Yes, but I drew a copy."

"But what about his father's half? If he don't have it, then we're right back where we started from."

Kitty pushed her barely touched glass away and got up and went to the stove and the pot of stale coffee on top.

"I can heat that," Opal offered.

"No need." Kitty found a mug and filled it, then sat down again.

Opal frowned. "Well, go on. What about McCloud's map?"

"Ryder didn't have it."

"What?" Opal screeched, leaping to her feet, then collapsed in her chair. "Then how in the hell did you think he was going to find the damn gold with just yours? And what kind of bargain was that, anyhow?"

"You don't understand." Kitty knew her argument

was weak, but it was all she had to offer. "He said he had a good idea where his father's map was."

"Which was a trick. You know he had it all along, and now he's got both pieces, and he'll find the strike and keep it all for himself. So there's nothing to do but forget about it. Your copy is worthless without his."

"Not necessarily."

Opal's eyes narrowed. "What do you mean?"

"Do you remember the numbers we saw on the map?"

"Yes. We couldn't understand the meaning."

"Ryder figured out they were actually numbers for a Bible verse. He said the chapter would probably be on his father's half, and we'd need that before we could see what it was . . . what it meant. He said he thought maybe his father might have started reading the Bible in his later years and become a religious man."

"So?" Opal threw up her hands. "Like I said—you're right back where you started from."

"And like I said—not necessarily. Ryder said we could probably find out the location from my map, or close to it, but we'd need his father's part to get the clue from the Bible verse."

Exasperated, Opal said, "I'm confused."

Kitty's smile was cold and sinister. "There's no need to be. All I have to do is use my copy of the map to follow Ryder. Then I'll hide and watch him find the gold, then take my share."

Opal rolled her eyes. "And I think you've lost your mind, because he'll wind up killing you. After all, he's half-Apache, half-gunslinger, which can only be a deadly combination."

"And you forget I'm also good with a gun, and can be cunning, too, Opal."

"I still say you're crazy."

"And I say it's my only chance. I'll know which direction he headed once I get my copy of the map, and I'll follow him."

"Where is it?"

"In the vault at the bank. As soon as it opens in the morning, I'll be ready to leave."

Opal shook her head. "I think it's too dangerous. I don't want you to do it."

"I have no choice."

Opal banged her fist on the table. "Yes, you do. You can let Nate go with you."

Kitty stiffened. Taking Nate was the last thing she wanted to do, but she knew she had to choose her words carefully lest Opal be offended. "I . . . I'd rather go by myself," she said slowly, evenly.

"Why? You'd be safer with Nate, and you know it. And Roscoe could go along for extra protection. Between the two of them, you'd have nothing to fear from that half-breed." She smiled confidently. "And don't worry. Nate and Roscoe's pay would come out of the share of the gold you said you'd give me, so's you don't have to worry about paying 'em out of your pocket."

Kitty knew she was on the spot. "It . . . it isn't that, Opal."

Opal sat up straight, hands gripping the edge of the table as her face twisted into an angry mask. "What, then?"

"I . . . I just prefer to go alone."

"Oh, yeah? Well, I don't believe you. No woman in her right mind would want to go chasing after a gun-totin' savage when two good, able-bodied men are willing to go with her. I think you've just changed your mind about sharing with me."

"Opal, I promise you that's not true."

"And I say you're lying."

"No, I—"

"Get out." Opal bolted to her feet. "You've used me all you're going to, damn it. You never had any intentions of sharing with me. You just needed a place to stay, somebody to help you find a job, and if that son of a bitch hadn't run out on you, you wouldn't be here now. But enough is enough."

Kitty felt tears spring to her eyes to think Opal believed she was capable of doing such a thing. "I'd never do that to you, I swear. I'm your friend, Opal. And I'd never have asked for your help if I hadn't thought you and Daddy Wade weren't close, and—"

*"Daddy Wade,"* Opal mimicked with a snort. "You didn't give a hoot about him, neither. All you ever wanted was his gold." She kicked her chair across the room. "Now I'm telling you for the last time—get out of here."

Kitty got up and began backing toward the door. "Opal, I swear to you that you've got it all wrong. I *do* intend to share the gold with you if I can find it. Even when I made the bargain with Ryder McCloud to split it fifty-fifty, I was going to split my half with you."

"If that was so, you'd have no objection to Nate and Roscoe going with you."

Kitty had never known such frustration. "That's not the reason."

"There can't be any other."

"Oh, yes there can." Kitty sucked in a sharp breath and let it go, along with her resolve to keep from hurting Opal's feelings. "The truth is, I don't like your brother, and I don't trust him or Roscoe, and I'd rather take my chances alone than have them with me."

For a few seconds, Opal could only stare at her, lips twitching. Then her anger erupted. "You've got no cause to feel that way. Nate apologized to you for what he did. He told me so. You're just uppity, that's all. You think you're too good for the likes of him, and me too."

Kitty took a step toward her. "That's not true—"

Opal held up an arm to fend her off. "Don't you come near me with your hugs and lies. I want you out of my house now. Folks that don't like my brother aren't welcome here."

Kitty knew there was no use in trying to reason. Opal was fanatically loyal to her brother and would stand for no criticism of him. "All right, I'll go. But you have my word that if I am able to find the gold, I'll see to it you get your share."

"Oh, yeah, I'm sure you will," Opal cackled as she followed her to the door. "And folks in hell are gonna want ice water, and pigs will fly."

Kitty rushed into the night.

Opal went back to the table and the whiskey, intent on drinking herself into a stupor.

"You can come out now," she said dully.

The curtain at the rear of the kitchen parted, and Nate entered, a smug look on his face.

"I told you the bitch was two-faced," he said, picking up the bottle and turning it up to his lips. He took a deep swallow, then wiped his mouth and said, "She only came here tonight wanting you to stake her to go after him. She never intended to share with you."

"I know that now," Opal sadly agreed. "But I was hoping you were wrong, and that she'd let you and Roscoe help her."

"So what do we do now?"

She yanked the bottle away from him and took a drink herself, then fiercely declared, "You follow her and when she and that half-breed find the gold, you take my share, goddamn it."

Kitty knew it was not safe to be on the streets at such an hour. Hurrying along, she went straight to the livery stable. No one was around, and she quickly scurried up the ladder to the loft to once again bed down in the hay.

She planned to be at the bank as soon as it opened, then be on her way to make Ryder McCloud regret, by God, that he had double-crossed her.

Weariness carried her away to slumber so deep she was unaware when someone took up vigil below to await her next move.

The river was a liquid ribbon, curling through and around the rocks and boulders.

Overhead, hawks rode the breeze, soaring endlessly without need of flapping their wings.

A rabbit peered from a hole to watch as the horse and rider passed by, then dove back into the earth to wait for safer conditions to scamper forth.

Kitty pulled her hat lower on her forehead against the unrelenting sun. Her shirt was wet with perspiration and clung to her like a second skin.

She paused often to allow her horse to drink his fill from the cool river waters, and she frequently dismounted to submerge her whole head in an effort to find relief from the smothering heat.

Judging from the shadows, Kitty estimated it was perhaps three or four in the afternoon. She had been at the bank when it opened at nine and left right after, so she had covered a good distance. It would have been more, however, had she not allowed the horse to go slowly, lest he succumb to the scorching heat of the day.

Delighting to find a spot of shade beneath a cottonwood tree, Kitty dismounted for much-needed respite.

She did not tie the horse but allowed him to graze his way along the bank. He would wind up in the water, but she was not worried he would run away.

Taking a few bites of hardtack and a cold biscuit

from her saddlebag, Kitty sat down and settled back against the tree trunk to once more study her map.

The numbers she made out were 18:27. Part of the preceding was missing, but she could make out the phrase "unto the Lord." Ryder had been positive it held an important clue, and she hoped he had already figured it out. It would make things so much easier if all she had to do was find him somewhere ahead, then settle back and wait for him to do all the work. Then she would take him by surprise, guns drawn, and demand her part.

She had made up her mind never again to think that the passion that surged so fiercely between them might lead to something else—like caring . . . and love. Damn it, she had made a big enough fool of herself. She was not about to let him think she had been falling in love with him.

Still, despite feeling humiliated, Kitty allowed herself to think how she had actually been drawn to two men—two different, distinct beings. Whitebear, the fierce Apache warrior, and Ryder, the gunfighter who also possessed charm and a rollicking sense of humor. The two halves combined into a man, Kitty knew, who could have held her heart in the palm of his hand.

But no more.

Betrayal was not something she took lightly.

She would get what was coming to her and then ride out of his life and never look back.

At least that's how she hoped it would happen.

She could not control the dreams that haunted her nearly ever night . . . dreams of what was . . . what might have been . . . and, painfully, would never be.

Folding the map, she tucked it inside her hat band. She had almost memorized it, anyway, but was puzzled by a huge X in the middle. If she had the other side, she thought she might be able to figure it out. As it was, it appeared to be marking a cabin of some sort, for there was a crude drawing of one. At least, it seemed that was what it was. But perhaps it would not matter. Ryder would probably already be there by the time she arrived at that vicinity, and, having the entire drawing made by his father and her uncle, he would have figured it all out.

She noted that the horse had waded out into the stream, no doubt to get cool rather than drink. Then it dawned on her that with no one around, she should do the same. There was time. In fact, she figured she would have to camp overnight before reaching where she expected to find Ryder.

Unbuckling her holster, she carefully laid it beneath the tree, took off her boots, then peeled out of her shirt, trousers, and underwear. Naked, she ran down the bank and waded in.

It felt wonderful, and she swam till she was tired, then flipped over on her back to float lazily.

She heard nothing . . . saw nothing. And it was only when she emerged a half hour or so later, squeezing water from her hair, that she froze in horror to realize that her clothes were not where she had left them.

And neither was her holster.

She whirled about, expecting to see—what? Indians? They would not play such a trick. They would have charged right in to either fill her full of arrows or capture her. Neither would outlaws have taken time for pranks.

Then it dawned on her.

Ryder.

Evidently he must not have been as far ahead of her as she had thought. He had managed to see her and was teaching her a lesson, but enough was enough. She wanted her clothes back, along with her guns, because if he were mean enough to take them and keep on riding, she was in big trouble.

"Ryder, that's enough," she indignantly called out

in the stillness. "Give me back my things, and let's talk."

She had backed against the tree, arm across her breasts, hand covering her crotch. She felt so vulnerable, which was making her furious. "Do you hear me, damn it? This isn't funny. Now give me my clothes, or—"

"Or what?"

The man stepped from behind a boulder only a few feet away. His hat was pulled low on his forehead, and a bandanna covered the lower part of his face. And while he wore a holster, he had not drawn his gun. There was no need, for Kitty was unarmed.

"Leave me alone," she said in a voice braver than she felt as he advanced toward her. "I don't want any trouble, so get the hell out of here."

"Soon as I get what I come for, I will."

Panic stabbed like a knife as Kitty pressed farther back against the tree.

"Wouldn't of been no need for all this if you'd left the map in your room."

Fear was shoved aside by rage. "You're the one who ransacked my room." She ached to see his face, for surely she would recognize him as someone who had frequented the Oriental, knew Opal, and had heard her ramblings.

"No, it wasn't me," he said lazily. "My partner's the one who did that, and if he'd found it, you wouldn't be here now. But maybe you'll be glad you are, 'cause I'm gonna show you what it's like to have a real man."

He licked his lips and squeezed his crotch and kept walking toward her.

Kitty waited till he drew close, then lowered her head and ran for him, intending to butt him right in his gut, knock the wind from him, then make her escape before he could rally to his senses.

She had not, however, realized just how huge a belly

the man had—huge and hard. She bounced right off of him, and with a vicious laugh he grabbed her by her throat with one hand and slapped her with his other.

Still clutching her neck, he hit her again. She felt herself slipping away in a storm of pain and blackness and struggled to cling to consciousness. If she passed out, he would have his way with her. As long as she could hang on, there was a chance she might find a way to disable him.

Through the haze of anguish that fell like a shroud about her, Kitty heard a second man's voice.

"That's enough. Leave her alone. Ain't no need to beat her to death."

Her attacker continued to hold her and cackled maniacally, "Oh, I ain't gonna kill her. Not now, anyways. I'm just breakin' her spirit so I won't have to work so hard to get between her legs."

"If you beat her senseless, she can't tell us where the map is."

He gave her a violent shake that set her head bobbing to and fro. "Shit, we don't even know she's got it." Then, to Kitty, "What'd you do with it, bitch? Hand it over, and I'll go easy on you."

"She's got it," the other said confidently. "Otherwise, she wouldn't have got this far. She knows where she's goin', all right."

"Well, I'm gonna make her tell."

Kitty's eyes flashed open in time to see his fist coming straight toward her face, and suddenly she screamed—a long, piercing howl fueled by rage, as strength she never knew she possessed suddenly coursed through her veins.

The villain was stunned, caught off guard, and loosened his hold just long enough for her to make a lunge for the pistol in his holster.

"Watch it," the other outlaw yelped, grabbing her.

It was a wild tussle, and in the midst of it all, shots

rang out, and the men, abandoning Kitty, scrambled for cover.

Staggering, she looked about wildly, trying to figure out who was shooting and from where.

A familiar voice boomed from behind the rocks. "Get out of the way, Kitty. I can't get a clear shot for you."

She dropped to her knees at once, at the same time hearing the sound of horses as the outlaws made their getaway.

Ryder scrambled down from the rocks and rushed to where she was slowly getting to her feet. "Are you hurt?" He helped her on up.

"I . . . I'm fine," she managed to say, head still throbbing from the vicious blows. Then anger took over. "You double-crossed me, you lying sneak."

"That's not true. You're the one who ran off. When I got back to camp, you were gone."

"You weren't supposed to leave till dawn."

"That"—he grinned to admit—"*was* a lie. I had to go look for my father's piece of the map while it was dark."

"I don't understand."

"You would if you knew where I had to go to get it."

"Then you did find it? But where—"

He shook his head. "Believe me, you're better off not knowing.

"Anyway," he continued, "when I saw you weren't there, I knew what you had to be thinking—that I had double-crossed you, so I went to town to look for you. It took me a while to get there, though, because I had to buy new clothes, get a hot bath, and by then you were gone. I knew, because I went to the livery stable, and your horse was missing. I figured you'd made a copy of the map you gave me like you said you were going to and set out on your own to try to catch up with me. Thank goodness I was behind you instead of in front and heard the commotion."

Kitty was washed with relief. "Then you didn't abandon me after all."

"No, but I should have." He furrowed his brow in a mock frown. "Especially since I was taking a chance riding back into town now that the soldiers know I'm half-Apache, thanks to Opal. But tell me," he pressed, "how did those men know to follow you?"

"They're the ones who ransacked my room. They were looking for my map. They know all about it."

This time his frown was genuine. "Probably the whole Arizona Territory knows about it, thanks to Opal."

"She was just frightened for me. Only now she's angry, because she thinks I won't give her half of my share like I promised."

"We'll worry about that later. Right now we've got to keep an eye out in case those men come back and try to track us."

Kitty was able to smile. "Then we're still partners?"

"Oh, yeah," he said, dark eyes twinkling as they raked her up and down. "And I like it even better this way."

Innocently, she asked, "What way?"

He winked. "You naked."

"Oh, no . . ." In the excitement she had completely forgotten she was, and began to turn around, arms waving helplessly as she looked for her clothes.

"Over there," Ryder said, pointing.

With cheeks burning, she ran and put them on quickly. She could feel him watching and cursed herself over and over for having allowed herself to become so embroiled in the situation that she could actually forget she was standing before him without a stitch on.

Finally, she strapped on her holster and turned

around. Without meeting his mocking gaze, she said, "All right. I'm ready. And I just hope those bastards come after us."

"Forget it. We don't have time for revenge, but"— he pointed to the wound on her cheek—"we'd better take time for you to wash that cut in the river."

Kitty felt her lips pull in a mysterious smile. "This cut is why I *want* them to follow us."

Exasperated, he repeated, "I told you—we don't have time for revenge."

"Not even for the murder of your father and my uncle?"

His face went tight. "What do you mean?"

She was rocked with emotion. "I saw a ring on his finger when he was about to hit me with his fist—a *turquoise* ring."

"I don't understand. How does that prove they were the murderers?"

"When my uncle's body was found, one of his fingers had been cut off in order to get that ring. I know, because Opal told me about it. My uncle wanted me to have it, and Opal described what it looked like."

"And you're sure that ring fit her description."

"Positive."

He nodded grimly. "Then we'll be sure *not* to cover our tracks."

# Chapter 23

They had made camp for the night after nearly reaching the spot on the map where they thought the gold might be located. Supper had been a rabbit Ryder had caught with a snare and then spit-roasted. Kitty had made beans and tortillas like an expert, and they were finally stretched out lazily beside the dying embers of the fire.

Enjoying the night breeze and the canopy of stars overhead, Ryder seized the first real chance for conversation by asking, "Are you sure you don't know who those men were?"

Kitty thought hard, then said, "I didn't see their faces, and the voices weren't familiar. They could have been any of hundreds of men that passed through the Oriental every night."

"But they knew about the map," he said resolutely.

"Probably everybody in Tombstone does by now, thanks to Opal. It couldn't have been anyone but her who told them, because I sure never confided in anybody—till you," she added sharply.

There was the hint of a smile on his lips. "Still don't trust me, do you?"

"Not really. After all, you're actually two different people." *And also devastatingly handsome,* she thought as her gaze dropped to his bare chest. He had taken off his shirt, and his muscles rippled and gleamed in the light of the campfire.

"So which one don't you trust?"

"I haven't made up my mind," she laughed to say, "because I can't decide which one you are. Probably both of you, though."

He laughed with her. "Well, you're a good one to talk. First you were a wild-haired, husky-voiced boy, and then you turned into a beautifully soft woman with a voice like melted butter."

"And you don't know which is the real me?" she teased.

He rolled to his side to grin and wink. "I think I found out back in the cave."

Kitty glanced away, feeling her face turn warm. She sat up, cleared her throat, and abruptly changed the conversation. "So where did you find your father's map?"

"Like I said before—you don't want to know."

"Actually I'm more interested to find out why it's such a big secret . . . why you seem determined not to tell me."

"All right then." He crooked his arm and propped his head on his hand. "I found it in Boot Hill."

She was stunned. "Why on earth would your father hide it in a cemetery?"

"He didn't. It was buried with him."

Kitty tensed. "Are you saying it was still on him? But the murderers would have searched him thoroughly."

"They didn't know where to look, which was under the sole of his boot. I remembered he always kept a little money there so he'd never be caught without any. He'd pry off the sole, stick the money in, then tack it back in place. So when I heard how he said with his dying breath that he was taking his secret to the grave with him"—he shrugged—"I knew what he meant."

"So why didn't you tell me that? All you said was

that you had an idea where it was, which made me think you really didn't know."

"I didn't think you needed to hear that I was going to have to dig up his grave and open his coffin to get it. That's why I had to make sure you had your half before I went that far."

Although macabre and horrible to contemplate, Kitty began to understand why things had happened as they had. "So that's why you had to do it at night . . . why you left me."

"Exactly. I couldn't dig him up in daylight, when someone might see me."

"That also"—she swallowed past a knot of revulsion—"explains why you had to take the time for a bath and get new clothes."

"Right again."

"Oh, dear Lord," she murmured, her heart going out to him for having to perform such a grisly task. "It must have been awful."

"I tried not to think about it and worked fast. But now we've got the whole map, and, after studying it, I think we'll reach the area of the strike tomorrow. Then the real work begins, because we've got to try to figure out what the Bible verse means."

Kitty had also scrutinized the map after it was finally put together. "I can see the reference is the book of Genesis, chapter eighteen, verse twenty-seven. There was something about dust and ashes, but I can't make out the words."

"I couldn't either. His half is in pretty bad shape."

Kitty felt a wave of defeat. "And I don't suppose you happen to have a Bible in your saddlebag."

"No. I should have thought to get one before I left town, but I was in a hurry to find you and didn't think about it."

"Then we're out of luck."

"Maybe not." He leaned to pick up a stick and stir

the fire, sending a spiral of ashes skyward. "Maybe it's not as complicated as we think. Dust and ashes could mean the strike is hidden near a chimney or stove of some sort."

She did not share his optimism and sarcastically asked, "How many chimneys have you seen since we left town, or, for that matter, how many cabins?"

"They had a shack. It wasn't much of one, according to my father, but they threw it together to have shelter in the winter. You may not know it, but they'd been digging for several years."

"I knew it had been a while. What I never understood was why they didn't go ahead and record their claim and be done with it. Why all the secrecy? It seems to me if they had a rich strike they'd have gone about it in the right way—dug deep shafts and had carts and mules, men to help. I heard miners talking in the saloon sometimes, and they all dreamed of being able to finance big operations to bring out the *mother lode,* as they called it."

Ryder's eyes took on the mischievous twinkle Kitty had come to know so well as he made the barb, "The reason they didn't do all that is because they trusted other folks about as much as you trust me."

She fired back, "If they had the same reasons I have, then I don't blame them."

His laugh was loud, robust, as he rolled to his back once more. "Hell, woman, how can I expect you to trust me when you don't even *like* me?"

"Sometimes trust and like go together."

The humor slipped from his voice. "I can't see that I ever mistreated you . . . even when you were a captive."

"That was because of your mother. She wouldn't allow it."

"That's not why, Kitty," he said quietly. "Our band of Apache are more civilized than others. Besides, we didn't want a slave. We're renegades, and all we're trying to do is survive. And you know the only reason I wanted the gold—and still do—is to take care of my people till they can get settled in Mexico and start a new life. Otherwise, I'd never have led a raid on a stagecoach or anywhere else."

"So let's find it quick," she said, uncomfortable to feel as though she had been soundly chastised. "So we can go our separate ways."

But even as she spoke, Kitty felt a stirring in her heart that made her wonder whether that was really the way she wanted it.

"Tell me more about your people," she urged to end the tension that had sprung between them. She also liked to hear him share Indian folklore, for she had become fascinated with the Chiricahua Apaches and their sad plight.

So he talked, on into the night, telling her stories of war and famine along with peace and plenty, and she listened intently.

When he finally lapsed into silence, with apparently no more yarns to spin, she said, "I hope your people will find what they're looking for in Mexico. I'll think about you and wonder."

He was quiet for a moment, then said so low she had to strain to hear him, "You could go with us."

She had stretched out on the ground, propping her head on her saddle to stare up at the silver-velvet night as he talked. Now she turned to stare at him in wonder. "What did you say?"

"I said you could go with us."

The idea had never entered her mind, and she was astonished at the suggestion.

"Where else do you have to go?" He made his tone light, as though it were an idea born of politeness rather than what he had begun to feel for her the past weeks.

Kitty was still reeling and stammered, "Well, nowhere . . . yet. Opal wants to go to California. I don't know . . ."

"It would make my mother happy," he said, thinking how it would make him even more so. "I can tell she likes you very much."

Kitty smiled. "She liked Billy Mingo."

"She likes Kitty Parrish even more. And so do I," he added soberly.

A nervous laugh escaped her lips as Kitty pointed out, "I'm not Apache. I'd never get used to your ways."

"So you could teach us yours. Besides, once we get settled, I plan to build a school and find someone to teach the children all they need to know, and that someone could be you. Times are changing, Kitty, for all of us. The old ways will fade away. It's time to learn new.

"There's a lot we could teach each other," he added as he moved closer.

She had been staring into the fire but brought her gaze up to meet his eyes as she felt a little shiver within.

He leaned to tilt her chin with outstretched fingers. "I've fought against what I've come to feel for you. I want you to know that. But I'm burning inside, Kitty, like I've never burned for any woman in my life. I don't know what it means, but I'd damn sure like to find out."

Kitty was mesmerized and could no more have drawn away from him than change the winds or turn the tides. Once more she was his captive, held by invisible chains she did not wish to break . . . even though she told herself she should. She meant nothing to him but raw, savage pleasure, yet she could not deny herself this time of ecstasy.

"Tell me to stop," he commanded huskily. "Because I didn't mean for this to happen. I swore I wouldn't touch you, that we'd work together and nothing more, but damn it, being so close to you, wanting you, is driving me crazy. So tell me to go to hell, Kitty, if this isn't what you want, too."

For answer, she bent her head back, offering herself to him as she slipped her arms about his broad shoulders.

Smiling at her surrender, he cupped her cheek in his hand, gently stroking the cut made by the outlaw's stolen ring. "I want to take care of you, little one," he murmured, his thumb following the bow of her lip. "Don't be afraid. Don't ever be afraid . . ."

Leaning forward, he captured her mouth to taste the sweet quivering beneath his.

"Tell me you want me," he coaxed, tongue flicking across her lips. "Tell me you want me, or I'll stop and never touch you again, I promise. I can't let you think I forced you . . ."

Kitty stared at him, swallowing against the lump in her throat. Never had she seen such tenderness in a man's face, but there was something else, something more that made her heart swell to bursting. "I do want you, Ryder," she whispered tremulously. "I think I always have—as you, as Whitebear. I felt desire for the both of you, even though I tried to fight it . . ."

He pulled her gently down to lie beside him, as his mouth skimmed along her throat, lips emphatic and unbelievably warm. His tongue flicked over her flesh, making it quiver as her body seemed to melt against the length of him. Through the thin cotton of her blouse, her breasts and her nipples strained toward his hands, which were dropping lower.

Suddenly he took her lips in a kiss so ravaging that spirals of fire lanced through her. As his fingers tore at her blouse, his tongue swept into her mouth.

She arched into him, yielding to the kiss, at the

same time thrilling to feel him touch a breast and tease the nipple with his finger. He plucked it to a hard, tight bud, and waves of longing swept over her.

And then she was struck by the driving need to touch him, as well. Her hands moved down his back, then around to trace the rock hard lines of his chest and on to the flatness of his belly.

She heard his groan, deep in his throat, and then he was undressing her, and she was helping him, anxious to be naked and vulnerable to his sweet assault.

"So beautiful," he said thickly as he pulled back to rake her with lusty eyes in the fire's glow. "Had I seen you this way when you were my slave, I'd have never let you go and kept you naked all the time . . ."

His fingers went to her waist, pulling her roughly against him to feel the hardness of his need. "See what you do to me?" He slid it between her thighs, working to and fro, one hand moving to cup her firm, rounded buttocks, to lock her in his embrace.

His lips burned, his tongue devoured, and Kitty felt flaming heat consume her body.

He continued to hold her tight while moving a hand upward to once more cup and mold each breast in turn. And then he was lowering his head to feast and suckle, and her cheek lay against his thick, dark hair as she cradled his head and whimpered to urge him on.

"I've never wanted anyone more," he whispered, his tongue circling a nipple before drawing in as much of her breast as he could take.

She slid her hands down to grip his shoulders, then ran her fingers along his back to feel the heavy cords of muscle tighten at her touch.

She felt him move to skim her flesh, downward to her navel and on below.

A shudder sparked in her loins to feel his long, slim fingers dance through the hair at the juncture of her thighs, then ease them apart to slip inside.

"No . . . oh, no . . . ," she whispered.

He brushed her mouth with yet another fiery kiss as he plunged a finger in and out to send hot, damp tremors up and into her belly. He paused to caress the swollen bud hidden within her sex and tease, "Are you telling me you don't want this? Are you telling me to stop? I promised I would, little one. Just say—"

"Yes . . . I mean, no," she cried, thinking how she should be embarrassed, but hot, burning need was taking over, sweeping her helplessly into a storm surge of emotion, and with the deep, thrusting rhythm of his finger she could only melt into moaning sighs of pleading for him to go on, to take her all the way to paradise.

But he was enjoying the honeyed torture he was inflicting upon her and continued to make her writhe and sob with pleasure beneath him.

Pushing her onto her back, he bent her legs to prop them on his shoulders as he positioned himself between.

Kitty closed her eyes and threw her head back in readiness to feel the first, hard thrust of his manhood. Then her legs stiffened, and she gave a little cry to feel not his shaft but his tongue instead.

He began to circle the tiny nub with his tongue, then drew it between his lips to lick and explore. He was, she realized in sweet-hot panic, devouring her. She thought surely she would die if he did not stop. Hot needles of pleasure that were almost painful stabbed to the very core of her being.

She held tightly to him, nails digging into his shoulders as he continued to feast, turning her blood to liquid fire as her heart pounded so fast she feared it would burst from her chest.

And then it happened—deep, twisting, gnawing licks of pleasure like blows from a whip. Within, without, over and under. Her insides were exploding, and she began to undulate her hips, striving to get closer to him as he plunged yet deeper, harder, almost bruising, fingers digging into the softness of her hips.

She twisted her head from side to side, writhing in the most delicious rapture she had ever known, and he held on tightly, making her ride with his rhythmic assault.

At last, he released her, but not for long, as he tore out of his clothes and positioned himself above her once again.

And this time she did feel the hard plunging of his desire and clung to him yet tighter, reveling in the feel, for the afterglow of her own pleasure burned as bright and hot as the embers of the campfire that refused to die.

Ryder took himself to glory quickly, for it had been all he could do to hold back as he had consumed her with his tongue, his mouth. He had wanted to send her into a frenzy of longing, to teach her the pleasures of her body she had not known existed. But it had taken every ounce of willpower he could muster to hold back.

For a long while, they clung together, arms and legs entwined, then finally they drew apart, gasping for breath.

"We . . . we'll never find the treasure like this," Kitty said, attempting humor in the wake of embarrassment to have so lost control.

"Maybe," he said as he drew her into the circle of his arms once more, "we've already found it."

Ryder lay awake a long time after Kitty had fallen asleep.

Nothing had been resolved.

She had made no commitment.

He had no reason to think she felt anything for him beyond passion, but then she was a stubborn sort. So he dared to wonder if perhaps she were fighting an inner battle, fearing that to love would mean giving up the independence she so fiercely clung to.

He worried, too, that the same obstinacy and spirit that had drawn him to her might be her ultimate downfall.

Coyotay had found her when she was overly confident in thinking she could find the camp.

The outlaws had tracked her because she was not experienced enough to cover her trail.

Both were mistakes that could have cost her her life, and they worried him, because if she did go her separate way when their quest was over, what was to become of her?

But all he could do in the time they had together was to try and make her love him . . .

. . . *as he loved her.*

# Chapter 24

"I'm starting to think we'll never find it," Kitty said, feeling discouraged.

It was mid-morning, and they had set out at dawn to take advantage of the cool, crisp air before the sweltering heat settled in.

"It shouldn't be much further," Ryder said without looking at her. They rode side by side, but he was ever alert for any sign of danger, eyes constantly darting about. "How's your water holding out?"

Kitty unlooped her canteen from the saddle horn and shook it. "I'm afraid there's not much left."

"We'll run into the San Pedro again beyond those buttes. We can fill our canteens and let the horses drink, because after that we'll be heading away from the river. And unless we happen across a stream, we might be in for a dry spell."

Kitty wanted to get her bearings. She did not like having no idea where she was. "The trail has been so crooked. How far would you say we are from Tombstone?"

"Probably a day's ride." He flashed a crooked grin. "We got kind of sidetracked, you know."

Kitty blushed and felt a stirring warmth to think of the splendor they had shared in each other's arms.

He pointed to a distant mountain of rock and sparse vegetation. "My people's camp is only a half day's ride through that pass. Once you reach the other side, you'd see familiar signs and know where you were. But I'd never risk going that way again. It's on the fringe of Comanche country to the north, and they keep sentries in the pass. It's a death trap."

"But you made it through."

"Yes, by riding like the devil was on my heels with arrows flying over my head. You can't see it from here, but the pass is very narrow, with lots of outcroppings and ledges where the Comanche can hide. I knew it was dangerous when I did it, but I was in a hurry to get back to camp. I had gone to find special herbs found only on this side, that my mother needed for a sick baby, and there was no time to waste."

"And did the baby live?"

He smiled. "Oh, yes. My mother is very good with her potions. A medicine man didn't escape the reservation with us, but she's the next best thing."

"A medicine *woman,*" Kitty said pleasantly.

"Well, she can't be called that. She would have to convince everyone that she had a special gift—the ability to interpret dreams, omens, and subject herself to long fasts and vigils. She would have to go off by herself to meditate and communicate with spirits, especially at night. She doesn't care about that. She just mixes her potions and minds her own business, and people can call her what they want to."

He looked at her suddenly, sharply. "Have you given any thought to what I said last night about your going with us to Mexico?"

"Some." She was not about to confide she had thought of little else.

"Even if we find the gold, it will be a struggle. Shelters have to be built, herds of cattle started, crops planted."

"And without the gold?"

"Some will starve before spring, because there won't be money to buy food to see us through the winter. I can understand why you wouldn't want to go."

She hedged. "I need to think about it," she said. After all, he had only said he loved her—not that he wanted to marry her. And even that revelation might have been inspired by the heat of the moment.

No, she could not make a momentous decision that could affect the rest of her life unless she was completely sure it was what she wanted. After all, she still had much to learn about the other side of Ryder— the side that was Apache. Perhaps custom demanded he marry one of his own kind. Maybe Adeeta would be his choice. What then? Would he make her his mistress? She did not know about such things, only that she could never share him with another woman.

She dragged in a heavy breath. She was weary from riding doggedly in the sun, as well as exhausted from the delicious hours of lovemaking the night before.

They reached the river, and the cool, dark waters proved irresistible in the miserable heat. Kitty, soaked with perspiration, peeled down to her undergarments and waded right in.

Ryder, however, hung back, and Kitty called, "Aren't you coming in?"

His grin was wry. "You seem to forget what happened when you went swimming yesterday. Somebody needs to keep watch. I'll go in when you're through."

She did not tarry as long as she would have otherwise. They needed to be on their way, and she wanted him to have his turn in the water.

Soon she took over the vigil, but Ryder swam only briefly.

When he came out, she was sitting beneath the sparse shade of a cottonwood tree, knees drawn to her chin. A slight breeze had begun to stir but not enough to cool the fires smoldering within her, for he had stripped completely.

Their heated gazes locked as he walked directly toward her, passing his clothing which he had left on the ground.

He dropped beside her, still imprisoning her with his lust-filled eyes.

A small sound seeped from her throat as he reached for her. Hands clutching his shoulders, her lips softened beneath his almost-bruising kiss, she allowed her tongue to slide gently into his mouth.

He groaned softly, and she pulled back long enough to tease, "No one is standing guard, you know."

"Outlaws be damned," he growled, claiming her lips once more.

His long fingers tugged at the ribbon at the front of her chemise, which was wet and plastered to her body. His mouth moved slowly across her shoulders.

With the ribbon untied, her breasts tumbled forth, and he bent his head and kissed each in turn as though it were a delicate, succulent fruit that must be caressed only with tenderness, lest it bruise.

Hooking his thumbs in her pantalets, he pulled them down over her hips and off her ankles to be cast aside.

He stretched her out on the ground and settled beside her as he kneaded the curve of her waist, then moved warm hands lower to smooth over her buttocks and slide between.

Deftly he laced his fingers through the damp, curling hair at the apex of her thighs before diving downward to stroke and tease the folds of her sex.

She arched against him, flames of desire licking from head to toe, the core of her throbbing with damp, slick heat. She pulled him closer, wanting him and sobbing deep in her throat to think how in that burning moment she would surely die if she did not have him.

"Take me," she moaned. "Please, please, Ryder . . take me."

And he did so, spreading her thighs and positioning himself between. "Put your legs around me," he urged, "and your heels on my back. Then ride me, sweetheart. Ride me with everything you have."

He plunged into her, and the gasp of ecstasy came from her very soul.

She matched his every thrust with one of her own, her nails digging into the rock-hard flesh of his broad back. He did not wince but urged her on, his face contorted with the tension of holding back to ensure she reached her own pinnacle before he released his seed into her core.

At last, they came together. For long moments they lay quietly in each other's arms, rocked by the splendor of their passion.

With great effort, Ryder finally forced himself to draw away from her. "We've got to ride, sweetheart," he said, kissing her fevered brow. "We've got the rest of our lives for this."

*The rest of our lives.* Kitty mulled the words over as she hurriedly dressed.

They could mean nothing.

Or everything.

Only time would tell.

It was nearly sundown when Ryder cried triumphantly, "That's it. Beyond that cluster of boulders. It's the camp. It has to be."

They dug their heels into their horses' flanks and galloped the rest of the way, charging around the rocks and into the clearing to share shouts of jubilation.

There were a few tools about—shovels, picks, and empty barrels—and sacks of feed for mules no longer there. A well was situated near a small wood shack.

Quickly dismounting, they went first to the shack.

It had a small porch, with two old rocking chairs that had seen better days.

Kitty felt a wave of sadness as she sank into one and began to rock to and fro. "He sat here," she said in wonder. "My uncle actually sat here, probably in the evenings after a hard day digging. However did they get them here, though?" she marveled.

"On pack mules," Ryder said. "And, yes, he probably did sit here after a hard day digging, but where in the hell was the dig?" He scanned the barren clearing surrounded by boulders. "I don't see any signs, much less the opening to a mine shaft."

"Maybe this was just where they ate and slept, and they mined somewhere else."

"Not according to the map. It leads right here and nowhere else."

Kitty jumped from the rocker. "The fireplace. This shack has a chimney. I saw it. So there will be a fireplace, and maybe that's what the Bible verse meant."

They went inside to see that the shack had but three walls, the back wall actually being the side of a boulder. It was only one room with a dirt floor. There was a table made of a board laid across two large rocks, and two benches made in similar fashion.

On each side was a mattress made of sawgrass, with animal skins for cover.

The fireplace was crude but adequate. A few cooking pots were scattered around, along with utensils made of tin or clay. Ryder gestured to the coffeepot. "I wish it was full and piping hot."

"It can be," Kitty said cheerily, indicating the supplies stacked in a corner. "I see coffee, as well as flour. I can make tortillas for our supper. Maybe you can snare a rabbit."

"Right now I'm not concerned with food." He squatted in front of the fireplace and leaned inside to look up, then said, "I can see daylight up there, so it's not a false chimney."

He checked all around it. "Nothing. No loose stones. No signs of digging." He lifted the lid of the wood box beside it. "Just a few pieces of kindling wood." With a sigh, he straightened. "I think we can forget anything to do with fireplace or chimney.

"But there's something we'd better notice real quick," he said suddenly, sharply, as he spotted the stack of boxes in another corner. "Dynamite. They must have left it here to keep it from getting wet if it rained. Probably did it just before they left, because they wouldn't have been so stupid as to keep it near where they had a fire going.

"This means," he whirled on her, eyes shining, "that the dig has to be around here somewhere. If we only had a Bible to try and figure out the verse—"

"We do," she cried, rushing to the mattress closest to her. She knelt and picked up the worn Bible from where it lay, partially covered.

"This must have been your father's bed," she said, almost reverently, as she pointed to a candle in a wax-covered jug nearby. "He probably read from his Bible every night before he fell asleep."

Ryder took it from her and immediately opened to the front and the book of Genesis.

"So you do know a little about the Bible," she said. "Like how the chapters are arranged."

"The missionaries introduced me to it, yes," he said absently as he turned the pages. "Here," he cried. "Chapter 18, verse 27—'Behold now, I have taken upon me to speak unto the Lord, which am but dust and ashes.'

"Which doesn't mean a damn thing to me," he concluded lamely.

"Me, either. So what do we do now?"

"Think about it while I get this dynamite out of

here. It makes me uneasy. You can draw some water from the well. I'll get a fire going once I get the dynamite out, and then you can make us some coffee."

"I can help you with the smaller boxes." She started toward them.

"No," he spoke so loud she jumped.

"No," he repeated, softer, then explained, "The blasting caps are in the smaller boxes and may be more dangerous than the dynamite."

Reaching into a box, he gingerly took out a small, tubular-shaped object. "In order for dynamite to explode, it has to have a heavy jolt—like this cap. It's made of something known as *fulminate of mercury*. You put it in the dynamite stick and then set it off with either a spark or a light concussion. But caps alone can blow up and take a hand—or even a life. They're nothing to mess around with."

"How do you know about such things?"

"I worked in a mine once to make a few dollars when the army didn't need me as a scout. They had me doing the dynamiting, and, believe me, I learned quick so I wouldn't make a mistake. Blasting is slow, however. It advances a tunnel by maybe three feet each explosion."

"Wasn't it terribly dangerous for my uncle and your father to transport it here?"

"Oh, yes, and you can believe they packed everything very carefully and moved easy to keep from jarring it."

He picked up a box of dynamite and carried it out.

Kitty went to the well, and groaned when she saw it was boarded over.

"It must have gone dry," Ryder said when she told him. "But don't worry. I'm stacking the dynamite on top of the rocks just above it, and I spotted a watering hole on the other side. Probably it's fed by an underground stream. We can get water there.

"By the way," he added, lifting another box, "I noticed something interesting up there. It appears that's where they kept the dynamite when it wasn't in the shack. I found some caps strewn about."

Kitty felt renewed hope. "Then the dig has to be somewhere around here, Ryder."

"That's what I'm counting on. But it's going to be dark soon. We'll have to wait till morning to try to find it."

Alone, Kitty wandered about the tiny shack, deeply moved to think this was where her uncle had lived. How she wished she could have seen him one more time to tell him how much he truly meant to her. And if the gold could not be found, she was glad to have come so far, if only to visit what had been his home.

Finding a knapsack, she opened it and immediately wept to find the letters she had written to him through the years. Tied with a pink ribbon, they were packed with a worn, moth-eaten sweater she had knitted for him the year she tried her hand at ladylike crafts. It was the one garment she had been able to complete, and though it was crudely made, he had apparently treasured it.

She sat on the floor and cradled the sweater to her cheek as childhood memories came sweeping back. The years with her uncle had been the only truly happy ones she had known. She wished now she had run away to follow him to Arizona. She could have cooked for him, cared for him, and things would have been different for both of them. And his life would not have been cut short so tragically, and—

A strange noise was coming from inside the wood box.

Thinking it was a rat or a snake, she raised up on her knees and drew her pistol, then cautiously reached to lift the lid.

Just then it banged open with a loud clatter, kindling sticks scattering as Ryder poked his head up to find himself staring into a gun barrel. "Don't shoot."

Wide-eyed, Kitty holstered her pistol. "How did you get in there?"

He climbed out and dusted himself off. "When I was stacking the dynamite I noticed a large hole beneath the edge of one of the larger rocks. I looked inside and realized it was actually a tunnel of some sort, so I climbed in to see where it went, hoping it would lead to the mine shaft. It led here instead."

Kitty rocked back on her heels. "Why on earth would they have done that?"

"Obviously for an escape route in case they got trapped in here by outlaws or Indians. There's no telling what we're going to find around this place, and—" He saw the open knapsack beside her. "What do you have there?"

"The letters I wrote my uncle over the years. Looks like he kept every one of them."

He saw her sadness and gathered her close. "It hurts, I know. They shouldn't have died. They should have given up the damn map, told where the gold was."

He rested his chin on top of her head as he continued to hold her. "I keep thinking how my father hinted he'd be going to Mexico with us, and the look on my mother's face when I told her. I realized then they never stopped loving each other. It was going to be a chance for them to be together and make a new life.

"I hope we don't lose *our* chance," he murmured his cheek brushing her hair.

"I hope not, too, Ryder," she said shakily, pressing closer against him, delighting in the warm, masculine scent of him and how she felt so protected, so cherished, in the circle of his arms.

He bent his head and kissed her, long and deep

and possessing. She yielded, twining her arms about his neck.

Then, lifting her up, he carried her to lay her down on one of the mattresses. "I think supper will have to wait awhile," he said huskily as he began to undo the buttons of her blouse while raining kisses over her face, "because we're having dessert first."

As he worked on her blouse, she tore at his shirt, his trousers, wanting to be flesh to flesh, heart to heart.

When they were naked, he lay back and spread his thighs, then gently settled her on top of him. She shuddered with delight to feel his swollen shaft enter and began to undulate her hips against him.

He clutched her buttocks tightly, lifting his own to match her sensuous rhythm.

It did not take long. They felt themselves peaking together. Kitty threw back her head and gave a soft cry as Ryder clutched her tighter in his own journey to bliss.

Afterward, she collapsed beside him, soaked with sweat and exhausted.

"You're like a wild mustang," he whispered, caressing her cheek as she snuggled against him. "You can be tamed, but your spirit will never be broken. And that's how I'd want it, Kitty. I—"

It was like a hailstorm of lead as an explosion of bullets suddenly hit the front wall of the shack.

Kitty screamed, but Ryder, no stranger to sudden danger, reacted quickly. "Stay still," he ordered, holding her tight against him.

The firing lasted for interminably long moments, then there was silence.

"Now," he commanded, lunging for his gun in the near-darkness. "Shoot back, goddamn it, and let them know we're still alive before they rush us."

Together they fired off several rounds. Ryder dared

peer out a window, to see several men running for the cover of the rocks.

"Get your clothes on fast. Then reload."

Hands shaking, Kitty obeyed. She had never been in a gunfight, and knowing how to shoot was little consolation, she feared, when outnumbered. "How many are there?"

"It's hard to tell. I can't see. It's almost dark." He was rapidly stuffing bullets into the gun's cylinder. "I'm glad I tied the horses by the water hole on the other side. Otherwise, they'd probably have been hit."

Kitty fed her own guns. "There were only two at the river yesterday."

"Evidently they rounded up a gang. Damn it, maybe I should have covered our tracks, but if they are the murderers, I wanted them to follow."

"So did I, but I never thought they'd bring all their friends."

"We're going to have to clear out of here. I had one more box of dynamite to move, and if it gets hit, we'll be blown to bits. We can use the tunnel under the wood box. Once we get to the top of the boulders, all we have to do is scramble down the back side to the horses and ride out of here."

"But what about those murdering bastards?" she protested. "Are we going to just let them get away?"

"Hell, no. I'll leave you someplace safe, then go back to my camp and get my warriors."

"That means riding through Comanche Pass."

"I don't have a choice." He slid one last bullet in the cylinder and gave it a spin, then clicked it in place. "Go now. I'll hang back to cover a few minutes, and then I'll be right behind you."

Kitty worried. "But if they start shooting and hit the dynamite— "

"Go." He hooked a hand around her neck to yank

her close for a quick kiss, then released her. "Don't worry about me." He gave her a gentle shove.

She took a few steps, then turned to look at him once more, barely able to see him in the shadowy darkness as he crept toward a window.

A shot rang out, then another, and he yelled at her to get the hell out as he started shooting back. But Kitty could not abandon him and rushed to the other window to take aim.

He saw her and yelled, "I told you to get out of here, damn it— "

And then he was hit.

With a grunt, he pitched forward.

After a few moments, the firing stopped, and Kitty was able to rush to him, but he pushed her away. "Go on. Get in the tunnel."

"But you're hurt. I can't leave you."

"You've got to. It's my leg. I can't run, Kitty. Now go. I'll hold them back."

"I won't leave you," she repeated sharply. "Let's fire a few rounds and then we'll both go. I'll help you through the tunnel."

"You're going to get both of us killed," he fumed. "God, woman, I should have beat that stubborn streak out of you when you were my slave."

"Start shooting." She raised to the window and emptied one of her pistols, then ducked as a hail of bullets was promptly returned.

"Now," she said. "We can get out while they reload. Put your arm across my shoulders. Hurry . . ."

He shrugged her away.

"Now who's being stubborn?"

"Go. I'm coming. I promise."

But Kitty refused to climb down into the wood box, insisting he go first. "You know the way, how the tunnel curves, and I'll be behind you in case you pass out."

She could imagine the fury etched on his face as he snapped, "I'm not going to pass out. I've been hurt worse than this."

She knew he was bleeding bad. "Wait a minute." She bent and quickly tore a strip of material from the bottom of her skirt and wrapped it tightly around the wound.

When she was finished, he braced himself against the anguish of moving his wounded limb and lowered himself into the box.

Kitty was close behind.

It was pitch dark, and the way was narrow, forcing them to stoop. She knew he had to be in agony.

They began to move upward, stretching, reaching, climbing. Kitty wondered how he was able to endure, and marveled at his strength and courage.

At last, he pulled himself up into the night that had finally descended.

"Are you all right?" she whispered anxiously when she reached his side.

"I think so. The bandage helped."

"They haven't fired at the shack anymore."

"They'll likely wait till morning since we aren't shooting at them. They figure they've got us pinned down, and they don't want to waste any ammunition firing wild.

"At first light," he went on, grasping her shoulders tightly and wishing she could see his face to know he meant business, "you're getting out of here. I can't go with you. I'd hold you back, and we'd both get caught. But you're going to slip down the back side, get your horse, and ride to Tombstone. You can cut around the boulders so they don't see you, then hit the trail. You should be able to follow it. Find Marshal Earp and tell him your uncle's killers have got me pinned down here. Tell him to round up a posse and get here as quick as he can."

"But you can't hold them off by yourself," she protested. "Not wounded like you are. You might pass out from loss of blood, Ryder. Then they'll be all over you. And what about your own ammunition? Once they rush the shack and find us gone, they're liable to find the tunnel and track you up here. You won't have a chance."

"Oh, won't I?" He chuckled. "You're forgetting I've got my own personal arsenal up here with all this dynamite. And the way it's stacked, it won't be hit by a stray bullet. I can hold the bastards off for days. And the first thing I plan to do once you're out of here is blow up the tunnel to keep them from getting up here that way. Now don't argue."

She gently touched his wound and could feel that while the bleeding had slowed, despite the arduous trek through the tunnel, the bandage needed to be thicker. She tore another strip from her skirt.

"The bullet is going to have to come out," he said as she wrapped him.

But Kitty was not listening as she thought how once she got to the Chiricahua, they could be back before day's end. That meant Ryder would not have to hold off the outlaws as long as he would if she went to Tombstone, which was where he believed she was headed.

She was confident she could make it through Comanche Pass. Her horse was strong and fast, and she was an expert rider. All she had to do was dig in her heels, keep her head down, and ride like thunder through the pass.

She would do it, by God, because it might be the only way to save Ryder's life. After all, she had no assurance Marshal Earp would even gather a posse and come to his rescue. By now, Opal might have done so much talking that no one would lift a finger to help Ryder, regardless of the circumstances.

"Sleep now," she said. "I'll keep watch. I just wish we had something for you to eat. You're going to need your strength."

She could imagine his mocking grin as he murmured, "That's what I get for having dessert first."

She was about to tell him it would always be that way, because she loved him too much to ever refuse him anything . . .

But suddenly a voice rang out, clear and booming in the still of the night, directed toward the shanty.

"You might as well come on out, McCloud. And the woman, too. You're surrounded. And I ain't gonna lie to you and say we'll let you go once you hand over the map, neither. I'll just do you the favor of killing you quick so you won't suffer like your daddy and Parrish did 'cause they was stubborn sons of bitches."

Kitty made a whimpering sound, and Ryder was quick to clamp his hand over her face to muffle the sound.

"Last chance," the outlaw bellowed. "You make us sit here till morning to get you out of there, and I'll make you beg to die once I get my hands on you."

And then chills rolled over them to hear another voice, speaking low, directly beneath the boulder where they were hiding.

"You're wastin' your breath, Nate. We might as well let some of the boys stand guard while we get some shut-eye. We'll get 'em first thing in the mornin'. But remember I get my turn with the girl before we kill her."

"Yeah, yeah. But after me, Roscoe."

Had Ryder not continued to press his hand over her lips, Kitty's cry of rage would have carried farther than that of the coyotes howling miles away. For she knew, as did Ryder, in that heart-stopping moment when time seemed to stand still, who the outlaws— the *murderers*—were.

*Nate Grimes and Roscoe Pate.*

# Chapter 25

The night wore on, but Kitty and Ryder did not take turns sleeping, for neither could rest. Ryder was in too much pain, and Kitty was shaken with rage to know Nate and Roscoe were the murderers.

Below them, the outlaws kept their vigil on the shack. Every so often Nate would call out his taunting threat again—how he would make them suffer a slow death if they did not surrender themselves *and* the map.

Ryder whispered, "He figures we'll destroy it to keep them from getting it and can bargain to kill us quick if we hand it over. To hell with him," he snarled. "He doesn't know the Apache."

"My uncle wasn't Apache," Kitty reminded. "And they couldn't make him give up his part."

"Sorry." Ryder gave a low chuckle. "How could I forget you're living proof of the stubborn blood in your family?"

Kitty ignored the good-natured barb and continued her furious brooding out loud. "When Nate offered to help me look for the gold, he said he'd just found out about the map from Opal, but I think now he was lying. I also think he was the one who ransacked my room, and that's why he made the offer—because he couldn't find it and didn't know what else to do without arousing Opal's suspicion."

"Exactly when did he offer to help you?"

"The night before I left to find your camp. He followed me to the livery stable. I had to sleep in the hayloft, because I couldn't find a room. Thank goodness I·left before dawn. Otherwise he'd have followed me."

"As he did when you thought you were following me. Did you sleep in the hayloft that night, too?"

"Yes. Like I told you—Opal got mad when I wouldn't agree to Nate and Roscoe searching with me. She accused me of not wanting to share any of the gold with her and threw me out of her shanty. Nate must have been close by and trailed me to the livery stable and waited for me to leave the next morning."

Ryder nodded to the darkness. "Oh, I have an idea now he knew where this place was all along. He had probably been stalking my father and your uncle but couldn't figure out where the dig was and finally attacked them. Now he thinks *we* know where it is."

He was leaning back against a rock, wincing against the pain in his leg. "The bullet has to come out," he whispered suddenly. "Use the knife my mother gave you."

Kitty knew even if she could dig it out, the bleeding would be worse. She opened her mouth to argue, but he did not give her the chance.

"If it doesn't come out, I'll have lead poisoning and lose my leg. So do it and be quick about it."

Kitty knew his mind was set, just as she knew he was probably right. Taking the knife from inside her boot, she said, "I'll try, but how am I going to see in the dark?"

"You aren't. All you can do is feel for the hole, cut into it till you feel the bullet, then dig for it."

Kitty swallowed hard.

"Do it," he hissed.

Sucking in a deep breath, Kitty found the hole and stuck the knife in before she had time to think about it. She felt him go stiff and knew the pain had to be excruciating.

The knife tip hit something hard. "How do I know it's the bullet and not bone?" she asked, hysteria bubbling within her.

"Feel for it," he said between clenched teeth, "And hurry. I don't particularly enjoy having a knife stuck in my leg."

"And I don't enjoy sticking it in there, either," she fired right back. Then, with another hard breath drawn, she plunged her thumb and forefinger into the hole she had widened with the knife, then gave a soft cry of relief to fasten about the bullet.

With a mighty tug, it pulled free.

Blood began to flow heavily, and she quickly ripped at her skirt for bandages to try and slow it.

"I'm wrapping this real tight," she explained to Ryder as she worked. "You can loosen it in the morning if it looks like the bleeding has stopped. I'll leave some more strips of cloth in case you need to change it.

"I wish I had some whiskey to give you for the pain," she continued. "Even water might help. How are you feeling now?"

He did not answer.

Panicked, she pressed her head to his chest. He was breathing, but she knew he had quietly passed out from the ordeal.

Kitty endured the rest of the night alone, biting back rage each time Nate or Roscoe would shout their taunts and threats to the shack, believing she and Ryder were inside.

And during the long, miserable hours till dawn, she knew she was, indeed, capable of taking a human life, for how easy it would have been to kill them if given the chance.

When the first watermelon fingers of dawn began

to creep, Kitty gently shook Ryder awake. "I'm leaving now, but you have to wake up and be ready should they realize you're up here."

She felt a rush of alarm. "Do you have matches to light the dynamite?"

He patted the pocket of his vest. "I found some in the shack."

She checked his bandage. It was soaked but seemed to be drying. "Are you sure you aren't able to come with me?"

"You'll move faster without me."

In the scant light she saw the look in his eyes and knew he was not altogether telling the truth. "That's not it. You want to cover me, don't you, so I can get away. You think they're going to hear me once I'm on my horse, and—"

"And you talk too much." He managed a lopsided grin. "And you're also wasting time. Now, get out of here."

Kitty started to rise, then threw her arms around his neck and whispered, "I've made up my mind. I'm going to Mexico with you and your people."

"Then I have even more reason to be here when you get back," he murmured, before claiming her lips in a kiss that left both of them shaken.

"Now go," he urged, gently pushing her away. "Get to Tombstone as fast as you can."

Kitty turned away, fearing he might sense she had no intention of going there.

Though her instinct was to hurry, she moved slowly, careful not to send rocks tumbling over the side to draw the outlaws' attention upward to the boulder.

Working her way down, at last she dropped to the ground. Untying her horse, she did not bother with a saddle, instead leaping on him bareback and taking up the reins.

Again, she forced herself to hold back, wanting to

get as far from the area as possible before setting the horse into a gallop, to lessen the chance of being heard.

That hope was quickly dashed as someone yelled, "Hey, they're gettin' away."

Kitty leaned across the horse's neck, dug her heels into his flanks, and yelled, "Go," just as a bullet whizzed over her neck. In a few seconds, she was around a huge rock and no longer a target.

Maybe, she dared hope, Nate and the others would think both she and Ryder had got away. Then she realized with a heavy heart that they would find Ryder's horse and know one of them was still around.

But there was no time to look back or worry, because her reaching the Indian camp was Ryder's only chance of survival. Not only was it doubtful he could hold the outlaws off with dynamite long enough for her to go to Tombstone and back, but also his leg needed medical attention.

She whipped the end of the reins from side to side, urging the horse into full gallop.

The pass loomed ahead. The land was still only slightly bathed in light, rosy and pale, and she dared think she might be able to catch the Comanche sentries off guard at such an early hour and make it through before they realized what was happening.

Digging her heels in harder, she was thundering straight into the pass when she heard the explosion.

She did not slow but turned her head to see the smoke and dust shooting skyward and knew Ryder had blown up the tunnel.

But another blast followed, and terror shot through her. They had discovered he was on the boulder, and he was attempting to hold them off, and she prayed he could do so.

She gave the horse his head, and he sprinted around

the big rocks. Sure-footed, he did not stumble and charged ahead.

Kitty heard the enraged scream from above at the same time an arrow whizzed by. Without looking up, she raised her gun and fired off several rounds to let the Comanche know she was armed.

At last the end was in sight.

She was going to make it.

Once through the pass, it was as Ryder had said it would be—she saw signs, got her bearings, knew where she was.

On she rode, stopping but once, at a watering hole for the horse to drink and rest a few moments. Then she was on her way again.

The sun was high in the sky when she saw the familiar saguaro cactus at the spot where she and Pale Sky had come down off the mountain—two green, spike-covered arms jutting to the left, toward the eastern horizon, and one to the west, and taller than her by three heads, at least.

But she had no sooner turned up the trail when three warriors with fierce expressions leaped to block her way, all holding bows with arrows pointed.

"Coyotay," she gasped, out of breath. Her horse was lathered and also heaving. "I must see Coyotay at once."

They exchanged glances. They knew very little of the white man's tongue but understood she spoke Coyotay's name.

One of them motioned to her holster. She knew what he wanted and quickly unbuckled it and tossed it to the ground, then said in a rush, "Pale Sky. Take me to her."

Their eyebrows lifted at the sound of yet another name they knew.

"Take me to her. Or Coyotay. Please," she begged.

"Whitebear is in big trouble. He's going to die if we don't get to him right away."

Hearing Whitebear's name rang the final bell.

One of the Indians leaped behind her on her horse. She leaned forward, not wanting to touch him, for she could feel his hatred. But he reached around her, taking the reins, and she found herself helplessly pressed against him.

In silence they rode the rest of the way, and as soon as they reached the camp, the Indian began yelling for Coyotay.

In an instant, Coyotay rushed from a wickiup, his face twisting with fury to recognize her.

He ran forward and roughly yanked her from the horse and threw her to the ground. Towering over her, legs apart and fists clenched, he spoke his rudimentary English to demand, "Why you come? Why you here? Where is Whitebear?"

Kitty did not cringe and scrambled to her feet despite his menacing stance. "Whitebear is wounded and trapped on the other side of Comanche Pass. Gather your warriors and come with me."

His lips turned back in a snarl. "You lie. You bring pony soldiers."

Exasperated and desperate, Kitty screamed at him, "Damn it, you don't see any pony soldiers, do you? If I had brought them, they'd be all over the place by now. I don't have time to argue. If you want Whitebear to live, get your men and follow me. I'll take you to him."

Pale Sky, hearing the commotion and Kitty's voice, rushed from her wickiup. "What is this? My son is wounded?"

Kitty quickly told her what had happened, how Ryder was trapped on top of a boulder overlooking the camp where they believed the gold strike was located. "And we have to get to him, fast. He has dynamite to hold them off, but he's hurt. He could lose consciousness, and then they'll overtake him and kill him."

She grabbed Pale Sky's shoulders and gave her a shake. "The men who have Whitebear trapped are also the ones who killed his father and my uncle. Make Coyotay understand that."

With an angry roar, Coyotay lunged to tear her away from Pale Sky, but Pale Sky held up a hand to stop him. "We must listen to her. She speaks the truth."

Coyotay's eyes narrowed. "How can we be sure? It could be trap. Pony soldiers could be waiting to ambush when we come down off of mountain."

Pale Sky shouldered him away from Kitty to stand before her and look deep into her eyes. "I do not see lies. I see love—love for my son. Go, Coyotay. Take the warriors and go with her."

Coyotay shook his fist in Kitty's face. "If you lie, you will die a thousand deaths."

"I already am dying a thousand deaths," she told him, tears filling her eyes, "to think of what it must be like for Ryder—*Whitebear*—back there. Please, Coyotay. Hurry."

He threw his head back and began to shout out orders in Apache.

The camp came alive, as warriors gathered their weapons, while their women and children hurried to ready their horses.

During the mad rush, Pale Sky embraced Kitty. "Thank you, my child, for what you have done. I know of the danger of Comanche Pass, how you risked your life to go through it. You must love my son very much."

"I do," Kitty avowed. "And when this is over, I'm going with all of you to Mexico to be with him."

Pale Sky was taken aback. "Are you sure? The life will not be easy."

"I'm sure."

"He has asked you to be his wife?"

Kitty lifted her chin, trying not to show how it hurt that he had not, for she now knew, beyond doubt, that she truly loved him. There would be differences, true, due to their backgrounds, but her love would see her through.

"No," she admitted finally. "He has not spoken of marriage. He has said he loves me, though, so maybe in time—"

Frowning, Pale Sky interrupted. "Do not cling to that hope. He may fear you do not have the courage to live our life. You would have to prove it to him first."

Then, seeing the forlorn expression that swept Kitty's face, she offered, with a smile to comfort, "But who am I to say, child? Perhaps by what you have done you have already proved your courage."

On horseback, Coyotay charged up to where they were standing, barely reining to a stop before running into Kitty.

She did not leap out of the way but faced him defiantly.

"We go now," he said. He turned to Pale Sky. "And if she lies, I will bring you her scalp."

Kitty embraced Pale Sky one last time and managed to smile. "Don't worry. If he brings back a scalp, it won't be mine."

She ran to where a warrior was holding her horse and mounted.

With another yell, Coyotay led them from the camp.

Though Kitty did not know it, the Indians marveled at her riding skills. Coyotay had feared she would be unable to go as fast as they wanted, but she led the way at full gallop.

At the pass, Coyotay reined in his warriors to tell them once they started through, they could stop for nothing.

Kitty did not understand, for he spoke in Apache, but when he finished he told her of his instructions to the warriors, then grimly said, "Tell Coyotay the way to go should you die in the pass."

Despite the tension, Kitty had to laugh. "Don't be so quick to bury me, Coyotay. I made it through once, and I'll do it again."

"You tell Coyotay," he said fiercely.

Knowing he was right, she described as best she could the direction they should go once they reached the other side of the pass. "Attack the campsite," she advised, "but try to take the outlaws alive."

He sneered. "They will all die."

"No, Coyotay. There are two that must live to face white man's justice for murdering my uncle and Whitebear's father. And since you don't know which ones they are, you must let them all live."

He grunted. "Whitebear will have Indian justice for the one who killed his father."

Kitty hoped not . . . hoped that he would take a different way as an example to his people. But there was no time to worry about it. "Just please don't kill unless you have to. Now we have to hurry," she urged. "Whitebear will be on top of the boulder above the well—if he is still alive."

With the war cry of the Apache, Coyotay kicked his horse into a wide open run.

Kitty was swallowed in the lineup behind him as they all charged through the pass. Unlike the Indians, she did not shriek wildly but instead kept her head down by leaning forward to press herself against the horse.

Two warriors were felled by arrows. Everyone kept on going, as Coyotay had ordered.

And then they were through the pass and heading straight for the campsite, another quarter hour's ride away.

Coyotay did not slow, and neither did Kitty and the others. It was only when they reached the outskirts of the site that Kitty cut to the side and went to the rear of the boulder. The others attacked, firing their arrows and rifles.

The air exploded with the sound of gunfire and screams of rage and pain as the Indians routed the outlaws. Those that were not sprawled on the ground dead or wounded lifted their hands in surrender.

Kitty saw Ryder's horse still tied. Dismounting, she scurried up the rock, calling his name as she went, slipping, sliding, falling, getting up again. The flesh was torn from her hands and knees, as she took no time to pick her way carefully. She had to get to him, had to know if he was all right . . .

Finally reaching the top, she was washed with panic to see he was not there.

She raced about, looking in every nook and cranny, but the only signs he had ever been there were blood-stains and the empty dynamite boxes.

Terrified not to find Ryder, she crept to the edge to look down on the camp and was grateful to see that Coyotay and his men were now in command.

Spying Nate Grimes, arms stretched over his head as Coyotay held him at bay, she cried at the top of her lungs, "Damn you, Nate, where is Ryder? What have you done with him?"

He glared up at her. "I ain't done nothin' with him, but I wish to hell I had."

She hurried down the boulder to rush him and demand, "You know where he is. Tell me or I'll—" She took note of Coyotay's fierce expression and warned, "I'll tell the Apaches to *make* you talk."

Nate paled. He was worn and weary and hungry, and there was no fight left in him. "I swear I don't know." His face was screwed in desperation for her to believe him. "He blew up two of my men, and when he finally ran out of dynamite, he just disappeared. We circled to the back to take him by surprise, but he was gone. We been lookin' all over for him, 'cause his horse is still there."

"Then he has to be here somewhere."

Coyotay drew his knife and held it to Nate's throat. "Tell us what you have done with Whitebear, or I will cut out your tongue."

Nate's eyes bulged. "No, no. I swear. He just disappeared . . . like some kind of ghost."

"Where's Roscoe?" Kitty asked.

Nate pointed to a body lying facedown. "There. The injuns got him."

Kitty walked over to him, and, sure enough, the turquoise ring, set in silver with snakes entwining the band, was on his finger.

Nate saw her staring at it and whined, "Yeah, that's Wade's ring. Roscoe cut it off his finger. I told him not to, that it won't right, but he did it, anyway."

Kitty knelt and, after a few hard tugs, removed the ring. She did not know what she would ever do with it, only that she did not want the fiend that murdered her uncle to have it any longer.

"Don't kill him," she said to Coyotay, who still held a knife under Nate's chin. "Tie him up. He'll hang for what he did. Right now, though, we've got to find Whitebear. He's hurt and needs help. Tell the warriors to spread out and look for him."

Coyotay gave the orders in Apache, then spoke English to Kitty as he offered an apology for having misjudged her. "You told truth. I am sorry to have doubted." He grinned. "I will not take your scalp this day."

"Or any other day." She was smiling, but her eyes were solemn; her voice, firm.

She drifted away to search for Ryder on her own. Passing by the well, she noticed that the boards had been shoved aside. Nate and his men must have been looking for water.

She started on by but paused to hear a sound that seemed to come from the well.

It came again, and, heart slamming into her chest, she realized it was someone calling her name, and that someone could only be Ryder.

Shoving aside the rest of the boards, she gripped the edge of the stone wall around the well and frantically called down, "Ryder, is that you?"

Joy flooded to hear him shout back, "Yes. I'm down here."

Never had she been so grateful or relieved in her life. "Are you all right?" she called anxiously. "How is your leg?"

"It bled some when I jumped in here, but it's slowed now. I heard Nate and his boys coming up the back of the boulder and knew I had to hide. This seemed the best place."

Kitty was amazed he was able to make it with his injury but knew all too well how courageous he was.

"I heard the war cry. Where did you find Apaches willing to help? On the way to Tombstone?"

"I rode through Comanche Pass to get them. They are your warriors, Ryder—Chiricahua. It would have taken too long to go to Tombstone."

"You—what?" he bellowed, then, "We'll talk about that later. Right now I want you to get a rope and climb down here quick."

"No. We'll haul you up." She called to one of the Indians to bring a rope.

"Kitty, you don't understand. I've got to show you something."

He sounded excited and urged her to hurry and climb down.

"Let us pull you up instead," she begged. Whatever he wanted her to see could wait until his wound was properly tended. They would be coming back. With Roscoe dead and Nate awaiting the hangman's noose, they would not stop until they found the gold strike.

The Indian brought the rope and dropped one end over the side.

"I'm not coming up till you come down, Kitty."

"And you call *me* stubborn?" Kitty sighed and climbed over the side, hoping the Indian understood he was to hang on to the rope and not let her fall.

Ryder was waiting to grab her by her waist, then set her on her feet.

He was about to kiss her, and she was about to eagerly let him do so, but then she stared beyond him and nearly choked on a gasp of wonder.

There was light behind him—lantern light—and a tunnel.

Breathlessly she asked, "Does this mean what I think it means?"

"It does," he said exultantly. "I haven't explored too far. My wound won't let me. But I did find a lantern and lit it, and I can see the tunnel winds way on back. This is where they were digging, Kitty. The boards were put over the well to make it appear that it was dry. It was a decoy.

"And I also know," he rushed to tell her, "what the Bible verse meant." He gestured about them. "The reference was to dust and ashes. My father was wanting us to think of something dusty and worthless—like a dried-up well. It was under our noses all along."

"Ryder, it's wonderful." She hugged him as hard as she dared, for he seemed a bit unstable, leaning against the rock wall for support. "Now let us get you out of here. We'll leave some warriors to stand guard in case anybody else happens by, and when you're well, we'll come back and get the gold."

He lifted a brow in mock indignation. "You think you're taking over, don't you? Giving orders to me and my warriors. You've got another think coming, sweetheart, and—"

"And I don't have time for your whining," she retorted with feigned bossiness. "Now, get that rope tied around your waist, so we can lift you up."

"Not yet, sweetheart." He tossed the rope aside and swept her into his arms. "Not till I kiss you till you can't breathe and tell you how much I love you till you're tired of hearing it."

She yielded to his lips and swayed with joy when he released her.

"I'll never get tired of either," she said huskily.

"Then you're coming with us to Mexico?"

"Try to stop me," she laughed.

"This time *I'm* the one with conditions."

She thought he was going to chide her for making the run through Comanche Pass and ask her to promise never to defy him like that again. "All right," she gave an exaggerated sigh. "Let's hear it."

He had been smiling, but Kitty saw in the lantern's glow how his face had taken on a stern expression. And the way his eyes were locked with hers made her uneasy, for he was so intent.

"I only have one condition, Kitty . . . that you marry me."

Her mind began to spin as she frantically wondered whether she had heard him right. After all, he was weak, probably feverish, and—

"You said you loved me."

She did not hesitate then. "And I do. More than I ever thought I could love anyone."

"Then marry me," he said as though it were all quite simple . . . as though he were not a great Apache warrior and leader of his people, and she an easterner who had barely got western dust on her boots.

"I've had a lot of time to think, Kitty, and I've realized you are the woman I want to spend my life with, to bear my children, and help me lead my people."

"Oh, Ryder, are you sure? I have so much to learn about you and your ways. I might disappoint you *and* them."

"That could not happen. You're a woman of courage, and they respect that." He kissed her deeply, then said with the tug of a smile on his lips, "And once my wound is healed, I'll show you how sure I am. I'll take you captive again till you say you'll marry me."

"But I'm saying it now," she cried, tightening her arms about him. "I love you, Ryder, and I'll be proud to be your wife."

From above, Coyotay called impatiently to Ryder in their native tongue.

Ryder answered in Apache, as well. They talked back and forth for a few moments, and then Ryder said something and laughed, and Coyotay seemed stunned.

"What was that all about?" Kitty asked as Ryder wrapped the rope around his waist in preparation to being hoisted up.

His eyes were twinkling. "He wanted to know what I found down here."

"And now he's excited to hear you located the gold."

"Yes, but he's also trying to figure out what I meant when I said I'd found something else . . . something even more precious."

He pulled her close. "I found my future . . . I found *you,* Kitty, and I swear I'll do everything in my power to make you happy."

"I already *am* happy, my darling," she declared fervently, raising her lips for his kiss. "I already am."